Emily Forbes is an award-winning author of Medical Romance for Mills & Boon. She has written over twenty-five books and has twice been a finalist in the Australian Romantic Book of the Year Award, which she won in 2013 for her novel *Sydney Harbour Hospital: Bella's Wishlist*. You can get in touch with Emily at emilyforbes@internode.on.net, or visit her website at emily-forbesauthor.com.

Sue MacKay lives with her husband in New Zealand's beautiful Marlborough Sounds, with the water on her doorstep and the birds and the trees at her back door. It is the perfect setting to indulge her passions of entertaining friends by cooking them sumptuous meals, drinking fabulous wine, going for hill walks or kayaking around the bay—and, of course, writing stories.

D0488901

A GIFT TO CHANGE HIS LIFE

EMILY FORBES

FROM BEST FRIENDS TO I DO?

SUE MacKAY

MILLS & BOON

Published in Great Britain 2021
by Mills & Boon, an imprint of HarperCollins*Publishers* Ltd,
1 London Bridge Street, London, SE1 9GF

www.harpercollins.co.uk

HarperCollins*Publishers*
1st Floor, Watermarque Building,
Ringsend Road, Dublin 4, Ireland

A Gift to Change His Life © 2021 by Emily Forbes

From Best Friends to I Do? © 2021 by Sue MacKay

ISBN: 978-0-263-29779-9

10/21

MIX
Paper from
responsible sources
FSC® C007454

This book is produced from independently certified FSC™ paper
to ensure responsible forest management.
For more information visit www.harpercollins.co.uk/green.

Printed and bound in Spain using 100% Renewable Electricity
at CPI Blackprint (Barcelona)

A GIFT TO
CHANGE HIS LIFE

EMILY FORBES

MILLS & BOON

For my children.

I am so proud of you both,
and watching you chase your dreams
and achieve your goals gives me great pleasure.

I hope you continue to
live the lives you're dreaming of,

With love, for ever,

Mum

CHAPTER ONE

THE SUN WAS starting to drop in the sky, casting shadows over the sand as Jet steered the jet ski past the surf break, parallel to the beach. He kept an eye on the ocean, paying close attention to the three rips that were starting to run as the tide turned.

The jet ski had been launched as a precaution as the late afternoon swell picked up. The long blue rescue boards were hard to manoeuvre over large waves, making it difficult for the lifeguards to get out past the break in an emergency. The motorised ski was faster to respond in big seas but not easy to use when the water was crowded as it was today.

It was the last week of spring, less than five weeks until Christmas, and Bondi Beach was busy. Not anywhere near peak capacity, which could regularly reach forty thousand people at the height of summer, but busy enough to keep the lifeguards on their toes. School had ended for those students in their final year, exams were over and the graduates were making the most of their new-found freedom. Those who hadn't ventured off to the popular hot spots of Bali, the Gold Coast and Byron

Bay mingled with the university students, backpackers, tourists and families.

Jet scanned the waves, lifting one arm to shield his eyes from the afternoon sun, as he looked for anything untoward and any sign to indicate swimmers who might get into difficulty—those who weren't strong swimmers or who had overestimated their abilities as well as those who'd been drinking. Alcohol was banned on Bondi Beach but there were several bars in close proximity and Jet knew there would be plenty of beachgoers who had smuggled alcohol onto the sand. While he'd been living in Bondi and working as a lifeguard for the local council for the best part of five years, he had grown up in Byron Bay on the north coast of New South Wales and he'd been part of many end-of-school parties so he knew from experience it was easier to avert disaster than to have to respond to it.

He reached the south end of the bay near Bondi Icebergs, turned the ski one hundred and eighty degrees and headed north. The one-kilometre stretch of beach curved around on his left, bookended by two rugged headlands, while the distinctive circular lifeguard tower held centre stage.

'Jet? We've got a swimmer in trouble near the middle break.' Gibbo's voice came through the radio that was slung across Jet's chest. 'Hands have gone up.'

He pressed the button through the waterproof casing to reply. 'On my way.' He opened up the throttle on the ski and cut through the water.

He scanned the water, looking for raised hands, looking for something to guide him to the site of trouble.

Middle break was several hundred metres away and, while he wanted to cover the distance as quickly as possible, he needed to take a wide berth, adding metres to the journey, but his trajectory allowed him to avoid the swimmers and surfers.

There was a man in the water with his hand in the air. He could see people looking in his direction and although he couldn't hear them over the noise of the jet ski it was obvious they were calling for help. He slowed the ski and cut the engine as he drifted in amongst the swimmers. Two swimmers were treading water while they supported a third man between them. The man's face was grey, his eyes were rolled back in his head and he wasn't breathing.

Jet turned around on the seat to face the back of the jet ski and reached into the water. He grabbed the man under his armpits and pulled him onto the rescue mat that was attached to the rear of the ski. He didn't know what had caused the man to lose consciousness and the possibility of a spinal injury hovered in the back of his mind. He hoped he hadn't been speared into the bottom of the ocean by a large wave as there was no option but to drag the man onto the sled and get him back into shore. He couldn't be treated here.

'Can you climb on too?' He nodded at one of the swimmers who had been assisting in the water. 'I need you to hold him onto the board for me, make sure he doesn't fall off.'

The man nodded and Jet helped him out of the water before getting on the radio and calling the tower. 'We've got a resus,' he said. He knew Gibbo would call for an ambulance and send lifeguards down to the water's edge to assist Jet. They would have work to do before the paramedics arrived. 'Send a couple of rescue boards too,' he added. The men who had helped in the water would be fatigued from their efforts. Jet had no idea how competent they were; if they weren't strong swimmers they might need help to get back to the beach and it was always better to pre-empt that rather than wait for another call. Things could turn very nasty very quickly in big seas.

Jet's heart was pounding as he steered the ski towards the sand. There were so many things that could go wrong, and his mind was racing as he sifted through the scenarios. He knew he had to focus. He'd made a decision and now he had to work out what came next. He would still need to get his patient off the rescue mat and onto the beach for treatment. He needed help but he could see one of the lifeguard buggies racing along the shoreline, coming to meet him. The ATV came to a stop in line with Jet's path and Bluey and Dutchy, two of his fellow lifeguards, were waiting for him as he drove the jet ski onto the sand. A third lifeguard ran past; he was carrying a blue rescue board and was heading into the ocean to check the other swimmers.

Jet jumped off the ski and with Bluey and Dutchy's help lifted the unconscious man off the mat and carried him out of the shallow water and laid him on the hard sand beside the buggy.

He still wasn't breathing.

Jet held his fingers over the man's wrist at the base

of his thumb, feeling for a pulse. He moved his fingers around, searching, but there was nothing.

Bluey held the man's head while Jet and Dutchy rolled him onto his side. Salt water poured out of his mouth but he didn't regain consciousness.

The man who had helped bring the patient into shore had followed Jet and the other lifeguards up the beach. 'Do you know him?' Jet asked.

He hadn't stopped to ask that in the water; there hadn't been time and it hadn't mattered then but now he'd like more information. Starting with whether the patient had any pre-existing health conditions. But the other man shook his head.

'Do you have any idea what happened?'

Another shake of the head.

If they weren't going to get any additional information they'd have to treat the patient as best they could.

They rolled the patient back into a supine position so that Jet could begin CPR. Bluey got an airway in and attached a bag ready to pump air into the man's lungs between Jet's compressions.

Dutchy had fetched the kit containing the defibrillator from the buggy and was preparing it for use while Jet counted out his compressions. Dutchy worked around Jet, wiping the patient's chest, drying it off so he could stick the defibrillator pads on.

Jet lifted his head as he continued the compressions. He looked towards Campbell Parade, hoping to see the flashing lights of an approaching ambulance, but a crowd had gathered to watch the resuscitation effort and they'd formed a wall of people, obscuring his view.

Jet counted to thirty and took a break while Bluey squeezed the bag and Dutchy stuck the defibrillator pads onto the patient's chest. He put his hands back on the patient and resumed his pressure while Dutchy plugged the defib leads into the machine.

'I think I've got a pulse,' Bluey said as Jet sat back, listening to the defib's instructions.

'Analysing rhythm.'

'No shock advised.'

'Yep, definite pulse,' Bluey confirmed.

They rolled their patient onto his side again and this time he vomited and opened his eyes as the crowd clapped and cheered.

Above the noise of the crowd Jet heard the 'toot-toot' of the horn of a second buggy and the wall of people split as the ATV pushed its nose through. Jet could see Ryder Evans, his future brother-in-law, at the wheel, with two paramedics on board.

He recognised the first; Alex often partnered with Jet's sister Poppy, who was Ryder's fiancée, but today she wasn't the other paramedic. The other paramedic, while female, was petite with dark hair. She was the complete opposite to Poppy, who was tall and fair like Jet.

Bluey had strapped an oxygen mask over the patient's nose and mouth and was talking to him, telling him what had happened.

Jet stood up, stretching out his tall, lean frame. He rolled his shoulders to ease the fatigue as Ryder hit the engine's kill switch and Alex and the second paramedic jumped out of the buggy. He frowned as the female paramedic leaned into the back of the ATV and lifted a medical bag out. There was something familiar about her, about the way she moved, but he didn't think he knew her. He wondered if it was just the adrenalin in his system after the rescue and resuscitation heightening his senses, increasing his awareness. His heart was still racing and blood was pumping around his body.

He had a sense of déjà vu as he watched her and a name popped into his head. Mei.

Was it her?

She was wearing sunglasses and a navy cap with 'Ambulance' stitched across the front. Her dark hair was pulled back in a ponytail, her skin was smooth and lightly tanned and her lips were full and pink but that was all he could see of her. It wasn't enough to be certain it was her. He hadn't seen her for years—would he really recognise her after so much time?

She paid him no attention as she gathered her equipment and Jet decided he must be mistaken. He must be confusing her for someone he knew a long time ago.

She knelt in the sand beside the patient as Alex walked over to Jet. Jet knew he needed to give him an account of the incident and of the treatment they had given but he continued to watch the other paramedic while he spoke to Alex. For reasons he couldn't explain he found it impossible not to.

The lifeguard beeped the horn on the buggy and the crowd parted to let them through. This was Mei's fifth day on the job as a Bondi paramedic and her third callout to the famous beach. Although she'd grown up around Bondi she wasn't a fan of the beach, but it was becoming apparent that attending to incidents here would become a regular part of her new job. She'd experienced a traumatic incident in the water when she was young and had tended to avoid the beach after that but, despite this, she had applied for a transfer to Bondi Ambulance Station as it would halve her commuting time. Traffic in Sydney could be a nightmare and working closer to home would give her back precious time to spend with her daughter instead. As a single mother she figured that commuting time could be better spent on more important things.

She hopped out of the buggy, stretching her legs over the blue rescue board hooked along the passenger side, leaned into the back of the ATV to grab her kit bag from beside her colleague and glanced towards the patient. She'd been glad to hear the patient was an adult male; she found dealing with children hard, especially ones around the same age as her daughter. The patient was lying in the recovery position and her heart skipped a beat when she looked that way, but it wasn't the patient who got her all flustered but one of the lifeguards at the scene.

Tall, blond, tanned and lean, he was standing beside the patient. The late afternoon sun shone on him, appearing to deliberately single him out. It was a silly notion, the sun must have been falling on dozens of people but to Mei it felt as if the sun was purposely, and solely, landing on just one person.

Jet.

She'd last seen him eight years ago in Byron Bay

on the New South Wales central coast and last she'd heard he had moved to Hawaii. What was he doing on Bondi Beach?

All those sleepless nights she'd spent wondering where he was. All those years when she'd pictured him travelling the world, surely he hadn't been right here, in her own backyard?

What did this mean? Was it fate or fortune? Was his presence going to turn her life around or simply upend it? Whatever happened, she had no doubt it would be life-changing.

The sun made his bronzed skin glow and his golden hair shine. It might have been eight years since she'd seen him, but she'd thought about him every single day with a trace of anger mixed with regret. She waited now for those familiar feelings, but it was nervous excitement that she felt instead. He was even more gorgeous than she remembered and seeing him in the flesh made her heart race and her hands clammy. Her knees wobbled and her breath caught in her throat, just like the first time she'd seen him. They'd been on a beach and he'd been lit by the glow of a bonfire instead of the sun, but she still hadn't been able to take her eyes off him.

But she couldn't afford to let her attention be diverted. Not now. Not again. She had a job to do.

Perhaps he wouldn't recognise her, she thought as she walked towards the patient. She had never forgotten him, but she didn't for one moment expect the same could be said for him. She was wearing sunglasses and a cap, and her uniform was hardly flattering. She suspected she couldn't look more different than the eighteen-year-old girl she'd been when they'd first met. There was no reason for him to remember her. If he didn't recognise her, if he didn't speak to her, she knew she'd be able to maintain focus.

She kept her head down as she went to the patient and knelt in the sand. She and her partner had been given a brief outline of the incident—a successful resuscitation on a middle-aged man.

She could hear Jet summarising the incident for her colleague, Alex. His voice was deep and it coursed through her like music. She felt as if her nerves were guitar strings and each word and syllable plucked at the strings and reverberated through her body. It was an unexpected but pleasant sensation.

But she had other things to focus on, so she tried to block him out. She would work out later how to deal with this surprising turn of events.

She unzipped her bag as she got the patient's name— Paul—from a second lifeguard who had introduced himself as Bluey.

'Paul, my name is Mei; I'm a paramedic.' She talked quietly to him, asking him to squeeze her fingers as she checked for spinal injuries. His grip was strong as he followed her instructions.

She clipped an oximeter to his finger and moved her hands to the soles of his feet. 'Push down against my hands,' she said, relieved to feel responding pressure.

'Do you remember what happened?' she asked the patient as Alex squatted beside her. She resisted the urge to turn her head to see if Jet was still there. She couldn't be concerned about his whereabouts right now.

'Not really. The last thing I remember is a tightness in my chest and difficulty breathing and then I woke up here.'

'He was found floating in the water by some surfers,' Alex told her. 'The priority was getting him to shore.'

She knew what Alex was implying—the priority had been getting Paul out of the water, not looking for spinal injuries.

'Muscle strength is normal,' she said, letting her partner know she had checked. She had done a couple of shifts with Alex, but they were still getting familiar with working together and she knew he couldn't assume that she had performed the right checks. 'But we can pop a cervical collar on, just to be safe.'

Alex nodded and grabbed the collar. 'Just popping this on as a precaution, mate,' he said as he slid it under Paul's neck and fastened the Velcro straps.

'Have you got any history of heart problems?' Mei asked Paul. 'Are you on any medication?'

'No.'

Their priority now was to get Paul stable enough to transfer him to hospital. He needed a cardiac assessment.

'We'll need to take you to hospital. Is there anyone with you?'

'My son is here.'

Mei looked around and saw a young man crouching in the sand to her left, watching the proceedings anxiously. She knew it must be a distressing experience for him. 'If you've got all your things you can come with us,' she told him.

She packed up their equipment as Alex organised the lifeguards to help them roll Paul onto a spinal board, ready to be moved to the buggy.

She knelt in the sand by Paul's right shoulder. Alex was to her left, ready to support Paul's head as they rolled him. Bluey knelt opposite Mei with Ryder beside him. She felt the air stir as a fourth person knelt beside her. She didn't need to turn her head to know it was Jet. He smelt warm and salty; he smelt of the sun and the sea; he smelt just like she remembered.

Mei kept her gaze fixed on the spinal board, which she held across her knees, ready to slide it under Paul when Bluey and Ryder turned him. Jet reached for the handles in the edge of the board. His fingers brushed against Mei's, making her heart skitter. She kept her eyes averted—she wasn't brave enough to look at him.

Ryder and Bluey had their hands on Paul's shoulders, pelvis and knees, ready to log roll him. 'On three,' Alex issued instructions.

'One, two, three.'

Mei and Jet slid the board under Paul before the others rolled him back.

The moment Paul was safely on the board Jet was on his feet, leaving a void of empty air beside Mei. The air stilled and the energy that had been buzzing around her dissipated as Jet moved away.

She knew she was being ridiculous, but her memories were flooding back. This was the same reaction she'd had to him all those years ago—immediate and completely out of her control. It had been all-consuming, leaving her feeling distracted. Eight years ago, she'd let herself get carried away. She had been looking for excitement, for adventure after graduating from high school and she was overwhelmed by her reaction to Jet and had given herself over to him willingly. But eight years ago she'd been young, naïve and impressionable. None of those things could be said about her now.

She couldn't afford to be irresponsible any more. Her life now was rational, measured. She had responsibilities and commitments; there was no room in her life for fantasies, infatuations or affairs.

She had consigned Jet to history and she'd like him to stay there, even though she knew that was impossible.

There was no way she could ignore him, or the fact that he had changed her life. He had given her the most precious gift. One he had no idea about. They had a daughter. It wasn't a secret she'd intended to keep from him but Jet had disappeared and now, eight years later, she knew she was about to change his life.

They carried Paul to the buggy and loaded him on, ready to transport him across the sand. Bluey drove her, Alex and their patient back to the promenade. Several lifeguards then helped carry the stretcher to the ambulance, but Jet wasn't among them. He stayed down at the water's edge but, even so, Mei's breathing didn't return to normal until she shut the rear doors, closing Alex in with their patient, jumped into the driver's seat and headed to Bondi General Hospital.

She was disappointed but relieved that Jet hadn't recognised her; she wasn't ready to revisit their history. She knew it was inevitable but she needed time to prepare.

She needed to work out how to deal with this unex-

pected turn of events, but she had time. She had two
night shifts coming up and then four days off. She had
time to put things in perspective before she would see
him again.

She knew what the end result needed to be—she just
had to decide the best way to get there.

Jet stood and watched as Bluey drove down the beach
towards the lifeguard tower. The crowd had dispersed
and he had a clear view of the buggy as it headed into
the distance with the paramedics and their patient. He
turned around, knowing he had work to do, but that
didn't stop him from wondering about the petite, dark-
haired paramedic.

He was disconcerted as he tried to marshal his
thoughts. She looked familiar, she felt familiar, but she
didn't seem to recognise him. Had it been her?

He helped Ryder pack up the equipment, picking
up the detritus and returning the oxygen cylinder and
mask to the second buggy. Job finished, he grabbed a
drink of water.

'I haven't seen that paramedic before,' he said, trying hard to sound offhand. 'Have you?'

'Nope,' Ryder replied. 'She said she just transferred
to Bondi Station a week or so ago. Why?'

'She looked familiar. Did you get her name?'

'May.'

Mei.

It had to be her. Didn't it? But she didn't seem to
recognise him. Was it a coincidence? Was that sense of
déjà vu simply a figment of his imagination?

He didn't think so—he wasn't given to flights of fancy. But he figured time would tell. The paramedics were called to Bondi Beach frequently, so he'd find out soon enough.

'Do you know her?' Ryder asked.

'I'm not sure.'

He could see from Ryder's expression that his answer wasn't a satisfactory one, but he didn't want to share his thoughts. Something made him hesitate. It had been years since he'd seen Mei—maybe he was mistaken and he wasn't about to have a discussion about a girl he once knew eight years ago. Ryder would want details. Jet had a reputation for brief dalliances and Ryder would be curious to know what it was about a girl from all those years ago that made her unforgettable. Jet wasn't sure he'd be able to explain.

'I can ask Poppy about her if you like? Or you can. They must have met at work.'

He knew Ryder was fishing but there was nothing he was prepared to say.

Ryder and Jet had grown up together but Ryder had moved from Byron Bay to Perth when they were seventeen. He had left before Jet met Mei and he had never mentioned her to his friend. He wasn't about to mention her now either.

The past was the past. Their relationship had been a fleeting one, like all Jet's relationships. Work and training took up his time. He had been twenty, happily drifting along with vague plans to become a professional surfer. Mei had been eighteen and on holiday in Byron Bay celebrating the end of her school days with friends. They had been chalk and cheese. She was driven, focused and determined but naïve. She had a plan; she set goals that she knew she would achieve. He was a dreamer, a risk-taker, he had no real plans; his priorities were to have fun and spend his days surfing and he'd figured life would take him where he needed to go. But, despite their differences, there had been instant attraction and amazing chemistry and nothing else had mattered.

He wasn't even aware of their differences initially and, to be honest, didn't care. He was interested in her physically, not in her mind. At least not at first, but over the course of seventy-two hours she had challenged him and changed him. And he had changed her.

They had parted ways at the end of the weekend, content to return to their different lives having had a taste of other things, having had their horizons expanded. Mei had experienced spontaneity, she'd relaxed and had perhaps learnt not to be her own harshest critic, that the world wasn't going to end if she took five minutes to enjoy herself. He had learnt that he would need to set some goals and apply himself if he wanted to achieve international surfing success. He'd realised that most people who achieved their dreams had an element of talent, determination and effort to thank, and didn't rely solely on good fortune.

The one thing they did have in common had been loneliness. It wasn't that that drew them together, that had been purely and simply chemistry, but their loneliness had given them a bond, an understanding of each other and that connection had made them feel safe enough to share their thoughts with each other in a way he knew he had never done before.

It was crazy to think that a girl he'd met on the beach in Byron Bay, at a party he hadn't even planned on attending, had managed to have such a profound effect on him.

He had never had a serious relationship, not then and still not now. He'd never felt comfortable expressing his feelings so he'd never been able to give women what they craved—his emotional side. He could share himself physically but opening up emotionally was difficult and he knew it was a barrier to forming a lasting relationship. He told himself he was fine. Told himself he didn't have time, but he craved the attention and recognition he'd never received from his parents.

He'd wanted someone to take him seriously, someone to believe in him. His parents had never been ones to show pride or love or to shower him or his sisters with praise or affection and it was something he longed for. He hated the fact that he felt that way, but he knew that the only way he would get that attention was through his sporting endeavours.

But Mei had been different. Mei had made him feel seen.

They might have been young, and they might have only spent a weekend together, but she had learned more about him in those seventy-two hours than any other woman and taught him more about himself than anyone else ever had.

She'd made him want to be a better person, to strive to achieve. She had made him realise that he couldn't keep hoping for his parents' praise, that he had the chance to set his own goals, to chase his own dreams and to do it for his own satisfaction. Mei had set him on his own path, had freed him to be himself. He hadn't achieved everything he wanted, not yet, but she had been partly responsible for making him who he was today. He wondered what would she think of that.

But that was a long time ago. He wasn't that twenty-year-old with unrealistic expectations any more. He had a career as a lifeguard, which would serve him well for the next few years while he chased his dream of qualifying for the Ironman World Championships. His dreams of becoming a professional surfer had been relatively short-lived and he'd discovered he was far better suited physically to the rigorous, gruelling competition that was the professional Ironman.

He was about to turn twenty-nine; he had years before he needed a serious relationship. In fact, he wasn't convinced he needed one at all and right now he had other things to concentrate on, including two Ironman events in the next month. Mei belonged in the past. He had no time to devote to thinking about her. He was looking forward, not back.

'Do you want me to find out more?' Ryder repeated when Jet didn't respond. 'I'll see Poppy tonight. We're going to look at that rental.'

Ryder and Poppy's relationship was moving at a rapid pace. Apparently they'd had some sort of connection back when they were teenagers, unbeknown to Jet or the other Carlson siblings, but they'd only officially been together for a few weeks. Jet couldn't understand the urgency, but he didn't begrudge Ryder and his sister their happiness. Ryder made Poppy happy, he was a good guy and Jet was glad to welcome him as a brother-in-law. But he didn't envy them. As selfish as it might seem, he was quite content with his bachelor lifestyle.

He shook his head in reply to Ryder. 'Nah. It doesn't matter. I've probably got her confused with someone else.'

'I can believe that.' Ryder laughed as he let the subject drop, just as Jet had intended. His relationships might be fleeting but they were also numerous and he knew Ryder would believe that he'd lose track.

But he knew it was her.

That sense of déjà vu. The spark he'd felt when his hand brushed hers.

He'd been waiting for a sign that she remembered him, but she'd ignored him completely, seemingly unaware of him. He wasn't used to that. He was used to women noticing him and his ego was bruised to think she'd forgotten him.

That, or the alternative—that she knew exactly who he was but had chosen to ignore him—wounded his pride and he vowed to get her attention.

CHAPTER TWO

FOR THE REST of her shift, each time there was a lull, Mei's mind returned to Jet and the weekend they had spent together and she could think of nothing else on the drive home.

Eight years on and that one weekend felt like a lifetime ago. For her it was. Her life had completely changed in that time. She wondered how different he was.

She'd had no idea he was in Sydney. In Bondi. The last time she'd seen him was in Byron Bay. At the age of twenty he'd been gorgeous, charismatic, full of energy, full of life and she'd been swept off her feet. She'd been ready for some excitement, ready to cast off the stress after years of studying and she'd let herself throw caution to the wind, not concerned with consequences, the future or anything that came next.

She'd never done that before and it had felt liberating.

She'd thought at the time she would be fine, but she should have known better than to tempt fate. She could still hear her mother's voice warning her she would pay the price for any reckless behaviour, for her mistakes, and her mother had been half right. Mei didn't consider her behaviour wayward, it had been her choice, but she hadn't escaped unscathed, although she had learned to live with her mistake. To love her mistake. And she wouldn't change a thing.

Well, almost nothing.

The smell of garlic and spices greeted Mei as she walked from her car to her back door. The dinner service at her parents' restaurant was well underway. Her stomach rumbled as she climbed the stairs to their apartment above the restaurant. She'd shower and change and then go back downstairs and see what her mother was cooking. She hoped the restaurant wasn't too busy. Her mother ran the kitchen and her father ran the front of house with a couple of regular waitresses and if it was busy Mei often lent a hand. But she was tired today. The mental and physical strain of her job had been compounded by the stress of a new environment but, on top of that, seeing Jet again had taken up a lot of her concentration and she wasn't sure she had enough in reserve to be a gracious hostess. Thank God it was Tuesday, usually the quietest night of the week, with most customers opting for takeaway.

Her parents had opened Lao Lao's Kitchen when they emigrated to Australia twenty-four years ago, when Mei was two years old and her brother, Bo, five. Running the restaurant had enabled her parents to raise their children in a new country where they didn't have the extended family support they had been used to in Hong Kong. Mei's parents had worked in one of the five-star hotels—her mother had been a chef, her father was a manager—but he'd had concerns about the future of Hong Kong and together they had made the decision to emigrate and open a restaurant of their own.

Mei and her brother had grown up in the apartment above the restaurant, but she hadn't ever envisaged that she would still be living with her parents at the age of twenty-six. But then, there were a lot of things about her life that were different to what she'd imagined. She knew her parents didn't mind having her there, but she still dreamt of a life of her own. One day.

Mei slipped her feet into her slides and headed for the restaurant kitchen. If she needed to give her father a hand in the dining room she'd have to change again.

The sound of clattering pans and frying food assailed her as she pushed open the swinging door. Her mother was directing the kitchen staff and didn't notice Mei's entrance.

A young girl sat at the stainless-steel workbench, carefully decanting sauces from a large jug into small condiment bowls. Mei smiled at the look of concentration on An Na's face.

'Hey, gorgeous girl,' she greeted her daughter. She bent down and kissed An Na's forehead.

'Careful, Mummy, you'll make me spill it.'

'Sorry, darling,' Mei replied as An Na looked up and smiled.

Mei caught her breath as Jet's smile flashed across her daughter's face. Albeit missing one front tooth. She'd always known An Na had his smile but seeing it today when Jet's face was fresh in her memory was a jolt she didn't need.

'Hi, Mama,' Mei greeted her own mother as An Na returned to her task.

Mei's mother put chopsticks and a bowl of steamed dumplings in front of her. The dumplings were varied in size and shape.

'I helped Lao Lao make those,' An Na told her. 'They're prawn and chicken.'

Mei remembered being seven and learning to make dumplings. She'd loved the precision of the task, the effort to try to make each one identical. It had taken a long time to master.

'They look delicious,' she said as An Na handed her a bowl of dipping sauce. She knew that even if they were a little misshapen they would taste amazing.

Mei gobbled the dumplings as she listened to An Na chatter about her day at school, about the Christmas decorations they were making and the songs she was learning for the Christmas concert.

'Is everything okay? You're very quiet,' her mother asked as she took the empty bowl.

Mei nodded. 'Just a hectic day at work.' It had been busy but that wasn't what was keeping her preoccupied. She wasn't thinking about work and she was only half listening to An Na. She was too busy thinking about Jet.

'Does Dad need help in the restaurant?'

'Not tonight. You can take An Na upstairs—she did her spelling homework with your father after school.'

Mei spent the night tossing and turning over Jet. Every time she closed her eyes visions of him came to mind. His startling blue eyes. The smooth warmth of his bare chest. His long fingers stroking her skin. The taste of his lips on hers. Her hormones were going crazy and it was hard to be annoyed with him when her body was flooded with heat.

She blamed her reaction on the recent lack of sex in her life and told herself it was just a chemical response, but she knew she needed to stay away from him until she'd worked out how to maintain her self-control. She'd dated occasionally over the past eight years, but not terribly successfully. She didn't want to be a single mother but she hadn't really given herself the opportunity to meet someone. It wasn't easy when she still lived with her parents. Normally dating and sex were the furthest things from her mind, but seeing Jet again awoke a lot of long-forgotten feelings and impulses.

It would be okay. She had time to work out what this meant. What seeing him again meant. For her but more importantly for An Na.

In the meantime, she'd have to figure out how to work with him. She'd been wanting the transfer to Bondi Station for months; she couldn't let anything derail her.

'Bondi Eleven, do you copy?'

'This is Bondi Eleven, go ahead,' Mei responded to the ambulance command centre. She and Alex were heading for the station at the end of a night shift but, as so often happened, a call came in before they could get back and hand over to the day shift crew.

'We have a call from the Bondi lifeguards requesting assistance. They have an injured surfer with a nasty gash to the upper thigh; it's bleeding heavily and they haven't been able to control it. They've brought the patient to the tower.'

Mei frowned. It was just after six in the morning; what time did the lifeguards start work?

'On our way,' she said as she flicked the switch for lights and sirens and Alex swung the ambulance in a one-hundred-and-eighty-degree turn and headed for the famous beach.

The streets had been decorated in preparation for Christmas. Somewhere in the past twenty-four hours the shops and restaurants seemed to have mutually decided to launch into the festive spirit. Decorations hung from the light poles and even their ambulance had a Christmas bauble hanging from the rear vision mirror. Mei loved Christmas but it did seem to arrive earlier every year. She supposed her parents would soon be digging out the decorations for the restaurant and she and An Na would be busy stringing lights and tinsel. She wondered if Jet loved Christmas.

Perhaps he would be at the tower. 'What time do the lifeguards start work?' she asked.

'Six a.m. And they're on duty until seven at night.'

She hadn't realised they started that early. She'd been preparing herself to see Jet again next week, when she was back on day shift. What if he was on duty today? She wasn't mentally ready for this. It was only two days since she'd seen him on the beach at Paul's emergency and she hadn't anticipated seeing him again so soon.

She took a deep breath and told herself to relax.

Maybe he wasn't rostered on. Maybe she was stressing over nothing.

But of course he was the lifeguard who greeted them at the door to the tower.

Her heart was racing. She was glad she was short; that way she didn't need to look him in the eye but instead she was face to face with his bare chest. Yet again. Didn't the man own a shirt?

She looked past him, trying to ignore the fact he was tall, lean, golden and glorious.

She didn't want to think of him that way. She didn't want to think of him at all.

But her head had been full of memories for the better part of the past two days and she was struggling to think about anything else.

She tensed as Jet greeted Alex. She had no cap or sunglasses to hide behind today, but maybe he still hadn't recognised her? Maybe he hadn't remembered her? Maybe she was getting herself all worked up over nothing.

'Hello, Mei.'

So he remembered her. That pleased her, appealed to the little bit of vanity she had, but she wished it didn't. It didn't make the situation any easier. Any less complicated. She was equal parts flattered that he hadn't forgotten her and annoyed with herself that she cared, but right now she needed to ignore both those feelings and get to work.

Would she be able to work with him? It was obvious it was going to be a regular occurrence. She'd have to find a way. She had a job to do. She had to focus on her job. On her patient. Their patient.

'Hello, Jet.'

Her voice was husky and she fought the urge to clear her throat, knowing that would just draw attention to her flustered state. She brushed past him as she stepped inside the tower, aiming for nonchalance, hoping not to let him see how much he affected her and eager to get on with treating her patient, eager to have something else to focus on.

A treatment plinth was tucked against the wall in the lower section of the tower. A dark-haired woman with a pale face lay on the bed. Her skin was grey and covered with a sheen of sweat. She clutched a small green whistle in her hand and as Mei watched she put it in her mouth and sucked on it like a lollipop, seeking the pain relief from the drugs it administered.

'Hello, I'm Mei,' she said as she put her medical bag on the floor beside the bed, taking care not to knock the woman. 'I'm with the ambulance.'

Mei had hoped that treating the patient would have focused her attention, but Jet stood beside her as she introduced herself to the patient, giving her no space to gather her thoughts.

'Amandine is from France.' Mei could feel Jet's warm breath on her neck as he spoke.

'Do you speak English?' Mei asked.

The woman nodded but did not let go of the green whistle. Mei knew she was in pain and would find talking difficult, so she wasn't surprised when Jet stepped in to provide the history of the injury. 'She's got a nasty gash in her thigh. It's pretty deep and we had trouble stemming the bleeding.'

Someone had put a blanket over Amandine's torso but her legs were bare. Mei could see a tourniquet around Amandine's thigh, above the bandage. Blood had soaked through the layers, staining the fabric red. That didn't look good.

'This was a surfing accident?' Mei looked up at Jet, forgetting in her confusion that she was trying to avoid eye contact, but she couldn't figure out how Amandine could have cut her leg so badly while surfing.

Jet nodded. 'The fin on another surfer's board cut across her thigh.'

'The fin on a surfboard did that?' Mei hadn't realised they were sharp enough to cut skin and, by the sound of Jet's description, right through the skin and into the muscle. But hopefully the sharpness would at least mean they would be dealing with a neat wound with no jagged edges. Mei wondered if she should take a look at the wound. Would it be better just to transport Amandine to hospital? What if it wasn't as bad as the lifeguards thought? She didn't want to make a drama, but there was no reason to doubt them. They had seen the wound, dressed it, and it was still bleeding. She must attempt to stem the bleeding before moving the patient.

'Is it all right if I take a look?' She needed to know what they were dealing with. Could they move her safely or was that likely to cause more bleeding? How much blood had she already lost?

Amandine nodded but it was obvious she was feeling uncomfortable. That made two of them, Mei thought.

The tower was crowded. Every square inch of space had a purpose and there wasn't much room around the bed. Jet was on Mei's right, standing close, filling the space. He was close enough that she could feel his body heat and his proximity made the skin on her forearms tingle.

He smelt of the ocean. Of salt and sun.

He smelt the same as he had eight years ago.

Mei wondered if she could give Jet a job to do, something to get him to move out of her space.

'Alex, can you give me a hand?' She'd replace Jet with Alex, she decided. Together they'd have a look at Amandine's wound. Alex moved in as she pulled on a pair of gloves, but Jet only moved to Mei's left.

He brushed past her, his leg grazing her bottom as he squeezed behind her. Mei's hands trembled as she unwrapped the bandages to examine Amandine's injury. She took a deep breath to focus her mind as Jet kept up a conversation with their patient.

'Is this your first time in Australia?'

'*Oui*, I arrived yesterday.'

Jet continued chatting to Amandine and Mei knew he was distracting her deliberately, giving her something other than her injury to focus on.

She was well aware that Amandine's eyes were fixed on Jet, that she couldn't care less what Mei and Alex were doing. Which was just as well. Her leg was a mess. Mei kept her eyes fixed on her patient. She couldn't afford to be distracted by Jet's voice as well.

Amandine had sustained a nasty injury. The gash in her thigh was deep into the muscle. She needed to go to hospital and would probably need the skills of a plastic surgeon. Luckily, the fin of the surfboard appeared to have missed all major arteries, but she would have a nasty scar as a reminder of her holiday in Australia.

Mei cleaned the wound and did her best to hold the edges together with butterfly strips before rewrapping Amandine's thigh with fresh sterile bandages.

'You'll need to come with us to the hospital,' she told Amandine. There was nothing more they could do for her here in the lifeguard tower. They needed to get going. *She* needed to get going.

'I'll get the stretcher,' Alex said, and he ducked out of the tower before Mei had a chance to respond.

Mei gave Amandine an injection for the pain and then finished bandaging her thigh. She looked around, wondering how they were going to get the stretcher into the tower. She knew it wasn't going to fit easily and there was no way Amandine could walk out of there on her injured leg or after sucking on the green whistle.

'The stretcher's not going to fit in here,' she said as she taped the bandage in place and began to repack the kit, looking for tasks to keep her hands and mind busy.

'I've got this,' Jet said as the tower door opened, announcing Alex's return. 'Keep sucking on the whistle, Amandine, while that injection takes effect. I'm going to carry you to the stretcher,' he said and, before Mei could ask what he was doing, and before she had time to wonder if it was safe, Jet had slid one arm under Amandine's thighs, another around her back and she was clinging to him with her free hand as he scooped her up.

Mei stepped back, out of the way as Jet spun on his

heel and carried Amandine out of the tower. And then she forgot to move. She stood, rooted to the spot, transfixed by the sight of Jet effortlessly lifting this woman. Amandine wasn't a big girl, but she wasn't tiny either, and while Jet's muscles bulged he didn't appear to be struggling.

As Jet gently lowered the patient onto the ambulance stretcher Mei finally got her feet moving just in time to see Amandine gazing adoringly at Jet. The effects of the green whistle often induced a feeling of euphoria and Amandine was no exception. She had completely forgotten about her pain, probably due to a combination of the pain relief and being in Jet's arms, and Mei couldn't blame her. Jet was gorgeous.

Alex strapped Amandine onto the stretcher as Mei dumped the medical kit at her feet and released the brakes, in a hurry now to get away from the beach. She knew she wouldn't be able to think straight until she put some distance between herself and Jet. Between herself and his golden gorgeousness. Between herself and the sight of his tanned perfection and blue eyes.

Mei pushed the stretcher to the ambulance and Jet followed behind her. She locked the stretcher into the rails and pushed the button to load it into the ambulance before climbing into the back with her patient. She turned her head, waiting for Alex to close the doors, but Jet was there instead.

He smiled and winked at her as he pushed the rear doors shut and Mei could feel a blush staining her cheeks. He hadn't said anything, thank God, as Mei knew she wouldn't have been able to formulate a sensible response; her brain felt like scrambled noodles.

She needed to get herself together. She needed to work out a plan. A strategy.

The sun was well and truly up over the horizon by the time Mei and Alex handed Amandine over to the hospital staff and returned to the station to knock off. Mei was eager to get home in time to take An Na to school. Normally after a night shift she would then go home and sleep for a few hours, but she was far too wound up. She messaged her sister-in-law, desperate to meet for a coffee after school drop-off.

Somehow she got An Na organised and to school. Thank God, at the age of seven, her daughter was too engrossed in the day ahead to notice her mother's distracted air.

Mei arrived first. The café was playing Christmas carols and listening to songs about sleigh rides in the snow when the Australian sun was high overhead and it was almost thirty degrees Celsius at ten in the morning always made Mei smile. It was quite incongruous, but it didn't diminish the excitement that started to build in her at this time of year. She loved Christmas, loved the time spent with her family, loved the traditions her family celebrated. When her family had moved to Australia from Hong Kong her parents had combined the more formal British and Chinese Christmas traditions with the laid-back Australian style and Mei loved the uniqueness of their celebrations.

She hummed along to the music while she scrolled through photos of An Na on her phone and waited for

Su-Lin. She noted some similarities between An Na and Jet that she'd forgotten about. They had more in common than just their smile. The tilt of An Na's head when she was deep in thought and her long fingers had been inherited from her father, but Mei wasn't certain she wanted to see the similarities.

She put her phone away as her sister-in-law arrived, pushing a pram; Mei's nephew was fast asleep.

'What's the emergency?' Su-Lin asked as she parked the pram beside the table.

'Thanks for coming,' Mei said. 'I hope I haven't interrupted your day.'

'You have—' Su-Lin laughed '—but I'm glad of the interruption. I could murder another coffee. I feel like I've done a day's work already. I had to get Dan to daycare, Vivian to school and Kai has got his vaccinations today, but I'm guessing, given that you're still in your uniform, that I'm not going to get much sympathy from you. I have no idea how I'm going to manage when I go back to work. Three kids are *so* much more work than two.'

'I thought you were going to have help?' Mei asked. Su-Lin was on maternity leave from her job as a lawyer and Mei's brother was a dentist. They could afford help.

'Bo wants me to find a nanny—it would make sense, rather than paying for two lots of childcare—but I haven't started looking yet.'

Mei had always thought her brother and sister-in-law's life looked easy in comparison to her own. They had plenty of money and there were two of them to raise the kids. She wasn't jealous but envious. She knew she was lucky to have not only their help but that of her parents, but she still dreamt of being independent. She could move out of her parents' apartment, but she told herself they would miss An Na. Even though she knew she stayed put because it was easier for her. She didn't see the point in disrupting everyone's lives just to make her own harder.

'How much longer until you go back to work?' she asked.

'A couple of months. February,' Su-Lin said as Kai woke from his nap and started gurgling in his pram.

Mei picked him up, keen to have a cuddle.

'You need to have more kids,' Su-Lin told her.

'You just said how hard it is!'

'You don't have to have lots, just one more. Babies suit you.'

'I do adore babies,' she admitted. She loved their smell, their softness. She loved imagining the possibilities for them. She would actually love to do it all over again, but she had promised herself she'd do it differently next time. For a start she'd plan the pregnancy. She didn't want another surprise; she wanted to enjoy the excitement, the anticipation, and not be terrified of the future. She wanted a partner to support her, she wanted to get some sleep and enjoy being a mother.

She knew some of her fears would ease the second time around, although she suspected she would always be scared of failing in her parenting duties somehow. It was a constant worry, probably heightened by the fact that, for An Na, she was it. But having a partner might help to allay some of that fear. It would have to, surely?

'An Na is old enough now,' Su-Lin said. 'You should start dating. We need to find you a man.'

'That's what I needed to see you about.'

'What? Really? Have you met someone?' Su-Lin clapped her hands in excitement.

'No. It's not that,' Mei said. 'I wanted to talk to you about An Na's father.'

'The surfer?'

Mei nodded. Su-Lin knew all about Jet. Su-Lin had married Mei's brother, but their families had been connected since they were babies. Both Mei's parents and Su-Lin's had emigrated from Hong Kong to Australia when Mei was only two years old. Su-Lin had been like an older sister to her and she was the one Mei had turned to when she'd discovered she was pregnant.

When it had been too late for a termination and Mei was beside herself, worried about her parents' reaction and knowing she couldn't possibly manage seven years of med school with a baby, she had turned to Su-Lin. She'd been terrified that she wouldn't cope, that she'd ruin not only her own life but her child's as well. But Su-Lin and Mei's brother, Bo, had been supportive and had certainly helped to smooth over what could only be described as a rocky patch in Mei's life and also in her relationship with her parents. She knew they'd been disappointed in her, she'd been disappointed in herself, but they had crossed that bridge and ever since they had been an amazing support for her and for An Na.

It had taken them all a while to get to where they were now. For Mei to stop feeling ashamed that she'd put herself in this position and that she couldn't manage on her own. For her to accept her parents' help without feeling guilty. For a long time she'd felt she'd let everyone down, but now they had their routine, their roles and An Na was loved and supported by her extended family.

Su-Lin had been the one who had gone back to Byron Bay with Mei in search of Jet eight years ago. She had comforted her when they hadn't been able to find him. She and Bo had supported her when she'd told her parents about her pregnancy. She'd been with her when An Na was born and she'd been beside her every step of the way since. Su-Lin was her best friend and had always given her unwavering support and sage advice and she needed her wisdom and practical advice again now.

How would Jet fit into the roles they had all adopted for themselves? How would his presence change the dynamic? How would his presence affect An Na? And Mei?

What if he didn't like the way she'd brought up their child? It hadn't been his fault that he wasn't around, no matter how irritated Mei had been at times that he hadn't been there to help. What if he was critical of her parenting skills? She was just beginning to feel that she knew what she was doing after all these years. What if he found fault?

She had a thousand questions and she needed Su-Lin to help her make sense of it all.

'What about him?' Su-Lin asked.

'He's here. In Bondi.'

'You've seen him?'

Mei nodded.

'Where?'

'At work.'

'He's a paramedic?'

'No.'

'A patient?'

'No.'

'A policeman?'

'No,' Mei huffed. 'If you let me finish, I'll tell you,' she said. 'He's a lifeguard on Bondi Beach.'

'A lifeguard! How long has he been here?'

'I have no idea. I didn't get a chance to find out.' She didn't admit she hadn't tried.

'And does he know about An Na? Have you told him?'

'Not yet.'

'You will tell him?'

'I'll have to.'

'How did you feel, seeing him again?'

Conflicted. She couldn't deny that she was still attracted to him, that she was still drawn to him. That had surprised her. She had never reacted like that to anyone else—that strong sense of fate, inevitability. She was trying to put that to one side; there were more important issues than her hormones.

But how did she put her feelings into words?

Despite wanting Su-Lin's advice, she knew she couldn't tell her how she really felt. She didn't need advice about her emotions. She needed practical advice.

'I'm not sure how I feel,' she admitted. 'I've spent so many years being angry with him...' That was true but, seeing him again, that anger had diminished. It was still there but it wasn't as overwhelming, as all-encompassing. Anger and irritation had been moved aside to make room for a host of other emotions. Seeing him, hearing his voice and feeling his fingers brush her skin had made her feel alive, afraid and apprehensive. Anxious and excited.

'You're still angry with him? After eight years?'

Mei nodded.

'How is that even possible?' Su-Lin wanted to know.

'Because every time I have a bad day—when An Na was not sleeping, or not feeding, or teething, or crying because she didn't want to go to daycare, I would imagine Jet, somewhere in the great big world, surfing, dancing, having fun. In my mind he had no responsibilities, he was out there enjoying his life and that would annoy me. I never wanted to give An Na up but I resented the fact that I was raising her on my own.'

'To be fair, he didn't know about her.'

'I realise that. I know I'm being unreasonable, but it's how I felt. How I feel. All this time he's been right here in Sydney, living his life, while I've been raising An Na. He got to chase his dreams, while I had to give mine up.'

'You can't blame him for things he's known nothing about. Was it his dream to become a lifeguard? I thought he was going to travel the world and try to make it as a professional surfer?'

Mei nodded. 'He did want to be a professional surfer. At the time I thought that sounded romantic and exciting and adventurous. Once I had An Na I thought it just sounded unrealistic.'

'So, while you're angry at him, you don't actually

know how his life has turned out. You don't know what has happened to him over the past eight years. What has happened to his dream. It's probably fair to say that being a lifeguard wasn't his dream. Maybe this is your chance to sort things out. To forgive, in a sense. To move on and make a fresh start. You need to talk to him.'

'I know. I will. I just need to work out how and when.' She was incredibly nervous about what would happen next.

'Is he married?'

'I have no idea,' she said as a realisation hit her. 'What if he is? What if he wants to take her?'

'He can't just take her.'

'Oh, God, what a mess.' Mei put her head in her hands. 'This could get complicated.'

'Don't start worrying about things that might not happen. We'll work this out. You liked him once; I'm sure he's still a decent guy.'

'Do you think I should get a family lawyer?' Mei asked, completely ignoring Su-Lin's advice about not stressing over things she couldn't control or that hadn't happened yet.

'I don't think that's necessary at this stage, but family law isn't my area of expertise.' Su-Lin worked as in-house counsel for a large bank. 'If you like, I can ask a friend who is a family lawyer. I'll see if she is free over the weekend and if she minds if you pick her brains. We've got a dinner to go to on Friday, but we'll be home on Saturday. I could ask her over then.'

'Saturday is no good; it's the ambulance Christmas

party. I've said I'll go. It's a good chance to meet all my new colleagues.'

'You're going to a party?'

'You don't need to sound quite so surprised.'

'Why not? This is a big deal for you. What are you going to wear?'

'I haven't thought about it.'

'Just make sure it's something other than your paramedic's uniform or jeans.'

'I have absolutely nothing else in my wardrobe.'

'You know you're welcome to borrow something of mine.'

'Your clothes are far too glamorous for me.' Su-Lin's wardrobe was extensive and she was always immaculately dressed. Even today, when all she was doing was running errands, she looked as if she had stepped off a catwalk, but Mei had long since given up comparing her style to Su-Lin's. She knew they were chalk and cheese.

'Don't be ridiculous. I've got a red dress that will look gorgeous on you and perfect for a Christmas party. Why don't Vivian and I pick An Na up on Saturday and bring the dress over and help you get ready? An Na and Vivian would love to see you getting dressed up. And then we'll take An Na home with us; she can spend the night.'

Mei knew she'd accept Su-Lin's offer of a sleepover. She knew how much An Na loved spending time with her cousins, plus it would give Mei a chance to sleep in.

'And that way,' Su-Lin continued with a smile, 'if you meet someone nice, you don't need to rush home. You don't need to come home at all.'

'It's a work show,' Mei protested. 'I'm not about to hook up with one of my colleagues!' Her days of reckless behaviour were well and truly behind her. She had other responsibilities now but, even if she didn't, one big mistake was all she was prepared to make in her lifetime. 'I'm quite happy with my life.'

'It's not you I'm thinking of,' Su-Lin said. 'It really is time you started dating. An Na needs a father figure and your parents expect you to get married.'

Mei knew her parents wanted her married. The fact that she'd had an unplanned pregnancy and was now a single mother was a source of disappointment to them. She was disappointed in herself—not because she was a mother but because her mistake had cost her her dream of becoming a doctor. It was her only regret, but one she'd learned to live with. It would have been impossible to manage; she wouldn't have had the time or energy to cope. Something would have failed, she would have failed, either at being a doctor or being a mother, and that was a risk she hadn't been prepared to take.

She was only just coping now with raising a child and working and that was with the help of her extended family.

'I don't have time to date,' she told Su-Lin.

Mei had never really dated anyone seriously despite her sister-in-law's best efforts at matchmaking and she'd always been adamant that she was happy alone. But she knew that wasn't true. She wanted a relationship, someone to share her life with, but she was terrified of mucking things up, of not choosing wisely.

She'd worked hard to make a happy, uncomplicated

life for An Na and she was trying not to put unrealistic expectations on her. She understood why her parents had raised her and her brother the way they had, but she wanted her daughter to live a more carefree childhood and Mei didn't want any of the dramas that could come with failed relationships. An Na had good male role models in her grandfather and uncle; her life wasn't lacking but Mei's was. But she didn't want to risk failure.

'I'd need some sort of guarantee that it was going to work out before I expend precious energy on dating.'

'That's ridiculous,' Su-Lin protested. 'You can't know in advance. You have to give someone a try.'

But Mei wanted—needed—a guarantee next time. She'd given her heart to Jet, unintentionally; she hadn't meant to fall so hard for him, a holiday fling. She'd known it would never work—he was a young man with no bigger goals than to travel the world. He was headed for the surf breaks of Hawaii, and she was headed for med school—but that hadn't stopped her from falling for him.

They'd had instant chemistry, but that wasn't what she'd fallen for. She'd fallen for his soft heart and the loneliness that lay beneath a veneer of confidence. The loneliness that mirrored her own. She'd known he'd needed her and she was happy to give herself over. She hadn't expected not to get all of herself back though. But that was exactly what happened. She'd taken a piece of him with her when she'd returned to Sydney but left a piece of her heart behind.

Next time she gave her heart away she needed a guarantee that it wasn't going to hurt. Next time she gave her heart away it was going to be to her true love.

CHAPTER THREE

MEI READJUSTED THE straps on her borrowed dress, checking that she was still decent. Su-Lin's idea of a party dress revealed a little more cleavage than Mei was comfortable with, but she had nothing else to wear. Her wardrobe consisted of jeans, T-shirts and her uniform and she had to admit Su-Lin had been right; red suited her and it did feel good to dress up for a change. She'd even relented and let Su-Lin do her make-up. While it could still only be called minimal it was more than she normally wore. Her job as a paramedic was far from glamorous whereas Su-Lin, as a corporate lawyer, was a dab hand at applying make-up and had transformed Mei's look from tired, suburban single mum to a festive twenty-something. On the outside at least.

Satisfied that all her parts were where they were supposed to be, she climbed the stairs to the Bondi Pavilion. She wasn't nervous. She was used to making conversation and, being a work party, she would have something in common with everyone here, but it had been a long time since she'd gone to a function on her own. Since she'd gone to a function at all.

The sound of live music greeted her as she pushed open the door. She ducked under some low-hanging mistletoe and looked around the room. Christmas lights and decorations were strung around the room and a band was set up on a stage in the opposite corner. There was already a crowd on the small dance floor and the room seemed to be bursting with people. Surely they couldn't all be from the Bondi Ambulance Station? Perhaps a few stations had combined their celebrations.

She spotted some of the paramedics she'd shared shifts with standing in a group near the stage and headed in their direction. She'd start with Alex and Poppy, two familiar faces; there'd be time to meet new people later.

'Hello, Alex. Poppy.'

'Mei! Hi,' Poppy greeted her. 'You look great; that's a fabulous dress.'

Mei squirmed under the compliment, aware that it drew everyone's attention to her. She preferred to fly under the radar. 'Thank you,' she managed to reply as she resisted the urge to check that everything was in the right place yet again.

The lifeguard who had driven her to the resuscitation job was standing beside Poppy. His name popped into her head as she wondered what he was doing there.

'Hello, Ryder,' she said. She would have loved to have a quick glance around to see if there were other lifeguards at the party, to see if Jet was there, but her back was to the room. She didn't turn; she wasn't sure if she wanted to see Jet or not. Equal parts yes and no.

'You've met?' Poppy asked.

Mei nodded. 'We met at the beach, on a job.'

Poppy tucked her arm through Ryder's. 'He's my fiancé.' She was looking at Ryder as she said, 'I still can't get used to the idea that we're getting married.'

'Congratulations.' Mei relaxed. Ryder was there with Poppy. She wouldn't be bumping into Jet. 'When is the wedding?'

'We're not sure yet,' Poppy said.

Ryder answered at the same time, 'I'm thinking March.'

'You are?' Poppy sounded surprised. 'March?'

Ryder nodded and kissed Poppy. 'I'd marry you tomorrow if I could. I don't see any reason to have a long engagement.'

Poppy looked very much like a woman in love as she beamed at Ryder before she turned back to Mei, who was beginning to feel a little as if she was intruding on something private, despite the fact that Alex was also still standing there.

'Are you married? Dating?' Poppy asked Mei.

'Stop it,' Ryder said.

'What?'

'You're doing the thing that all couples do—trying to set everyone else up.'

'It's fine,' Mei said. 'I'm single but I'm not looking to be set up. I've got too much on my plate at the moment with the new job and all.'

'Well. If you change your mind, Ryder knows plenty

of eligible men. Half the lifeguards are single. He can introduce you to some tonight if you want.'

'Tonight?' Mei looked around the room, suddenly nervous.

'Yes. The lifeguards are here too. The party is for all the Bondi first responders and emergency services—the firies, police, paramedics and lifeguards, because we all work so closely together it's become an annual tradition to celebrate together.'

'I hadn't realised that the party was for everyone,' Mei replied. Her heart was racing at the thought that Jet could be here too.

'Christmas is a crazy time in Bondi,' Alex added. 'So we have to celebrate early—we'll be working flat out for the next month, right up past New Year's Day.'

Ryder was looking at his empty glass. 'I need a beer and you need a drink, Mei. What can I get you? Champagne? Wine?'

Mei wasn't much of a drinker, alcohol tended to go straight to her head, but it was Christmas. One champagne couldn't hurt. 'I'd love a champagne, thanks.' The idea that Jet might be at the party had made her jittery; perhaps a drink would help to calm her nerves.

'Alex, do you need another?'

Alex checked his drink and drained the last mouthful. 'I'll come with you.'

The men headed for the bar, leaving Poppy and Mei alone.

'How are you settling in at the station?' Poppy asked.

'Good. Apart from the sand. I swear I empty half

the beach from my boots every night. I hadn't realised how often we'd be called to the beach.'

'It does keep us busy, especially at this time of year. There can be forty thousand people at Bondi on a summer's day, that's the population of a large country town, so there's plenty for us to do there. Where were you working before?'

'In Western Sydney, but this is closer to home. I've been applying for a transfer for ages, but I've only got a few years' experience and I kept missing out to more qualified paramedics. How long have you been at the station?'

'Only a couple of months.'

Mei smiled. 'So, you're one of the ones I was competing against. Where did you move from?'

'Brisbane.'

'Did you move with Ryder?'

'No, we grew up together but we hadn't seen each other for twelve years. I bumped into him again here.' Poppy looked past Mei towards the bar and smiled. Mei didn't turn her head, but she could tell from Poppy's dreamy expression that she was looking at Ryder. 'I can't believe we're getting married.'

'That's twice you've said that. Don't you want to get married?'

'Funnily enough, I do, but I never expected that I would. I didn't grow up in a traditional family so this is a big deal for me.'

'Where did you grow up? Brisbane?'

'No, I grew up in Byron Bay.'

Mei's heart thudded in her chest at Poppy's mention

of Byron Bay. She'd been thinking about Byron often over the past week but to hear someone else mention it, to hear she had lived there, was a little surreal.

'I grew up with Ryder. He was a friend of my brother's,' Poppy was saying and Mei forced herself to focus. 'Speaking of the devil, here he comes.'

Poppy was looking over Mei's shoulder and this time Mei turned to see who was in her field of vision. And then immediately wished she hadn't.

Jet was walking towards them.

'Jet is your *brother*?'

She hoped Poppy was going to say no even while she knew it was inevitable that the two of them were related. Seeing them together, both tall, blonde, tanned and gorgeous, it was obvious they were related.

'You know Jet?'

Surprise made Mei incapable of stringing two words together and when she nodded in reply, Poppy concluded, 'Of course, you would have met him at work. Yep, he's my big brother.'

Mei took a deep breath as she tried to quell the rising panic. She had an overwhelming sense that she wasn't keeping up, that things were spiralling out of her control. She hadn't been able to decide if she wanted Jet to be here tonight or not, and now he was walking towards her and she was totally unprepared.

She knew she wouldn't be able to avoid him for ever, but she wasn't ready. In a social setting there was no easy way to escape. At work she could avoid difficult conversations and she always had an out—at some point she always needed to get back into the ambulance and leave the beach. She could leave the party but she hadn't been there long and her intention had been to socialise with her new colleagues. She wasn't going to let Jet scare her off.

He was smiling as he came towards them, fixing Mei to the spot as she got a glimpse of An Na. She let her eyes run over him, wanting, needing to avoid getting entranced by his beautiful face. He was wearing lightweight trousers and a blue shirt that matched the colour of his eyes. The shirt was decorated with surfing Santas and his outfit made her smile.

Too late, she realised he would think she was smiling at him. For him.

'Hello, Mei. Ryder sent me over with drinks for you both.'

Mei hadn't noticed that he was carrying two champagne flutes and what appeared to be a water. She had been far too immersed in his eyes.

'Is the water for me?' Poppy asked.

'No, it's mine. Why?'

'I'm not drinking. I have to work tomorrow.'

'You'd better check with Ryder. I don't think he got that memo.' Jet grinned as Poppy excused herself.

'And then there were two,' he said, still smiling, as he held out a glass to Mei. 'Champagne?'

'Thank you.' Mei took the glass Jet offered. 'You did that on purpose,' she said as she tried, unsuccessfully, to ignore the heat that spread through her as Jet's fingers brushed hers.

'Did what?'

'Brought Poppy the wrong drink.'

'And why would I have done that?' His smile widened and Mei's knees wobbled.

Mei didn't answer. She'd imagined it was his ploy to get her to himself but she couldn't say that. At best, she might be wrong; at worst, it would make her look conceited.

'Would it be so that I could speak to you alone, without my sister around?' he asked.

Perhaps it had nothing to do with wanting time alone with her but simply a desire to keep Poppy in the dark about how they knew each other. She hadn't thought about that.

She sipped her champagne, using it as an excuse to avoid answering his question as she cautioned herself to relax. She realised her insecurities were carrying her away. She didn't need to try to work out what he was thinking—more than likely he wasn't thinking anything at all—and he certainly would have no idea about the thoughts in her head, the ones that were threatening to drive her crazy. She would relax and try to pretend that he was just a casual acquaintance and not a man who could send her hormones wild and make her go from annoyed to weak at the knees with just one smile or the briefest touch of his hand. She'd pretend he was a casual acquaintance and not the father of her child.

'You look worried,' he said. 'I won't tell anyone about our wild weekend if that's what's concerning you.'

Shit, maybe he could read her mind! But that wasn't what she was worried about. Well, not the only thing. Jet could promise to keep it a secret but what he didn't realise was that everyone was going to find out about their history anyway. She couldn't keep An Na a secret for ever. What *she* hadn't counted on was that 'everyone' included Jet's sister, which meant that her new colleagues would also be privy to that history. Would they judge her harshly?

'I'm not worried,' she lied. She wasn't only worried—she was nervous too. But it wasn't their history making her skittish, it was Jet. The way she felt around him unsettled her. The moment she saw him she forgot to be angry. She forgot about all the years when she'd been literally left holding the baby and all she could think about was how she'd felt when he'd held her in his arms, when he'd kissed her, when he'd made love to her. She could feel a blush start to rise in her cheeks and was grateful that the room was only lit by strings of Christmas lights.

'Catch me up,' he said.

That might have been possible if it hadn't been years since they'd seen each other. If her whole life hadn't changed. 'On the last eight years?'

'Is that how long it's been?'

'Almost to the day.'

He was still smiling as he said, 'You must have lots to tell me then.'

If he only knew.

'You're not married, are you?' he asked and before she could respond he had reached for her left hand, holding her fingers gently in his and turned her hand over, looking for a ring.

His thumb brushed her knuckles and her hand trembled as heat raced up her arm and filled her chest.

Her heart was pounding as she shook her head. 'No, never married.'

She wondered what he'd say if she said she had a daughter. She was tempted to see what sort of reaction she would get but she knew that was irrelevant—she was going to have to tell him at some point, but she wanted to find out what sort of man he'd become first. How his life had turned out. What would she be dealing with? What if he had other children? What if An Na had siblings? If he had a family, would they accept An Na?

Did he have a wife? A girlfriend? Who would Mei be competing with?

Where had that thought come from? She knew she was getting carried away. Creating issues before she knew what the situation was. She needed to slow down. 'What about you? Married? Kids?' she asked.

He laughed. 'No, that's not on my agenda.'

He was two years older than her, which would make him twenty-eight, or maybe twenty-nine now. She was partly relieved to hear that the added complication of Jet having a wife and kids didn't exist but then she wondered if he'd ever want to get married. If he'd ever want a family.

He had a mischievous gleam in his eye as he asked, 'So, are you still behaving scandalously?'

'No!' She withdrew her hand from Jet's hold.

'That's too bad.'

She recalled his devil-may-care attitude. Rules and conventions didn't faze him, and while she couldn't imagine behaving scandalously again—she had certainly paid a price for that last time—she did wish she'd retained a little of the spontaneity that she'd found in Byron Bay, a little of the spark that Jet had brought out in her. But she knew that had been lost under the weight of responsibility and parenthood.

'What we did, what *I* did, was completely out of character for me. I *never* would have done that if I were in Sydney.'

'Why not?'

'I was too afraid of what people who knew me might say.'

'What did your girlfriends say? They were with you in Byron that weekend.'

'They were far too busy having their own adventures, celebrating the end of our school days and the start of their freedom, to worry about me.' She'd lost touch with those friends over the course of the next few months. An unexpected teenage pregnancy had been a sure way of sending her on a different trajectory to her peers and her embarrassment had ensured that she'd deliberately cut those ties.

'You know,' he said, 'I wasn't sure it was you, that first time I saw you on Bondi.'

'No?'

He shook his head. 'You looked familiar but beneath your cap and sunglasses it was hard to be certain. And you said you were going to study medicine. I wasn't expecting to see you working as a paramedic. I thought you had planned to be a doctor.'

'My plans changed,' Mei responded. 'I thought *you* were going to travel the world and live the life of a professional surfer.'

'My plans changed too,' he said. He looked away, but not before Mei had seen the shadow that crossed behind his eyes. What had caused that? Had she offended him?

She immediately wondered if she should apologise. Not that she was sure what for, but that was a habit of hers. She spent her life feeling pressured to live up to certain expectations and then apologising if she didn't meet them and that impulse spilled over into other aspects of her life. But before she could say sorry or ask him what was wrong he changed the subject.

'Do you like being a paramedic?'

She sipped her champagne as she considered her answer. 'I enjoy the fact that every day is different and that I'm helping people, but I still wish I was a doctor.'

'What's stopping you?'

'So many things,' she sighed. She had never let go of the idea of becoming a doctor, but the dream had faded as the reality of life took over until, eventually, she'd had to let it go.

'Regrets?'

She nodded. 'Some,' she said honestly. 'What about you?'

'Regrets? I've had a few...but then again—' he laughed '—I don't want to talk about regrets.'

'No?'

'No.' He was watching her closely now, his blue eyes intent on her face. They were standing close together, the volume of the band made it impossible to hold a conversation at a distance, but Jet stepped even closer. He bent his head until his lips almost brushed her ear and his voice was low and soft as he said, 'I want to dance. With you.'

She remembered how well he could dance. Mei had spent years in ballet class, dancing was something she loved, and Jet's dancing ability had been one of the many things that had attracted her to him. He was light on his feet, balanced. He had good rhythm and enjoyed dancing almost as much as she did.

He enjoyed dancing almost as much as he enjoyed sex.

She knew it was dangerous to accept. She knew she should say no, but no words came out of her mouth.

He took her drink and then he took her hand.

She hadn't said she'd dance with him. She hadn't needed to. They both knew she would.

The song ended and the band started a slower number but still she let him lead her to the dance floor.

Jet was well over six feet tall and he towered over her. Mei was only five feet four inches tall, and even with heels on she was little, but she didn't feel insignificant as she stepped into his hold. She felt delicate, but safe. She felt precious.

She closed her eyes and the years fell away as the music took her back to the night when they'd first met. It was almost as though she could feel the sand of Byron Bay between her toes.

She remembered how it felt to be in his arms, both dancing on the sand and in his bed. Whoever had coined the phrase about dancing leading to sex had got it right as far as she and Jet were concerned. Dancing with Jet on the beach had led her down the path towards her future.

Their first dance had been around a bonfire on the beach. She'd been with her group of girlfriends when she'd seen him, dancing on the opposite side of the fire. He'd been hard to miss. Tall and blond, he'd glowed in the firelight; his white gold hair had caught the glow of the flames, shining like a beacon against the black darkness of the night.

He'd locked eyes with Mei and he'd moved around the fire and joined the circle of girls. He'd danced with them all as a group until, at some point, it had become just the two of them together. Still separate, not touching, but definitely dancing as a couple.

And then she'd been in his arms. She'd been attracted to him immediately but once he'd held her in his arms she was done for. That was all it had taken. That was when she'd known she would sleep with him.

And then they hadn't been dancing at all. He'd bent his head and kissed her, brushing his lips over hers, and she'd lost her mind. Her feet had stopped moving but her knees wobbled. He'd held her up, supported her as she kissed him back.

She hadn't even known his name at that point.

She'd let him take her hand and lead her to a blanket on the sand. They'd listened to the music and kissed until the fire was just glowing embers.

At some point her girlfriends had told her they were going home to bed. They hadn't wanted to leave her with a stranger, but he hadn't felt like a stranger by then.

She'd gone home with him just as the sky was beginning to lighten in the east.

Home was a caravan on a block of land behind the beach. It was tiny but clean and had a bed just big enough for two.

She hadn't fallen in love. Not that night. It had been lust, pure and simple, and she'd made a conscious decision to give in to her desires. To give herself to Jet.

There had been no commitment, no promises, no expectations of anything other than fulfilling their desire.

She hadn't told him she was a virgin and he hadn't asked. She had danced for years, there'd been no pain, and he never suspected that he was her first lover.

He hadn't asked about contraception either and she hadn't thought to mention it.

That had been her only mistake.

If she'd known then what she did now, would she have danced with him at all?

She knew she would. She was doing exactly the same thing tonight, but this time she would be cautious. This time it would just be a dance. One dance where she could enjoy the feeling of being in his arms before she went home. It was highly likely that he was going to be a part of her life in some way, given he was the father of her child, but she couldn't let herself fall for him. They would always be connected but she didn't need to fall in love.

'Jet, you promised me a dance.'

Mei opened her eyes to find a pretty blonde woman standing beside her. It took her a minute to get her bearings, she'd been firmly lost in the past, but as the song ended and the tempo of the music changed she finally realised the woman was cutting in on her.

Jet looked as though he might be about to ask if she minded but she didn't have a monopoly on him and she knew the wisest course of action would be to put some distance between them.

'Thanks for the dance. I'm going to grab a drink,' she said before he had a chance to speak. She turned to the blonde, 'He's all yours.'

Giving him up willingly was one thing, watching him dancing with myriad other women was another thing altogether. Mei tried not to notice who he was dancing with, she tried to keep engaged with conversations with her colleagues, but it was impossible to ignore the fact that Jet had no shortage of partners on the dance floor. It wasn't surprising, a man who could dance was always going to have plenty of partners, but it made her wonder if that held true in all aspects of his life as well. She suspected it would. He exuded charm and confidence. He had grown into a man who was comfortable in his skin and that was a highly attractive trait. Combined with his physical attributes, she knew he would have no shortage of female attention and companionship.

Eight years had passed since they'd spent a weekend together. She'd slept with two men since. She knew her experience would be vastly inferior to Jet's and that put her at a disadvantage. She couldn't blame her inexperience on youth any more and watching him with other women, women who she assumed were vastly more confident and knowledgeable than her, convinced her that there was no way Jet would be remotely interested in her now.

It was probably just as well. She didn't need a playboy in her life.

Mei turned her back on the dance floor, thinking perhaps out of sight out of mind would work, but as the music stopped and the band announced a break between sets she felt the air around her begin to hum with an invisible energy and she knew Jet was nearby.

His hand brushed her hip as he stopped beside her. She had no idea if his touch had been intentional or not and, while he didn't seem aware of the contact, her heart leapt a little inside her ribcage.

'That took longer than expected,' he said.

'What did?'

'Getting off the dance floor.'

She was pleased that he'd come straight back to her, that he'd chosen her company in preference to one of his other dance partners, but she was also a little annoyed that he'd waited until the music stopped. He didn't have to keep dancing.

Mei took a deep breath as she gathered her thoughts. Jet made her feel so conflicted, so nervous and anxious, annoyed and excited. He made her feel things she hadn't felt in years, things she didn't *want* to feel, and that irritated her.

She felt vulnerable and exposed. Over the past few years she had learnt to be strong and independent and she didn't want someone else to influence her emotions or her character—especially not Jet. He'd had enough impact on her life.

'Will you dance with me again when the band come back on?' he asked.

Mei shook her head while she thought of an excuse.

She couldn't afford to let her guard down…she couldn't afford to step back into his arms.

'No, I'm about to head home.'

'Already? The party's only just getting started.'

She knew that wasn't true, but it was also far from over and she couldn't stay. She needed to put some distance between them. 'I have to be up early in the morning.'

'Are you working?'

'No.'

'Then surely you can stay a little longer. Can't you sleep in tomorrow?'

She shook her head again and decided to test him. 'No. There's no sleeping in when you have a child.'

'A child?' She heard the surprise in his voice and saw it on his face. She watched his expression and she could tell he was scrolling back through their earlier conversation, wondering if he'd asked that question and then realising he hadn't.

He'd asked if she was married. *She'd* asked if he had kids.

'You're a mother?'

She nodded. 'A single mother.'

She waited for him to ask if she had a son or a daughter. Then waited to see if he'd ask how old her child was and panicked that if he asked that question it would lead her into a conversation she hadn't prepared for. But she needn't have worried. He didn't ask anything more and he didn't try to convince her to stay.

'Okay, I get it,' he said.

He didn't physically step back but she could see in

his eyes that her status as a single mother had doused any interest he might have had in her. Telling him she had a child had been a test and Jet had failed. That was fine, she told herself. At least she knew where she stood, but she was disappointed in him and annoyed with herself for caring.

Seeing him withdraw made her realise she had been entertaining ideas of a happily ever after for her and for An Na. She'd been hoping he would embrace his instant family, embrace his daughter, embrace her. She'd pictured them building a life together, but finding out he was no longer interested in getting to know her again because she had a child was deflating.

But she tried to convince herself it was far better to know that now, before she got even more caught up in her fantasies of a happily ever after. Before she made another mistake.

It was their mistake that got her pregnant, but it was her mistake for choosing to sleep with a man she'd only just met. A man she barely knew. At least knowing how he felt saved her from making the same mistake again.

She'd be fine. She and An Na didn't need Jet in their lives.

But, for the first time in years, when she crawled into bed in a dark and silent house, the other side of the bed seemed very empty and Mei was swamped with loneliness. If An Na had been home she would have sneaked in with her, but she knew it wasn't her daughter's company she was missing. It wasn't her daughter's warmth that she craved. It was Jet's.

CHAPTER FOUR

JET AVOIDED THE dance floor after Mei had gone. He didn't want to dance with someone who wasn't Mei. The party had lost its spark and his mood had soured since she'd left. He was restless, off-kilter. He didn't feel like celebrating but he didn't want to go home yet either. He didn't want to go home alone. Earlier in the evening he had been anticipating spending time with Mei, perhaps even going home with her at the end of the night. He hadn't anticipated she'd be going home to a family.

It shouldn't matter, he told himself. He'd barely thought about her for the past eight years, even if he'd thought about her plenty over the past few days, and he could put her out of his mind again. Maybe he'd find someone else to take home.

But as he looked around the room he realised there was no one else who captured his attention the way Mei did. He hadn't been able to take his eyes off her all those years ago and it had been the same tonight. She had mesmerised him with her symmetrical doll-like features and dark eyes that seemed to be able to read his thoughts. There was a strong connection between them; it had been there eight years ago and it was still there now. He was drawn to her and he was powerless to fight it. Not that he wanted to.

There was something about her that made him feel less alone in the world. He felt that, even without talking, she understood him. Normally he wasn't fussed about people being on his wavelength, understanding him; he was quite happy as a solitary man and if he wanted a female opinion or point of view his sisters were always happy to oblige, but there was something about Mei that made him want to impress her. Something that made him want to be more than what he was. Who he was.

But finding out she had a kid changed all that.

He had decided long ago that he didn't have the skills needed to be a parent. He didn't want to risk making the same mistakes he felt his own parents had made. And if he had no intention of being a father he definitely had no intention of being a stepfather, which meant it was easier not to start a relationship with a woman who already had a child. So, unless he was prepared to break his own rule, Mei was off-limits. There were plenty of women in the world. He didn't need to chase after one with a child.

'You look like you could use a drink.' His brother-in-law-to-be was by his side, holding out a beer. Jet hadn't had a drink all night, he had a big training session tomorrow, but one beer couldn't hurt. Maybe it would help him to sleep, help to keep his mind off Mei.

'Where's Mei?'

Jet sighed. Couldn't Ryder have picked a different subject? Anything else would have been good.

'She's gone home.'

'Already? What did you say to her?'

'Nothing.'

Well. Almost nothing. Maybe he should have said something. But what? Her announcement had taken him by surprise, but even with warning he wouldn't have changed his mind. He had a rule. He didn't date mothers.

Mei was exhausted. Because of Jet she'd experienced myriad emotions in the space of a couple of hours. Surprise, desire, disappointment, anger.

And now she was annoyed with herself. She wished she could dial down her physical reaction to Jet, she wished she could forget about him, but he was clearly at the forefront of her mind and almost the first thing she mentioned to her sister-in-law when she went to collect An Na in the morning.

'Did you have a good night?' Su-Lin asked.

Had she? She wasn't sure how to describe the evening exactly. 'It started off okay.'

'What happened?' Su-Lin switched on the coffee machine as she prepared to listen to Mei debrief.

Mei was happy to stay. An Na was not in a hurry to leave her cousins and Mei needed a sounding board. Su-Lin was always the voice of reason.

She sat at the kitchen bench and started talking. 'Jet was there.'

'With a partner? Is he dating a paramedic or married to one?'

'No. The party was for all the local first responders, I hadn't realised that. I was a little unprepared.'

'You talked to him?'

'Yes,' she said, although she neglected to mention she'd danced with him. That seemed irrelevant now. As did the fact that she was still attracted to him, that he made her feel things she hadn't felt in years. If she was going to be completely honest, which she wasn't, she hadn't felt like this about anyone else, not before and not after Jet. But it didn't matter how she felt when she was in his arms. He'd made it perfectly clear that he wasn't interested, and Su-Lin didn't need to hear all of that. It wasn't important now.

'Did you tell him?'

'I told him I had a child.'

'That was it?'

'It was hardly the right environment to share the whole story and it was obvious he wasn't interested in me once he knew I was a single mother.' Mei checked behind her, making sure that none of Su-Lin's brood or An Na had come into the kitchen without being noticed. 'At least I don't need to worry about him wanting to take An Na away. He's not interested in being a father.'

'He said that?'

'He didn't need to.'

'He might change his mind if he knows he already has a child. You are still planning on telling him?'

Mei wasn't convinced. 'An Na and I are okay; maybe there's no need. We don't need to upset the apple cart.'

'Mei, it doesn't matter what you think. Jet needs to know. You need to think about An Na. What if she wants to find her father one day and then finds out you have kept them apart? You might not want Jet in your life but you can't make that decision for An Na. Or for Jet.'

'And what if he doesn't want anything to do with her? With us?'

'That's his call to make and it's one that is better coming from him, not from you. You have to give him all the information and then see what choice he makes. You can't condemn him without giving him the facts. He needs the chance to make an informed decision.'

'What would you recommend?'

'You should tell him sooner rather than later, but if you do want to speak to a family lawyer first I can give you a couple of recommendations,' Su-Lin offered for the second time. 'It might be a good idea to get some information about custody situations.'

'I really don't think he's going to want custody,' Mei said. She could talk to a lawyer, but nothing would change the fact that Jet was An Na's father and if he wanted to be part of her life Mei knew she would let him. She would never deny her daughter that.

'What about child support then?'

'Child support? I'm not going to ask for child support. An Na is my responsibility.'

'The court won't see it that way.'

'I thought you said you weren't a family lawyer.'

'I have plenty of friends who have been through divorces.'

'I don't need a lawyer. Not yet,' she decided. 'I'll talk to him first. We're both adults. Hopefully he'll want what's best for An Na and we can work things out between us.'

She thought about how she'd felt last night in Jet's arms.

Maybe things would be okay. She just needed him to be honest with her.

Could she trust him to do that?

She thought so. She hoped so.

Jet was coming back to the lifeguard tower after a coffee run when he saw an ambulance driving down Campbell Parade. His heart started racing and he picked up his pace as he wondered if the ambulance was headed for the beach, wondered if Mei was in it.

He ducked across the promenade and reached the tower just as Ryder stepped out.

'What's going on?' he asked as the ambulance turned onto the promenade and headed in their direction.

'We've got an elderly lady with a suspected fractured hip.'

'Do you know who the ambos are?'

Ryder grinned. 'Not Mei, if that's what you're asking.'

He bit back his disappointment. He hadn't seen her since the Christmas party and he hadn't been able to stop thinking about her.

'Why don't you call past the station and ask her out?' Ryder suggested. 'You know you want to.'

'I told you, I don't date women with kids. That's too much responsibility. I prefer to keep things simple.'

'Maybe you should make an exception. She's clearly

got under your skin; you've been grumpy ever since the Christmas party. It's your rule so there's no reason why you can't break it.'

Jet shook his head. 'No. I don't need to complicate my life. There are plenty of single women out there without kids,' he replied.

'Trust me, you don't want to live with regret. You should take the chance…that's assuming she's interested in you.' Ryder laughed and slapped him on the shoulder before going to meet the ambulance.

Jet returned to the tower, coffee in hand, and picked up a pair of binoculars to scan the beach. The beach was busy enough to keep him occupied while he tried not to think about Mei. There were plenty of other women in the world, in Bondi even.

That might be true, but he knew there weren't a lot of women out there who made him feel like Mei did.

But was she interested? He had no idea.

Was Ryder right? Should he test the water or would he be getting in over his head? Mei was different. Was that a good thing or a bad thing? Would he be asking for trouble?

He debated with himself for most of the morning, backwards and forwards, until finally he had enough. Until he finally realised there was only one option. He would put the ball in her court and see what she said.

He scribbled his number on a piece of paper and stuck it in the pocket of his shorts. If it was still there next time he saw her, if he hadn't gone into the ocean and destroyed the paper, he'd give her his number and leave it up to her to call him if she was interested. The decision would be Mei's.

He picked up the binoculars again and kept his eye on a group of teenage boys who were standing in a circle and kicking a soccer ball around. Ball games were banned on Bondi as the beach was often too crowded for ball sports to be played safely. He watched them for a few minutes, hoping they'd pack the ball away of their own accord, but when that didn't happen he decided he needed to go down to the sand and put a stop to their fun. He didn't enjoy spoiling someone's day but he'd seen too many accidents from wayward balls and knew it was better to be safe than sorry.

'I'm going down to speak to those boys,' he told Ryder when he returned to the tower.

He jogged through the soft sand towards them and, as he approached, one of the boys completely missed the ball and kicked another boy in the ankle. He collapsed in a heap and hadn't stood up by the time Jet reached them.

His ankle swelled immediately and he was unable to bear weight. Jet suspected the teenager had a fractured fibula and he called for the buggy and an ambulance. He crossed his fingers, hoping the ambulance would bring Mei.

By the time he got the boy into the buggy and back to the tower he could hear the siren of the approaching ambulance. The door opened and Mei appeared. Jet's heart leapt at the sight of her and he fought hard to keep the smile off his face.

'We're going to need the stretcher,' he told her as Alex started to assess the patient.

Mei nodded and turned on her heel to fetch it from the ambulance. Jet went with her but he knew she was wondering what he was doing.

'I don't need help,' she said as she opened the rear doors.

'I know. I have something for you.' He took the folded piece of paper from his pocket and handed it to her.

'What's this?'

'My phone number. I thought we might have a coffee some time.' He was surprised to find he was nervous.

She was frowning. 'I got the feeling you didn't date single mothers.'

Had he been that obvious or that easy to read?

'I don't,' he said. He didn't bother lying, there was no point; she could easily find out the truth from anyone who knew him. 'It's just a coffee,' he added, trying to downplay the invitation.

Mei nodded and tucked the paper into her chest pocket before pulling the stretcher from the ambulance and turning her attention to their patient. She gave him nothing and left him feeling that he might have just made a complete fool of himself.

'An Na, time to get ready for bed.'

An Na had been making dumplings, but she should have cleaned up her workstation ages ago. She was normally compliant about bedtime, but she was being resistant tonight and she was testing Mei's patience.

Mei was tired. She'd had a busy day at work and she was stressed over Jet. She had unfolded the piece of paper with his phone number on it so many times over the past few days that it was in danger of falling apart. She hadn't been able to bring herself to put his number into her phone but if she didn't do it soon the paper might disintegrate. Knowing she now could contact him, that he had unwittingly put the ball in her court, was making her fractious and she wasn't handling An Na's difficult behaviour well. Maybe she'd take over from her dad in the restaurant and he could put An Na to bed.

'An Na, do you want Ye Ye to read you a story?' she asked.

'If you're going out the front, can you take this order out?' her mum said as she handed her a takeaway order.

'Dad, do you want to take a break?' she asked as she put the carry bags on the counter. 'Would you mind reading An Na a bedtime story? She's resisting going upstairs but I think she'll listen to you. I'll look after things here for a bit.'

Mei was keen to get upstairs too, but she didn't have the energy to deal with An Na. It was one of the many difficult things about being a single mum. She thought again about how Jet had managed to escape all the hard years, the long hours. She realised he'd also missed out on all the joy, although some days, when she was so exhausted that her bones ached and she felt forty-six instead of twenty-six, it was harder to remember the good times.

She turned her head as the bell above the restaurant door jangled and Poppy walked in.

'Poppy, hello!'

'Mei! What are you doing here?'

'This is my parents' restaurant.'

'Your parents?'

Mei nodded. 'This is my dad—' she gestured a hand in her father's direction '—and Mum is the chef.'

'I had no idea!' Poppy declared. 'Ryder and I have eaten here so many times, the food is incredible. It's amazing that I've never seen you here.'

'I'm not regular wait staff, although I do help out around my ambo shifts,' Mei explained as An Na appeared from the kitchen.

'Hello, An Na,' Poppy greeted her.

'You know An Na?' Mei asked.

Poppy nodded. 'Of course, she's looked after us often when we eat here. She brings our menus and our water.'

'Hello,' An Na acknowledged Poppy before asking Mei, 'Mum, is Ye Ye going to read to me?'

'An Na is your daughter?'

Mei nodded—she could hardly deny it but she felt a flutter of anxiety coupled with a spell of light-headedness. She held onto the counter for support as her worlds collided. How had she never seen Poppy and Ryder in the restaurant before? How could Poppy know An Na?

Poppy was Jet's sister. Jet hadn't asked An Na's age but what if Poppy said something? He could put two and two together as easily as the next person. There were too few degrees of separation now.

She really needed to speak to Jet. Preferably before

Poppy did, but she couldn't ask her to keep An Na a secret without giving an explanation. Mei looked at the name on the takeaway order that her mum had given her; she hadn't paid attention to the name but it was obviously Poppy's.

'This is your order,' she said as she passed it over, hoping that would be enough to get her moving. Mei needed some time to think. 'Enjoy your dinner.'

Poppy left and Mei's father and An Na headed upstairs, leaving her alone at the counter. Why couldn't Poppy have come in ten minutes later, after An Na had gone upstairs? She knew it was only a matter of time now before Jet learned the truth. And she knew he needed to hear it from her.

'Has she called you yet?'

Jet and Ryder were sitting on the deck at Lily's house overlooking Bondi Beach and waiting for Poppy, who was picking up a takeaway on her way home from the ambulance station. All three of Jet's sisters—Lily, Poppy and Daisy—were living together and Jet, and Ryder, were frequent visitors.

'No.' He didn't know what to make of it. It had been a few days. He'd been sure Mei would call. But what if she didn't?

'So maybe your concerns about dating a single mother are unfounded. Looks like you might not get a chance.' Ryder laughed.

Of course, with Jet's competitive nature, the minute someone told him he couldn't do something he'd become desperate to prove them wrong. But he wasn't used to being in this situation. He wasn't used to waiting for a woman to be interested. He'd always been popular with women, had always been able to pick and choose, but now Mei had all the power and it was unsettling.

'Perhaps this is a good thing,' he said. 'I'd like to get to know her but it's not like I can just pretend her kid doesn't exist. It's probably better if she doesn't call. I don't like complicated women.'

'What makes you think she's complicated? There's a difference between a complicated woman and a complicated situation. I don't think you should give up on her yet.'

'Who are you talking about?' Poppy asked as she stepped out onto the deck and dumped the bags of takeaway on the table.

'Mei Chen,' Ryder said as he poured her a glass of wine.

'That's a coincidence,' Poppy said. 'I just saw her when I was picking up dinner. Her parents own Lao Lao's Kitchen. Why are you talking about her?'

'Your brother has given her his number but she seems to be resistant to his many charms and he's not sure what to do about it.'

'You're waiting for her to call you? Why don't you just ask her out?' Poppy said when he nodded.

'Because I have a rule—I don't date single mums. You know she has a kid?'

'I do.' Poppy nodded. 'She has a daughter and she's the cutest thing.'

'You've seen her?' Ryder asked as he unpacked the takeaway containers.

'Yes, you've met her too. It's An Na.'

'The waitress?'

'Waitress?' Jet was surprised. He hadn't asked her daughter's age but she couldn't be old enough to work. She must only be little. 'How old is she?'

Poppy laughed. 'Only young. She helps out in the restaurant, but waitress is a bit of a fancy term for a child. She's about seven.'

'Are you sure?'

'She's six or seven, around about that age. Why? Does her age make a difference?'

It didn't. At least, not in the way Poppy was thinking, but hearing that Mei's child—Mei's daughter—was that old made his head spin.

After Poppy's announcement it was impossible to focus. Dinner was a blur. He couldn't remember what he ate or the conversation. He hoped it mostly focused on Poppy and Ryder and their wedding plans. He hoped there wasn't anything he'd promised to do.

He kept doing the sums, over and over, in his head and as soon as they'd finished eating he excused himself.

His mind was racing as he walked down the hill towards home. Churning through multiple possibilities.

He'd been twenty when they'd met. Eight years ago. If Mei's daughter was six, he was off the hook. But what if she was seven? Who was the father?

Was he?

But surely Mei would have told him?

It mustn't be him. There was no real reason to think

he had anything to do with it. Which meant it was either someone else...or was Mei not sure?

But he didn't think Mei was the type of girl who would have had multiple partners.

Which left the very real possibility that Mei's daughter could be much younger than seven. Poppy hadn't been certain of her age.

Or maybe Mei didn't want him to know?

His mind was still spinning when he reached the corner of his street. He needed an answer, one way or the other. He needed to know if he was a father. If he had a daughter.

Instead of turning for home, he continued walking. He was halfway to the Junction. Halfway to the Chinese restaurant that apparently Mei's parents owned. There was only one way to solve the puzzle. He'd go and see if the restaurant was still open. If Mei was there.

He'd find Mei now and confirm that her daughter wasn't his and then he'd get on with his life.

He was only a few metres from the restaurant when the outside lights were switched off, leaving just the sign over the awning illuminated.

He stopped at the door and peered through the glass. He could see a figure at the back of the restaurant. Was that Mei?

He rapped his knuckles on the door and waited as Mei crossed the room. She was peering through the darkness and her expression when she reached the door and saw it was him was not one of surprise. He noticed her hesitate before she unlocked the door and he had the feeling that if the door hadn't been glass, if he hadn't been able to see her, she would have left him standing on the footpath.

'You've seen Poppy,' she said as she opened the door. Her voice was flat, her words a statement, not a question.

He nodded. 'Your daughter,' he said as he wiped his clammy hands on his thighs. 'Is she mine?'

CHAPTER FIVE

'YOU'D BETTER COME IN.'

Mei stepped back and let him into the restaurant. The chairs had been upended on the tables in preparation for cleaning the floor and she lifted one chair off a table for two near the window and set it on its feet. Jet lifted the other and collapsed into it. His legs felt as if he'd run a half marathon and he knew if he didn't sit down he'd fall.

Mei sat opposite him. She hadn't turned on the restaurant lights but there was enough light coming through the window from the street to illuminate her face. She was biting her lip and looking anywhere but at him.

Jet's heart was racing and his hands trembled. He clenched them into fists to stop the shaking and said, 'She's mine, isn't she?'

Mei looked at him then, her eyes huge and dark, her face pale.

She nodded and Jet exhaled, letting go of a breath he hadn't been aware of holding. He felt nauseous, nervous, terrified. That wasn't how he wanted to feel but he couldn't control it.

Mei was watching him. She looked worried and he wondered if she was afraid of his reaction.

One of them had to speak, but what was the right thing to say? What was the appropriate response? He realised he'd convinced himself that Mei's child wasn't his. He'd expected her to say no. But that wasn't the case. With one nod Mei had upended his world and changed his life.

He had a child.

He was a father.

Was he prepared for that?

He knew he wasn't. Far from it.

He wasn't emotionally or mentally prepared. He had no idea how to be a parent. His own parents had hardly set a fine example and fatherhood was something Jet had been doing his best to avoid. This wasn't a situation he'd ever spent much time considering and he found himself floundering now.

He should have a thousand questions but his mind was blank. The idea that he had a child, a daughter, that he was a father, was quite incomprehensible. He needed some time to process the information.

'Her name is An Na.' Mei had obviously given up waiting for him to say something, which was fortunate as he couldn't think of a single sensible, suitable comment.

'An Na.' The unfamiliar sounds rolled around in his mouth. He had a daughter; she was real. A small piece of him existed in the world, separate and distinct from him, but a part of him all the same.

'It means quiet and graceful.'

'Is she?'

Mei smiled and her expression softened, changing in an instant from one of concern and caution to one of unconditional love. Jet recognised it and wondered if that was an emotion that was innate or learned. He suspected the former. Surely if love for your child could be learned his parents would have been more loving. But if it couldn't be learned he was in trouble.

'She can be.' Mei paused before adding, 'Just not very often.'

'And she's seven?'

Mei nodded. 'She turned seven in August.'

'Were you planning on telling me about her?'

'Of course.'

'When? When she was eight or eighteen?'

'I've been trying to work out when and how. I didn't want to spring it on you out of the blue after all this time.'

They sat in silence as Jet tried to sort through his emotions.

'What happens now?' Mei asked. He was glad she didn't try to justify her position any further.

'I have no idea. I need time to think. You had time.'

'No, I didn't,' she argued. 'One day I was a teenager, planning on going to medical school, and the next I was an eighteen-year-old girl who was pregnant and having to make choices about something I had never considered. But I get that this is a shock, I get you'll need time, but please consider An Na in all of this. I know you said kids were not on your agenda, but none of this is her fault.'

'I know.'

He heard what she was saying but he couldn't make any promises. Not yet.

'Are you working tomorrow?' he asked.

'Night shift.'

'Can we meet for lunch?' He didn't know if his head would be any clearer by then, but he also knew he couldn't delay a serious conversation indefinitely. They would have a lot of things to talk about and work through.

'Shall I meet you here?' he asked when she nodded.

'No! Not here.'

'How about Tamarama Beach then?' Jet thought it would be good to be able to see the ocean; it would give clarity to his thoughts and Tamma was quieter than Bondi during the week.

'Can we go somewhere else?'

'Why? We'll get more privacy at the beach than we would in a restaurant.'

'I'm happy to avoid restaurants but I hate eating at the beach; there is nothing worse than sand in your food.'

'Okay, let's meet at Bronte Park,' he suggested as a compromise. There was a picnic area on the headland that overlooked the ocean but avoided the sand and it was usually quiet on a weekday. 'I'll meet you at the surf club; I'll bring something to eat and we can have a picnic. That way, we won't have any interruptions.'

'Let me bring the food. My parents own a restaurant after all.'

Jet wasn't sure that he could face another meal of Chinese food. Tonight's dinner was sitting heavily in his stomach but he knew that wasn't a fault of the cooking or the food. It was purely and simply stress.

'No, it's okay, I've got this one.'

Jet walked the streets after leaving the restaurant as he tried to figure out what had just happened. He knew he was in shock, nothing life-threatening or critical but he was reeling from the news that he was a father. It was a surreal notion.

He knew it wouldn't feel real until he met her.

He should have asked to see a photograph of her. Mei must have had dozens on her phone. But he was so stunned he hadn't known what to say, what to think.

He wondered what his daughter looked like. Did she take after him at all? Had he passed on any traits?

What would she be like and what would she make of him?

Could he be the father she wanted or needed?

How would he know? He and his sisters had grown up in an unconventional family. He knew they'd had an unusual childhood and that their experience was vastly different to the majority of kids and that meant he had no real idea about what was normal.

And what did all this mean for him and Mei? He had never dated a single mother, but she was no longer just any single mother—she was the mother of his child. That didn't change the fact that he was still drawn to

her, that she still set his pulse racing. But what did this
news mean for them? What would their future look like?

He wasn't about to walk away from his responsibilities, but did those responsibilities extend to Mei?

What was the right answer? Was there one?

Mei checked the time on the clock in her car. She was
running late to meet Jet and, to make matters worse,
she couldn't find a parking space. She slowed to a crawl
as she watched the pedestrians—hoping one of them
would get into their car and create a space for her—as
she tried to organise her thoughts before she saw Jet.

She'd tossed and turned all night, worried, stressed
and anxious about today's discussion, but a quick catch-
up with Su-Lin after dropping An Na at school had
calmed her nerves a little. Mei had dissected every one
of Jet's few words from last night's conversation, trying to guess where his head was at.

She had hoped he would be more enthusiastic but,
once again, Su-Lin had been the voice of reason, pointing out that the news had been rather sprung on him.

Mei hoped he would embrace the idea of being a father because how would she explain the alternative to
An Na? How could she tell her she'd found her father
if he didn't want anything to do with her? With them?

A young girl up ahead had her keys in her hand and
Mei pulled her car to the left, narrowly missing scrap-
ing her side mirror on a parked car as she waited to see
where the girl went. She breathed a sigh of relief as the
girl got into her car a few metres in front. Fortunately,
the space was large enough for Mei to avoid needing

to reverse park. It was never her forte and she knew in her current mindset it would be a risky manoeuvre. She parked without incident and was heading for the surf club when she heard Jet call her name. He was waiting by a picnic table and he looked relieved to see her. Was he not certain she'd turn up?

She had been tempted to postpone before realising there was no point in delaying the meeting. There was nothing to stop him from coming to the restaurant again and she was desperate enough at this stage to want to avoid that at all costs. She didn't want anyone to see him there and start asking questions, especially An Na.

'Hi. Thanks for coming.' He took one step towards her before stopping in his tracks and dropping his hands to his sides. She knew he'd been about to greet her with a kiss. It had been an instinctive move and one she would have been happy to receive but she saw the hesitation on his face. Saw the moment he second-guessed himself, the moment he wondered if he would be overstepping boundaries.

How was it possible that she could interpret the thoughts and expressions of a man she barely knew and hadn't seen for eight years? Some thoughts, she told herself. She had no idea what he was thinking with regard to An Na. Maybe she was just projecting her feelings, maybe they didn't have a real connection.

She would have been happy for him to kiss her, but it was probably wiser that he didn't. She knew it would cloud her thoughts and sway her judgement and she needed a clear head for the discussion that was to come. They had a lot to work out, not least what her news meant for them. Where it put them. But An Na had to be her priority.

'That's okay. Thanks for not making me go to the beach,' she said, extending an olive branch.

'I didn't realise you were so against the beach. I would never have guessed that about you, considering where we met.'

'I was only there because my friends were, but I don't hate the beach. I just really prefer to keep my food and sand separate and I'm not a strong swimmer.'

'So...' Jet smiled and her heart melted just a little. 'Apart from the sand and the sea, you have no objection to the beach.'

'None at all,' She laughed. 'An Na, on the other hand, loves the ocean. Any water. She'd spend her life swimming if she could.'

'Really?' He looked pleased and her heart softened a little more.

She nodded. 'She must get that from you. A definite case of nature over nurture.' She'd brought An Na into the conversation because, after all, that was why they were there, to discuss their daughter, not to exchange personal titbits about their lives as if they were on a first date. It wasn't a date.

She didn't want to feel the tingles, the connection. She needed to separate Jet, An Na's father, from Jet, the man who made her lose her train of thought, who made her heart race and her breath catch in her throat.

'I'm glad to know we will have something in common.'

'She has your smile too.'

'She does?'

Mei nodded. She took out her phone and showed him a photo. He still hadn't asked to see his daughter but she wasn't going to wait. The photo had been taken almost a year ago, but she'd chosen it deliberately—it was the one that most reminded her of Jet. The one that showcased An Na's smile—and the resemblance to Jet was unmistakable.

He looked at the photo in silence and this time she couldn't tell what he was thinking.

'I don't understand why you didn't tell me when you found out you were pregnant. I get that telling someone you don't know all that well they have a seven-year-old child isn't an easy thing to do and I appreciate you were intending to tell me, but why didn't you do that eight years ago?'

'I tried to. I came looking for you. I drove up to Byron Bay with my sister-in-law. We went to your caravan but someone else was living there and they didn't know where you had gone. They didn't know you.'

'So that was it. You stopped looking?'

'I didn't know what else to do. We went to the beach, watched the surfers, but you weren't there. You'd told me you were going to travel. You were going surfing in Hawaii. How was I supposed to find you? I didn't even know your last name. For all I knew, you had already left town. If I had found you, what do you think you would have wanted? How would you have felt? Did you want to be a father at twenty-one?'

'No. Did you know right away you were going to keep the baby?' he asked.

'By the time I figured out I was pregnant it was too late to do anything else,' she answered honestly. 'I knew this was going to change my future, but An Na didn't deserve to pay the price for something I'd done. I chose to sleep with you, it was a conscious decision, and I chose to keep An Na. Getting pregnant was my mistake; it wasn't hers.'

'It was *our* mistake.'

Mei nodded. 'Maybe,' she agreed, 'but I don't think of it as a mistake any more.'

'Were you scared?'

'Terrified,' she admitted. 'But I think that's how every new parent feels.'

'So, it's not just me then?'

'No, it's not just you.'

'But you had time to grow with An Na. To learn, to make mistakes. If I make a mistake there's nowhere to hide. An Na will know. I don't want to let her down but I have no idea how to be a parent.'

'Do you have nieces and nephews?'

'No. I have three sisters but none of them have kids.'

'Your job is to love An Na, to guide her, to encourage her, to support her. To teach her that she can do anything, be anything. Teach her to be kind, help her to be happy.'

'But how do you do that? My sisters and I weren't taught any of that by our parents. My father loves two things—surfing and my mother. In that order. And my mother...' he sighed '...the best thing I can say about her is that she was distant. She had a difficult upbringing. She ran away from home, fell in love with my father.

She sees him as her protector and sometimes I think he is *all* she sees. She isn't maternal at all. I don't think she ever really wanted kids and I certainly don't think she planned any of her pregnancies. Lily, Poppy and I were born within 22 months of each other. That's the very opposite of planned pregnancies. The only thing our father taught us was how to surf.'

'Who brought you up?'

'We grew up in a commune. Supposedly we were raised collectively, although I really think we raised ourselves. I moved off the commune and into my caravan the minute I turned eighteen. I got a job in a pub and spent my days surfing. I'm guessing your story is a bit different; most people are.'

'Our childhoods were probably chalk and cheese,' she admitted.

'Are you close to your parents?'

Mei smiled. 'I'm Asian, I don't really have a choice, but yes, I am. I still live with them. Things were rocky when I fell pregnant. That wasn't the life my parents had envisaged for me when they emigrated from Hong Kong when I was two. It wasn't the life I imagined either, but they have been supportive and An Na had has good male role models in my brother and my father. I'm not saying it's been easy, but we've got this far.'

'And now what? Where do we go from here?'

'I guess An Na and I need to know if you want to be a father now. It's a full-on commitment. What does your life look like now? Are you still surfing, travelling the world? That could make things complicated.'

'Surfing is just a hobby now. I enjoyed it but I wasn't

having great success. I told myself I was too tall but the truth is I simply wasn't good enough. But while I was in Hawaii I competed in the Ironman series, a competition which started in Australia but I'd never been involved. Turns out my height and long limbs were an advantage in that sport, so I switched over.'

'Is that a professional sport too?'

'Semi-professional. I'm training and hoping to qualify for the World Championships next year. There is prize money for some events, and I have a couple of sponsorship deals, but I couldn't live off what I make. I need my job as a lifeguard.'

'So, you're still chasing your dream. I used to imagine you, travelling the world, chasing your dream. I resented you and your freedom after I gave my dream away.'

'Medicine?'

She nodded.

'Did you start the course?'

She shook her head. 'I knew it was going to be impossible to study medicine as a single mother. I wouldn't have the time or energy for years of intense study. I needed an income.' She shrugged. 'Paramedics seemed like a good compromise.'

'Has it been?'

'In a way, but I still have regrets. I still dream of being a doctor.'

'What's stopping you?'

She stared at him in disbelief. 'For the last seven years my purpose has been to raise An Na, to be a mother to An Na, to make sure I didn't fail her. I couldn't do both. Yes, I regret I didn't become a doctor, but I wouldn't change anything. I wouldn't give up being An Na's mother to be a doctor.'

'I'm not suggesting you have to give something up. I'm just asking what the barriers are.'

'I still need an income, for one thing, if I'm ever going to be able to move out of my parents' house and into one of my own, and even if I worked part-time a thousand other things are stopping me. Time, money, logistics.'

'We can work something out financially. An Na is my responsibility too now.'

'We don't need your money.' That wasn't true but her pride wouldn't let her admit it. Besides, it didn't sound as if he had much money to spare.

'Maybe not, but it is my responsibility. I want to help.'

'What we need to do is to work out a plan going forwards. I need to know how involved you want to be. Are you going to be a part of An Na's life or just send a cheque in the mail once a month?'

'You know no one sends cheques any more, right?' Jet was smiling.

'This isn't funny.'

'Mei,' he said. He reached across the table and held her hand and her stomach somersaulted in her belly. 'I spent most of the night thinking about this and I have to admit that I haven't come close to getting my head around the situation. I have no idea how to be a father. It wasn't something I ever thought I'd be, but I don't walk away from my responsibilities. I am a grown-up, an adult. I'm not twenty any more. My concern is that I might not be able to be a good father and will that do An Na more harm than good? I need some time to process this but I would like to meet her.'

Mei nodded. She knew it was a reasonable and logical request, but she wanted him to think about what that meant before he met his daughter.

'Once you meet her you are committed to being her father. Walking away then would be more damaging to her than not knowing I'd found you in the first place. If I introduce you, do you understand you're making a commitment, a promise to her?'

'I do.'

Mei took a breath. 'Okay, give me a few days to break the news to her. Why don't we meet for breakfast on Sunday? You can meet her then.'

CHAPTER SIX

JET WATCHED THE beach from his post in the North Bondi tower. The morning sun had finally risen high enough so it was no longer shining directly into his eyes and he removed his sunglasses and picked up the binoculars as he scanned the water. The conditions weren't favouring the surfers but there were plenty of swimmers making the most of a warm Saturday and the beach was busy. The north end was popular with families and also with the teenagers who were constantly coming off second best when launching themselves into the ocean from Flat Rock.

Jet was working with a rookie lifeguard who was full of questions. Usually he would be impressed with his enthusiasm but, this morning, he just wanted peace and quiet. He needed time to think. Tomorrow he would be meeting his daughter for the first time and he was on edge.

What if she didn't like him? What if he didn't know what to say? He'd had limited experience with kids and he'd been wondering if he should seek advice from his sisters, but what could they tell him that he couldn't figure out for himself?

Lily was the one he usually turned to for advice but he was worried about discussing An Na with her, given her situation. Lily's marriage had broken down after she'd suffered a miscarriage and Jet knew she still hadn't completely recovered. He didn't want the news about An Na to open old wounds. He could talk to Daisy, she was a paediatric nurse and was brilliant with kids, but she would also have myriad questions for him and he doubted he would have the answers.

He needed some more time to figure things out before he divulged his news. He needed a chance to make arrangements with Mei before his sisters chimed in with their ideas. He knew they would mean well but they wouldn't be able to help themselves and he wasn't sure their input would be taken in context by Mei. She might consider it interfering and, after raising An Na for seven years on her own, he knew she had a right to her opinion. Besides, what guidance could his siblings really offer? They might know how to talk to kids, but they certainly couldn't offer any parenting advice. None of the Carlson siblings had any idea of what normal parenting looked like. Their upbringing had been unconventional to say the least.

He also knew that the moment he told his sisters about An Na they would want to meet her and he didn't want to swamp Mei or An Na with his family. He needed time to establish a relationship with his daughter first.

And what about his relationship with Mei? What would that look like going forward? He was having difficulty separating the idea of her as a mother, his daughter's mother, and someone he felt emotionally and physically drawn to.

He needed to prioritise the issues, he had to consider one thing at a time and the first thing needed to be An Na. His first priority was working out how to be a father. He didn't think he could handle starting a relationship with Mei at the same time. That was too much pressure. He had no experience in either of these areas and it was highly likely that he would be biting off more than he could chew if he pursued a relationship with Mei while he was trying to figure out parenthood. He didn't want to fail. His focus had to be An Na, which meant that everything else would have to wait.

He needed some thinking time but it was difficult when he was being peppered with questions by the rookie lifeguard. He was about to suggest to the rookie that he go for a walk to patrol the water's edge when a radio call came through from the main tower.

'North Bondi, this is Central.'

'Go ahead, Central.'

'We've got reports of bluebottles at the south end. They'll be heading your way. You might want to alert the swimmers.'

'Roger that.'

The bluebottles, officially known as Portuguese man-of-war, were jellyfish whose long tentacles could wrap themselves round swimmers and inflict painful stings. While they were venomous, the most common symptom amongst the beachgoers was intense pain.

Jet had seen many people suffering extreme pain and

those under the age of thirty seemed less able to stand the discomfort. The beach had plenty of people in that age group today. Rather than wait for the inevitable as treating bluebottle stings had a tendency to stretch the lifeguards' resources, Jet would do his best to warn the swimmers and clear the water.

The red and yellow flags were flapping in the breeze, indicating the change in the wind direction. He knew the little sails on the tops of the jellyfish would be catching the wind and it was only a matter of minutes before the troublesome sea creatures would arrive at his end of the beach.

'Lewis, the southerly is blowing bluebottles into shore—we need to clear the water,' he instructed the rookie lifeguard. 'I'll head down to the water to let the swimmers know. Can you erect some warning signs?' Yellow warning signs were stacked underneath the tower, but Lewis would need to dig some holes in the sand to hold them. That was a job for a junior, Jet thought as he grabbed the megaphone and backpack and leapt down from the tower.

Before he reached the water's edge he could see several people already emerging and complaining of stings.

'Don't pull the tentacles off with your fingers,' he warned a pair of teenage boys. 'It'll just transfer the venom to your hands as well.' He pulled a disposable glove from his backpack and handed it to them. 'Use this and then head up to the pavilion; a hot shower is the best remedy.' The quicker they got under the shower, the sooner their symptoms would ease and usually within a half hour of being stung people had recovered. They might be left with angry welts on their skin but the pain normally settled relatively fast.

As he finished with the teenagers a man standing in the shallows called out and waved Jet over. 'I need help, please. My niece has been stung—she's having trouble breathing.'

There were three young children, two girls and a boy, with the man and Jet could see red welts on their skin. Two of the children were yelling in pain but one young girl was quiet and Jet was immediately on high alert. The volume of a child's reaction to an injury was usually a good indicator of the level of pain and the quieter a child was, the more the lifeguards worried.

Allergic reactions to bluebottle stings were rare but Jet knew they could occur. The man had picked the girl up and she was clinging to his side while the boy continued to wail. Jet could see an angry red welt on the girl's throat. Stings on the limbs or trunk were painful enough; he could only imagine how one on the tender flesh of a throat would feel and if it was associated with swelling it was a dangerous situation.

'Is she allergic to anything else? Bees?'

'I don't think she's ever had a bee sting.'

The girl's eyes were wide with fear and she was going pale. She was still breathing but Jet knew time was critical. He needed to get her to the tower. Quickly. He needed two buggies and an ambulance.

He called the tower requesting backup and then spoke to the girl's uncle.

'Give her to me and I'll meet you at the tower,' he told him. 'I need to get her there quickly. Other lifeguards are on the way and they'll help you with the other children.'

He took the little girl. She was light but limp in his arms and he was breathing heavily as he jogged through the sand, heading for the tower and keeping an eye out for the buggy.

'You're going to be okay,' Jet told her as Ryder pulled up in the ATV. Jet jumped into the passenger seat, cradling the girl on his lap. 'Go, go,' he said to Ryder. His priority was to get her to the tower to treat her there. He just prayed the ambulance would hurry.

Ryder parked the buggy at the steps to the tower and Jet was out of the vehicle before Ryder had killed the engine. He ran up the stairs and laid his patient on the treatment plinth. She was as limp as a rag doll and barely breathing.

Gibbo was waiting for them. 'The ambos are a couple of minutes away, but they've said to administer the EpiPen if her condition is still deteriorating.'

The girl's eyes were closed and Jet knew she wasn't aware of her surroundings.

'I think we have to,' he said. Her condition was critical and they couldn't afford to wait another minute, let alone two.

Gibbo handed him the adrenalin pen. Jet removed the blue lid and pressed the orange end against the girl's thigh, pushing hard until he heard it click. He counted to three and held it a fraction longer, just to be sure the adrenalin had been administered, before lifting it off her leg. He looked at the clock on the wall above the desk and noted the time, hoping he wouldn't need to give a second dose and knowing he'd need to tell the paramedics the time he'd injected the first.

He slipped an oxygen mask over her face as an extra precaution and stood beside the treatment plinth and watched, willing the drug to work as he waited for the girl's breathing to ease.

He could hear the ambulance siren now, its volume increasing as it approached, and he felt the tension dissipate from his body as his shoulders relaxed.

There were still some tentacles clinging to the girl's arm and leg and he pulled on a pair of surgical gloves and began to gently remove them while Gibbo sponged the welt on her neck with hot water, trying to take some of the sting out of the venom.

The ambulance siren cut out as Jet lifted the last tentacle from the girl's thigh. Her breathing had improved but she wasn't out of the woods yet and he was eager to hand her care over to the paramedics.

The door to the tower opened and he immediately looked over, hoping to see Mei. He knew she was working today, but it was the girl's uncle who entered. Jet took one look at him and could see he was still in a state of panic.

'She's okay,' Jet reassured him. 'She's breathing more easily and the ambos have arrived.'

The girl's uncle turned to face the door as it opened again, this time admitting Poppy and Mei. Mei led the way and he tried to catch her eye over the heads of the others but, before she could look in his direction, the girl's uncle had intercepted her.

'Mei!'

'Bo? What are you doing here?'

Jet listened in slight confusion, trying to work out the relationship between them as the uncle explained the situation. 'Mei, it's An Na—she's been stung.'

'An Na?'

Jet turned back to the plinth. An Na? This little girl was An Na? His daughter?

'An Na.' Mei pushed past the lifeguards, forcing her way through the congested space until she reached the plinth.

She was standing next to him, but Jet knew she hadn't seen him as she slid her arms under her daughter and held her.

His first instinct was to do the same for Mei. To hold her, to protect her, to comfort her and reassure her, but she wasn't even aware of his presence. She was completely oblivious to everything around her, intent only on her daughter. She hugged her and then laid her flat again. She brushed An Na's hair from the side of her face with one hand, tucking it behind the strap of the oxygen mask and held An Na's wrist with the other, feeling for her pulse as she watched the rise and fall of her chest. An Na's breathing was still laboured and her skin was crisscrossed with angry welts.

'What happened?' Mei was speaking to him now, but he still wasn't sure if she was taking things in. She would have been told the details of the incident when she'd received the emergency call, but it was clear her mind had gone blank. Her eyes were glazed and he suspected she just saw a random lifeguard. He certainly didn't think she'd registered that it was him she was speaking to.

'She had an anaphylactic reaction to a jellyfish. She's been given one dose of adrenalin.' He tried to set her mind at ease, but he doubted she was really listening. It was impossible to expect her to be impartial, to respond as a paramedic when the patient was her own daughter. He needed to let Poppy know what had transpired.

He turned around, desperately seeking his sister.

'This is Mei's daughter,' Poppy explained. She was talking to him as if this was just any patient and he was momentarily confused, but of course, from Poppy's point of view An Na was just an ordinary patient.

'How long ago did you administer the adrenalin?' Poppy asked as she wrapped a blood pressure cuff around An Na's arm and clipped an oximeter to her fingertip.

Jet checked the clock. 'Ten minutes.' He frowned. Had it really only been ten minutes? It felt like a life-time.

'And her breathing's improved?' Poppy confirmed.

Jet nodded.

'Mei? Does An Na have any other allergies?' Poppy spoke quietly to her colleague, gathering information but not expecting any contribution in terms of treatment from her.

Mei shook her head as Jet stood there, not sure what was needed of him, not sure if he was needed at all, but he couldn't bring himself to step away. He remained in place, as a spectator. There was no role for him. An Na didn't know him and, with the exception of Mei, no one knew he was An Na's father.

'Okay, she's stable,' Poppy said as Jet let himself relax just slightly, 'but she needs to go to hospital for observation.'

Jet knew there was a danger of a second allergic reaction once the adrenalin from the EpiPen wore off. 'Are you ready to move her now?' he asked Poppy. The ambulance stretcher didn't fit inside the tower and it was always easier to carry the light patients out rather than transfer them to a chair or spinal board, but he wasn't going to give anyone else the opportunity to carry An Na. She was his daughter and the incident today had terrified him. He could have lost her before he'd even met her.

Poppy nodded, giving Jet the all-clear, and he touched Mei's shoulder. 'Mei, let me carry her.'

Mei finally registered his presence. She nodded and stepped back as he scooped An Na up off the plinth.

Her head rested on his chest and he hugged her to him. She'd opened her eyes briefly when Mei had spoken to her, but her eyelids had fluttered closed again. Her eyelashes were thick and dark against the pale skin of her cheeks and this time Jet concentrated on how it felt to hold his child in his arms.

He wanted to feel a connection. He'd imagined there would be some sense of recognition when he first met his daughter, although he hadn't imagined it would be under these circumstances, and it disappointed him to know that he'd had no inkling, that there had been no sense that she was part of him. She was delicate and warm, but she felt like any other child in his arms.

He badly wanted to feel a connection and now he just had to hope it would develop, but he was terrified that it wouldn't. Perhaps he would turn out to be like his parents.

Poppy opened the rear doors of the ambulance and pulled the stretcher out but didn't disengage it from its rails. Jet laid An Na on the sheet and Poppy strapped her in securely.

'Are you going to be okay in the back with her?' Poppy asked Mei, obviously thinking she was in no fit state to drive. 'I can call for backup if you like.'

'No, I'm okay.'

Poppy pushed the stretcher into the ambulance and made certain it locked in place. Mei climbed in and Poppy closed the doors and Jet lost sight of his daughter.

As the ambulance departed he knew he couldn't just let them go like that. Not An Na or Mei.

Dutchy was off-duty but at the beach and Jet convinced him to take over his shift. 'I need to go,' he told Dutchy and Gibbo. 'There's something I have to do.' He stalled any questions by adding, 'I'll explain later.'

Poppy was loading the empty stretcher back into the ambulance when Jet arrived at the hospital. He waited until she turned away from him before he ducked through the emergency entrance. He didn't want to answer questions about what he was doing there—he wasn't completely sure himself—but he couldn't stay at the tower; he had to get to the hospital.

He'd been consumed with fear at the idea that he could have lost An Na and his fear was tinged with anger at Mei for keeping her secret, even though he knew he was being unfair.

He'd managed to avoid Poppy on his way into the emergency department, but he hadn't counted on running into Lily.

'Jet! What are you doing here?'

Bumping into Lily was probably a good thing. He wouldn't be able to see An Na; he had no rights. He was her father but only as a technicality, not legally. Not yet.

'The patient Poppy brought in…a little girl? Do you know if she's okay?'

'You know I can't discuss my patients with you.'

'So, she is your patient?' All he needed now was for An Na to be admitted onto the paediatric ward and for Daisy to be the nurse, but he couldn't subject An Na or Mei to all his sisters in one go. Not here. Not today. His life was complicated enough, but somehow he had to find out how An Na was. 'Is Mei with her?'

'What's going on?'

Jet ignored her question. He really didn't have time to explain. 'Can you tell Mei I'm here? I need to speak to her.'

'I don't think she'll want to leave An Na to come out and talk to you,' Lily said. 'What is this about?'

'I'll explain later. Please, just pass on the message.'

Lily frowned but agreed. She left him pacing backwards and forwards in the emergency department as she went to deliver his message.

Jet imagined this was how expectant fathers would

have felt back in the day, waiting for news. Things had changed now though—if Mei had told him about her pregnancy he would have been in the delivery room, not pacing the corridors and wearing out the linoleum floor. But would his twenty-one-year-old self have wanted anything to do with a baby? The truth was he wouldn't have been ready then. He'd still been growing up himself. He'd been self-absorbed, focused on his dreams, his goals—would he have wanted to derail those? He knew the answer was no, but what about now? Was he ready now?

He still hadn't achieved his goal of qualifying for the World Championships. It was so close he could almost touch it, but what if he had to give it up for An Na? Was he prepared to?

He didn't know the answer and he wasn't about to abandon An Na and Mei, at least he didn't think he was, but he was considering turning around and walking out of the door to give himself time to think when Mei appeared.

'The doctor told me you wanted to speak to me,' she said. 'She's another one of your sisters?'

Jet nodded.

'She didn't seem to know why you needed to see me.' She paused while Jet shook his head. 'You haven't told your sisters about An Na?'

'No. I wanted to meet An Na first. To get to know her and for her to get to know me before I introduced you both to my sisters. Is An Na okay?'

'She will be.'

'Can I see her?'

Mei nodded and Jet followed her into the treatment bay.

An Na was sleeping.

'I can't believe she's mine,' he said as he studied her face, searching for any similarity, anything to connect her to him, but all he could see was a little girl, covered in red welts, who looked just like her mother.

'She looks like you when she is smiling. She walks like you too, light on her feet and bouncy, and she has your long fingers.'

'How did you know what I was thinking?'

Mei shrugged. 'It makes sense that you would be looking for traces of yourself in her, but I often feel like I know what you're thinking.'

'Are you able to stay with her? What about your shift?'

'Alex is coming to relieve me. Poppy is waiting out the front in case we get called out on a job before Alex can get here and my sister-in-law is on her way. She'll stay with An Na if I can't.'

'And tomorrow?' They were supposed to be meeting for pancakes in the morning.

'An Na should be fine. I'll message you later to let you know and I'll confirm in the morning. Okay?'

Jet was reluctant to leave but he knew he couldn't stay. There was only supposed to be one relative with An Na at a time. He left Mei with An Na and returned to the waiting area, where he ran into Lily again.

She looked enquiringly at him. 'What's going on?'

'An Na is my daughter.'

'Your *what*?'

'My daughter.'

Lily's mouth fell open but before she could ask any more questions her pager went off. Jet thought for a moment she was about to ignore it, before common sense prevailed.

He knew she would have to go but he also knew there would be explanations needed and it would be easier for him if he only had to tell his story once.

'Can we get together tonight?' he asked. 'All of us? Poppy and Daisy too. I'll explain everything then.'

CHAPTER SEVEN

JET'S SISTERS' QUESTIONS were flowing thick and fast after his announcement about An Na but he didn't have the answers for many of them.

'How long have you known?'

'Only a few days. I knew Mei had a child, but I assumed it was little…two or three at the most,' he said to Poppy. 'When you said you'd met Mei's daughter, and told me how old she was, it made me wonder and I went to see Mei. That was when she told me.'

'When did you meet Mei?' Daisy asked.

'Obviously about eight years ago,' Poppy said.

Daisy glared at her while Jet replied, 'She came to Byron Bay for a holiday when she finished school. I met her then.'

'Why didn't Mei tell you about An Na years ago?'

'She says she tried to find me but by the time she realised she was pregnant I'd left the country. Gone to Hawaii.'

'I can't believe you're a dad. And we are all aunties! What are you going to do now?'

'I don't know. We haven't had time to figure it out. I

hadn't met An Na until today. Mei was going to bring her to meet me tomorrow.'

'How are you feeling?'

'Overwhelmed. Worried. Nervous. I have no idea how to be a father and Mei doesn't seem overly confident in me either.'

'What did she say?'

'She said she thought I wouldn't want the responsibility or commitment of being a father. She didn't think I was someone she could rely on and that she and An Na would be better off with her family.'

'She said that now?'

'No. That was when she found out she was pregnant, but what if she still thinks that?'

'You're not born knowing how to be a parent. You'll learn as you go.'

'But it's different learning with a baby. An Na is seven; she'll know if I muck things up and so will Mei. She's had years to get it right. What if I fail? It's not like we've had great role models.'

'Your responsibility is to teach her how to be a good person. How to be kind. To love her. You can do that,' Lily told him, echoing Mei's sentiments.

'I feel like if it was going to be a natural or instinctive thing I would have felt a connection today on the beach. When I was holding An Na, I should have had some sort of sixth sense.'

'I think you're being a little harsh on yourself.'

'And what about Mei?' Poppy asked. 'I know you like her—does this change anything?'

'I don't know. Probably. My priority is getting to know An Na. I can't think about Mei right now.'

Mei and An Na were already at the North Bondi RSL Club when Jet arrived the next morning. As he approached their table he heard Mei tell An Na to go and ask for some colouring pencils. The tables were covered with white paper for kids to draw on but he did wonder why she sent An Na off as soon as he arrived.

'I haven't had time to tell her about you yet,' she explained when he asked the question. 'I was going to tell her last night but the trip to hospital put paid to that. Is it okay if we don't say anything this morning? You can just get to know her a little?'

He nodded in agreement, knowing there was no time for discussion.

'An Na, this is Jet,' Mei introduced him when An Na returned to the table clutching a cup filled with pencils. 'He's one of the lifeguards who helped you yesterday when you got stung by the jellyfish. Do you remember him?'

'No.'

'Hello, An Na. You tangled with a pretty nasty jellyfish yesterday—how are you feeling today?' He was a little hesitant to ask as he didn't want to raise any fears she might now have. He wasn't used to second-guessing himself and he wanted to make a good impression on Mei and An Na.

'I'm okay. A bit itchy. Do you want to see the marks?'

'Sure.'

An Na pushed the sleeve of her T-shirt up to show

him the welts on her arm. They had faded but were still obvious. 'I had to go to hospital.'

'I know.'

'Are you going to have breakfast with us? We're having pancakes.'

An Na chatted away almost non-stop throughout breakfast. She was more than happy to have a captive audience and all that was required of Jet was to make a few interested remarks occasionally. She told him about her cousins and school. She told him about her favourite movie and her favourite subjects.

'And when you're not at school—what do you do then?'

'I go to ballet and tap classes and I'm learning the violin.'

'That sounds busy. Do you like that?'

'It's okay, but I really want to have surfing lessons. Do you know how to surf?'

'I do, actually.'

'Can you teach me?'

'If it's okay with your mum.' He knew he wasn't playing fair, but he didn't think Mei would refuse and he was happy to offer. It would give him a chance to spend some time getting to know An Na. His daughter.

He had no doubt that there were plenty of other skills she would need that he was not equipped to teach her, but this was something he could do and he was pleased to know the bluebottle incident hadn't put An Na off the beach.

'I guess so.' Mei nodded.

'Can we go surfing now?'

'No,' Mei replied. 'We have some things to do today. We'll sort out a time later.'

'Promise?'

'I promise.'

Jet paid for breakfast and walked with Mei to her car while An Na skipped ahead.

'She's amazing,' he said, 'but I'm wondering if you chose the right name for her. She's anything but quiet. It won't take long before I feel like I know her.'

Mei smiled. 'I think I just imagined that she'd take after me a bit more. I was quiet.'

It was blowing his mind that this little girl was part of him. He wanted her to know who he was. He stopped in his tracks and turned to Mei. 'I want to tell her who I am.'

'Now?'

'Yes. You know we'll be telling her at some point and if I'm going to take her surfing this week I think it's the right thing to do.'

'You're going to start this week?'

'I can pick her up from school.'

An Na turned back and tugged on Mei's hand as they walked down Campbell Parade.

'Can I have an ice cream?'

'You just finished breakfast!'

'I'm still hungry.'

'I reckon I could fit an ice cream in too,' Jet said. 'Why don't I buy us both one? You can have one as well, if you like, Mei, and then we can sit on that bench over there and eat them. What's your favourite flavour, An Na?'

'Chocolate.'

'Mine too.'

Jet caught Mei's eye as he paid for the ice creams and raised an eyebrow. She gave a slight nod but said nothing until they had their ice creams and were sitting on a bench looking over the sea.

'An Na, we have something to tell you.'

An Na looked at her mother and then at Jet. 'Are you Mummy's boyfriend? Isabella's mummy has a boyfriend.'

'No, that's not it. You know how I told you your daddy lives overseas?'

An Na nodded. 'In Hawaii.'

'Yes, that's right. Except he doesn't live there any more. Now he lives here, in Sydney.'

'He's here?'

'He's right here. Jet isn't my boyfriend, he's your dad.'

An Na turned to look at Jet. Ice cream dribbled down her arm, but she didn't seem perturbed by that or by Mei's announcement. 'Did you come to see me?' she asked.

'Yes,' Jet told her. It seemed like the best answer.

'Are you going to live with us?'

'No, I have my own house.'

'Are we going to live with you?'

He should have anticipated there would be plenty of questions, but he didn't know the answer to this one. He looked to Mei.

'No. Lao Lao and Ye Ye would miss us.'

'They could come too.'

'They need to stay at the restaurant.'

'Do you have other children? Do I have a brother or a sister?'

'No.' Jet finished his ice cream and licked his fingers. 'Why don't I take you for your first surfing lesson after school one day this week and you can ask me as many questions as you like then?'

'Okay.' An Na slipped her hand into his as they walked around the corner to Mei's car. Her little hand was soft and somewhat sticky, but with that gesture Jet knew what it felt like to be a father. He knew he would do whatever it took to make An Na proud of him.

'Thank you,' Jet said to Mei as An Na climbed into the car.

'What for?'

'You obviously haven't dragged my name through the mud as far as An Na is concerned. She doesn't seem to hold any ill will towards me.'

'I had no reason to try to set her against you. You did nothing wrong by her,' Mei said as she slid behind the wheel.

As she drove away he wondered about what Mei hadn't said.

Did she feel he'd done wrong by her?

'Mummy, Mummy, did you see me? I was surfing!'

An Na ran up the beach to where Mei was sitting on a towel. She was bursting with excitement and Mei hugged her daughter tightly and said, 'That looked like so much fun.'

Over the top of An Na's head Mei could see Jet coming towards them, his surfboard tucked under one arm, and from behind the safety of her sunglasses she admired his long lean frame, taut abdominals and broad shoulders. She wasn't a fan of the ocean but she could see that there were certainly some benefits to spending time at the beach.

'Can I go back in the water?' An Na asked as Jet lowered his board to the sand.

'Don't go in too deep,' Mei cautioned as An Na skipped back to the waves.

'And stay between the flags,' Jet added.

'She absolutely loved that, thank you. I wish you could have seen the expression on her face when you stood her up on the board.' Jet had been standing behind An Na; he'd lifted her onto her feet as they'd surfed in on a wave, not once but several times. The delight and sheer joy on An Na's face had made Mei's heart sing. 'Actually, you might be able to. I took a video. It might be clear enough.' She picked up her phone and opened the video as Jet sat on the sand beside her.

He didn't bother drying off and the water droplets on his skin glistened in the late afternoon light. He smelt of the ocean and she could feel the coolness of the water radiating from his body in contrast to the warmth of the day. She resisted the urge to lean in against him. But it wasn't easy. Whenever he was near she could feel herself being drawn to him and it took all of her willpower to control her impulses.

She passed him her phone and prepared herself for the rush of heat she knew she would experience when their fingers touched.

He hit 'play' and she waited while he watched the video. 'She's got good balance,' he said as the video finished. 'She'll be surfing in no time. Imagine what she'd be like now if she'd started surfing a few years ago.'

'If our paths had crossed earlier, you mean?'

'I'm not having a go, but I keep thinking about all the years I've missed. If you didn't have such an aversion to the beach we might have crossed paths again sooner,' he said as he smiled and returned her phone to her.

'It's not the beach I dislike, it's the ocean. I got washed off a sand bank and caught in a rip when I was about An Na's age. It absolutely scared the life out of me and ever since I've been wary of the water.'

'I can take you in. You'd be safe with me.'

Mei could almost imagine how it would feel to be in the water with Jet. To have his arms around her as if they were dancing. She wouldn't be afraid of drowning while he held her in his arms, but she would be afraid of other things.

'I'm okay here, thanks. If you can teach An Na to surf that's enough for me.'

'Well, let me know if you change your mind.'

'I will.'

Mei closed her eyes for moment as she let her mind wander. What was the future going to look like for her and Jet? Did she dare ask?

Was there a possibility that they could have a relationship? Not as An Na's parents but as a couple? Would there be a chance to explore that, or had that opportunity passed them by?

She couldn't ignore the fact that she was still attracted to him, but how did he feel about her?

Mei arrived home from work and headed for the restaurant kitchen, eager to find out how An Na's second surfing lesson went today.

'Where's An Na?' she asked, expecting to find her making dumplings or doing homework at the bench, but she wasn't anywhere to be seen.

'In the restaurant. She's having dinner with her father.'

'With her father?' Mei swallowed nervously. Jet was here? Her hands were suddenly sweaty and she wiped them on her trousers before going into the restaurant.

Jet and An Na were sitting at a table sharing a bowl of dumplings and Mei's stomach rumbled as she sat down with them.

'Mummy! Guess what? I surfed all by myself today!'

'You did! That's fantastic. Well done!' Mei congratulated her daughter with a kiss on her forehead before turning to Jet. 'What are you doing here? I thought Bo was bringing An Na home?'

'An Na wanted to show me what she made at school today.'

'Oh?' She turned to her daughter. 'What did you make?'

'We decorated our tops for the Christmas concert. And Daddy said he'd come to watch me.'

'You did?'

Jet nodded. 'I did. So, I had a good day. I got invited out and I got to meet your parents. I wasn't sure when you were planning on introducing me.'

She wasn't sure either. She'd been nervous about that meeting but was kind of relieved now that he had taken it out of her hands.

'You can relax. I think your parents like me,' he said.

Did he know she'd been worried about that? She had been reluctant to introduce them, nervous about how it would go and what her parents might say. Although they understood that Jet hadn't known about An Na, she knew they would now expect him to take responsibility. She was sure he'd charmed her parents, but did he understand their expectations? Would he be prepared to step up?

She needed to know what his plans were—she needed some time alone with him to suss out his thoughts. Mei picked up the empty dumpling bowl and passed it to An Na.

'An Na, can you go and ask Lao Lao for some more dumplings, please?'

'Out with it,' Jet said as soon as An Na had disappeared into the kitchen.

'What?'

'There's obviously something on your mind. You sent An Na off so you could ask me something in private. What do you want to know?'

'You've taken An Na surfing twice and met my parents. You've obviously got an idea of the direction this is heading with An Na and I'm just wondering if we're going to have a chance to sit down together and have a conversation about what we're doing.'

'Are you asking what my intentions are?'

'Maybe.'

'To be honest, I haven't figured that out yet. I think getting to know An Na needs to be my priority. I don't know if I can do more than that at this stage. But if you want to organise a time to talk you can. I gave you my number—you *can* call me.'

'Oh.' Was she going to have to make the first move? She wasn't sure if she was brave enough for that.

'Mei, it's okay.' Jet reached out and placed his hand over hers and squeezed her fingers as An Na returned with more dumplings. 'Gibbo and his wife are hosting a barbecue for the lifeguards in a couple of days. It's a Christmas tradition—he does a turkey, we sing carols, everyone dresses up. Come with me, have some fun and I promise we will find time to work out a plan going forwards.'

'That dress suits you,' Jet said as he opened the car door for her and took her hand to help her out.

'Thank you. An Na and Su-Lin picked it out for me.'

Mei was wearing one of only a few dresses she owned, a black silk dress with spaghetti straps and a flowing skirt. Su-Lin had chosen it for her and had helped her with her make-up. She'd applied red lipstick and a thick coat of mascara with just a touch of powder to highlight her cheekbones. Her hair was pulled back off her face. Su-Lin had gone for the casual, effortless, 'I'm not wearing any make-up' make-up.

'An Na didn't mind that you were going out without her?'

'No, she loves staying with her cousins overnight; she'd happily do it every night. But she did want me to invite you to do something with us tomorrow. She told me you had the afternoon free.' Mei wondered when Jet might think to share his schedule with her rather than her having to hear it from An Na.

'I'm doing a half day, starting at six, finished by one. Does that fit in with your plans? What are you doing?'

'Going to the mall to see Father Christmas. We can go in the afternoon if you'd like to come.'

She could see a moment of hesitation on his face. 'Are you busy?'

'No, I'll work around it. I don't want An Na to feel that I don't have time for her. I know what that's like and I don't want that for her. I'll be there.'

'Thank you.'

Mei took a deep breath as they opened Gibbo's front gate. She was nervous. This was the first social occasion she had been to with the lifeguards since they'd found out about Jet's history with her...since they'd found out about Jet's daughter...but she needn't have worried. Everyone was lovely and welcoming and she soon relaxed.

Jet was attentive and she actually felt like part of a couple. It was a good feeling. They still hadn't had a conversation about what the two of them were doing but the sparks were flying.

As the sun went down and the food was cleared away Dutchy picked up his guitar and started playing Christmas carols. Jet pulled Mei onto his lap as everyone joined in the singing. He snaked his arm around her hips and rested his chin on her shoulder. His breath was warm on her bare skin. She relaxed, happy to lean against him in the dark. It reminded her of the night they'd met. A warm summer's evening, music playing, the scent of frangipani in the air.

She could feel the heat of Jet's hand through the thin silk fabric of her dress. His hand slid down the side of her leg and under the hem of her skirt. She closed her eyes and pictured each fingertip where it rested on her thigh. Jet's thumb was making tiny, lazy circles on her skin and Mei stopped singing, focusing only on the sensation of his touch. She shifted in her seat, wanting more, until Jet's hand slowed and he whispered, 'Do you want to get out of here?'

'Now?'

She felt him nod.

'And go where?' She knew where his train of thought was heading; she could feel it. Her heart was thumping in her chest.

'This can go one of two ways,' he said. 'We can decide to pretend that we don't have chemistry and focus on working out how we are going to raise our daughter as single parents or we can explore the spark between us and see what happens.'

'And if it just fizzles out? What happens to An Na then?'

'Nothing happens to An Na. She still has two parents. She doesn't need to know about any of this. Not until we figure it out. What do you think?'

The logical part of Mei's brain had shut down. The

part that told her she wasn't eighteen any more, the part that said she needed more than chemistry, the part that said she needed someone who could be a partner for her and a father for An Na. An equal. She wasn't after a bit of fun any more—at least that was what she thought— but her body was crying out for his touch. Right now, she didn't care if they only had one night. She would willingly take that over the alternative of nothing. She wanted to see what happened. She wanted to take that chance. She was older and wiser and she wasn't about to repeat her mistakes. This wasn't a spontaneous or rash decision—she had thought of almost nothing else since the moment Jet had reappeared in her life. If she passed it up, she knew she'd regret it and she had plenty of regrets in her past already.

She still thought she might be crazy, but she wasn't going to say no. Was she setting herself up to fail? She'd never tried anything without knowing she could do it before. And giving herself over to Jet, letting him have half the control was scary for her, but if anyone could make her relinquish control it was him. She wanted to give herself to him, to see if it was the same as before. She missed that feeling, that connection to another person. Had their relationship been just a teenage dream, a holiday romance? Or could they sustain it, develop it into something more? She wanted to know. She needed to know.

'Let's go,' she said.

CHAPTER EIGHT

'THIS IS NICER than I expected,' Mei said as Jet unlocked the front door and led her inside.

'Were you imagining the caravan? I have grown up a bit since then.'

The house was freshly painted with polished wooden floorboards and a new kitchen. Surfboards were racked on one wall of the living room but, other than that, it didn't overtly look like a bachelor pad.

'I didn't mind the caravan.' She smiled. 'I have some fond memories of that weekend.'

'Is that so?'

'But it seems like a lifetime ago,' she said as she followed him through the house.

'Let me see if I can jog your memory,' he replied as he pushed open the door to his bedroom and switched on a lamp. He reached for her hand but before he led her into his room he said, 'Are you sure about this, Mei?'

He had to know she wanted this as much as he did.

Mei nodded and stepped inside his room. He closed the door as her hands went to the side of her dress. She unzipped it and pushed the straps from her shoulders and he watched, mesmerised, as her dress slithered to the floor.

Automatically his eyes had followed the movement as gravity took hold and his gaze was now focused on her dress where it lay in a pool of black silk around her ankles. His eyes travelled up the length of her bare legs, long and brown, to her slim hips.

Through the lace of her panties he could see the dark triangle of hair at the junction of her thighs. His mouth was dry and his legs were shaky as all the blood in his body rushed south. A severe lack of oxygen to his brain had left him light-headed and had robbed him of the power of speech. But he could admire. So he did.

Mei was almost naked, and she was gorgeous. She was still thin, but she'd filled out nicely and had curves in all the right places. His gaze travelled higher, over her flat stomach and her round belly button to her small, bare breasts and erect nipples. She was perfect.

He could see the pulse beating at the base of her throat, her lips were parted, her mouth pink and soft, her eyes gleaming. She was stunning.

He remembered how comfortable she'd been in her skin when she was eighteen. How years of ballet had shown her what her body could do. How she'd shown him. He remembered how she'd wrapped her body around his, how soft she'd looked, but how strong she'd been.

She lifted her hands and removed the clip that held her hair in place. Her hair tumbled over her shoulders as she reached for his hands.

He was almost afraid to let her touch him. Afraid of losing control.

'I want this,' she said. 'I want you.'

Jet swallowed. There was only so much temptation he could stand. He forgot about his daughter. He forgot about Mei being a mother—he forgot about everything as desire took over. With one step he closed the gap that had opened between them.

Her hands were on his arms as his fingers cupped the curve of her bottom. He pulled her to him and bent his head. She tipped her face up to him and he closed his eyes as their lips met. Her lips were soft and sweet. He stroked her cheek with a thumb and her lips parted. Her mouth was warm as she pressed against him. He could feel his erection, hard and stiff, between them.

Mei's fingers flicked open the button on his shorts and he kicked off his shoes as she slid his shorts from his hips. Her hands slid under his shirt and he broke their kiss as he impatiently pulled his shirt over his head. Now they were both semi-naked.

He scooped her into his arms. Her skin was warm and so soft, and inches of her bare flesh pressed against him as he held her. She wrapped her arms around his neck as he carried her to the bed. One, two, three, four steps across the room until he could gently lay her down.

He ran his fingers up her thigh, cupping the curve of her bottom. Mei closed her eyes and arched her hips, pushing herself closer to him. He bent his head and kissed her. She opened her mouth, joining them together as he slid her panties from under her, pulling them off in one smooth movement.

He ran his hand over her hip and up across her stomach. His fingers grazed her breast and he watched as her nipple peaked under his touch. She moaned softly and reached for him but he wasn't done yet. He was calm and excited all at once but he was in no hurry.

He pushed her hair off her shoulders and bent his head, flicking his tongue over one breast and sucking it into his mouth. He supported himself on one elbow while he used his other hand in tandem with his mouth, teasing her nipples until both were taut with desire. He slid his knee between her thighs, parting them as he straddled her. His right hand stayed cupped over her breast as he moved his mouth lower to kiss her stomach.

He took his hand from her breast and ran it up the smooth skin of the inside of her thigh. She moaned and thrust her hips towards him as her knees dropped further apart.

Jet put his head between her thighs. He put his hands under her bottom and lifted her to his mouth, supporting her there as his tongue darted inside her. She was slick and sweet and she moaned as he explored her inner sanctum with his tongue. He enjoyed oral sex, giving and receiving, and tonight was no exception.

Mei thrust her hips towards him again, urging him deeper. He slid his fingers inside her where she was wet and hot, her sex swollen with desire. His fingers worked in tandem with his tongue, making her pant, making her beg for more.

'Jet, please. I want you inside me.'

But he wasn't ready to stop. Not yet.

He knew she was close to climaxing and he wanted to bring her to orgasm like this. He wanted to taste it, to feel it.

He ignored her request as he continued to work his magic with his tongue, licking and sucking the swollen bud of her desire. He continued until Mei had forgotten her request, until she had forgotten everything except her own satisfaction.

'Yes, yes…oh, Jet, don't stop.'

He had no intention of stopping.

He heard her sharp little intake of breath and then she began to shudder.

'Yes. Oh, Jet.'

She buried her fingers in his hair and clamped her thighs around his shoulders as she came. Shuddering and gasping before she collapsed, relaxed and spent.

Mei felt as if she'd shattered into a thousand pieces and it took her a few moments to gather herself together again. It was years since she'd slept with anyone, but she'd had no reservations. Her body had responded to Jet's touch as if she'd known him for ever. It felt as if every cell in her body recognised him. As if he could bring them all to life simultaneously until she exploded. All her concerns had ceased to exist. There had been no room in her head for a single conscious thought. It was all she could do to remember how to breathe as Jet reminded her of how it felt to let go, of how it felt to be a woman.

And now it was his turn. This time Mei took charge.

His boxer shorts came off with one tug of her hand and as his erection sprang free Mei's groin flooded with heat and she felt the wetness between her thighs. She spread her legs and straddled him. She cupped him and then encircled his shaft with her hand. It was thick and hard and warm and pulsed with a life of its own as she ran her hand up its length. She rolled her fingers over the end and coaxed the moisture from his body.

Jet gasped and his body trembled. 'In the drawer by the bed,' he panted, 'I have protection.'

Mei opened the drawer and found a condom. She tore open the packet and watched his beautiful face as she rolled the sheath onto him. His blue eyes darkened as she brought herself forward, raising herself up onto her knees before lowering herself down. Jet closed his eyes and sighed as she took his length inside her.

She lifted herself up again, and down, as Jet held onto her hips and started to time her thrusts, matching their rhythms together. Slow at first and then gradually faster. And faster. Mei tried to stay in charge, but she found it impossible to control her body. All she could think of was how good this felt and that she wanted more. And more.

'Oh, God, yes.'

'Keep going. Don't stop.'

And, just when she thought she couldn't stand it any longer, Jet shuddered and she could feel his release as he came inside her. She held her breath as she let herself go and her body shook with pleasure as his orgasm was joined by hers. Their timing couldn't have been better.

Mei rolled over, tender and spent, and lay along Jet's

side. He wrapped his arm around her and she felt as though her every wish had just been granted and she had everything she could ever want or need as she lay in Jet's embrace.

An Na had been chattering non-stop all day about all things Christmas. About the school concert, about what present she might get from her dad and about the afternoon's visit to see Father Christmas. She was frenetically excited, but Mei could understand how she felt. Mei felt the same way, only she was getting in a flap because of Jet, not because of the season.

She could scarcely believe that they had slept together last night. Or that their lovemaking had been as good as she remembered it being. Often over the years she'd wondered if she was looking at that weekend through rose-coloured glasses. If she had imagined the connection, the pleasure, the sheer ecstasy she had found in Jet's arms. She wondered if she had made it up as a way to soften the blow of falling pregnant, if she'd pretended to herself that she hadn't been able to resist, that they'd been destined to meet, to have a child. That their fate had been sealed somewhere in time without their knowledge. If she could blame fate then it wasn't her naivety, or her stupidity that had got her pregnant. She had been powerless. And after last night she knew she hadn't made it all up. She'd been powerless again.

It was almost as if Jet had a force field around him that drew her in. She couldn't fight it, she didn't want to fight it, and last night she'd relived that fateful weekend all over again. And she was now hoping and praying that she would get another chance. And another. She almost needed to pinch herself.

She kept her eyes peeled for Jet. She and An Na had come to the mall early to do some Christmas shopping and Jet was meeting them here after he finished work.

She could see his blond hair in the distance, above the crowd which had gathered to visit the department store Father Christmas. She'd sent him a text, letting him know they were in the queue, and her body responded as she watched him weave his way towards them. She could feel her tummy tremble and her pelvis throbbed slightly. Her sex was still a little swollen and tender after last night. She smiled to herself as she wondered what he'd say if she told him that. Would he be shocked?

Jet reached them and greeted An Na with a kiss before kissing Mei. She'd turned her cheek, not wanting to answer questions from An Na if she let him kiss her properly. If she let him kiss her like she wanted him to.

An Na stood in front of them in the queue and Jet had his hand on Mei's waist. He let it drop to her bottom and she leant in against him as he winked at her. She hummed Christmas carols as they waited for An Na's turn.

'Hello, An Na,' Father Christmas greeted them when they finally made it to the front of the queue, 'and who have you brought with you this year?'

'This is my mummy and my daddy.'

'And have they been good?'

'Mummy has. Daddy, have you been good?' An Na asked.

'I've tried my best.' Jet held his hand over his heart and answered with a smile.

'And what about you, An Na?'

'I've been *very* good.'

'And what would you like for Christmas?'

'I'd like Mummy and Daddy to get married.'

Mei gasped. 'I thought you wanted a surprise from Father Christmas, An Na?'

'That would be a surprise,' An Na replied.

'It might be a bit tricky to fit Mummy and Daddy and a wedding into my sleigh,' the jolly man said, 'so why don't I get my elves to mark down a surprise for you this year and we'll see what happens after that, okay? Now, are you ready for your photo?'

'Okay,' An Na replied. 'Mummy and Daddy, are you going to be in the photo too?' she asked as both her parents hung back.

Jet was the first to agree and he stood behind Mei and rested one hand on her hip. She liked the way it felt. She liked the weight, the warmth, the strength and the security.

Once the picture had been taken and the visit completed, all they had to do was wait for the photo to be checked and emailed to Mei.

'Can I go on one of the rides while we wait?' An Na asked, pointing at the carousel that was set up in the toy department of the store.

Mei and Jet moved to stand by the roundabout, watching as An Na chose her horse and climbed on. Mei reached into her handbag and handed Jet a ticket.

'What's this?' he asked.

'Your ticket for the Christmas concert this weekend. We had to reserve tickets so the school knows how many to expect.'

'It's this weekend?'

'Yes.'

'I've got an event in Port Macquarie on the weekend. It's a qualifying event for the World Championships.'

'This weekend?'

He nodded.

'Which day?'

'Saturday.'

'Oh, well, that's okay,' Mei said, relieved. 'The concert is on Friday. You can do both.'

'No, I can't. I'm leaving on Friday.'

'Can't you leave on Saturday?'

'It's a four-hour drive, just to get to Port Macquarie. The race starts at six in the morning and takes over four hours to complete. There's no way I can drive up in the middle of the night and then be fresh enough to compete.'

'So you'll miss her concert.'

'It looks that way.'

'But you promised her.'

'I didn't know when it was.'

'You should have asked,' Mei snapped. He shouldn't have agreed to the concert without checking the details. She couldn't believe he was letting An Na down already.

'I didn't think to ask,' he admitted, 'but there's nothing I can do.'

Mei was annoyed. She'd love to have no responsibilities. She'd love to be able to chase her dreams. 'What's more important? Your race or An Na's concert?'

'I can't change the race.'

'And I can't change the concert.'

'But she'll have other concerts. This race is important.'

'So is An Na. I thought you said you didn't want her to feel like you don't have time for her. This concert is important; she is so excited that you are coming. I can't believe you're going to let her down. Having kids means that your plans change at the drop of a hat. You have to be flexible. You can't put yourself first.'

'Mei, you're not being fair. There's nothing I can do.'

Mei was close to tears. All the joy and delight from the past twenty-four hours evaporated in the space of a few minutes and one argument and it was obvious Jet was not budging. Their bond was tenuous and she could feel it starting to unravel under the weight of the disagreement but if he wasn't going to prioritise his daughter she didn't know what she could do about it.

'You'll have to tell her that you can't make it,' she said.

What did this mean for their future as a little family? Would he always have other priorities? She was juggling motherhood, a career and helping her parents in the restaurant. His life revolved around training commitments.

Had he been right when he'd said he worried about not being father material? It was obvious he didn't get it.

'Bondi Eleven, we've got a call for assistance at Ben Buckler.'

'This is Bondi Eleven, go ahead,' Poppy responded.

'We've had a report of a person on the rocks at Ben Buckler. Bondi lifeguards have requested assistance.'

'We're on our way,' Poppy replied as she started the ambulance.

'Who or what or where is Ben Buckler?' Mei asked as she clicked her seatbelt into position. It didn't sound as if the dispatcher was going to give any more information about the location.

'It's the area at the northern end of Bondi Beach. Near the golf course. Have you not been there before?'

'No. Should I have?'

'It where the big cliffs are.'

'Oh.' Now she knew where Poppy was talking about. 'You get a lot of calls for help out there?'

Poppy nodded.

'The person on the rocks—they're talking about the base of the cliffs?' Mei asked. She could imagine the type of incidents that would occur there.

'Yes. It's a popular spot for rock climbers. Most of these calls usually involve a mishap with one of them, rather than anything more dramatic or mental health related, although we get those too.'

Mei relaxed and hoped that was the case today. She hoped the outcome wasn't going to be disastrous or tragic. But the location presented other challenges. The cliffs were high and imposing and access would be difficult.

'How do we get down to the bottom?'

'That depends. Obviously, we can't get down there— it would need the special ops team—so the lifeguards usually go in from the water.'

'The lifeguards will do the retrieval?' She wondered if she would see Jet. They hadn't spoken since their disagreement at the department store and she had no idea if they were going to be able to get past that.

'If they can. Sometimes Lifeguard One is called in.'

'Lifeguard One?'

'The helicopter. We're just on standby really; we wait and see what the situation is and what decision is made regarding retrieval. If the person's injuries aren't serious, and the lifeguards can extract them using the jet ski and rescue mat, we'll meet them at the beach. If it's more serious than that the helicopter team will come into play. We'll go to the headland first though, so we can get a handle on what's happening.'

A crowd had gathered by the time they reached the headland. Poppy and Mei got out of the ambulance as the jet ski rounded the base of the cliffs. Ryder was driving the ski and Mei could see Jet on the back.

There was a body on the rocks. Immobile.

'How will they reach the patient?' Mei asked.

'Jet will jump off the ski and get onto the rocks.'

'He'll do what!?'

Waves crashed onto the rocks. Mei knew they would be slippery underfoot and she couldn't imagine how Jet could safely negotiate his way from the ski to the base of the cliff. 'Isn't that dangerous?

'Jet knows what he's doing,' Poppy reassured her. 'He can read the ocean and the swell—his years of surfing experience will hold him in good stead. He'll be okay.'

Mei's heart was in her mouth as she watched Ryder time the swell of the ocean and she saw Jet leap from the ski. She had her hands clasped tightly and she held her breath, but somehow Jet landed safely on the rocks.

She breathed a sigh of relief as he moved away from the edge, away from the impact zone where the waves were still crashing onto the rocks. At least now she didn't have to worry about him getting swept off and into the ocean.

He scrambled across the rocks and knelt beside the patient.

'Now what?' she asked.

'Now we wait. Jet will assess the patient and determine the extent of his injuries and make a decision about evacuation.'

Poppy was holding the radio from the ambulance and it crackled to life as the communications centre relayed the information Jet was reporting to the tower.

'Male, age thirty-two, fell while rock climbing. Bilateral simple ankle fractures.'

'He's not walking out of there,' Poppy said as they heard the call go out to Lifeguard One.

'So that's us done? We're not needed?' Mei raised her voice to be heard as the helicopter flew overhead but her voice wobbled with fear. The patient had been safely extracted but Jet was still at the base of the cliffs, alone on the slippery rocks, and Ryder was sitting on the jet ski fifty or so metres out to sea. Somehow Jet had to get off the rocks and back to the beach. She might be annoyed with him but she didn't want any misfortune to happen to him.

Poppy nodded. 'We'll just wait and make sure Jet gets back out to Ryder, but we're done. Are you okay?'

No, Mei was far from okay. She was extremely anxious. Her hands were tightly clenched together and her heart was racing.

She shook her head. 'I'm worried about Jet and I'm not sure if I should be.'

'He'll be fine; he knows what he's doing and this spot isn't as dangerous as it looks. He'll come back to you, safe and sound.'

'That's partly what I'm worried about.'

Poppy frowned. 'I'm not following you.'

'I'm worried for his safety, of course, but I know he understands the water. Far better than he understands me or me him. That's what concerns me. That he won't come back to me. That he's not interested in being a father or in having a relationship with me.'

'And you are?'

Mei nodded. 'I've never got over him. When I bumped into him again here I thought maybe my feelings were so strong because of An Na and the connection I felt through her to Jet, but it's more than that. It's much deeper. But his priorities are very different to mine—too different. I fear for us to be able to find some middle ground. For us to find our way to each other with any sort of permanence.'

'And that's what you want?' Poppy asked as they watched Jet dive off the rocks into the ocean and swim out to where Ryder waited on the jet ski.

Mei nodded. 'For me and for An Na. But I think Jet and I are on completely different wavelengths and I don't get the sense that he is ready to take on a serious relationship. He seems caught up in his solitary bachelor life and his training and I don't think he has room for me or wants to make room. He's trying with An Na, I get that, but I want him to try harder and I'm worried that this little bit of him that we're getting is all he can give. I'm worried I'm wishing for something that is impossible.'

'Have you told him how you feel?'

Mei shook her head as they returned to the ambulance. 'I think we've got enough on our plates with figuring An Na out without complicating it. I can't demand something of him that he can't give me.'

'But you like him?'

Mei nodded.

'Maybe you need to take the first step. Tell him how you feel. Our family isn't great at expressing our emotions. I know he's besotted with An Na and I've seen the way he looks at you.'

'How?'

'Like you are the sun, the moon and the stars. Like you're precious and delicate and he can't believe you're real. Give him a chance. He isn't great at communicating and I know he's worried about his ability to be a good father. We didn't grow up in a conventional family and none of us really know if we've got the skills to raise a family of our own. You'll have to teach him.'

'I don't know if he's ready to learn. I'm scared there are too many hurdles for us to get over.'

'Be patient. It's a big adjustment. But he's a good guy. He's loyal and kind but he needs something, someone, to anchor him. Not to tether him or tie him down but someone he can rely on to be there when things don't go his way and who will celebrate the successes with him. Someone who will be proud of him and support him. Our parents weren't like that.'

Mei's family had always been there for her. Even when she fell pregnant they stood by her. She knew they would never abandon her.

'Jet has always had our support, but he needs more. He needs you,' Poppy said as she started the engine. 'He needs encouragement and attention. He's afraid of being rejected if he fails. He needs to know you'll be there for him no matter what. If you can give him that you'll reap the rewards.'

Mei wasn't sure she and Jet would be able to make this work but she vowed to be more supportive. One of them had to act like a grown-up and perhaps she was being unfair, expecting him to drop everything and change his life because of a decision she'd made eight years ago.

She wished she could turn off her feelings but she couldn't. He made her giddy, nervous and excited and she didn't want to let go of that. Not without a fight. If she wanted to make this work, maybe she needed to heed Poppy's advice.

CHAPTER NINE

MEI HAD MADE a promise to herself that she would be patient, that she would be supportive, but she found it hard to remember her promise when An Na's Christmas concert was ten minutes from starting and not only was Jet absent but she knew he hadn't told An Na about his schedule clash. She was furious that he was going to let her down. That he was going to let them both down.

She had delayed going into the school hall, hoping in vain that Jet might still turn up, but she could see the hall was nearing capacity. Su-Lin and Bo were saving her a seat in the second row and if she didn't claim it soon other parents would have it in their sights.

She bit back her frustration. She was disappointed in Jet, disappointed for An Na, disappointed for herself. She was being a romantic, dreaming of a future that wasn't going to happen. Surely it was better to know now.

She wiped a tear from the corner of her eye, straightened her shoulders and pasted a smile on her face. She didn't want to ruin An Na's day any further by letting her daughter see her cry. She would smile and enjoy the concert even if she felt like screaming. The person she wanted to scream at was God knew where and it wasn't fair to take her frustrations out on anyone else.

She excused herself as she side-stepped past other parents and took her seat beside Su-Lin. Her sister-in-law reached across and squeezed her hand in support as the school's principal stepped on stage. Mei did her best to ignore the empty seat on her left, the one Su-Lin had optimistically kept for Jet.

'You okay?' Su-Lin asked.

'Not really.'

Poppy had told her she needed to give Jet time. People kept telling her what Jet needed, but were any of them giving him advice? Were any of them telling him what *she* needed? That she wanted someone to step up and share the responsibility of parenting. She didn't want someone who was only prepared to do the fun stuff, the surfing lessons and the visits to Father Christmas. She wanted someone to help with the boring, mundane but important day-to-day stuff too. She needed someone on her side.

Mei could feel the tension in her jaw and shoulders and she tried to relax as the principal introduced An Na's class. She smiled as her daughter came onto the stage and soon discovered that watching An Na's enthusiastic performance was the perfect thing to distract her from the thoughts relentlessly swirling around in her head. She even managed to make it through the pieces and songs that the other classes presented.

She knew she was biased but she thought An Na was brilliant. She sang carols with her class before she and some of her friends who attended the same ballet classes performed a dance. Mei clapped and smiled as the little girls finished their routine. An Na did a half-curtsey and waved to Mei, but her attention was quickly diverted and Mei saw her waving towards the rear of the hall. She turned in her seat to see who had caught her daughter's attention and her heart skipped a beat when she saw Jet leaning against the back wall. What on earth was he doing here? Had he cancelled his plans? Was he putting An Na first?

She fidgeted through the last few performances, wishing they would be over, wanting to go to Jet. Her concentration was completely shot and all she could think about was making a beeline for him to find out what was going on. What had made him change his mind.

The entire junior school was on stage to sing the final carol and as soon as they filed off Mei was ready to spring to her feet. But as the applause died down the principal came back onto the stage with her final message and Mei sank back into her chair. Would this never end?

At last the audience was excused. Mei stood and turned towards the back of the hall, but her view was now obscured by all the other parents. She had no chance of seeing over people's heads; her line of sight was level with people's chests. The parents on her left were in no hurry to move and Mei didn't want to push past them again, but if they didn't hurry and gather their belongings she would have no choice.

Finally, they began to move and she was almost treading on their heels in her haste to get out of the row.

'I'll meet you outside,' she told Su-Lin. If her sister-in-law wondered where the fire was she didn't say.

Mei dodged and weaved past the dawdling parents but when she eventually made it to the back of the hall Jet was nowhere to be seen. She stepped outside and scanned the grounds but there was no sign of him. She knew she hadn't imagined his presence so where was he?

'Mummy! Mummy! Did you like my dancing?'

Mei almost overbalanced as An Na came running towards her and threw her arms around her waist. She scooped her up and took a step backwards, regaining her feet as she smiled at her daughter. 'I thought you were magnificent,' she told her. 'I loved it.'

'Did you see Daddy?' An Na asked as she set her back down on the ground.

So she *hadn't* imagined him. That eased her mind. She nodded. 'I did.'

'Look what he gave me.'

An Na's fingers were at her neck. She was holding a delicate silver chain between her thumb and forefinger and Mei could see a tiny charm hanging from the chain. She squatted down to get a closer look. It was a girl on a surfboard.

'It's me!' An Na exclaimed.

'I can see that,' Mei replied and wondered why Jet was buying An Na gifts this close to Christmas. She knew she was looking for flaws in his behaviour and she didn't like the way that made her feel about herself.

She saw Su-Lin heading towards them and she held up one finger and motioned 'one minute' to her as she took out her phone. She needed to speak to Jet.

'Hi, where are you?' she asked as he answered her call.

'In the car on the way to Port Macquarie.'

Mei frowned. 'But I saw you at the concert.'

'Yes. And now I'm in the car.'

'But we're going out for pizza.'

'Mei…' She heard him sigh. 'No one said anything about pizza and I couldn't stay. I shouldn't have stayed for the concert, but Ryder offered to drive me up the coast tonight and I thought I could make it work.'

'Can't you leave in the morning?' She hated the fact that she was almost begging when really she should be thanking him for being there for An Na, but the words were out before she could stop herself.

'I've changed my plans once already and no, I can't go in the morning, the race starts at six am. As it is, I should have been up there tonight to prepare. Ryder is driving me so I can sleep in the car. It's not ideal preparation but a promise is a promise and I didn't want to let An Na down.' He paused and she knew he was waiting for her to respond. Waiting for her to say it was okay, but the words stuck in her throat. She wanted him there. With An Na. With her. 'Mei, I don't know what else you want from me. It seems like nothing I do is good enough.'

He'd done the right thing by An Na, he'd watched her concert as he'd promised, and Mei knew this shouldn't be about her, it *wasn't* about her, except that she wished it was. She wished she was a priority for Jet too.

Mei nibbled on a shortbread biscuit that An Na and Daisy had baked and sipped her champagne as she watched Lily and An Na decorate the Christmas tree. She was tired and on edge, wound tight from lack of sleep and stress. She'd spent the past few days rehashing her post-concert conversation with Jet and thinking of all the ways it could have gone differently. And now he was back from Port Macquarie but things between them had definitely not improved. The tension was palpable and the air frosty.

Jet had come fourth in his race and Mei was feeling guilty. He had needed to finish second or higher to get automatic selection into the national team for the World Championships and Mei couldn't help wondering if he'd stuck to his original plan and travelled to Port Macquarie the day before the race, rather than arriving at the last minute, he would have been better rested and the result could have been different. He hadn't said anything to her about the race but she knew he was disappointed and was now pinning all his hopes on the final qualifying event which was being held four days after Christmas in Bondi.

Jet had barely spoken to her. For once she had no idea what he was thinking. Was he annoyed or upset with her? Did he think she was too demanding? Unreasonable? Or was he simply upset about the race? She knew he'd been surprised to see her here, but he hadn't questioned her presence, but still, she needed to get him alone. They needed to talk but he was doing his best to avoid her.

Mei appreciated that Jet's sisters seemed determined to try to fix things between their brother and her. She knew that was why Lily had invited her and An Na to join them today, to help decorate the Christmas tree. Lily had explained it was her tradition, albeit a relatively recent one that had begun when she'd married and moved into this house, but whichever of her siblings were in Sydney were always invited to help decorate the tree. An Na could have gone alone but Lily had insisted that she come too, and Mei didn't have the heart to suggest that their efforts to mend bridges would be in vain. Jet was proud and Mei knew she would have to fix this.

She looked up at the tree as she finished the shortbread. It was looking festive and she was hoping the sight of the tree would lift her spirits a little and restore some Christmas cheer. Lily had chosen a blue and silver theme this year, which Mei had to admit had surprised her at first. Her family celebrated Christmas too but their decorations had always stuck to the traditional red. She wondered if that was a throwback to her parents' youth, growing up in Hong Kong under British governance, or if it was because the Chinese associated the colour red with good luck and fortune. She'd never thought about it before but she liked the idea of choosing a theme. And the blue and silver made it feel like a fresh start, a new beginning.

Maybe she wouldn't get quite the new beginning she'd been hoping for, but if An Na could get to know her father and be happy that was enough for Mei. She would learn to be content with that.

Jet was lifting An Na up so she could place the angel at the top of the tree when Lily's phone rang. He might have been avoiding Mei but his attitude towards An Na was unchanged and for that she was grateful. Jet might want nothing to do with her but it looked as if he intended to keep his promise to be a part of An Na's life.

Mei was watching Jet and An Na but she could see Lily too and her attention was caught when she saw Lily freeze. She went absolutely still as the blood drained from her face.

'Lily, what is it? What's wrong?' Mei crossed the room and made Lily sit down; she looked as if she might faint. 'Who's on the phone?'

'Mum,' Lily said as she ended the call.

Mei saw Poppy's head swivel towards them. 'What did she want?'

'Dad is in hospital.' Lily was looking at her siblings but Mei could tell she wasn't really seeing them. 'He's in a coma.'

'What?' Daisy asked. 'What happened?' she asked.

Everything came to a stop as they all waited to hear what Lily had to say. 'It sounds like he's had a ruptured brain aneurysm.'

That wasn't good. Mei looked around the room, waiting for someone to say something, but all four of the siblings were silent. She assumed they were in shock and she knew someone needed to take charge.

'He's in Byron Bay?' she asked.

'Yes,' Jet replied as he handed An Na another piece of shortbread.

Mei wanted to yell at him, to tell him this was no time for shortbread.

'Okay, so what do we need to do? How will we get you all there?' she asked.

'Where?'

'To Byron, to see your father.'

'Why?'

'What do you mean "why"? Your father is critically ill; you need to go to see him.'

'We'll have to drive,' Lily said, coming out of her trance. 'Who's going to come?'

Mei frowned. Why would Lily ask who was going? Why would that be up for discussion? Surely, they would all be going.

'I'll come with you,' Daisy said.

'Poppy?'

'I guess so.'

What was wrong with this family?

'Jet?'

'I'm supposed to be taking An Na surfing tomorrow.'

'Don't be ridiculous,' Mei told him. 'That doesn't matter. Your father is much more important.'

Jet was shaking his head. 'He doesn't need me there. We don't have a close relationship.'

'Jet, you need to go with your sisters,' Mei insisted. 'If you don't want to be there for your dad you should at least go to support your mum.'

'She doesn't need us either. Our family is not like

yours, Mei. Goldie doesn't need us—she only ever needed our father. He is her world.'

'All the more reason for you to go then,' Mei said. 'He's in hospital. She doesn't have him to lean on. She will need you.'

'You can't have it both ways, Mei.' Jet's tone was abrupt and Mei felt it slice through her like a knife to the heart.

'I think you should take your discussion out to the deck,' Lily interrupted. 'Away from little ears.'

Jet and Mei both looked towards An Na before heeding Lily's warning.

'What do you mean, "both ways"?' Mei asked as they stepped outside.

'One minute you're telling me I'm not prioritising An Na, I'm not committing to my promises, that I'm not meeting your expectations of what a proper father should be, and the next telling me your family doesn't matter.'

'I was talking about a surfing lesson,' Mei replied. 'A surfing lesson can wait. Your family has to come first.'

'But a few days ago you thought my race could wait. Why do you get to decide what is and isn't important?'

'Is that what this is all about? You're blaming me for what happened in the race?'

'No. I'm blaming myself for that. But it seems that, no matter what I do, it's never enough for you. Never the right thing. I don't know what you want from me but I'm beginning to suspect that I will continue to disappoint you, that I cannot be the man you want me to be. And perhaps we need to think about that.'

* * *

'You okay?' Jet asked Poppy as they sat outside the critical care unit of the Byron Bay hospital. The drive from Sydney had taken eight hours and it was late in the day, but they had gone straight to the hospital and were now waiting for their mother to come out and give them some information about Pete's condition.

'I don't know,' Poppy replied. 'I haven't seen Mum or Dad for a year, and it feels strange to be waiting to see them in a hospital. Dad always seemed so fit and healthy. I know these things happen out of the blue, I've seen it often enough in my job, but it just isn't making sense. I'm a bit out of whack, but I'll be okay. It's you I'm worried about.'

'Me?'

Poppy nodded. 'Things seem a little strained between you and Mei. What's going on there?'

'I'm not really sure, to be honest. This is all new to me and I feel like I'm constantly mucking things up. I know we think Mum and Dad didn't do a great job of raising us, but bringing up a kid is harder than I thought.'

'You're doing well with An Na. You're a natural with kids and she adores you.'

'Maybe.' Jet shrugged. 'But I'm not doing so well with Mei. She's got high expectations and I want to live up to them but I'm not sure that I can.'

'Perhaps, when we get home, the two of you need to sit down and have a proper discussion about your goals and expectations. About what your future looks like.'

The idea of that terrified Jet. He knew he would fail

to live up to Mei's expectations. But wouldn't it be better to fail Mei than to fail An Na? As much as the thought of that conversation terrified him, he knew Poppy was right. There was no avoiding the fact that they needed to talk, and he was about to agree with Poppy just as their mother emerged from the CCU.

Jet got a shock when he saw Goldie. Like Poppy, it was over a year since he'd visited and Goldie, who was only forty-eight and usually looked younger, appeared to have aged ten years.

Lily stood up and went to hug her. Jet, Poppy and Daisy stayed in their seats. Goldie seemed dazed. She let Lily hug her but she didn't return the hug. Her arms hung limply at her sides.

'I don't understand how this happened,' Goldie said as Lily released her. 'Pete is fit. He'd been surfing. I don't understand.'

'Mum—' Lily put her hands on Goldie's shoulders and forced her to make eye contact '—tell me what happened.'

'He'd been surfing and complained of a headache. He collapsed on the beach and was brought to hospital.'

'What has the doctor said?'

'The doctor?' Goldie repeated. 'I don't know.'

'Did they say anything about surgery?'

'I can't remember. He might have said something about draining fluid.'

Lily turned to her siblings. 'Stay with Mum. I'll go and find someone to talk to.'

They waited in silence for a while but when Lily didn't return Jet started asking questions.

'How does this happen, Poppy? What causes it?' he asked.

'It can be genetic,' Poppy said, 'and can also be related to illness or drug use, but often there's no specific cause. You can have aneurysms that never burst—they just sit there and you wouldn't know they existed.'

'I've spoken to the surgeon,' Lily said when she came back. 'He's put a catheter in to drain the fluid off Dad's brain. He's recovered consciousness but the next twenty-four hours are critical. There's a high risk of another bleed in that time frame. They want to operate.'

'Operate? On his brain?'

Lily nodded. 'They have two options. In one they insert a catheter through an artery in the groin and then push a soft wire through that into the aneurysm and seal it off. In the other they remove a section of skull and clip the aneurysm directly to stop the blood flow.'

'They cut open his skull?'

'Yes.'

'Will they do that here?'

'No, they need to move him to Brisbane and there are risks associated with both options.'

'What sort of risks?'

'Post-op pulmonary oedema is the biggest concern. That can cause heart attacks. The surgeon has spoken to Dad about his options; he's going to discuss it with Mum but he wants to see each of us one by one first.'

'Who does? The surgeon?'

'No, Dad. He's conscious.'

Jet sat and waited as his sisters each had their turn. The hospital was decorated for Christmas and it seemed completely surreal to be sitting outside the critical care unit surrounded by tinsel and sparkling lights.

'Your turn,' Poppy said as she emerged from the unit. Her eyes were red and Jet was surprised to see her upset. Of his three sisters, Poppy was the most self-contained. Lily and Daisy were far more emotional. Had Pete said something or was his condition really critical? Lily had said there were surgical options and Jet had just assumed that meant it was a problem that could be fixed. Had he misunderstood? What were they really dealing with? What was he walking into?

He was dreading what was about to happen. He wasn't ready to deal with this. It was way beyond his emotional experience. His heart was racing and his palms were sweating. He knew it was anxiety. Nervousness he could handle. He was nervous before a race but he'd learned to use that surge of adrenalin to focus his body and mind on the physical effort that awaited him. He'd trained for those situations but today was something new. He was unprepared—woefully unprepared—and he felt certain it was going to be a disaster. He was bound to say the wrong thing or have nothing to say. Which would be better? Which would be worse?

His thoughts turned to Mei. She'd know how to calm him down, to focus his thoughts, and she'd know what to say to Pete too. Jet was completely lost.

He wished Mei was with him. But she wasn't. He was on his own.

He wiped his hands on his shorts, trying to get rid of the clamminess. He took a deep breath, stood up, pushed open the door and stepped into the unknown.

His father was blond and tanned, an older version of his son, and he looked incongruous lying in a hospital bed. If it wasn't for the tubes protruding from him and the leads connecting him to the machines, he would have looked perfectly fine.

He was awake.

Jet knew he should be pleased that his father was conscious, that he had survived, but all he could think of was that now he would have to make conversation and he and his father hadn't had a proper conversation for fifteen years.

He stopped himself from asking Pete how he was feeling. It would have been a ridiculous question, given the circumstances. He sat beside the bed and said the first thing that came to mind. 'I hear you've got a trip to Brisbane coming up.'

'Yeah, never much cared for the city.'

'Well, I expect they'll fix you up and send you back here as quick as they can.'

'I hope so but, in case they don't, in case something goes wrong, there are some things I need to say to you.'

Jet had not prepared himself for a personal discussion. He'd already forgotten, or chosen to ignore, the fact that Pete had asked to speak to each of his children individually. That should have served as a warning, but Jet and his father had never shared their thoughts and feelings. They had spent time together in the waves, but surfing hadn't involved much communication. And that was the way they both liked it.

'You don't need to rest?'

'No,' Pete said. 'I'm about to put my life in the hands

of some doctor I don't know, things might not go according to plan and there are some things I want to say that I might not get a chance to say later. I need to get this off my chest. I need to apologise.'

'What for?'

'For not spending more time with you. I feel that I don't really know you and I'm sorry about that. And now, faced with my own mortality, I realise I might never get that chance. Before today I would have blamed my own parents for the way I brought you all up, but the blame stops with me. Raising you kids the way we did was a conscious decision on my part. Along with your mother. My parents were strict, my father in particular was very demanding, and I vowed not to bring you kids up the same way. I wasn't going to insist you follow our rules or chase our dreams.

'My parents insisted I study medicine. I wasn't at all interested but that was what all the men in my family did and it was expected of me too. I hated it. I failed second year and then dropped out. I went travelling and ended up here, where I met your mother. Once I met Goldie, that was it. I wasn't going anywhere. And we've been together ever since. I don't regret that but what I do regret is that I didn't set goals for myself. I always thought I would have time to do things later, but the opportunities weren't available in Byron back then. I ended up with the surf shop and surf school. I love that job, but I do wonder if I could have done more, accomplished more. It's too late for me now, but I'm really proud of you kids and what you've achieved.'

Jet didn't feel that he'd achieved very much yet—not

compared to his sisters. He believed he could do it but he realised now that he needed someone else to believe in him, to make him try harder. He needed someone to impress, someone to be proud of him. He needed a reason to set an example, a reason to do his best, and Mei had given him that reason. He would try, not just for An Na but for Mei as well. She had achieved so much as a single mother—her career, raising a daughter—and Jet realised he needed to step up and show her that he had what it took. That she could rely on him, that he wouldn't give up.

'I didn't want to pressure you kids like I'd been pressured,' Pete said. 'I figured we'd give you freedom to make your own decisions, your own mistakes.'

'Kids need boundaries,' Jet said. He hadn't known that, growing up. He'd revelled in the freedom he'd been given, but as he'd become an adult and interacted with the lifeguards and their families and with the teenagers on Bondi, he'd learned the value of boundaries. Growing up in the commune, they'd had no restrictions and Jet now knew that his life could have gone in a whole different direction. He'd been a wild teenager who could have so easily gone off the rails.

'I know. But I wanted to give you space. I wanted to be your friend, not your father. I probably needed to find a happy medium, but I didn't want to turn out like my father. You'll probably say the same one day.'

It wasn't that Jet was desperate not to be like him, but he wanted to do a better job than his father had done.

'That's what worries me, that I—probably all of us, but me in particular—won't know how to parent. How to show love and affection but still set boundaries, how to encourage without spoiling, how to discipline without damaging.'

'It sounds like you are already a step ahead of where your mother and I were. All I could think about were the things I didn't want to do, not what I should do. And Goldie had even less idea than I did about how to raise a family. She'd never had an example set. She was raised in foster homes and ran away at eighteen and when she fell pregnant she didn't know what she was doing and neither did I. If it wasn't for everyone in the commune rallying around us we wouldn't have survived. It took us a long time to work things out. Goldie kept getting pregnant and she was never emotionally equipped to deal with the hard aspects of raising kids. We put each other first when we should have prioritised you kids. I feel like we've let you down and I'm sorry. But, despite all our mistakes, you're doing well and I am proud of you. I wish I could say we helped. I know you'll do a better job when it's your turn.'

'It's my turn now.' Jet hadn't meant to say that. He'd had no intention of divulging anything personal to his father, but An Na and Mei had been in his thoughts since he'd arrived in Byron Bay and he'd spoken without thinking.

'What do you mean?'

'I have a seven-year-old daughter.'

'I have a granddaughter? And you never thought to tell us? You never thought we'd like to meet her?'

'I didn't know about her,' he said. 'I've only just met her, but no, I didn't think about introducing her to you.

I didn't think you'd be interested.' He knew he sounded harsh, but it was the truth. Introducing An Na to his sisters was one thing, meeting his parents was something else altogether. But, once again, he could hear Mei's voice in his head and he knew what her opinion would be. She would insist at some point that An Na meet her paternal grandparents, but he'd worry about that another day.

Right now, he knew that he would do whatever it took to ensure he didn't let An Na down.

As he sat by his father's hospital bed, he promised himself and An Na that he wouldn't make the same mistakes. An Na didn't need a buddy; she needed guidance, boundaries and love. He would be involved; he would make sure she knew she was loved.

Mei was doing a brilliant job but he needed to step up for both Mei and An Na. His daughter had one parent but she needed two. She deserved two.

Being a parent wasn't necessarily harder than he'd thought; he'd always thought it would be difficult and that he wasn't cut out for it, but that was irrelevant now. He was a parent, and it was his responsibility to be the best he could be and he vowed to do a better job than his father had.

He could do better. He *would* do better.

He didn't want to be a part-time father, and he didn't want An Na looking to anyone else for a parental figure. It had to be him and he didn't want to be without Mei. He wanted to raise An Na with Mei. He was determined to be a father and a husband and that meant he had to set the wheels in motion to sort out how they were going to live their life. What his life—their life—was going to look like going forward.

He needed to put An Na and Mei first.

People didn't always get a second chance—he hadn't really even had a first chance with An Na or Mei—and he now knew exactly what he was going to do.

CHAPTER TEN

'Mummy, mummy, look, it's Father Christmas!'

Mei had been watching the beach, looking for Jet, when An Na began excitedly pointing out to sea. Jet had asked them to meet him on Bondi Beach at the end of his shift but when Mei arrived at the lifeguard tower Ryder had directed her down to the sand. She hadn't been able to see Jet anywhere on the beach and was wondering if he had made a mistake, but as she turned to look out to the ocean she realised Jet wasn't missing and Ryder wasn't mistaken.

An Na was right. Father Christmas was out on the water. To be exact, Father Christmas was coming towards them on a jet ski, standing up as he rode in to the shore, and there was something very familiar about the way he stood and the tilt of his head. Despite the costume, Mei knew instantly that it was Jet. What she didn't know was why he was dressed in a red suit, white beard and sunglasses and why he was balancing an enormous present under his left arm.

An Na was tugging on her hand, pulling her down

to the water's edge as Jet guided the watercraft into the shallows and came to a stop.

'Ho, ho, ho, Merry Christmas!' he said as he leapt from the ski, wrestling with the present at the same time.

It was late afternoon on Christmas Eve but there were still plenty of families enjoying the perfect summer weather and An Na and Mei had been joined by dozens of other children, all eager to see Father Christmas.

The lifeguard buggy pulled up behind them and Dutchy and Ryder jumped out. They were wearing Christmas hats and their lifeguard shorts and they each carried large red sacks.

Jet had the present he'd brought with him tucked under one arm. It was wrapped in red and white Christmas paper and shaped suspiciously like a surfboard. He put it into the back of the buggy and picked up another sack and proceeded to hand out individually wrapped chocolates and lollies to the crowd of children, assisted by Dutchy and Ryder.

Mei smiled as she watched the proceedings; she thought the lifeguards were having as much fun as the children.

An Na still hadn't recognised Jet but once the children dispersed, munching on their sweets, Jet removed his beard.

'Daddy!' An Na clapped her hands and ran to hug him. 'What are you doing?'

'I'm helping Father Christmas. He's got a busy day

tomorrow, so I thought I'd help him get a head start. He gave me something for you.'

'What is it?'

'I think it's a surprise. Do you want to see?'

An Na was hopping from one foot to the other. 'Yes!'

He took her over to the buggy and lifted the parcel out, standing it upright on the sand.

'This is for me?' An Na's eyes were wide.

Jet nodded and held the top of the present as An Na started to rip the paper from the gift.

'It's a surfboard! Is it really mine? Mummy, look, a surfboard!'

'It's fantastic, isn't it, darling?' Mei pasted a smile on her face. She'd known what it was—it was pretty hard to disguise a surfboard— but part of her was a little miffed that Jet hadn't discussed the gift with her because she knew his present was going to outshine hers. Although she couldn't deny he'd been quite clever, gifting it from Father Christmas, and seeing the delight on An Na's face she knew she couldn't begrudge the fact that Jet had chosen the perfect gift for their daughter.

But she couldn't help feeling that he was still getting to do all the fun stuff, the lighter side of parenting. She was still the disciplinarian, the one who figured out the day-to-day needs of her daughter—their daughter—and she was tired of doing it alone.

But she had to give him some credit. He hadn't abandoned them. He was trying.

She remembered Poppy's advice. She needed to give him time. She did owe him that. Finding out he was a father would have been a massive shock and to his credit he hadn't run away. It wasn't his fault that he coped with humour—that he didn't seem to be taking it seriously. That was her perception. She hadn't asked him how he was coping—she'd been too wrapped up in her own thoughts, her own needs. He deserved better than that. She needed to lighten up.

She knew she overthought things. She knew she could be too serious. Maybe she should take a leaf out of his book. The world wasn't going to end if she relaxed a little and gave him some space. Maybe she was asking for too much. She kept saying that all she wanted was for An Na to be happy and she was. Perhaps, with time, Mei could be happy too, but for now she'd try to relax, she'd try not to overthink things. She'd do her best not to expect too much or berate Jet for not meeting her expectations. She could admit that perhaps her expectations had been unrealistic. Time would tell, and in the meantime Jet didn't look as if he was going anywhere. Maybe things would still be okay.

'I love it!' An Na said as she let go of the board and threw her arms around Jet again. 'And I love you.'

'I love you too, my gorgeous girl.'

Mei caught her breath. She hadn't heard Jet tell An Na that he loved her before. She lifted one hand and wiped a tear from her eye, pleased that Jet and An Na were too preoccupied to notice her sentimentality.

What would he say if she told him she loved him? Was he ready to hear that? Was she ready to tell him?

She knew she loved him. Why hadn't she told him?

She knew it was because she was afraid that he wouldn't say it back. That he wasn't ready, that he might *never* be ready, and she couldn't take that rejection. While she kept silent she could keep the dream alive.

'You okay?'

Ryder was standing beside her. Mei nodded. She was overcome with emotion, which robbed her of speech as she wondered if Jet would ever say those words to her.

'Can we go surfing now?' An Na asked.

'In a minute, sweetheart,' Jet replied. 'I just need to ask your mum something.'

'I can take you, An Na,' Ryder offered. 'I have officially finished work for the day.'

Mei could tell An Na was torn between wanting Jet to take her and wanting to get into the water as soon as possible. 'That's a good idea, An Na,' she encouraged. She was keen to know what Jet wanted.

Ryder took off his Christmas hat and tossed it into the buggy when An Na agreed to let him surf with her. An Na was already in her bathers; Mei suspected she would spend the entire summer in swimwear and in the ocean with Jet if she had half a chance. Ryder picked up An Na's new board and the two of them headed into the surf. Jet stripped off his costume, leaving him bare-chested in his lifeguard shorts, and he and Dutchy loaded the jet ski onto the trailer attached to the buggy before Dutchy drove it back to the tower, leaving Mei and Jet alone at last.

'That's a very generous present,' Mei said as she watched An Na lie on her surfboard and start paddling. 'She will love it.'

'Should I have asked you about it first?'

She wanted to say yes but she knew it didn't really matter. 'No. It's fine.'

'Are you sure? I saw your expression when An Na unwrapped it; you didn't look as enthusiastic as I'd hoped.'

'It's not about me. An Na loves it; that's what counts. To be honest, I was just a bit miffed that you chose such a great present. You don't think you're spoiling her?'

'I probably am, but it's Christmas! I figured there's no better time and, just so you know, I plan on spoiling you too,' he said as he reached for her hand. 'You have given me the most amazing gift—our daughter. My life has taken a new direction with you and An Na. I want to see where it takes me next and I'm hoping that we can take that step together.

'Your family has welcomed me…you've supported me and shown me what a family can be. I'm never going to have the close relationship with my parents that you have with yours, but I've accepted that and realised that's okay. I have my sisters but now you have given me a chance to have a family of my own. If you'd asked me before I knew about An Na, I would have said I wasn't ready for that, in fact, I'm pretty sure I did say that, but now I can't imagine life without her. But I also can't imagine my life without you.

'You make me want to be a better person. You make me believe I can be that person. You inspire me to try harder, achieve more. With you beside me I feel that I can accomplish so much. I promised to take care of An Na—I want to make the same promise to you. I want to know if you think we could be a real family. Not just parents to An Na but if we could raise her together, as partners. As a couple.'

'A couple?'

Jet nodded. 'You and An Na have completely changed my life. I adore An Na—she is incredible, she is funny and warm and smart and I love her, and I feel the same way about you. I love An Na and I love you, Mei.'

'You love me?'

'I think I've loved you since the day I met you, but it's taken me until now to figure that out. When we first met, I was lost and lonely. The family I knew was gone—Lily was in Sydney, Poppy was in Brisbane and Daisy was only fourteen. Ryder, who was like my brother, had moved to Perth, three thousand kilometres away, and I was living by myself in a caravan. I needed something—someone—but I wasn't expecting you. I didn't realise at the time what a gift you were. I was young and foolish and stupidly thought there would be plenty of girls like you out in the world, but after all this time and all my travels I've never found anyone like you.'

'There must be dozens of women like me—dozens of women better than me.'

'No, you are the only one for me. You are more than I deserve. You are strong, you are brave, you are smart, you are loving. I found my tribe with the lifeguards, but I still needed to find my soulmate. I needed to find the love of my life, the person who gives me purpose and that is you. I want to be the husband and father you and An Na deserve,' he said as he dropped to one knee.

'What are you doing?' Mei had forgotten about An

Na, she was unaware of anything and everything else around her. All she could see was Jet, blond, tanned and gorgeous, kneeling in the sand at her feet.

He took her hand. 'I'm asking you if we can raise An Na together. I'm asking you to marry me.'

'You want to marry me?'

'I do. I want us to be a real family. I am already An Na's father but I want to be your husband. I knew you were special when I first met you. I believe we were destined for each other, there was a reason you fell pregnant, we are meant to be together. I love you and I want to build a life with you if you'll have me.'

'I used to hope that I'd find someone to share my life with, someone who would love me and An Na, someone who would want to be part of our future, but I never dreamt I would find you again.'

'And now that you have, now that we've found each other, what do you think?'

'I think you can make me stronger, braver and happier and I know I love you too.'

'Is that a yes? Will you marry me, Mei? Will you be my wife?'

'Yes. I will marry you.' Mei's eyes filled with tears and they spilled from her lashes as she nodded.

Jet stood up and wrapped his arms around her. He kissed her soundly and Mei was vaguely aware of the sound of cheering and clapping. Jet spun her around and standing behind her she saw her entire family and Jet's sisters and most of the lifeguards.

'Where did they all come from?'

'I was hoping you'd say yes, and I thought you might like to celebrate with everyone.'

'They all knew?'

Jet nodded. 'I had to speak to your parents. I needed to know if I was who they had in mind for a son-in-law, and then I had to talk to Su-Lin—I thought she could give me an idea about whether you'd accept—and then I needed to have Ryder on stand-by, because I figured An Na would want to go surfing. And of course he had to tell Dutchy and Gibbo and Poppy my plan and then she told Lily and Daisy. You don't mind, do you?'

'What, that I was the last one to know?' She smiled.

'Almost the last,' he said as An Na and Ryder came out of the water.

'Mummy, why are you crying?' An Na asked.

Mei bent down and hugged An Na. 'Because I'm happy. Daddy and I are getting married!'

'You are?' An Na threw her arms around Mei as she lifted her up.

Jet kissed An Na's forehead. 'An Na was the last one to know,' he whispered to Mei. 'I wasn't sure how good she was at keeping secrets.'

Mei laughed. 'I think you made a good decision—on all counts.'

'Did Father Christmas tell you to marry Mummy?' An Na asked.

'We might have had a little chat about it,' Jet told her with a grin.

'This is going to be the best Christmas ever!'

'I'm glad you think so.'

'So now can we live with you?'

'Yes.'

'All right!' Gibbo's booming voice carried over the gathering. 'I know you've all got Christmas Eve dinner to get to but the champagne is on ice if you want to come up to the tower for a quick toast.'

'We've *all* got Christmas dinner?' Mei and An Na were having dinner with Jet and his sisters to celebrate Christmas, as all the Carlsons had offered to work on Christmas Day, but Mei was confused about Gibbo's use of the word 'all'.

Jet took Mei's and An Na's hands as they headed for the tower. Ryder was bringing An Na's board in the buggy. 'Lily has invited your parents and Bo and Su-Lin and the kids to join us. We thought we could have a proper celebration.'

Mei smiled. 'You really are embracing family life.'

'Completely.'

Gibbo waited until everyone was crowded into the tower and the champagne had been poured before he raised his glass to make a toast. 'Firstly, I'd like to congratulate Jet on his choice; you are a lucky man. Mei, you've got yourself a good, genuine, honest and kind man and I have no doubt he will be the perfect partner for you. I'm sure the two of you and An Na and any future additions to your family will all be very happy. Congratulations to you both. To Mei and Jet.'

Everyone raised their glasses and repeated, 'To Mei and Jet,' as Jet kissed Mei again.

'And secondly,' Gibbo added, 'I'd like to congratulate Jet on his promotion. Three cheers for that! Hip hip hooray…hip hip hooray…hip hip hooray!'

'Promotion? What promotion?' Mei looked at him.

'I have a bit more news. You know Gibbo and Paula are moving to Melbourne?'

Mei nodded. Paula had taken a promotion in her job which meant a move interstate.

'Obviously that means Gibbo's position as Senior Lifeguard is going to need filling. I applied for the position and I've been offered the role. You're looking at the new boss.'

'Really? That's fabulous—congratulations!' Mei threw her arms around Jet. 'What does that mean, exactly?'

'More responsibility and a pay rise. But the best thing about it is I get to manage the rosters.'

Mei frowned. 'Why is that a bonus?'

'Because it means I can plan my shifts around yours and also around my sisters' shifts so that, between us and your family, there will always be someone around for An Na. Which means, my future wife, that if you still want to, you can apply for a post-grad medical school position and know that the rest of us will work around your study and paramedics commitments to take care of An Na. You can follow your dream.'

Mei eyes filled with tears. Again. She was turning into a fountain.

'What's wrong?' Jet's voice was filled with concern.

Mei shook her head and smiled through her tears. 'Nothing. Everything is perfect. I can't believe you're doing this for me.'

'I would do anything for you, Mei. I'm getting to follow my dream and you should get that too. I want us to show An Na that anything is possible. Your parents dreamt of a better life, a more stable, secure life, for you and Bo when they moved to Australia. I know you regret not studying medicine and I want you to have that chance. I don't want you living with regrets. I want to support you and I want us to live our best life. Together. How does that sound?'

'That sounds wonderful. I can't wait. I love you.'

EPILOGUE

'How long until we see Daddy?'

She knew An Na wasn't asking because she was bored but because she was excited to see Jet.

The race had started over three hours ago but Mei hadn't even attempted to watch the whole event. It was impossible for two reasons. One, a lot of the race was out on the water and the only way to see the action was on one of the big screens set up along the promenade at Bondi Beach and two, there was no way An Na's concentration would have lasted the distance. The final leg of the race was a ten and a half kilometre run which looped past the lifeguard tower three times. Mei knew that watching the last leg would be enough for An Na and it meant they could cheer Jet on from the sidelines.

Mei glanced over her shoulder towards the beach, but she couldn't see the water through the crowds. She looked up at the big screen and saw the first competitors jumping off their boards as they came out of the ocean. 'Not long now.'

Ryder had saved them a space at the finish line near the lifeguard tower and they were right at the front of the barrier, about twenty metres from the line. They would have a good view of Jet as he ran past.

'Help me with my sign, Mummy.' An Na was struggling with a huge cardboard sign that she'd spent hours decorating with drawings of fireworks, surfboards, medals and a sketch of Jet.

Mei unrolled the sign, before rolling it up in the opposite direction to flatten it out, and passed it back to An Na.

Mei watched the first runners on the big screen. They were about to come past for the first time. She could see Jet. He wasn't at the front, but he was part of the leading pack. 'Here he comes.'

An Na was jumping up and down beside her, holding her homemade sign above her head as Jet ran towards them. 'Daddy! Daddy! You can do it. Catch up!'

He was in fifth position. Mei willed him to go faster, do better. She really wanted this for him.

'Go, Daddy! Run faster!'

Jet raised a hand as he ran past them. Did he pick up the pace? Mei thought he closed the gap a little between him and the person in front.

Mei's eyes were glued to the big screen and her heart was in her mouth as the runners circled back around. The next time they ran past Jet was in third place. An Na was beside herself and Mei was also finding it hard to contain her excitement, although she felt sick at the same time. Could he do it?

He stayed with the leading pack as they approached for the third and final time. He needed to finish top two. He was now second.

Mei was cheering, her voice was getting hoarse but she kept yelling and didn't dare to uncross her fingers yet. There wasn't much distance between second and third but there also wasn't much of a gap between first and second. He wasn't guaranteed a top two finish yet. Anything could still happen.

There were one hundred metres to go.

Mei and An Na were screaming now, cheering Jet on.

He was sprinting as he ran past them, closing the gap on first place. Would he have time to catch the leader?

It was a race to the finish line, the final ten metres. Mei couldn't tell from her angle who was in front.

She looked at the screen as the two of them hit the finish line together and saw the ribbon streaming from Jet's waist.

He'd done it! He'd qualified for the World Championships.

'Did he win?' An Na was asking.

'He won!' She grabbed An Na's hand and pulled her through the crowd. 'Come on.'

Jet was at the finish line, searching for them.

'Daddy! You won!' An Na threw herself at him and wrapped her arms around his neck.

Mei reached out, ready to catch An Na, worried that Jet's energy might be completely spent and he wouldn't have the strength to hold his daughter. But she needn't have worried. He shifted An Na to one side, holding her with one arm, and reached for Mei with his other hand. He pulled her towards him and kissed her.

She kissed him back. He was hot and sweaty and he

tasted salty, but she didn't care. He had done it and she was so proud of him.

'Oh, my God, you did it! Congratulations!'

Jet was beaming. 'I did it for you. It's all for you.'

* * * * *

FROM BEST FRIENDS
TO I DO?

SUE MacKAY

MILLS & BOON

This book is for my family.

My man, Lindsay MacKay. And Hannah MacKay and her man, Phil Grigg, and Austin and Taylor Grigg.

You are all so special and I am lucky to have you.

PROLOGUE

MAISIE ROGERS SNIFFED, then blew her nose and wiped her eyes with her sleeve. Today her sister would've turned eleven. Instead she was stuck at ten— for ever. She'd never grow up and wear high heels or go on a date or become a ballet dancer like she'd wanted to be. All because of an ice cream.

No, Maisie, blame the driver of the car that hit her on the pedestrian crossing she was dancing across.

Scrubbing her face with her knuckles, she felt a change in the air, and stilled.

'Bad day, eh?' Zac Lowe sat on the bench beside her outside the classroom block at Queenstown High School.

'It sucks. It's the worst time since Cassey died.' Her heart began thumping weirdly as she looked at Zac. All out of rhythm.

'It is.' Zac rubbed his shoulder against hers like he was sharing something more than a bad day with her.

His touch was different to what she was used to. Usually he acted like a second brother. This prickly, excit-

ing sensation spreading out from her shoulder made
her lean closer for more. 'Thanks for being with me.'

'It's okay,' he muttered before shuffling sideways,
putting space between them as he glanced around the
grassed area in front where others were standing talking or girls strutting in front of guys.

Maisie leaned nearer again, not wanting to lose the
feeling he caused. She also needed his support and company. Today was truly awful. And now confusing.

Zac and her brother, Liam, became best mates a year
ago when they'd started playing in the same rugby team.
Now he was always there for her, and, like Liam, over-
protective since her sister's death. It was bad enough
having her brother and father watching over her friend-
ships and what she might be up to without adding Zac
to the equation. 'Everyone says it'll get easier with time.
I don't believe them.'

He straightened away from her again. 'I guess no
one really knows what to say.'

As usual, he was right. It didn't lessen her pain any.
'I wouldn't mind a hug.'

*To be held in your arms and feel what it's like to
press against your chest.*

Her cheeks heated.

Zac looked around, fixed his gaze on someone at the
far end of the block.

Liam stood yarning with some friends, looking over
their way, a frown marring his forehead. What was that
about? Since he'd brought Zac home after rugby prac-
tise one afternoon Zac had quickly integrated into her
family, her parents giving him support where he re-

quired it at school and with his sporting activities and in other areas when needed. Zac muttered, 'We're at school. Everyone's out here.' The gap between them had widened further.

'You can't hug me?' Her hands clenched and her head spun as she fought the need to throw her arms around him, to show him what she felt. He was cool. He didn't have a girlfriend. She didn't have a boyfriend. He was seventeen to her fifteen. What was the problem? More likely grief about her sister was screwing with her common sense, and it had nothing to do with Zac. Maybe he was just Johnny-on-the-spot.

The hell he was.

He was fun and strong and gorgeous, and she wanted to get close to him. She'd love to know him as a hot guy who might look at her similarly, and not as her brother's mate. To feel special as a girl, to have him want to spend time with her. To be the first guy to kiss her.

'No, Maisie.' He unfolded his long body from the bench and stepped away from her, leaving her lonely and cold.

'Why not?' Her feelings and needs hadn't been written all over her face, had they? Too bad, because they were real. Zac was amazing.

'Think about it. Everyone'd be talking about us. That's not happening. Some girls might get the wrong idea and upset you.'

'Stop trying to protect me from everything. I'm sick of you all doing that. I'm quite capable of looking out for myself.' Except she *was* hurting and it was getting her down. But she needed cheering up, not cosseting.

She needed Zac holding her against him, sharing himself with her, rubbing his hands down her back, touching her as she'd never been touched before. Except he'd just shown her he wasn't interested in her in that way. She'd have to hide her feelings and get over him as soon as possible.

Zac stared at Maisie, his heart in his throat. He wanted nothing more than to hug her, hold her close, feel her warm body pressed into his. He'd wanted that for a long time now. If only it was so straightforward. But. He drew a breath. It was a huge but.

He couldn't touch her, not even in a friendly way. One day her father had caught him watching Maisie with the hunger in his belly no doubt apparent in his eyes, and said, 'I'm sure there are plenty of suitable girls at high school for you to take a fancy to. Stay away from Maisie.'

She was too young, and too vulnerable since her sister's death. Being the quiet, unassertive one of the family, it was everyone else's role to make sure she was safe.

Given that this family had all but adopted him, given him the love and constancy he'd never had with his own parents, he'd known he had to shut down his feelings for Maisie. Touch her and he'd lose what was so, so important to him. Lose his go-to place and the people who'd enabled him to face the world with confidence when his parents didn't, and never had. They'd never been there for him, too busy with their seven-day superette and so tied up in themselves as though they couldn't accept they even had a second son. Their first had died before he was born. Which was why nowadays, if he had a problem, he went straight to one of Maisie's parents for advice and comfort.

It was so damned hard not to reach for Maisie and hold her as a young woman and not his sort-of-sister. Those big brown eyes with cheeky golden flecks were so hard to ignore, even when filled with sorrow. Especially then. But to tuck her against him now would only lead to more problems for them both.

So he turned away, saying over his shoulder, 'See you tonight.' There was going to be a special dinner at the Rogers house in memory of Cassey, and naturally he was expected to be there. This was the first time he'd ever wished he had an excuse not to be. The raw pain in Maisie's eyes had grown when he'd pulled away from her, making him feel guilty, and unworthy. He needed to toughen up, be the protective friend he was meant to be. Ask one of the girls in his class to go to the football team's end of season party next weekend if he wanted a bit of passion. That might quieten the hormones for a bit.

Sighing as he strode across to Liam and their mates, he knew there was more than hormones involved in how he felt about Maisie, but her father was right. This wasn't the time or place, if there ever would be.

CHAPTER ONE

MAISIE HANDED THE bridal bouquet back to her best friend, Mallory, who had just exchanged wedding rings with Josue, and hugged her. 'I'm so happy for you both. It's about time one of us was married.' Quickly turning away, she discreetly wiped her eyes, careful not to be seen so her friends couldn't give her a hard time about being sentimental. But hey, who wouldn't be when Mallory had tied the knot with a gorgeous Frenchman only minutes ago?

A sharp elbow prod from the second bridesmaid, her other close friend. 'Mallory looks beyond happy, doesn't she?' Kayla finger-wiped beneath her eyes.

Okay, so tears were allowed. 'About time she found her soul mate,' Maisie agreed. Mallory had done a better job of picking a great man than she had. *Her* marriage had been over within twenty-four months, and now she was a whole lot wiser about men and how they could lie to break her heart. When she'd met Paul, she'd naively jumped in without a thought, accepting his love and charm, believing she'd moved on from her teenage crush on Zac. Not once did she consider Paul might hurt her. But now wasn't the time to be thinking about that particular pain in the backside. Today she was happy for her friend, and also just plain glad to be back in Queenstown amongst family and friends for the wedding. She'd be back permanently in a few weeks.

Her gaze drifted sideways to scope out the guests. Zac stood with a group from the Search and Rescue crew, looking breathtaking in a dark blue suit and crisp white shirt. Stunning. Hot. He was not a man for her to be noticing that way—certainly not to be thinking he was even a *little* bit hot. She'd deliberately not thought any such thing about him since that day sixteen years back when she'd been so sad about Cassey and reached out to him because she'd yearned to get close, only to be rejected. At the time she'd wondered if he might want to be more than a friend, but he'd quickly dispelled that idea by walking away and joining her brother. She believed she could trust him to always have her back, but for anything else? When she'd learned the hard way not to trust any man with her heart? No, not even Zac. She'd read him wrong once, wasn't giving it a second crack, even if she was older and, hopefully, wiser.

She looked back to the bride, and sucked in air to settle her nerves. Zac was definitely hot, but nothing would come of that.

Mallory was laughing and saying something about how Maisie and Kayla should have another shot at getting hitched because it felt wonderful. Kayla replied it was too soon for her, and winked at Maisie. 'Guess that means you're next.'

No way. She so wasn't ready, and doubted if she would be this side of another decade.

Mallory suddenly threw her bouquet straight at Kayla, who caught it and tried to hand it back. Relieved it wasn't her who'd been targeted, Maisie laughed and hugged Kayla. 'They'll look nice in a vase on your table, if nothing else.'

'I could force them on you,' Kayla muttered.

'No, thanks. I'm happy being a free agent.' That was a loose term considering she wasn't on the dating scene at all. Again Maisie's gaze went to the men standing to one side of the aisle, and her skin tightened. Zac was looking at her with a hunger she'd not seen before. Desire for her? Surely not. In a blink the longing disappeared from his expression, replaced with the cheeky twinkle she'd grown up knowing. He must've realised she was watching him. Relief edged into her head, dousing the bizarre sense that something was out of alignment here. It wasn't like they'd ever been anything but friends. At fifteen she'd learned friendship didn't suddenly change to deep love and sex. She shivered. Zac and sex?

Not so hard to imagine. He was sexy. She'd always thought so. Occasionally, after leaving Paul, she'd wondered what might've transpired if she and Zac had got together when they were younger. Back then she'd been afraid to follow up on the feelings of tenderness and adoration, her lack of confidence stonewalling her. When he'd walked away that day, she'd accepted far too easily that he wasn't interested. The ensuing mixed emotions over Zac and her sister's death had caused endless sleepless nights and moods that drove everyone crazy for months.

Kayla said, 'Here comes the champagne.' She accepted two glasses from the young waiter's tray and handed one to Maisie.

Time to refocus on the happy couple in front of her and why she was here. 'We've all come a long way from three skinny little runts on the first day of school.'

Laughing, Kayla tapped their glasses together. 'Hopefully this will keep you from coming out with more daft things like that.'

And keep me from glancing across to Zac every few minutes trying to understand that look I saw in his eyes.

'You think?'

Except she didn't have to glance any more. Zac stood in front of her with a wicked grin as he raised a glass of champagne to her. 'You're looking very swish.' That *sounded* like the man she knew.

'I can scrub up with the best of them.' She sipped her champagne before looking directly at him, trying not to flinch as her skin tightened again.

His expression was clear of anything out of the ordinary. 'It's been a while since you last came home for a visit.'

'Over two years ago.' Before her world imploded. 'You know I'm moving home permanently for the job in the new paediatric department next month, right?'

'Your memory failing?' His grin was that silly brotherly one he'd given her most of their lives.

Disappointing for some reason, she thought, before getting back on track. 'I've already told you.' But she wasn't sure he'd remembered, because nothing seemed normal at the moment.

'Often.' His grin dipped as he sipped his wine, his eyes meeting hers over the rim of the glass, that cobalt shade sharper than she could recall noticing before. 'You're really ready to pack up and come home now?'

'The packing's all done.' Along with her family, he'd tried to persuade her to return to Queenstown before Paul's trial but she'd refused, insistent that she stay and face everyone who'd thought she'd been a part of the scam where her charming husband had convinced pensioners to invest their hard-earned life savings in his schemes. Schemes that were illegal and put money into his personal accounts, not investment plans. Some people, including a couple of friends, believed she had to have known and was as guilty as Paul. Others accepted she mightn't have, but she'd lived a comfortable life on the benefits so owed something to the victims. Few saw her to be as much a victim as they'd been. 'It's time to let the past go, to move on with my choices for the future.'

She was getting there by herself, without her brother and Zac butting in and taking over as they liked to do, and that made her feel good about herself. There was still a way to go, especially when it came to trusting people. She'd given her all to Paul, believed in love, believed he loved her back. Except she'd been wrong. He'd used her as part of his charm package to get older folk on side with his investment schemes that she'd had no idea about.

Those intense eyes were still locked on her. 'You know what you want?'

Her mouth dried a little. Because Zac *was* looking at her differently. As if he was seeing her as a woman and not the sister of his mate. Not his surrogate sister. But he couldn't be. She had to be making it up, seeing things that weren't there. Was she that desperate to find love? Not likely when she wouldn't trust a man with her heart again. Another sip of champagne moistened her dry tongue. 'I've got the job I'd been hoping for back in the town where my closest friends live, and Mum and Dad. It's all I've hoped for over the last year.' The plan was what got her through the worst days.

'It's something to start with and further along than you've been in a while.'

'I also intend buying a small apartment when I can afford it, but that's about it for now.'

Eventually a man I can love and trust would be great. A family too.

'You've never mentioned that before.'

'I don't tell you everything I hope to achieve.' With all the phone calls they'd shared over the last year, they'd covered a lot of ground but not everything. Certainly not another relationship or one that might involve children.

'Fair enough.' Did he have to look disappointed?

'I think so.' This discussion felt stilted, unlike the easygoing, almost intimate conversations they were used to having on the phone. Then again, she'd been stunned to see the way he was looking at her, and didn't quite know where she stood with him.

Zac took a gulp of his champagne, smiled crookedly. 'I'll talk to you about possibly joining Search and Rescue once you're settled in. We can always do with more medical personnel.'

The tension creeping in backed off. That smile always softened her heart. 'You're on.' She gave one back. 'I'm excited about coming home.' She'd been quick to get away from her over-protective family—and Zac—when she left school, and yet it was the first place she wanted to be when her world went belly-up. This was her comfort place where she knew so many people and fit right in.

During the last twelve months they'd spent more time on the phone discussing how Zac was coping after a shooting incident where he'd been injured when a gunman went crazy and killed one of the police team Zac had been a part of, and less about her and Paul. She hadn't wanted to share all the details with either Zac or her family, preferring to sort it out herself. So far she had, which made her proud, and stronger than the shy girl who'd left town twelve years ago at the end of school to train as a nurse.

When she met Paul, he'd charmed her, wooed her with an ease that should've been a warning. But she'd fallen in love instead, been too naïve and ready to forget how she'd once felt about Zac. Her family and friends never took to him, which only made her more determined to prove she was right and could look out for herself. She'd been too vulnerable, too ready to believe she needed Paul by her side, and thought love was supposed to be for ever, through thick and thin, good and bad. Yet she'd fallen out of love with him fast. How could she not when the exciting trips he took her on, the surprise dinners, the jewellery she'd find under her pillow as a surprise, had been paid for with other trusting souls' money?

'Photo time.' Kayla tapped her arm. 'You two will have to carry on catching up later.'

Maisie glanced to Zac. 'No problem. We'll have plenty of time after the dinner and speeches.' It would be fun to sit down with him and get back into the relaxed swing of things they usually shared. As long as she didn't put too much out there, like these mixed feelings of tension and longing filling her.

'Save me a dance later.' Zac grinned, this time looking comfortable.

'Sure will.' Dancing would be something new for them. Even more difficult were the tingles going up and down her spine, and the flare of heat in her cheeks.

They didn't just have one dance. The music that was played after the dinner was slow and sensual, and the air laden with laughter and happiness. Maisie couldn't have walked away from Zac if she'd tried.

He held her waist and led her around the floor so sure-footed that she relaxed into his arms and went with him, cosy and happy. His body was lean and muscular, his shoulders wide and strong. His face was endearing and his mouth soft yet firm. This was the man she'd known for ever, and she'd never seen him like this. Never felt hot and vibrant like this. Too much? Yes. Pull back? Impossible. Or was it that she didn't want to? Zac would never deliberately hurt her, but that didn't mean she wasn't vulnerable to him. More so, because she trusted him completely.

His hand was splayed over her lower back and she could feel each individual fingertip pressing into her. Protecting her from other dancers when they got too close.

'You know the moves,' he said beside her ear.

'Just following your lead.' It wasn't hard when her body was glued to his.

The music stopped.

'Want to continue?' he asked quietly against her ear.

'You bet.' She grinned. This was amazing. So different from anything she'd ever done with Zac. But then no one climbed trees or played cards at a wedding. 'I'm having a ball.' She really was, and waking up to a new side to Zac. A warmth that she'd not felt with him before, a tingle in her toes and heat on her skin.

Zac'd never do something so despicable as to rob people and abuse their trust. Nor would he con her.

Is this why I'm seeing Zac differently to the friend he's been? I can trust him, believe in him and not have everything thrown back in my face? Is this why I'm suddenly looking at him in a way I haven't since I was fifteen and buried my feelings? I'd be safe with him.

Or was she making another big mistake even considering Zac as more than a friend? Looking for a relationship she wasn't ready for because she knew he'd always have her back? Someone she believed she could trust? She'd thought she had that once before and look where it got her.

Rein it in, Maisie. Don't rush into these feelings and lose a special friend because you've been an idiot.

Straightening just a little, she held herself slightly away from that tempting body, and kept dancing.

'Zac, line three,' the police station receptionist called. 'It's Jamie.'

His Search and Rescue offsider calling during work could only mean one thing. Picking up the phone, Zac answered. 'We're on?' He was head of S and R, but sometimes the calls went direct to the fire station where Jamie worked.

'Yep. A thirty-two-year-old man's fallen off a climbing face in the Remarkables. We need to go in, retrieve him and get him to a point the chopper can safely lift him out. You available?'

'You bet.' It was after four and the day had gone on for ever, every hour dragging by as though two as he'd trawled though files on a cold case murder that new info had come in about. Better than the night hours spent thinking about Maisie and holding her supple body in his arms as they danced at the wedding. It had been everything he'd imagined for a long time—and more. She was real: warm, soft and so sexy when her body moved against him in time to the music. What a turn-on, and something he'd fought to keep in check. Since he was a teen he'd had feelings for Maisie, but suddenly they'd burst wide open. It was exciting, wonderful. Yet caution ruled. What did Maisie think about him? She'd moulded into him as they danced, which upped his hopes she might be changing how she felt. And reminded him of those long, sometimes intense, phone conversations they'd shared when he'd talked about the shooting and she talked a little about Paul's betrayal.

Since the wedding he'd had coffee with her once after helping move her few pieces of furniture left over from her marriage into her brother's apartment, which happened to be in the same complex he lived in. When he'd asked why she had so few items she'd snapped, 'I didn't want anything he bought.' He couldn't argue with that, and had struggled not to take her into his arms then and there and tell her he'd always be there for her. But he hadn't, because he was afraid he might show her his real feelings, and get knocked back. His parents had always ignored his attempts to show he loved them. They'd lost their firstborn at ten months old, and when he'd arrived unplanned for, they must have shut down on him for fear of going through the anguish they'd suffered over his brother's death. No wonder he'd grabbed with both hands the love and support offered by Maisie's family. He only hoped he could give as much love as he received, not only to his surrogate family but to the woman he longed to settle down with. Maisie.

'Hello?' Jamie cut into his thoughts.

Some fresh air and a bush rescue would be a perfect distraction to this love winding through him.

'We flying in?' It was part of his contract with the police department that he could drop everything for S and R.

'Sure are. I'll pick you up in five. Got one more call to make.' Click. Jamie was gone.

That one more call must've been to Maisie because

she was waiting on the footpath outside the hospital when they drove up. 'The man's companion describes severe injuries,' Jamie said as he braked. 'Who better than a nurse in the circumstances?'

'Can't think of anyone,' Zac grunted through the happiness spilling within him as he watched Maisie get into the back of the vehicle. So much for a distraction. Spending time with her only cranked up the need he'd come to expect every time he saw her these days. The feelings he'd had for her at seventeen had intensified over the years, added to by her being so damned attractive and sexy at Mallory's wedding. Then the dancing, holding her close, feeling her warm body under his palms, breathing the floral scent that was Maisie—of course he couldn't sleep the night through any more.

'Afternoon, Zac,' she said now.

'Hi. You were working late.'

'The ward was busy so I stayed on, keeping an eye on a six-year-old girl recovering from a ruptured appendix.'

'You've settled into the job quickly.' She'd been back in town three weeks and already seemed busy with work, S and R and her friends and family. Not so much with him. His choice. For now anyway. There was some thinking to be done about this need to get to know her in new ways. Once he'd have ignored it and got on with life but now he found he just couldn't put his longing aside. Deep down he had been hoping she'd return home and he'd be here for her. Maisie *was* special, more than a friend. 'What to do?' was the big question. Her family were a huge part of his life and getting too close to Maisie could jeopardise his relationships with everyone if it all went south. Her parents had taught him to be loved and to love back, but was he good enough to love their daughter? He could only work hard to prove he was.

'I love paediatrics more than any other specialty. All those kids needing my help and being able to make them smile or laugh always makes my day.'

Despite his misgivings, the pure joy in her voice made him smile. Quiet Maisie had toughened up a lot since Paul Harris came to light as a lowlife. Not that *he* or Maisie's family had ever liked him. Though there could've been a streak of jealousy on his part, having never quite managed to stop caring for her. Probably the reason his two attempts at relationships had failed.

Paul had been too full of himself and a right old charmer when it came to getting what he wanted. Maisie had fallen hard for him, and there'd been nothing anyone could say to change her mind. It had been a case of wait and be ready to step in after everything turned to dust. Except when it did, she'd refused help, shocking him and making him sit up and take even more notice of her. Maisie was still the same girl he'd fallen for, only with strength and determination added to the mix. Qualities he was happy to see. Add beauty and sexiness and there was no resisting her. She was gorgeous and those attributes had tightened his groin when watching her walk down the aisle in front of Mallory. Her laughter thickened his blood. And her smiles softened his heart.

How did Maisie see him? Still the guy who'd become a part of her family, to be teased, annoyed and loved like her brother? Whenever they'd talked about the shooting that saw him in hospital and Benji dead, she'd been caring and compassionate, intense sometimes, not quite Maisie as he'd known her. The phone calls had made him feel they were in a bubble, sharing their problems, having a laugh, even shedding a few tears once when talking about lost dreams. But he still had no idea if she might reciprocate his feelings even a little, though the way she'd danced so close to him at the wedding had him wondering if there was a spark there. Forget sparks, his body had reacted like an inferno.

This waiting and wondering wasn't doing him any good at all, but he knew this was something to take slowly, or there could be repercussions. If she wasn't ready for a new relationship, he could find himself on the outside of the family who'd taken him under their wing and given him so much, and no Maisie in sight. Though there was still his old job in the CIB back in Christchurch on offer if he messed up here and needed to get out of town.

Zac swallowed hard and leaned his head back against the seat, trying to focus on where they were going. 'What info do we have on this rescue, Jamie?'

'The man's unconscious, and bleeding from various wounds,' Jamie replied. 'Internally, who knows? It's very likely he's done some damage. The terrain's dangerous with a high risk of boulders falling down the cliff face so we'll have to carry him some distance to where the chopper can lift him out, according to his friend at the scene.'

'What were they doing climbing an unstable rock wall?' Zac wondered.

'We've seen many similar accidents over the years and still don't know what drives people to put themselves at risk. Not to mention the people who have to go out and collect them,' Jamie muttered.

'True.' He stared through the window at the airfield ahead. 'Looks like everything's ready and waiting for us.' The rescue helicopter was warming up, and three other S and R members were standing in the doorway of the aircraft.

'No time to waste,' Maisie said, unclipping her seat belt before Jamie came to a halt.

'Let's do this.' Zac took the heavy, extra medical pack for her, and stood back so she boarded first, smiling at her long legs dressed in fitted outdoor trousers.

No sooner was the door closed, and they were lifting off the ground. Maisie sat beside him, quiet and contemplative. Running through the medical scenario she might have to deal with?

'You okay?' he asked because he couldn't help himself when her hands flexed.

Her smile was tight. 'Yes.' She leaned sideways, away from him, and closed her eyes.

Like she'd prefer to be sitting beside someone else. He hauled in a deep breath, tried to swallow the hurt that created. Now he'd admitted to himself he cared for Maisie as a woman he kept looking for positive vibes coming off her. Not that he was expecting a sudden about-turn from friend to lover when her heart had been broken already. She'd be wary of taking another chance. Just because he was looking at her differently didn't mean Maisie would suddenly come on board.

The chopper rocked up, then down.

The pilot came through their headsets. 'Bit of wind up here, folks. Hope you're all belted in.'

'Hope it improves before we get to the Remarkables,' Maisie muttered.

'It's not going to be much better,' their pilot answered.

Maisie's hands clenched on her thighs. 'Damn.'

Zac tapped her foot with his. 'We'll be fine.'

'I know.' There wasn't a lot of positivity in her voice. 'Why does my fear of heights only affect me in helicopters and not planes?' Her lips pressed together.

'I think that's quite common.' Zac squeezed her hand. He'd prefer to keep holding her, but with these new feelings going on, he didn't dare. Slowly did it. Hopefully.

'Doesn't help, though.' Maisie stared at the floor, her arm against his, getting closer all the time. Leaning into him for strength? Whatever, the sparks were back. Another drop in the sky. Maisie gasped and slid her hand under his arm, nestled against his hip.

To hell with what the others thought. He held her hand. Maisie was scared.

'Sorry about that, folks. I'm going higher in an attempt to dodge the potholes,' the pilot told them.

Maisie remained still, tension rippling off her. 'Why did I volunteer for this?' she muttered. Small dents marked her bottom lip.

His heart squeezed along with his hand around hers. 'Because you're concerned about helping people.'

Because you're tough and caring and always putting others first.

One eyebrow rose and her mouth twisted into a wry smile. 'No getting away from that, is there?'

He nodded, returned her smile. 'Definitely not.' It didn't stop him wanting to protect her all the time. It was a given in her family. Unlike his. His relationship with his parents had been like living on the other side of the window: able to see in, unable to be seen by the two people who should've been looking out for him. Except when he did something wrong, and then his father knew exactly where he was, showing disappointment with loud admonishments and saying he had to be strong and sensible to get ahead in this world. Mix that with the easy way Maisie's parents treated him and he'd forged a rough line through life with a desire to help others on one side while keeping himself safe from any more hurt on the other. In the few romantic relationships he'd attempted he'd remained on that centre line, afraid to get in deep and be hurt, or hurt the woman he was with. Not to mention the buried feelings for Maisie that had escaped.

Against his arm, Maisie began relaxing and he realised the helicopter was flying without leaping all over the show. He relaxed with her. In this together all the way. As they were in so many things. Hope expanded, filled his chest, made him happy. The possibilities could be endless if he got really close to her—as in as lovers, not just friends. He glanced sideways and felt his gut tighten.

It looked as though she was reading his mind.

Zac swallowed hard. She'd better not be. Too fast, too soon. His gut clenched. His longing was so strong, going slowly might be impossible.

Her mouth tipped upwards in a wry way. So kissable. He could almost feel her lips under his.

Her smile widened.

Damn, she knew exactly what he was thinking. No, not possible. He knew Maisie.

And she knows you.

Too well, at that. But if she'd guessed his feelings, then she wasn't moving to the other side of the chopper. Or glaring at him as she used to do when she wasn't getting her way. But that had been years ago—when he and Liam had been interfering, bossy brothers who should've kept their noses out of her business apparently. Like the day they'd overheard Beau Coster make lurid suggestions to Maisie and gone in to haul the creep away for a 'chat.' She hadn't thanked them for what she called interfering, said she had it under control. She probably had, but they weren't buying it at the time. 'Feeling all right?' he asked to divert her attention from him.

'Couldn't be better,' she said, still smiling, and confusing him further.

The chopper began dropping height, then hovered. 'This looks the best spot for putting you down,' the pilot told them. 'It's the only flat ground I can see near where you need to be so I'll wait here. You'll have to walk east to find your man.'

'I've got the co-ordinates and this looks fairly close.' Jamie stood up.

Zac slung the medical pack over his shoulders without a glance at Maisie. He liked doing things for her, and didn't want her grabbing the pack off him. 'Let's do this.'

Zac walked beside Maisie whenever it was possible, but mostly they were pushing through low scrub in single file. 'It's not going to be fun carrying a laden stretcher through this.' With six of them they should be able to take breaks if needed.

'Hopefully the man isn't a giant,' Maisie tossed back.

He was average, Zac noted as he spotted the sprawled body ahead with another man sitting beside him. The cliff face towered above them. It was a miracle the guy had survived his fall. 'Hi, I'm Zac. How long ago did this happen?'

'Andy. It was more than an hour ago, likely an hour and a half. Brad's in a bad way. His breathing's all over the place and I don't like how his legs are lying. He slipped and bounced down that cliff.' His head tipped in the direction behind them.

Zac shivered. 'He'd better buy a lottery ticket when he's up and about.' Could be a long time for before that happened.

'I'm a nurse.' Maisie dropped to her knees beside the injured man. Her right-hand forefinger already pressing against Brad's carotid. 'There's a weak pulse.' She was scanning the man from top to toe. 'Brad, can you hear me? I'm Maisie.'

The guy didn't even blink.

Zac got down on the opposite side as Andy scrambled out of the way and delved into the pack for sterile pads and tape. 'That bone looks nasty.' He indicated the right arm.

'I agree. How many splints are in that pack?' Maisie asked.

'Two,' someone answered. 'Need both?'

'Please. I'll check for internal injuries. There's got to be some.' Using scissors, she cut through the front of the jersey and shirt to expose Brad's chest and abdomen. Running her hands over his body, she noted, 'Internal bleeding near the upper colon. And around the liver.'

Zac was taking the pulse rate. He glanced at her. 'Spongy tissue?'

'Yes.'

'Low pulse,' he said, before starting on the breathing rate.

'To be expected. We need to cover that bone, apply a neck brace and splints on his legs, then I'll administer pain relief. He's in a bad way. Jamie, can the chopper come any closer? The less time being carried through the scrub the better.'

'See what I can find out.' Jamie pulled the radio from his belt while moving away.

Zac opened the neck brace and he and Maisie put it in place.

'There's little I can do about the internal injuries.' Maisie placed two sterile pads over the broken bone and taped them firmly in place.

Zac nodded. 'I'll put that arm in a sling to prevent as much movement as possible.'

She gave him a brief smile, her focus entirely on

their patient. 'Can you remove a boot? I want to see if he reacts to any touch on his toes.'

They worked well together. Warmth touched his skin. It felt special. But then any time spent with Maisie was special. 'Spinal damage?'

'Very likely.' She glanced up at the rock wall behind them. 'That would've been some drop with no soft landing.'

'The pilot's going to fly as close as possible.' Jamie had returned. 'But he can't come too near to that cliff or the vibrations from the rotors might bring boulders down on us. He's also concerned that we're in a crevice with not a lot of room to manoeuvre.'

'Safety first,' Zac agreed as he eased a boot off the man.

'Totally.' Maisie flicked Brad's toes.

His foot twitched.

She did it again, harder.

Another twitch, stronger.

She nodded. 'Thank goodness. But we'll still go carefully. Put splints under his legs before moving him onto the stretcher.'

'I'll splint the right leg, but the straightening's up to you.' He didn't have experience of dealing with shattered bones, and the thought of causing Brad pain even when he was unconscious made his stomach churn.

'Fair enough.' Another quick smile came his way, again warming him. He liked her soft smile and the way her eyes widened while looking at him. Did it mean she was suddenly thinking of him differently?

As Maisie worked carefully with the fractured limb

a frown appeared. 'I don't want to tear an artery. Brad's got enough internal damage to be going on with.'

'We'll strap his legs onto the stretcher as well.' That'd prevent any movement while they carried him out. Zac took the strap Jamie held out.

Maisie moved nearer Brad's chest. 'Jamie, will you slide the stretcher up to Brad while Zac and I roll him onto his side? Get the stretcher as far under as possible.'

Zac crouched beside her, hands on the man's hip and thigh. 'Ready.'

'One, two three.' They rolled Brad onto his side and Jamie quickly slid the stretcher in place.

With Brad on his back again, Maisie strapped his legs onto the stretcher. 'Let's go. Easy does it as much as possible, everyone.'

The ground was uneven and the scrub whipped back whenever anyone pushed through but the main focus was on keeping the stretcher level and not bobbing up and down with their steps. Everyone was quiet, focused on walking through the rocks and bushes. It was hard going and the men not carrying the laden stretcher did their best to hold back branches or break them out of the way to make it easier.

Maisie walked at the end of the stretcher, keeping a firm eye on Brad. 'I'm pleased he's unaware of what's going on. It would be beyond painful if he was conscious.'

'You would've administered painkillers, surely?' Zac asked as he carried a back corner of the load.

'Yes, but they mightn't be strong enough for this scenario.'

The chopper was hovering, ready for the winch to

be lowered. Jamie talked to the pilot as they placed the stretcher on the ground, Maisie trying to protect the patient from the downdraught caused by the rotors.

'You'll be going with him,' Zac noted.

'You're not all walking out, are you?' she asked.

'No, we'll be picked up after you've been dropped off at the hospital.'

'I imagine our man's going on to Christchurch after the local emergency doctors have seen him so you might have a long wait.' Maisie had to lean close to be heard above the helicopter.

Zac breathed in sharply, and regretted the instant that floral scent wafted into his senses. It had nothing to do with the bush surrounding them. Instead it brought dreams, and longing for Maisie, rushing into him. 'Maybe we will start walking, then.' A hard hike would quieten the pounding in his blood, remind him he was supposed to be keeping distance between Maisie and himself.

But it was clearly impossible. He'd adored Maisie since he was a horny teenager, had wanted to get closer in every way, and now... Now he cared for her with all his being.

Except—his chest lifted—what if, when it came to it, he was unlovable? His parents hadn't loved him the way they had each other. His past two relationships had failed because he didn't love either woman enough, was always on edge about how much of himself to give. Becoming vulnerable felt impossible to do. Finally, after a lot of hurt for those women and himself, he'd owned up to himself Maisie was in his system and there was

no getting away from her. She did make him susceptible whenever he let her near—so he'd fought to keep
his distance. Only now he was ready to face his de-
mons to see if he could be the loving, openhearted man
he so wanted to be. If he succeeded, then he might finally accept he could be the father he'd always longed
for as a child.

'Maisie, we're sending you up first to unhook Brad
when the stretcher reaches the chopper.' Jamie held the
sling out to her. 'Zac, you're after Maisie. That stretcher's heavy and she might need a hand. You can stay on
board and hitch a ride back to town while the rest of us
slog our way out.'

So much for putting distance between them. But he
did like the idea, and the rules said two people had to
go with the patient if at all possible in case an emergency arose. So why not him?

Yes. He mentally fist-pumped. *Yes.*

As Maisie was winched up her face tightened and
lost some of the colour it had regained since they'd been
on the ground. Zac gave her the thumbs-up and hopefully an encouraging smile. It was good he was going
back with her. He'd be there in case the ride got bumpy.
'No argument from me,' he muttered at Jamie's back.

CHAPTER TWO

'HEY, MAIS, I wondered if you might still be here.' Zac stood beside the table in the pub where everyone from the rescue had gathered after being lifted out by another helicopter to wind down over a beer before heading home to their families.

Maisie smiled to herself. Not in a rush to leave—the warmth stealing through her suggested that deep down she must've been hoping Zac might drop by after he'd finished whatever he'd gone back to the police station for—she'd been taking her time over her wine after everyone else left. Maisie saluted Zac with her glass. 'Want to join me?'

Zac made her feel wanted for herself, and as more than a friend. There they were again—new sensations around Zac. Was their relationship changing? Getting deeper? Shifting to a romantic level? Excitement warred with worry. He'd never intentionally hurt her but she understood she didn't always read men correctly when it came to her heart. However, no denying she wanted time with him. Time to get to know him as a man, as someone she might fall for, more than a close friend. As long as they got it right.

'I'll get a beer. Want anything else? Another wine?'

Why not? She could always grab a taxi later if Zac wasn't going back to the apartment block. Except the Zac she knew would drop her off regardless of where he was going. 'Please.' He'd know what to get.

'Pinot Gris?'

Surprised, she named the brand. Since when did Zac ask her what wine she was drinking? Seemed he wasn't taking her for granted. Or she was probably looking for something that wasn't there, because of these new sensations he brought on whenever he was near her. Reaching for her glass she took the last mouthful and sighed. What was going on? She looked across the room and sighed again. No idea, but a tingle of excitement remained whispering in her veins.

Studying him leaning against the counter talking to the barman, she had to admit he was gorgeous. Those broad shoulders filled his jacket perfectly, and his bush trousers might be loose but they accentuated his muscular thighs causing her own muscles to spasm. Who was this Zac? Not the guy who'd hung out with her brother most of their lives. Not the man who'd tried to talk her out of marrying Paul and then wanted to help her pick up the pieces when her marriage crashed and burned. That man had been the protective second brother who always wanted to make sure she was all right and didn't get hurt. A great characteristic for a friend, even for a lover, but not when it was overbearing. Once, when she'd been fifteen and going through a rough patch over her sister, she'd thought he was quite the guy. But he'd pushed her away and she'd moved on. Or had she? She'd never forgotten how intense he made her feel, or how her skin used to warm whenever he was near. Still did, only forget warm, try hot.

With Zac and Liam always in her face she'd often had to fight them about letting her make her own choices about friends and hobbies. There was a day when a boy at school thought he could walk up to her, grab her to kiss and grope like he had all the rights in the world. She'd snarled at him to leave her alone, and was about to knee him where it hurt most when Zac and Liam appeared around the corner of the building and grabbed the guy for a 'talk.' Naturally they were on her side, but she'd been more than annoyed that they didn't give her a chance to deal with the boy herself. How else was she supposed to have become strong?

Gazing at Zac, she smiled to herself. Things were changing. She couldn't fault him. Her feet were itching to dance on the spot, and she fought to remain on her chair. That hunger in his eyes at the wedding had stirred her unexpectedly and she could no longer ignore him and these loving feelings. She was waking up to possibilities she'd buried as a teenager. He had all the qualities she wanted in a man. In a husband. Even as the father to her children. A lover. There was that word again. Wanting him sexually was a new reality that had been growing since the wedding when he'd looked at her with longing in his eyes, and had made her excited to come home to live. Zac was a hunk, no doubt about it. *And* she could trust him not to hurt her.

'Here you go.' A familiar hand holding a glass of wine appeared before her startled gaze.

Familiar but different because these days her body could imagine those fingers on her skin, feel the heat, the passion upping the tempo of her heart. Expanding the need for him that kept her awake at night too often. Maisie jerked and her hand knocked over a glass, fortunately the empty one.

'Careful.' Zac grabbed it as it rolled towards the edge of the table.

She needed a big mouthful of wine but the way her fingers were shaking she'd only spill most of it if she tried to lift the glass. Deep breath, one, two, three, four, five. 'Thanks.' For what? The wine, saving the glass or for setting her stomach churning and her blood warming?

Zac sank onto the nearest stool, watching her the whole time. 'Are you all right?'

Why was he looking at her so intently? He couldn't have noticed she was seeing him differently, could he? 'The rescue was full on, wasn't it?'

'Sure was. You did a great job with Brad,' he said, as though trying to keep some conversation going on.

He'd be doing a runner if she didn't get back on track and act normally. 'Everyone helped, making the whole show easier. And we worked well together despite it being our first time,' she added with forced heartiness. First time working with a patient. Could there be other, more personal firsts to come? Her elbows squeezed into her sides. Who knew?

'That's because we read each other easily.' Zac took up all the air and made her feel small beside his long frame.

Another thing she didn't usually notice. Nor did her tummy normally get into a knot just because Zac sat beside her. A hundred things sprang to mind to say, not one of them sane given she needed to stay grounded around him. Risking lifting her glass, she took another mouthful of wine, tried not to choke while hoping to keep this new desire from landing between them, there for ever and never to be taken back. It would create an awkward atmosphere that would change everything. Maisie wriggled her butt on the chair. Everything was changing already. Because she'd started seeing him as a man, not only a friend? 'You're right.' In lots of ways.

'The rescue gave me the same sense of fulfilment I get on the ward. Dealing with the unknown and whatever we find in less than ideal surroundings was great.' Working alongside Zac was an added bonus.

'A good outcome always makes me happier.'

Slowly the tension in her stomach loosened off, and she could breathe evenly again. 'It's all part of fitting back into the community.' But where was she at with Zac? Opening up to these unexpected feelings could mean playing with fire. There was a lot to lose if it didn't work out. For both of them. Another broken heart wasn't happening. She wouldn't recover a second time, especially if Zac was behind it. A lot of dimensions within her family would change, making it hard for either of them to drop by to visit her parents without wondering if the other was there.

'When I returned home from Christchurch after the shooting, I signed up for S and R fast so that I had something to do in my downtime to keep my mind quiet and let it recuperate so I could return to the city at some point, fit and ready to go.'

'Are you ready now?' If he went back to Christchurch what would that mean to her new awareness of him?

'Physically and mentally, yes. Do I want to? I'm not sure.' His gaze was on her, a gentle smile stirring her heart.

So he wasn't rushing away just yet. Good. 'I just want to get on with doing the things I enjoy.' She hadn't had much of that lately, being too busy staying out of the limelight while Paul hit the headlines regularly. 'And settle back into an uncomplicated life surrounded by those who are important to me.' Like Zac.

'Exactly.' He nodded and raised his beer. 'To us and new beginnings.' Then his smile faded as though he'd gone too far. Was Zac having issues about what he was going to do next with his career?

It was too much. She wanted to get back to normal, be relaxed with him. 'Let's go somewhere to eat. My shout.' When he started to reply, she added quickly, 'No argument. If you want to join me, that is.' She might not have much money to her name these days, but she would share what she had.

'Why wouldn't I?' he asked, though there was a hint in his expression saying he didn't know for certain he was being honest. Then he straightened those strong-looking shoulders and gave a teasing smile. 'Here or the Local?'

The Local—real name Queenstown Tavern—was where they'd all hung out in their late teens before everyone disappeared to places yonder. She, Mallory and

Kayla on the lookout for cute guys, Zac, Liam and their mates thinking they were the cute guys while keeping an eye out for her and her friends and who they were having fun with. These days the Local was quieter, but still used mostly by regulars. It would be good to go there, and being filled with old memories might help to get these alien feelings under control, if not completely out of her head. 'The Local, of course,' she laughed.

'Good answer.' Dark blue eyes locked onto her, drawing her in, making it hard not to reach for him, to hug him. She didn't usually hug Zac deep and hard, a quick winding of arms around him and that was that, and then only if there was a reason. Yet if she touched him this minute there'd be no letting go for a long time—no reason at all. She shivered.

Zac put his beer aside, unfinished. 'Let's go. I'm hungry.' And suddenly in a hurry to be out of here, judging by the speed with which he stood up.

Taking a long mouthful of wine she set the glass down and joined him, her hand tight at her side to prevent reaching for his to claim back that warmth and strength he'd just removed.

Outside she hesitated, shivering in the sudden chill. The weather had gone downhill since they'd flown back from the Remarkables.

Zac held out the jacket he'd slung over his shoulder. 'Put this on.'

'Don't mind if I do.' She slipped into it, the warmth immediate on her cool skin. The male scent honey to her senses.

'You're not worried I'll get cold?' Finally a smile. A smile that sent more shivers right down to her toes.

'You know me better than that.' Her laugh was tight. Could she be wrong? Snuggling deeper into his jacket, she mulled over the question. How well did they know each other? They'd always got along easily, no doubts about supporting each other and her brother. But—

Then his hand was on her elbow. 'This way.'

'My car's at work.'

'Worry about it later.'

This wasn't Zac's usual easygoing manner. His grip tightened on her elbow, holding her closer to that muscular body that she'd never noticed as anything but as a friend, before, and was now coming to appreciate more and more—*not* as a friend. 'Steady. Don't go tripping over yourself.'

She hadn't even noticed she had. Showed how skewed her mind was. He was just being protective. Typical. No getting away from that side of him. She needed to go home, get away from Zac, but as she opened her mouth she changed her mind. Running away didn't fix a thing, only complicated it further. She was strong. She'd deal with her feelings. Somehow or other she *would*. Starting with being the friend she'd always been, except she doubted that would be easy. She was getting in deeper every time she saw him, even when surrounded by other people. He was someone who wouldn't hurt her, could laugh with without having to prove she wasn't being coy and cute, was able to talk the truth about her feelings.

If Zac knew what she was thinking he'd probably laugh, suggest she got her head seen to. No one just suddenly started falling for someone they'd known all their life. She *wasn't* falling for him. Not at all. These new sensations came out of nowhere, blindsiding her at the wedding. Hands on her waist as they danced, a strong chest under her cheek when they moved slowly to the music. A well of longing and desire expanding throughout her as their bodies moved in unison on the dance floor.

This time she did feel her boot-encased foot trip on the flat pavement and tip her forward.

'Maisie, watch out.' Zac's grip remained firm. And warm. 'How many wines have you had?'

'Two, and don't start going all brotherly on me.' Shouldn't have said that. How else does he think he should act?

His hand tightened on her arm. Disorientating. She leaned closer to prevent another trip on her wobbly legs. And to suck in some of that man smell, to let his hand work a little magic on her arm through the sleeve of his jacket. Zac. Suddenly she felt as though she didn't know him at all. Blatantly untrue, and very bewildering. How could their relationship change after so long? Or had those feelings from her teens been simmering quietly in the background, waiting for her to wise up and move past the fact that Zac and her brother were best buddies and therefore she was almost like a sister to him, and not a woman with needs of her own that included him? But she'd married someone else quite soon after leaving home, which said there was more to these feelings than she was admitting to herself. Had Paul been an attempt to get over Zac? But she'd genuinely cared for Paul at the time, and wouldn't have married him otherwise.

'You're miles away,' Zac noted. 'Care to share?'

'Not really.' Physically mere centimetres away, but he was right. The gap between them was huge. Insurmountable? Only time would tell. Did she want to explore this? Her humming body indicated yes, but her heart was slow. Too much to lose. The pain of getting it all wrong would shut her heart down for ever, reinforcing the fact she wasn't good at choosing the right man. The Zac she knew was everything she hoped for, and usually trustworthy. But that was as a friend, not as a potential lover. He was so sexually attractive, he was becoming impossible to ignore. Becoming? He was already there, sexy as they came. Strange she'd never noticed his wide chest or muscular thighs before. He'd just been Zac, the boy in her life who grew into a man she hadn't really seen, except once as a teenager. Now there was no not noticing him. He oozed sexiness.

'Maisie, if you'd rather go home, just say so.' A crease appeared between his brows, like he was concerned about her behaviour and was about to turn around to head off.

'No way. I'm starving.'

For food, and life, and possibly you, Zac Lowe.

She headed inside. The place was humming, every table in use. 'I haven't been here in years.'

Zac stepped through the crowd, his arm around her shoulders, keeping her close—like he didn't want to let go either. Interesting. 'Let's sit at the bar and see if a table comes free.'

They could eat at the bar but that wouldn't be conducive to talking. Could be for the best though. Enjoy each other's company without getting into deep water. Minutes ago she'd wanted to get away from him because of these feelings, now all she wanted was to be with him. Yeah, he'd got her into a right pickle. She wanted him. She knew that wasn't the best idea she'd ever had. She needed to make up her mind. Go with this and see where it took her and Zac, or back off fast. She hadn't felt this alive and ready for a new adventure in for ever. Not since the police came knocking on the door with a warrant for Paul's arrest and she'd learnt he'd been using her for his own means and that when it all fell down around his feet she'd never really meant a thing to him.

'It's great to be out and about again. I haven't done much socialising lately.'

'So you're glad you came home?'

'Absolutely.'

'I am too.'

More warmth spread through her as she watched him from under lowered eyelids. That angular jaw begged to be touched with her fingers, those lush lips traced with her tongue.

'You heard from Liam this week?' Zac asked as they scrutinised the menus the barman handed them.

Liam? Oh, right. 'He rang a couple of days ago. Said he'd be coming for a visit within the next few weeks. Probably warning me to move out of his bedroom.' She was renting her brother's apartment off him until he made up his mind about buying a house in Christchurch. Somehow he seemed to be dragging the chain about that, and she suspected it was his way of helping her out.

'Think he's serious about this Sasha he's seeing? It's been going on for a while.'

'Haven't got a clue. He's not saying much. As per normal.' Maisie finally relaxed. This was her and Zac, shooting the breeze with no undertones to be heard. It was wonderful.

The only sour point was when she went up to pay the tab and the barman grinned. 'Already seen to.'

'Zac, I said I was shouting,' she growled.

'So you did.' He stared her down with a 'This is what I do' look.

Her heart twisted, and she relented. She rose onto her toes and brushed a kiss over his cheek, barely resisted his lips. 'Thank you.' What else could she say? It was as if they were on a date. Blatantly untrue, but she'd take it for now.

Zac was laughing on the inside as he drove them back to the apartment block. Maisie had looked ready to read him his pedigree when she learned he'd paid the bill. He got that she was independent and didn't expect him to do that, but that's who he was.

'Since my car's still at work, can you give me a lift to work in the morning?' she asked while staring out the window.

Not liking having to ask for help? That was new. But since Paul she had pushed everyone away when they wanted to help her. 'No problem.' He kept it light, didn't tease her as she'd probably expect. Instead he tapped the steering wheel in time to the music filling the warm air, and breathed deep. Maisie filled him, soft and warm, expanding his heart in a way that was foreign to him.

As he parked in his garage, she turned to him. 'Coffee? At mine?'

'You bet.' Hopping out of the car he raced around to open her door. 'I enjoyed tonight.' It wasn't over, but it also wasn't going to get cosy, or hot, or anything more than friendly. Not tonight. He needed to get more encouragement before he risked everything.

As she brushed past him her breast touched his arm, and he drew a breath. Friendly that was not. But it hadn't been a deliberate move. There wasn't a lot of space between the car door and the wall so he'd been close, too close apparently. Stepping out into the cool night air, he hauled in oxygen, let his body slowly relax.

She let them into her apartment, charging up the stairs as though trying to put space between them. Her long legs and sassy butt filled him with a need that coffee wasn't going to douse. It would have to. There was nothing else going down tonight.

So find something else to talk about. As he reached the top of the stairs he looked around and smiled. 'You've taken down Liam's favourite painting.' Where the abstract art piece in shades of grey and yellow had hung was now a large black and white photo of Lake Wanaka, waves pounding the shore, whitecaps everywhere, with a lone boat pitching abruptly.

'You honestly didn't think I could live with that hideous picture, did you? If you could call it a picture.' She shuddered, spilling coffee grains on the counter.

'True.' He looked around at what was now a cosy living room with soft pink cushions on the couch and chairs, vases and ornaments filling the shelves. Early irises stood in a narrow straight glass vase on a sideboard. 'This feels right.' A Maisie room. Warm and soft, inviting.

Leaning against the kitchen counter she nodded. 'It's me. I picked up most of the furnishings at the warehouse. It's amazing what you can do with very little to spend. Who needs Rimu tables and chairs, leather sofas?' A hint of bitterness darkened her voice.

'Hey, you've done well. And you're right. This is so you.' He stepped around the counter and reached for her, drew her in for a light hug. Not tight, not too close. Though he was fighting the need to wrap his arms right around her and hold on for ever. 'You're back, and you've made this place your home.'

She'd returned, and he had his old job waiting in Christchurch if he wanted to go back and pick up where he'd left off when the bullet took him down. He hadn't been rushing to go, and now Maisie was here, he was less than enthusiastic. Spending time with her was far more exciting than working every waking hour and then some to solve a murder. But the time for making a final decision was running out. The CIB wouldn't wait for ever. He held her tighter.

They stood there for a moment, quiet together. Then Maisie pulled away, looked everywhere but at him. 'You're right. And I'm happy.'

'Maisie?' If that tone was happy, then he didn't have a clue. 'You all right?'

She turned and locked her gaze on him. Fierce, and determined. 'I'm fine. Truly. Sometimes what happened gets to me, and then I remember it's over and I'm back amongst the people I care about the most in the world.' At last a full-on smile came his way. 'Including you, Zac.'

His heart melted. He could live with that for now. It helped taking things slowly a little bit easier.

CHAPTER THREE

ZAC SHOOK HIS head in exasperation. 'The man's holding the three-year-old daughter of his ex-girlfriend to ransom and I have to play nice.' All the hostage negotiating training Zac had done before returning to Queenstown for a quieter life didn't stop the pain he felt for that little girl he'd heard crying on and off over the last five hours, but he knew how to suppress it and get on with the job. 'Libby's traumatised enough as it is.' Sure, he understood traumatised was better than dead as had been threatened, but sitting here listening to Blake ranting about getting the child's father here was like watching the tide coming and going and nothing changing.

Hooper was at Shanghai Airport waiting for the first flight back to New Zealand and there was nothing anyone could do to get the poor guy here any sooner. Blake had been told so often it was like a record going round and round on the same groove. He refused to budge. Nor would he talk with the child's mother, who was desperate to get her daughter away from the monster.

'You're coping better than I could,' Colin, the station chief, muttered.

'Thanks.' Zac pressed the button on the phone. 'Blake, you need something to eat?' Anything to settle the guy down a little.

'Think I'm stupid?'

Yes, big time. But he was also evil and hurting a little girl. 'Blake, you hold all the aces. I have no intention of using a food delivery to attack you.' Zac rubbed his lower back where a dull throb had set in from sitting so long at the table trying to talk Blake out of his hyped-up scheme of holding Libby until her father turned up. The evil undertone to the man's attitude had the hairs lifting on Zac's neck every time he heard Libby cry.

'What the—?' Blake yelled.

Screams and shouts came from the speaker and through the open windows of the communications van Zac and Colin were sitting in with an internet special-ist. Who else was in there other than Blake and Libby?

'Where's Cathy?' Zac asked.

A scream answered him.

'That's Cathy? Inside? How the hell? She's supposed to be with a policewoman.'

'Blake, talk to me. What's going on?' Zac knew he'd be ignored and he'd lost the edge—if he'd ever had one—because someone else had entered the house. It wasn't his battle any more. That belonged to the armed defenders now swarming the building. But he leapt to his feet anyway. He might be able to talk to Blake in-side the house, talk him down from whatever high he was on.

'Get out or I'll hurt the kid.' Blake's roar came through the phone on speaker.

'Mummy.' Libby's small voice.

Zac froze. Why had the armed defenders gone in? They must've seen Cathy enter the house from the back, but if so they were supposed to notify him. But he knew from experience how fast these situations could change. How had the woman got in unnoticed? Someone was going to get a speech once this was over, and it wouldn't be pleasant.

'Stay down,' someone snarled. Not Blake so it had to be one of the armed defenders

Zac waited, every muscle screaming with tension and the urge to rush in to deal to the man who'd caused harm to the little girl. But others were doing that. It wasn't his job today. Damn it.

'Zac, you listening? It's Reed.' One of the armed defenders. 'You're needed in here.'

'On my way.' He leapt out of the van and ran. What now? They must have Blake under control, or something had gone horribly wrong. Heart in throat he raced for the building.

Libby was safe, held in her mother's tight grip as a policewoman escorted them out of the room to the ambulance now parked outside instead of around the corner.

Blake was face down on the floor, cuffed, and spewing vitriol.

'What happened?' Zac asked. 'Why was Cathy in here?' The mother should've been along the road in a police car out of harm's way, not risking harm to her daughter.

'She said she had to go to the toilet and came here

instead. She attacked him with that.' An armed defender nodded at the baseball bat.

Great. Did she not understand what could've happened to her daughter if she'd made a mistake? The man was big, she was small. How she'd beaten him was beyond him. But now wasn't the time to say anything. He turned around, stepped up to the man he'd spent the last five hours talking with. Now he could stop being 'nice' and get serious, read him the charges with satisfaction. 'Cut the noise, Blake. It's over.'

Maisie's teeth were grinding as she sponged the little girl's face, removing the smears of tear-streaked dirt plastered to the abrasions on her cheeks and chin. What had that monster done to her? 'There, there, I'm cleaning you up so we can make you better.' They'd be able to fix her physically but emotionally was going to take time and patience from the experts and the child's parents.

Rinsing the cloth in disinfectant, she moved onto Libby's hands, extracting first one and then the other from Cathy Hooper's grip. The mother hadn't let go of her daughter the whole time Maisie had been with them. But then, why would she? It must've been terrifying every second of the hours she couldn't see her daughter, didn't know if she was all right. She'd refused to stay in the emergency department to be treated for her own injuries when Libby was transferred to the paediatric ward. So one of the doctors had come here to stitch up the wounds she'd received when she'd tackled the man who'd abducted her daughter.

'Baby, you're safe now. Mummy's here.' Cathy's voice hitched with unshed tears.

Libby wasn't saying a word, staring around as though wondering where the monster had gone and if he was coming for her again.

Maisie's heart squeezed. Life was so unfair at times. She'd heard Zac had been the negotiator. He was experienced in these situations and would've been focused on the task, but now it was over would he be okay? Did he need to vent or did he write up the paperwork as his way of dealing with the event?

The air shifted, and her skin warmed, as though someone special was near. Glancing over her shoulder, she smiled her relief. He was here, and *safe*. No one had been able to tell her anything more than he'd been the negotiator and had been called to go inside towards the end. 'Zac.'

His shoulder was against the doorframe, holding him upright. Exhaustion had etched lines in his face and dulled his eyes. But there was a hint of relief there too as he fixed on her. 'Hey.'

It took all her control not to race over and embrace him. Not that anyone would give her a hard time if she did, but right now she had a wee patient to look after who needed her more. 'You okay?' Silly question. Zac took negotiations involving children hard because he knew what it was like for a family to lose a child. His family and Maisie's had suffered, though with his parents he'd come on the scene after his brother died from SIDS and had lived with the consequences.

He nodded. 'Sure.'

Giving him a quick once-over, she smiled, liking his strength and tenderness. So lovable. Yikes, better focus on cleaning the torn skin on Libby's hand, and not Zac. But she was aware of him, couldn't ignore his presence, and knew the moment he straightened and came across to the bed.

'How is she?'

'Sore, bruised, and there are a few abrasions, but no serious injuries.' He'd know she wasn't referring the mental ones.

How Zac managed to stay calm after what he'd dealt with was a mystery but spoke tons about his strength. She couldn't do it. That's why she was a nurse. She got to care for the victims of accidents and illnesses—and abductions—to help try and make them better. She didn't see the anger and rage as it unfolded, and never wanted to, especially after hearing Zac talk about the shooting that saw his friend and colleague killed, and put him in hospital with a gunshot to the abdomen. He'd taken the hit in an attempt to save the officer in charge. He said he'd done it without thought for the consequences, a reaction, was all. He didn't see himself as a hero, but she did. So did a lot of other people, especially in the police force. 'A good result.'

Zac winced. 'He's off the street, yeah.'

Maisie looked him over. 'Are you sure you're all right?'

'Yes. Got a blinding headache to be going on with, is all.' A crooked smile changed his face.

Ka-thump went her heart. He really was something else. Someone special. Someone who made her want to sing. She laughed. That would have security rushing to haul her outside. Placing her hand on his upper arm, she squeezed gently. 'You're amazing.' Really and truly amazing. Her kind of man. If—*if*—she could risk her heart.

'Don't go all soft on me, or…' He spluttered to a halt.

'Or what?'

'I'll have to take you out to dinner again.'

Now there was a good idea if ever she'd heard one. 'You're on. Now sit down before you fall down.' He was looking wobbly on his feet, now she was studying him as a nurse and not that woman who wanted him in her arms, against her body.

'I need to talk to Cathy for a moment.'

'I'm not leaving Libby.' The woman cuddled her daughter possessively.

Maisie said, 'I suggest you both sit over in the corner, on the other bed, speak quietly so the wee one here can't hear what you're saying but won't lose sight of her mother. She mightn't be saying anything but she can hear very clearly and I'm sure neither of you want to disturb her any more than she already is.'

Dark blue eyes locked on her, glittering with agreement. And amusement at her 'I'm in charge here' tone? Zac conceded, 'You're right. Come on, Cathy. Your daughter couldn't be in better hands.'

Relaxing, Maisie chuckled to herself. He wouldn't have heard her talk like that before. It was strictly a work voice. They were in a two-bed room with no other patient going to be brought in here while Libby was a patient. She'd made certain everyone knew no one was to come near Libby and her mother unless for medical reasons. 'Libby, think you can drink some water for me?' Maisie aimed for distraction to make everything easier on her mother, and to help her stop thinking about Zac's compliment.

Libby's eyes followed her mother the short distance to the other bed, didn't leave her when Cathy scrunched down on the edge and kept her vigil as Mummy talked to Zac.

There was a difficult time ahead for the child and her mother, Maisie sighed. 'Here, Libby, take a few sips.' She held the plastic mug to the girl's lips and urged her to respond. 'That's it. Good girl.' Now for some more cleaning up of abrasions, this time on the legs.

'Want a hand?' Jill appeared quietly at the side of the bed.

Nodding at the nurse, Maisie said, 'Can you bring some fresh warm water and more swabs? I don't want to leave her even for a minute.'

Libby had stiffened when Jill spoke but she hadn't looked her way, remained fixed on her parent, her hand reaching for Maisie's, gripping tight. 'It's all right. Jill's a nurse like me and she wants to look after you too.'

Jill went to get what was needed. When she returned, Maisie suggested, 'You clean those abrasions and I'll keep hold of her hand.' Libby was shaking a little. Time for some food. Though the reaction would have a lot to do with shock and terror catching up. Reaching behind her to the tray on top of the bedside cabinet she picked up a plate with a sweet muffin on it. 'Libby, how about you eat this? Look, it's yummy, with chocolate inside.'

Silently the girl reached out and took the muffin, nibbled at the edge, still watching her mum.

Maisie glanced across to Zac. He wore his serious policeman face but worry darkened his eyes. He must've sensed her looking at him because he turned slightly to look at her, and then at Libby. His fingers touched his right shoulder. Telling her to check her patient's shoulder.

'That's the girl. You'll feel better when you've finished the muffin. It'll make your tummy happy.' Maisie ran her hand over Libby's right shoulder, shifted the neckline of the hospital gown and studied the skin and muscles. Minor bruises, no swelling. Pulling the gown back in place, she lifted her thumb towards Zac.

He nodded once. They were on the same wavelength. A team of two. It would wonderful to take that further. Couldn't be simpler. *Sure.* Just forget the hurt from the past and get on with the future jointly. Love. Marriage. Family. So easy. *Not.* Or was it? Give it a go? Hard not to with her skin heating every time he was near. But easy does it. One step at a time.

Next time Maisie looked across Zac was leaning against the wall, his hands in his pockets, his head dropped forward, staring at his feet. She crossed over, leaving her wee patient snuggled against her mother again. 'Libby's safe. Because of you, the team and her mum. You can be proud of yourself.'

'I am, but now the questions start. Who was responsible for what? How did Cathy get into the house when it was surrounded with armed defenders? That sort of thing.' He lifted his head and stared at her, his baby blues fierce.

Baby blues? Yes, sometimes. And that sparkling cobalt shade when he was smouldering with longing. His eyes were lovely—hot. 'You'll sort it. I know you, remember?' Though obviously not as well as she'd once believed if she now noticed how his eyes had layers of depth and twinkled even when he was serious. 'I bet you wanted to smash the guy to pieces, but you didn't. Instead you did what was required—remained calm and focused.' Her arms tightened, preventing her from reaching for him. That wasn't happening here in the ward where anyone could see them. Jill would tease her relentlessly, as she was always on her back about finding a man to have some fun with.

But she so wanted to show Zac she was here for him all the time as someone special and not so much as the friend he knew. She cared for him in ways that were stronger, and deeper, than she'd felt before. But she had to be careful because if she was wrong, and found she was looking for love with Zac because it was safe and had no real foundation, she'd lose one of her closest friends and that would break her heart even more. She stepped back. 'I'm due a break. Feel like a coffee?'

Her patient was dozing. Jill would keep an eye on them while they went to the canteen.

'Good idea.' He straightened up and touched her shoulder. 'I feel whacked. It's all catching up.'

Heading down the corridor and around the corner away from the ward the need to hug him grew. And grew. To hell with it. This was Zac. Why shouldn't she? Until she'd felt attracted to him she wouldn't have thought twice about it. Moving closer she took his arm, pulled him to a halt and wound her arms around that expansive chest, tight not soft and loose. This was what friends did, right? Even them. But today was different. The faint smell of aftershave wafted past her nose, making her shiver with delight.

Zac tensed.

She backed off some. He didn't want her hug?

Then he was holding her, chin on her head, his breathing slow and quiet.

Relief warred with guilt. She shouldn't be wanting to press closer, but trying to stop the prickles of desire lifting her skin wasn't working. This was magic. Desire and Zac all rolled into one. Tensing, she pulled back a little, instantly regretting it.

Zac dropped his arms to his sides and stepped back. 'We'd better go get that coffee.'

Her heart sunk. She got the message. They were *friends*, not lovers, and never likely to be. Had she given herself away? If she took a chance on following this desire filling her more and more often, he still mightn't change his feelings for her to something so deep it came with a love that was intimate and loving beyond what they'd always known. This felt like that day when she was a teenager and wanting him to hold her. He'd walked away then too. 'Right.' Not even close, but hopefully he believed her.

Along with Liam, Zac had always been there for her, since the day Cassey went to the shop to get ice cream and never came home. It had been an awful time for her family. Zac had felt the pain too. Cassey had been as much a part of his life by then as she and Liam were. It also made things harder for Maisie because the boys became extra vigilant around her. Quiet, shy and more inclined to appease people than argue with them for the sake of it, it became difficult to be strong and stand up for herself with the boys overseeing everything she did. She'd paid them back by becoming the pesky sister always following them around and trying to join in their games, but they never backed off watching out for her. Then she'd started wanting Zac's attention in other ways and he'd shunned her.

As a teenager she'd dug deeper, started working out who she was and what she wanted, trying to ignore what the guys thought best for her. She'd stuck to it pretty much ever since and made some disastrous decisions along the way. But they had been her choices, no one else's. Now, after wrapping up her marriage she was taking a break on being tough, quietly finding her way through life without pushing too hard for anything, being content with what she had. Throughout all the drama of being publicly derided as the wife of someone who could steal from the weak and therefore must've known what was going on Zac was always at the end of the phone whenever she wanted to chat.

Except she hadn't talked to him much about Paul and how he'd decimated her with his crimes and lies throughout their brief marriage. Her family had never cared for Paul, thought he was self-centred, and she'd been defiant about marrying him. She had loved him in the beginning, hadn't seen his ego and need to be wealthy as a problem until it was too late, so the last thing she was going to do was to go looking for sympathy from those who'd tried to warn her.

'Where have you gone?' he asked quietly, his gaze focused entirely on her, his breathing uneven.

She shook her head, giving him a smile. 'I'm here, with you.' In more ways than one. 'Come on. At this rate I'll have to return to the ward before we even get to the canteen.'

Three hours later Maisie parked in her garage and breathed a sigh of relief. The day was over and she could relax, forget about a little girl who'd been put through hell and concentrate on not being a nurse for the next twelve hours. Starting with a hot shower.

Through the lounge window she saw Zac sitting on his deck, head tipped back, and a bottle of beer in his hand. He'd be winding down, letting go the tension from earlier in the day which had probably ramped up at the debriefing he'd gone back to the station for after they'd had coffee in the canteen. Self-contained came to mind. Zac to a T—most of the time.

Turning away reluctantly, she headed for the bathroom and switched the shower on to warm up while she got clean clothes from her bedroom. Jeans and a navy top with green and lemon patterns that opened down to the beginning of her cleavage. Lacy underwear that no man ever saw any more. It was her hidden pleasure. Gorgeous lingerie made her feel feminine and desirable.

Would Zac appreciate her sexy knickers? A bra

that opened at the front? What would he think of them on her?

Where did that come from? Turning the dial closer to cold she stepped under the water and gasped. Thinking about Zac and sex twisted her insides and heated places best ignored for now. But a relationship with him would be exciting. This had to be the craziest thing she'd ever contemplated. Altering the temperature to bearable, she soaped herself all over and tried to forget what she'd been thinking. But what would she come up with next?

The sight of Zac sitting out on his deck, staring up at the sky—or were his eyes closed and he was thinking about his day?—sucked her in. Made her happier than she'd been in a while. Had her wondering if these new feelings for him really were real, and if they were could she find the courage to follow through?

Damn it. She was going over to his apartment to have a beer with him, and try to clear the muddle in her head. If she really wanted to follow up on these new feelings, then hiding out in the apartment wasn't the way to go about it.

Towelling herself dry she laughed. Wasn't that why she'd got out that particular top and those jeans that hugged her hips and butt like a second skin?

Her phone vibrated on the counter. Liam's name was highlighted.

Heard Zac was negotiator today. How is he? He hasn't answered my messages.

Exhausted when I saw him.

To be expected.

True.

Give him an elbow from me when you see him.

From the day the boys started school together they'd always elbowed each other in acknowledgement of something well done. It had been their way of sharing secrets in front all the other kids.

Will do. Maisie put her phone aside.

Liam hadn't finished. Glad you're there for him.

How'd Liam know she was about to go visit him? Duh. Her brother knew her as well as Zac did. Of course she'd call in on him. She didn't bother answering, instead headed to Zac's apartment.

'Hey.' Zac held his door wide, a startled look on his face as he sussed her out. Never noticed her dressed in fitted clothes before?

'Hi yourself,' she managed around a blockage in her throat. His weather-hewn face was so familiar it shouldn't send the wave of longing ripping through her so that her knees felt weak. Those lips looked so kissable it was just as well her knees weren't able to lift her onto her toes. She'd have made a fool of herself.

This is Zac, for crying out loud.

A man to be relied upon. Sounded boring put like that, because Zac was anything but boring. He was fun and exciting, loved getting out in the bush and on the mountains or in his boat on the lake. And sexy. She winced. She shouldn't have come. 'I came to see how you're doing with getting over your day.'

'I'm fine. Join me on the deck?' He was studying her as though he didn't know her.

Surprise, Zac, you don't. Not where I'm coming from at the moment anyway.

But then she wasn't sure she knew what was going on with her either. 'A beer would be good.' She stepped around him to head out to the deck.

'On to it.'

Maisie sank onto one of the woven outdoor chairs and tucked her legs under her butt. The sun was sinking fast behind the mountains, but the air was still warm. 'Winter will be here before we know it,' she said as she took the bottle Zac held out.

'You ready for snow this year?'

Tauranga had warmer winters and snow was unknown. 'Bring on the skiing. I'll be a bit rusty, but it'll be fun.'

'You never forget the moves. Not when you've skied since you were knee-high to a grasshopper.' Zac tipped his head back as he sipped his beer, his throat exposed.

She looked away, afraid to be caught staring. Her eyes were probably full of lust. Sipping her beer, she tried to find something to talk about. Nothing came to mind.

'How was Libby doing when you finished up at work?'

At least one of them was on track for normalcy. 'The doctor knocked her out with a mild sleeping drug as she got very fidgety and was crying nonstop. Distressing

for everyone, especially her mother.' She knew too well
from working in paediatrics that being a parent came
with a cost. But she also understood how much there
was to gain by being a mother.

Paul had been adamant they had to wait until he
was established in his career. For once, he got something right, if for wrong reasons. Having the father of
her child in jail didn't bear thinking about. Her head
turned towards Zac. One day she'd be a mother. When
she was sure of giving her heart to a man who wouldn't
treat her as badly as Paul had.

Zac would look after her.

Then again, he hadn't done well with his previous
relationships, had said he'd always felt uncertain about
his ability to love the way he'd seen her parents did. He
believed he wouldn't be up to scratch when it came to
his own relationships, yet that didn't add up when he'd
known nothing but love from her family, and never let
them down. But it was probably impossible to forget
his roots.

She was learning to trust her judgement, but it had
been quite the lesson. Paul's apparent kindnesses came
with a price tag. His generosity was at someone else's
expense. His need to be wealthy hadn't meant working
hard himself; it had been all about taking from those
who had. Love hadn't been about sharing their lives and
future, hadn't been about raising a family together. No
wonder she was reluctant to try again, which meant becoming a mum was way down the track, if it ever happened. Having a child on her own did not feel right for
her. She wasn't against women having a baby without a

partner, but just not her. Growing up in a loving family had given her strength and kindness that she wanted for her children. She'd be a good mother, but kids needed the balance two parents brought.

Zac's jaw was clenched. Thinking about his day?

She leaned over and gripped his hand. 'Don't. You can't undo what happened, or why it happened in the first place. His day in court's coming and then he'll be living in purgatory.' From what she'd heard growing up with her dad, who'd also been a cop, child molesters and attackers didn't do so well in prison. 'You aren't a violent person so stop even thinking about what you'd like to do because there's no chance you would.'

'Everyone has their point of no return.'

'Yes, and you haven't reached yours by a long way. Don't do this to yourself, Zac.'

His thumb slid back and forth over her wrist. 'We do know each other very well, don't we?'

'We do.' It was how it was, friends growing up, going through their teens and becoming adults and seeing each other's strengths and weaknesses and accepting them. Zac and Liam had a similar relationship. Yet she couldn't help feeling there was more behind what Zac had said than she understood. Nothing unusual there. He didn't always let on about what was really bothering him. After the shooting he initially talked in depth about his pain and anger, but he'd stopped fairly quickly.

Zac crossed to the barbecue and turned on the hot plate. 'I've got some steaks in the fridge.'

'Want me to toss a salad together?'

'All done.'

'You were expecting me to turn up?'

He grinned. 'What would have kept you away?'

See? No secrets. No surprises. Except she did have one—one she was keeping to herself. She was well on the way to falling for him.

CHAPTER FOUR

'BUSY LAST NIGHT?' Maisie asked Faye at swap over. She felt tired before she'd even started work. The few hours she'd managed had been restless. She'd finally fallen asleep as the sun was making itself known coming over the horizon. As she always woke at six regardless of what her day held, she never set her alarm so if Liam hadn't phoned for a chat on his way to work she might still be in bed.

'Fairly quiet.' Faye brought up the file on screen. 'Libby only woke twice and with her mother right beside her she nodded off quite quickly both times. But you'll be getting her up today.'

'The sooner she's moving around normally the better for her mental state too.' Poor little lamb was going to ache all over for a few days from those bruises on her arms and torso.

'Cathy talked a lot during the night. She might not be finished,' Faye warned.

'Letting off steam after a horror of a day.' Maisie got that. She'd been the opposite when she learned what Paul had done. Talking had not been possible. She got too angry, not to mention feeling a fool for ever believing in his so-called altruistic gestures that turned out to be ways of sucking people in to let him take care of their investments so why would she talk about him? Also, at the time, she hadn't known who to trust. Many people, including friends, believed she had to have been aware about what was going on and had condoned it to live a very comfortable lifestyle in a grand house with everything she could want. Yeah, right. She hadn't a clue. Naive and stupid, that had been her. Paul had been a lawyer and made a very tidy income. Coming from an average background she hadn't thought to question how much he made and how they could afford their property. Multiple properties, she found out later as she sat in court listening to the victims' lawyers.

Faye put the file aside. "We had one other new arrival: Debbie Bell, seven, lung infection. She's on strong antibiotics and beginning to recover. No changes with any of the other patients. Harper's still on for discharge after Reed checks him over this morning.'

'That'll make his family happy.' Little Harper had had ongoing battles with bowel infections since he was one, and this time he'd been taken to Christchurch to have surgery to remove a piece of his colon. He was sent back to Queenstown Hospital a week later, when he was well enough, so his family had more access to visit from their remote farm. 'He's such a cutey, and a stubborn little man as well.'

Standing up, Faye rubbed her lower back. 'I'm going to say goodbye to him and his dad, then I'm out of here. See you tomorrow.'

Maisie nodded. 'Will do.' Taking Faye's place at the desk she scanned the files for details entered during the night. A quiet shift. Since everything was in order she pulled her phone from her bag and pressed Zac's number. 'Hey, how'd you sleep?'

'Not bad considering. You at work?'

'It's what I do.'

'You need a life, Maisie. I'll come up with a plan for the weekend.'

Warmth spread throughout her. 'Sounds good to me.'

He was focusing his attention on her more than usual, and she liked it. 'Liam rang earlier. He says to call when you can. You're a hero at Christchurch PD for stepping between the gunman and your chief to take the bullet. So don't grump about that. Those guys know how hard it would've been yesterday.'

'I feel good about yesterday.' He knew she'd understand what he meant.

'Great. I'd better go. Talk later.' It would be too easy to curl up and chat the morning away, but she was on duty, and this may be a low-key department but she was the head nurse. That husky voice sucked her in with warm fuzzies.

'See you soon.'

Smiling like a loon, Maisie hung up and went to see her patients.

Straightening his back, Zac stepped into the paediatric ward, scanning the area for Maisie, not the two people he'd come to see, and felt his gut tighten. She was talking to the little boy dressed in outdoor clothes and with a big grin on his pale face, calm and relaxed.

He knew that feeling. Maisie had often calmed him over the months following the armed holdup with her soft voice full of warmth. Once he'd told her the pain his friend's wife suffered, it made him wonder about the people who could be hurt due to a cop's job. Maisie thought he was saying he'd decided not to seek a long-term relationship, but he'd said no. Bad stuff happened everywhere, and that was life, but it had taken time to get past the grief for Benji.

'Don't go chasing the chickens too much for the first few days you're home, Harper. I don't want you to trip over and have to come back here again, do I?'

'I'll be good, won't I, Dad?'

The exhausted-looking man sitting on the end of the bed raised his eyebrows. 'You'd better be.' He smiled.

Maisie ruffled the kid's hair and got glared at for her trouble. 'We're going to miss you but it's best you don't find a way to come back. Stay safe and strong, then you'll be able to help Dad on the farm again.'

She was great with kids and would make a wonderful mum one day. His gut clenched. If he ever accepted fully he could love his own children as the Rogerses had loved him he'd love it for her to have his children. They'd have her pert nose and twinkly hazel eyes, and long legs and—

Shut up, Zac. He took an involuntary step away. *Get a grip or get out of here.*

'Zac? Over here.' Cathy called from the door to the small room.

Zac saw Maisie look around as he headed towards Libby's mother. He sent her a smile before concentrating on Cathy. 'Morning. How was your night?'

'I stayed with Libby, too scared to let her out of sight. I wasn't going to sleep anyway. I can't get the images of Blake swinging Libby from his hand or forget the threats he kept making about what he'd do to her.' Cathy picked at the hem of her rumpled blouse, her eyes full of worry and exhaustion.

'It will take time to get past those pictures.' An image appeared in his head of Benji sprawled on the floor of the liquor outlet, bleeding to death while the gunman aimed his weapon at the chief. Others at the scene had said there was nothing else any of them could've done to change the outcome. The shooter had been out of his head on drugs and nothing would have stopped him from taking the money he'd entered the liquor outlet to steal. But accepting that hadn't been easy for Zac so he'd left the city to return here for a while where life was less frantic and supposedly not as many evil people lurked. He preferred the slower pace and had leapt at the chance to work with the Search and Rescue unit, as if he didn't already have lots to keep himself occupied. Something he had in common with Maisie, if for different reasons. 'Get all the help you're both offered.' The best help he ever received had been Maisie listening to him choke out his anger and pain over the phone. Her support had been fierce, made him strong again.

Cathy ran her hand over her daughter's head, brushing random hair off her face. 'Libby's doing as well as can be expected, I suppose. I don't know what she's thinking, she's still not talking other than to say "Mum" sometimes.'

'She hadn't said anything about what happened?'

'Not a word.'

Zac's heart slowed. The bastard who did this should get locked away for good. But he wouldn't. His sentence might be the maximum time behind bars that the law allowed but it would never be enough. 'What time does her father arrive?'

'In about half an hour.'

'There are more questions we need to ask you later today.' The paperwork had to be done. 'We need to get everything down for the trial while it's still clear in your mind.'

Despair darkened Cathy's voice. 'I can't believe I was so stupid to ever think Blake might be kind and caring.'

'Hey, we all make mistakes when it comes to people in our lives.'

Maisie appeared to stand beside him. 'Don't go blaming yourself, Cathy. It doesn't help, only makes everything worse, and harder to move on from.'

Zac agreed. It had taken him time to let go of the anger from the shooting that took Benji's life and changed the direction of his future. But he wasn't a hundred percent sure that Maisie had got past what Paul had done. Even after the trial judge stated Maisie was as much a victim as anyone else, she'd had to deal with people blaming her for being a part of the embezzlement, if only because she'd enjoyed the spoils.

His heart tightened whenever he thought about that.

She never talked about it, other than say she'd made a
foolish mistake. Like it was her fault Paul had been
corrupt. That she should've seen it even when the de-
tectives who first interviewed him on suspicion of em-
bezzling client's investments hadn't even when they had
some evidence to suggest otherwise. It had taken another ten months and four victims before they worked it
out enough to prove his guilt. And Maisie had secretly
helped them to get the results that put the man behind
bars. How could Maisie have done any better? As a detective he knew she'd been in the midst of Paul's corrupt
life and should've realised something was out of kilter.
As someone who'd known her all his life he understood
Maisie was very trusting and believed people for who
they presented themselves to be. She'd thrown herself
into the relationship with Paul, completely trusted him
not to hurt her, and lost so much. Now she was older
and wiser, and bruised, that was his Maisie.

His Maisie? Zac stepped back, looked around for a
quick exit, taking with him the image of Maisie's gentle
yet firm hands helping the young boy. 'I'll come back
later.' He needed to get away from her for a bit so he
could breathe again.

Maisie, Maisie. She had got under his skin. After
knowing her since he was a gawky teen he suddenly
felt as though he didn't know her as he'd thought. Certainly not how he wanted to. Even now in a hospital
ward filled with sick children she made him long to
touch her, to hold her close. To kiss her.

'Zac?' Maisie was behind him, consternation in
her eyes.

'Sorry.' He shook his head. 'I just remembered something I've got to do.' Like she'd believe a word of that, but he had to get away. Now. While he still had enough nous left to act slightly sensibly. His feet were already heading along the corridor. 'See you later,' he said over his shoulder. Whether he was talking to Cathy or Maisie he wasn't sure.

He'd see both of them at some time during the day. He had an interview with one and knew there'd be no avoiding the other when she knocked off at the end of her shift. She'd be ringing his doorbell before the day's end like she had last night to make sure he was all right even if he texted her to say he was fine and working. It's what they and Liam had always done for each other and there was no reason for Maisie to stop today. Damn it. He did not want her in his space filling the air with her perfume, rattling his bones with lust, stirring his brain into a mess that said he was seeing her through different eyes and wanting her in ways he was struggling to go slow with. He wanted her, all right, but pushing Maisie could end in disaster. There was only one chance to get this right. Her family were his family, and he owed them so much for the love and consideration they'd always shown him. What if he didn't love her as she deserved?

He'd always protected Maisie, looked out for her, wanted her to be happy. As did Liam, and her policeman father. He was one of the men in her life who'd always been there to make sure nothing terrible happened as it had to her sister. Yeah, and hadn't they all done so well. She'd suffered the consequences of a disastrous marriage, and there'd been nothing any of them had been able to do to prevent it happening—because she'd become so determined to live her life her way without her family interfering.

Damn you, Maisie. You've got to me in ways I'd never have believed possible. How am I going to explain that? To you? To Liam? Your parents? I've ignored my love for so long, pretended it was friendly when I've always wanted you. I'm ready to show you now.

Little did she know he'd been waiting for her to return home one day. Even when he was living in Christchurch he'd waited for the day she'd be back. Now she was here he could no longer deny his love. Nor was he keen to return to Christchurch and the job awaiting him. That'd mean leaving Maisie when he was finally getting closer as a man and not a friend.

What did Maisie think about him? Lately she'd been getting closer physically, as if she wanted more too. Was she open to a relationship?

Damn it, man. Which part of slowly, slowly didn't he get?

CHAPTER FIVE

'WANT TO COME in for a beer?' Maisie called from her front door when Zac climbed out of his car outside his apartment.

He shouldn't. He was exhausted. He'd spent the night tossing and turning while thinking about Maisie—her fingers touching and exciting him yesterday as they walked to the canteen, the tang of flowers as she leaned near, the tightening she brought to his body at the thought of holding her naked in his arms and making love. He wasn't ready to make himself vulnerable to Maisie, but it was already too late. He was defenceless around her. So he should head inside his own apartment and crack a bottle open alone. 'Thanks, but I'll take a rain check.'

'Fine.' Maisie nodded sharply and began to close her door, disappointment blinking at him across the driveway.

He couldn't do it. They were close, no matter how his feelings had changed. He wasn't about to stop being a part of her life. He longed for more of it, not less. 'Maisie, wait.' He strode towards her door, pinging his car locks over his shoulder. 'Of course I want one.'

A tentative smile was her reply, *and* she held the door wider.

Their relationship had changed. Zac suspected Maisie realised it too. Normally she'd have replied with something apt about his attitude and tell him to get over himself but not tonight. Instead she'd looked sad. Which didn't make sense—unless something awful had happened at work today. 'How was your day? Everything all right?'

'It was good.' She headed upstairs to the main living area.

Her jeans highlighted her thighs and butt, brought him out in a sweat. Those same jeans covering that sassy butt had wound him up tight last night and been part of what had kept him awake half the night. His skin began tingling. His mouth dried.

Go home while you can move without having to hide your need.

As if. Too late.

Upstairs he headed straight out to the deck and leaned against the railing to stare across the town below. His right hand tapped the balustrade. Bang, bang, bang. Like the rapid beating going on in his chest, in his veins. He'd always loved Maisie. She was such a part of his life, his being, he couldn't image being without her. Suddenly he was afraid of where this was going. Losing Maisie as a friend wasn't an option. But standing back and not getting involved as his heart needed wasn't an option either. He needed her. He loved her.

The scent of roses wafted around him as Maisie

handed him a beer. 'Here, get that into you and hope-fully that grumpy face will disappear.'

Grumpy?

Not even close, Maisie.

Confused, uncertain, yes, but not grumpy. He was with the woman he cared too much for. Taking a long draw from his bottle, he changed the subject. 'There's an award ceremony in Christchurch in a few weeks.'

She gaped at him, a silly grin on her face. 'You're up for one.'

'Yeah. Want to come?'

Throwing her arm around him, she planted a kiss on his cheek. 'Try and keep me away.'

'I figured.' Of course she'd be there. She was the first person he'd thought of asking, only he'd been putting it off. No idea why, other than his tumultuous mind that couldn't think straight for any longer than a few seconds. 'Thanks.'

Her grin expanded as she stepped away, leaving him feeling as though some part of him was missing. 'You hear from Liam today?'

'He'll be here Saturday. He's bringing Sasha.'

The new woman. 'That sounds serious.' Liam wasn't known for totting out his female 'friends' for them to meet. Liked to keep his relationships close to his chest. Something he understood all too well now that he'd ac-cepted he loved Maisie.

Maisie swung a bottle of cider in her fingers.

What would they do to his libido tripping over his skin?

'I agree. Not sure I want to hang around in the apartment while they're here,' she laughed, the old Maisie back in play. 'I'll be a spare wheel.' Even though she rented Liam's apartment, her brother still used it whenever he came back to Queenstown. He'd talked about selling it to buy something bigger than his bachelor pad in Christchurch and, if he did, Zac had first dibs. Not that Maisie knew that he was interested in the apartment as part of the property portfolio he was slowly building. If he did buy it, he hoped Maisie would continue renting the apartment from him until she was financially back on her feet.

'You can always stay at my place.' Instantly Zac sucked in a breath, as though he could retrieve the offer. Too late. Anyway, he liked the idea, wanted her to accept.

'Thanks, but I'll go to Mallory's if it gets too much.' She stepped inside. 'I'll get some crisps.'

His shoulders sank. Okay, she wasn't keen to spend too much time with him.

Fight for her, Zac.

'The offer stands. We'll be hanging out with them both most of the weekend and you might need a break.' Having Maisie in the spare room next to his bedroom while he tried to sleep and not dream about what he'd like to be doing with her mightn't be good for him, but he was stepping up.

Following her inside, he closed the door, shutting out the rest of the world, and bringing all his doubts pounding down on his head.

'What's up, Zac? You're all over the show tonight.'

'I am?' Guess he was in a way. He breathed deep, relished the floral scent that was his Maisie.

'Reliving the hostage situation, by any chance?' She'd returned, packet of crisps in hand, a frown creasing her lovely forehead. 'That little girl and how she was terrified?'

'Not at all.' His hands clenched on the bench in front of him. 'Though now you mention Libby, it was disgusting. Children are meant to be cherished, kept safe.'

Maisie leaned over to cover them with her hands, warm and soft, caring. 'There are some dreadful people out there, which is why you do the job you do.'

'True. But honestly, I'm not thinking about that.'

'If you say so.' Her smile was gentle, full of understanding and something else he was afraid to hope for. Love?

Was it the love he was looking for? Or was it the same love she'd always shown? Love that'd encompass him and maybe their children. All these questions. He was looking for trouble. Breathe. Deep. In, out. In, out. Pulling his hands away from that warmth, he said, 'Sometimes I wonder if I'll ever get up the courage to father a child; I'm so afraid of what's out there that might hurt them.'

Maisie stared at him like he'd just exposed himself. 'You do?' she gasped.

He *had* a longing he'd never put out there before. Might as well follow up or there'd be questions from here to Africa. 'Of course I do. It comes with the territory of being a cop.' That wasn't what she was asking though, was it? 'Yes, Maisie, one day I want to settle down with a wonderful wife and have a couple of ankle biters, and most of the time I accept the fact life's full of dangers for everyone.'

'You've never said anything about wanting to be a dad.'

'Why wouldn't I? I admit to sometimes worrying about how my upbringing might influence how I behave as a parent, but I do know better than that. Your family gave me what mine couldn't. What better example would I want?'

He supposed his parents did love him in their own way, though couldn't they have shown him a little bit? It would've been traumatic for them losing his brother, but Ross and Pippa lost Cassey and still loved Maisie and Liam to bits. They weren't afraid to show and act on it. His parents had worked all hours in their supermarket as though it was a shield from life's problems. They'd been afraid to love him which sometimes made him angry, sometimes worried he wouldn't be any better because of the example they'd set. Mostly he knew he'd been lucky to have the Rogerses show him differently and that he could do better.

With a thoughtful look, Maisie pulled back and reached for her drink.

Instantly he felt something was missing. Crazy when she was still close enough to touch without moving off the stool, but there it was.

'You should never doubt yourself. You've got a big heart, Zac.'

That heart began tightening as he listened to the

sweet cadence of her voice. Sweet *and* sexy. Hot. He poured cold beer down his dry throat.

'You'll be an awesome father. Any kid would want you for their dad.'

'Only those I have, I hope,' he cracked through the warmth her words brought on. 'I'm not taking on spares.'

Her smile flicked on, then off. Her fingernail began scratching the bench surface.

An ache started under his ribs. Her family were very protective of her and they treated him as a second son. Because of that Pippa and Ross might not like him crossing the line from friend to lover. Though they knew him, trusted him. Once again he was getting ahead of himself. 'What about you? Want to have a family sometime?'

Maisie winced. 'First things first. I'm back on my feet, but not rushing to find another man to fill the void. I won't have children without their father at my side.' A delicate shade of pink was filling her cheeks as she stared harder at the view.

'Maisie?' The urge to haul her into his arms was intense. His hands tightened into fists again, pressed into his thighs. He would not follow through on that need. Must not.

Slowly she raised her head and looked at him. 'Zac?'

Confusion tripped out of her eyes, ensnaring him, causing him to wonder what was behind it. 'Are you all right?'

Her breasts rose. 'I'm fine. I thought we were talking about you.' The last words came out on a long sigh.

This hip-hopping from subject to subject was normal, only tonight it felt awkward, as though they were unveiling more depth to their relationship than ever before. Not that either had said much, but that sense of giving away something personal was there. 'I changed the subject deliberately.' He found a smile to make her see he wasn't trying to be a pain in the butt, as she liked to call him.

She turned to face him. 'I'm glad I finally returned home. I missed this, us talking about anything and everything.'

Did you miss me? As in someone to get close to?

'We stopped talking when you got with Paul, remember?' The man had been possessive and jealous and Zac backed away from even the usual friendly phone calls to Maisie to save her any problems. 'Apart from after the shooting when I talked non-stop.' Sort of anyway.

'When I left Paul you kept saying I needed to talk and get it off my chest.'

Zac couldn't help it. His eyes dropped to those beautiful curves filling the front of her shirt.

Maisie hadn't noticed he was distracted. 'It was time to stand on my own two feet and deal with the chaos, the hurt and the public criticism myself. I couldn't hide behind my family or you. I needed to be strong, to grow a backbone, or I'd never trust myself to cope with anything major again.'

Dragging his head upward, he smiled around the lump of longing filling his throat. 'You did that in bucketloads. You've always been tough, going about things quietly, putting yourself out there as a force to be reck-

oned with. Not saying you aren't, because you always
are, but most people don't see that behind the shy face
and soft manner.' It was so true even her parents hadn't
always seen Maisie for who she really was. Her father and Liam wanted to fight her battles for her and
never stopped when she grew up and became a woman.
They'd expected the same of him, and to a point he
had, while also understanding Maisie needed space,
that it was her battle to fight. Maisie had pushed them
away, told them to let her sort it out her way for once.
And she had.

And he'd gone and fallen deeper for that strong,
tough, gentle and no longer shy Maisie. In bucketloads.

'I was seen as selfish in Tauranga. And on the news.'
She shuddered. 'It still gives me the creeps to think how
a person's life can be exposed so easily.'

He'd spewed vitriol at the screen some nights watching the media having a blast over Maisie's naivety about
what her husband had been doing. It got to the point
where he couldn't watch any more. Not because he no
longer needed to find out what was going on but because none of those reporters knew her and had filled
in all the gaps with whatever anyone told them. People
who didn't know Maisie, and some who did, had been
basking in a moment of glory in front of the cameras.

'I was vindicated with the judge's comments at the
trial. There'll always be people who believe otherwise,
but…' Her shoulders lifted, dropped. 'That's life and
I'm not losing any more sleep over it. Nor do I watch
the news very often these days. Can't believe half of
what I hear.'

'Onwards and upwards, eh?' Find another man to love and possibly have children with?

Me?

Zac coughed, grabbed his beer and gulped down another large mouthful.

Get over yourself.

Could it be as easy as telling Maisie he loved her with all his heart? He shivered. He was ready. Was Maisie? Did she find him lovable? His heart pounded. Excitement pulsed throughout his body, his head and heart.

'Onwards is enough. You know my head for heights.' A cheeky smile lit up her face and eyes.

Zac relaxed. Or he got close to it. 'Climbing walls not being your thing.' Go for the fun times.

'Climbing walls and flying in helicopters to name two,' Maisie agreed. 'I still don't know why I let you and Liam talk me into giving that wall climb a crack.' Liam would normally have said no, she shouldn't do it, but they'd had a teenage argument over who was driving Mum's car that day and he was paying her back in typical brotherly fashion. Typically, she'd taken his challenge on despite the fear winding through her. It was a phobia she'd never been able to ignore. That day it had been Zac who'd climbed up to talk her down when she froze twenty metres above the floor in the gym. Come to think about it, it was usually Zac who rushed in to rescue her. A hero. Her hero. If only she could reach across and lift his hand to her mouth, feel his palm with her lips, absorb his heat and strength.

'You were spitting mad at him.' He grinned, sending

her heart out of whack. 'I egged you on, thinking you needed to show us what you were made of. I didn't see then that there were other ways to be putting yourself out there in everyone's face to show strength.'

The compliments were flowing tonight. What was Zac after? Maisie chuckled. They weren't kids any more. Even when they were he'd never tried to charm her into anything. So what was this about? It made her feel good—she wanted to get closer. And confused—because she was probably totally wrong about what he was thinking. 'You after something?'

Charm was Paul's middle name. She hadn't seen that in Zac before, but then she hadn't been looking for it either.

'Another beer.' He headed to the fridge.

She kept watching him for something that'd explain why she felt different about him. The man in her kitchen was still the man she'd always known, only now he was exciting, sexier—make that sexy, since she never used to think sex and Zac in the same sentence, not since she was fifteen anyway. That had been buried deep, not allowed out again, though lately there was no denying she found Zac sexually attractive.

His eyes clashed with hers as he turned back. 'You want anything?'

Deep blue eyes, like cobalt metal in the sun. Razor sharp and heart-meltingly enticing. Her mouth dried.

This is Zac, for crying out loud.

Yeah, and hadn't she been getting in a twist about him for weeks now? 'No, thanks.'

Yes, you.

She wanted to know everything. The Zac behind the Zac she'd grown up with. Zac the man. Was this love? It felt different to last time, but then she knew a lot about Zac whereas Paul had been a stranger the day she bumped into him in a grocery store aisle. She'd gone for him, all part of denying any feelings for Zac.

Zac paced to the glass door to stare out at the darkening town beyond.

Maisie's heart rate went sky high. What was going on? This involved her. Don't ask how, but she knew it did. 'Zac? Talk to me.'

Touch me.

Maybe she wasn't alone in being confused about their relationship. Hoping for too much? Was she even ready to pursue that path? To find out what Zac was thinking? These feelings were scary because if she made a blunder by telling him, only to be gently put aside like last time, she'd fall apart. She'd have to leave Queenstown again, go find somewhere else to work and live and get a grip on reality. She could not stay here bumping into him at family and friends' places if she loved him as much as she was coming to believe and not have that reciprocated.

He came to stand in front of her and reached for her hands. 'I'm heading over to my apartment.'

Her stomach dropped. 'Do you have to?'

'Yes, Maisie, I think I do.' Sadness took the light out of his gaze.

'What's going on?'

His fingers tightened around hers. 'I'm not sure.'

She squeezed back. 'Nor am I,' she whispered and

stood up. They were close, not touching but so near her nerves tingled and her heart pounded.

Zac's eyes widened. His breath trickled across his lips and touched her cheek like a caress.

Gentle, drawing her in, filling her with longing so strong it was irresistible. Yet she waited, poised on the edge of change. Her lungs stopped, her heart lay waiting, filled with expectation.

Zac let go her hands.

Her stomach dropped.

Then he took her face in his palms, warm, firm and determined as he looked into her, deep, as though looking for an answer to a question she was uncertain about.

Time stopped. The world stopped. She was with Zac. He was touching her. Searching for something. And she was looking back, holding onto the hope that filled her. Hope they were on this journey together. That she wasn't alone in wanting to move forward together and explore where it might lead. Trying to show she was falling for him.

But what if they got it wrong? Could they go back to who they used to be together? She'd miss Zac in that way as much as losing an arm. He was such a part of her life. Always had been, always had to be. Stepping over the edge was risky—too risky. She stared at him, devouring his strong, beloved face.

He nodded, dropped his hands and stepped back. 'Goodnight, Maisie.'

The door clicked shut quietly behind him and still she stood there, her fingers on her cheeks, tracing where his palms had touched her, where his fingertips had pressed. And tears spilled, washing away any trace of Zac. Leaving her bereft. And just a little relieved because if they got it wrong, then she'd lose too much. She didn't want that. Zac was a friend. Those old loving feelings were back, taking over, and she needed to roll with them. Zac might just be the man for her. But did these feelings come from a sense of safety or were they real and encompassing? Time was required to work through this. Time spent together.

Now what? Could they carry on as though tonight hadn't occurred? What happened to being stronger? Why hadn't she laid her heart on the line by kissing him? A lost opportunity was never recovered.

Slowly sinking onto the chair, she placed her elbows on the metal table and dropped her head into her hands. Tomorrow Liam and his girlfriend would be here and of course he'd see Zac. They were all going for dinner tomorrow night with her parents for starters. Anyway, Zac and Liam were always in and out of each other's apartments whenever they were both here.

Her head throbbed. That look in his eyes wasn't about friendship. It had been deep and sultry, full of longing. The same longing she'd seen at Mallory's wedding. He *was* susceptible to her too. Couldn't they sit down and have an adult conversation about this?

The front door burst open and Maisie's heart soared. Zac was back.

'Sis, you here?' Liam's voice stomped her hope to ashes.

'Sure am.' Her heart thudded. Not Zac. Liam. What if they had leaned in closer and begun kissing? How would that look to Liam if he'd caught them? There'd be all hell breaking loose right now. Liam would never approve of Zac falling for Maisie. He was her second brother in Liam's eyes and that would be gross.

'Howdy.' Liam dropped his arms on her shoulders and pecked her cheeks. 'I finished work early so we decided to change our flight instead of waiting for the morning. Sasha.' He grinned. 'This is my sister, Maisie.'

Maisie's legs were shaky when she moved to greet Sasha, but she drew a deep breath and got on with this development. 'At last.'

Sasha laughed. 'I've been looking forward to coming down here ever since Liam and I got together.' She was relaxed and happy.

So was Liam. Maisie felt a wave of happiness for her brother. It had been a while since there'd been a woman who made him look so at ease, if ever now she thought about it. 'Glad you're both here. Zac's looking forward to catching up too.' He would be, despite tonight's botch-up. 'He's just gone home to get some sleep.' Ouch. He was more likely sitting on his deck contemplating his navel.

'How is he, really?' Liam leaned against the bench. 'Not stressing too much?'

'You know Zac. But he's on track dealing with this case.'

'Figured he would be, but I'll still check him out over a beer. It's been a while since I was last here and now you all get to meet Sasha.' He hugged his girl-friend close.

Which said she was special to Liam. 'I'm glad.'

Liam got serious. 'Has Zac mentioned the award ceremony coming up in Christchurch next month? He's being recognised for his bravery.'

Maisie nodded. 'Tonight, as it happens.'

Liam was giving her an odd look.

'What?'

'Nothing.' Typical of her brother.

She wasn't fifteen any more. Or twenty. She was divorced and strong, but so not going to ask anything more in case Liam actually came out with something she didn't need to hear. 'Your room's ready.' She used the spare room so that whenever Liam came home she didn't have to move out of his room. 'I'm not being rude, Sasha, but I'm heading to bed. I'm in need of sleep.' Like that was going to happen with the turmoil going on in her head.

'It's fine. I'm feeling weary too. I started work at six this morning so I'd get off early,' Sasha said.

'Right, see you in the morning, Maisie.' Liam looked relieved. 'Unless you're working? Zac's not.'

Bring it on. 'I've got the weekend off.' She should've put in to work it but she did want to spend time with Liam and Sasha.

And Zac. Definitely Zac, despite, or because of, tonight's fiasco.

CHAPTER SIX

ZAC SCRATCHED HIS stubbly chin. He'd slept in after spending most of the night tossing and turning while his mind replayed holding Maisie's lovely face in his hands. Damn but she was beautiful. Achingly so. Well, he ached anyway. Everywhere. Yep, especially there, where his body needed release. And wasn't getting it any time soon, if at all.

Last night they'd come so close to crossing that fine line running between friends and lovers. So damned near that it suddenly frightened him, made him sit up and look seriously at what he was thinking. But not what he was doing, because close as he'd come to kissing Maisie, he hadn't. Minutes before he'd all but decided to go for it, and then after touching Maisie intimately, staring into those deep hazel eyes and seeing a longing he had not expected, he'd gone and walked away. That need blazing out at him had frightened him, shown how serious this really was—as if he hadn't already known that. Made him realise how easily he could hurt her and get hurt himself.

Mentally Maisie followed him into bed when he got

home. Her fragrance, her teasing laugh, her breasts rising and falling when she was agitated, those soft cheeks under his palms. She'd given him a hard-on when she was four apartments away. This wasn't the Maisie he'd grown up with, protected, looked out for, argued with, teased and annoyed. This woman was in his heart, and he'd always look out for her, and probably argue with her, tease her, but now there was so much more depth to those things.

This was Maisie, hot, sweet, strong and smart. Maisie he was in love with. No denying that he probably had been most of his life. He'd do everything possible to make her happy if they got together. But she was more cautious when it came to relationships since her ex's deceitful escapade. No doubt she'd loved Paul, though sometimes she had said maybe she hadn't loved him enough or she'd have forgiven him. Right. Like that was going to happen. The man didn't deserve her.

Putting the kettle on for a strong black coffee, he stared out the kitchen window onto the street. He could go to the station for a bit before Liam arrived. Work was his go-to place when he needed to take a break from things stirring his mind. Most of the week it had been the rescue and the hostage crime, with a little Maisie thrown in. This morning it was all Maisie and nothing else so work would help. His colleagues usually told him he needed to get out more and find a woman to have some fun with.

Guys, I want more than fun.

His previous relationships had been hard work, his heart not totally in them because he'd hidden from his feelings for Maisie. He was just uncertain how to start down the rocky road. If he got it wrong, then Liam and Ross would roast him slowly on the barbecue spit while sipping a beer. Rule one in the Rogers household was protect the women. Rule number two was no different.

His phone buzzed. 'Get your butt over here, man.' Liam. 'The bacon's cooking and I'm about to crack the eggs.'

'When did you get here?'

'Last night. Just after you left Maisie.'

Huh? Liam had seen him and not called out? 'I didn't see you.'

He would've if I'd stayed to kiss Maisie.

Zac's heart thumped against his ribs.

'I figured. By the time I'd parked and hauled Sasha's three-ton case out of the boot and up the stairs I was too exhausted to come find you.' He laughed. 'Get over here so we do the talking with food and coffee going down.'

'On my way.' Relief pounded through his veins. All night he'd been questioning himself on why he hadn't stayed with her since he'd made up his mind to be open with Maisie and show her his feelings. But it had been the need for him in her face that had made him haul the brakes on. Temporarily, he hoped, to give them both time to get used to what seemed to be unfolding between them. And now he was having breakfast with her. Oh, and her brother and his new woman.

'Here, get this into you.' Maisie handed Zac a large mug of coffee. He looked as bad as she felt. Puffy eyes, tired mouth, drooping shoulders.

'Cheers.' He took the mug carefully, not touching her hand. 'You get a surprise when Liam arrived out of the blue?'

'I sure did. He'd finished work early so changed their flight from this morning.' That wasn't what Zac was asking though, was it? If things had gone in another direction their first kiss would've been interrupted and she wouldn't have thanked her brother for that.

Zac was watching her closely, as though looking for her take on last night. 'You all right?'

Smiling wasn't as hard as she'd expected. If they both felt a mess, then they were together on that at least. 'I'm good.' Disappointed and still not quite sure where she was heading with this, but surprisingly, she was okay with it for now. 'You'd better be hungry. Liam's cooking enough breakfast for the whole police department.'

'Typical.' His shoulders lifted a little as he continued watching her. 'Can I give you a lift to dinner tonight?'

Her smile grew. 'Sure.' The four of them could go in one car, but fingers crossed that wasn't suggested by anyone. Time alone with Zac would be just what she needed to get used to allowing her love to come to the fore. Apparently neither was Zac wanting to keep his distance. That had to be good. Bring on more alone time. 'The table's booked for seven.'

'Right, sorted.'

'There you are.' Liam burst into the room. 'Thought you hadn't understood how little time eggs take to cook.' He gave Zac a man hug. 'Looking a bit rough round the edges, mate. Too much off-duty fun going on?'

Hopefully Liam didn't see right through her and

recognise her feelings for Zac. Not until she and Zac cleared the air themselves and really got into something deep and meaningful.

'Still working my way through the hostage situation, dotting the *i*'s and crossing the *t*'s so we don't have problems further down the track in court.' Zac looked directly at Liam. No sideways glances to her going on.

'There's someone I want you to meet. Sasha, come and meet the biggest pain in the backside there is in my world.'

Maisie shook her head. Liam was serious about this woman. Heck, if he could fall in love when he'd been such a playboy, then hopefully she could get past her mistake and let love win out. Properly this time, with the right man, the one who'd never hurt her or let her down. Like she'd thought last night, safe? Yes, but not so safe there wouldn't be any fun or excitement. Because with Zac there'd be plenty of that.

Zac hugged Sasha and must've said something about Liam to make her laugh.

Placing plates on the deck table, Maisie listened to Zac interact with Sasha like he'd known her for ever. So relaxed, yet he'd sense Liam's commitment to her and would be sussing her out. Then he looked Maisie's way and grinned as if to say 'not bad.' She laughed. 'Come on, everyone. Let's eat and make the most of the brilliant weather.' It wouldn't be too many weeks before the deck would be the one place she didn't frequent in the apartment with snow covering the mountains and the wind bringing the freezing air to town.

'Winter's on its way.' Zac pulled out a seat for her.

'Then I can take you up to hit the slopes with those skis in your garage.'

'Can't wait.' She rubbed her arms, smiling. 'It's already cooler than it was a week ago.' It wasn't the air making her skin tingle. That was entirely down to Zac. This was new and exciting.

'Who's up for a bit of fishing after breakfast?' Liam asked.

Sasha shuddered. 'No, thanks. I'll take a stroll around town if that's what you've got in mind.'

'I'll join you,' Maisie added. 'I'm not into smelly fish that look at you with their big eyes as the guys knife them.'

'So you won't being eating trout if we catch any?' Zac laughed at her, knowing full well that was one of her favourite meals.

'I might.' She grinned.

'So guys on the lake and women spending money in the shops.' Liam rolled his eyes.

'Couldn't get any better,' Sasha retorted through a smile just for him, showing how close they were.

Maisie's gaze slid to Zac and heat filled her. He was watching her with an intensity that was riveting. Desire swamped her from lips to toes, sending little shivers up her spine.

'You lost your appetite, Maisie?' Liam cut through her daydreams.

Shaking her head, she tugged around to face her brother, her cheeks reddening. 'I wasn't that hungry in the first place.' Not for bacon and eggs.

Zac said, 'We had a big dinner last night, didn't we, Maisie?'

She'd managed some crackers and cheese on her way to bed, and that was it. 'I'm not in any hurry. Sasha and I don't have to be at the shops the moment they open.'

'You don't know Sasha yet.' Liam grinned.

Standing up, Zac said, 'I'll go and sort out the rods and gear.'

'I'll give you a hand.' Liam stood too.

'And leave us the mess to clean up,' Maisie retorted.

Zac leaned his head around the doorframe and winked. 'Anything to keep you happy, Maisie.'

Her stomach crunched around the little she had eaten. If this was what falling in love with Zac was like, then she was in for a ride and a half. *If* he was in the other seat, and somehow she was starting to think he was, then it would be exhilarating. 'See you later.'

That evening Zac waited at the bar of the restaurant while Maisie popped into the bathroom. Something about checking her makeup which looked perfect to him, especially the mascara that highlighted the gold flecks in her eyes.

'What can I get you?' the barman asked.

'One Pinot Gris and a glass of beer, thanks. Make it the top brand of Pinot you've got.' Nothing was too good for his woman. His woman? There he went again. Leaning his elbows on the bar top, he watched the barman pour the wine, feeling more alive than he had in a long time. It was great to spend time with his mate on the lake, rods out as they talked. Even better being here with Maisie.

She and Sasha had gone into town in the morning after he and Liam left with the boat. Bonding, Liam called it, his voice filled with hope. The relationship with Sasha was serious. No surprise there. It was pretty damned obvious from the look of adoration in both Liam's and Sasha's eyes every time they glanced at each other.

'Another wedding coming up?' Zac had asked. Would this be the third after Mallory and Josue having tied the knot, and Jamie and Kayla about to?

Liam said quietly, 'I think so. You up for best man when I pop the question?'

'I'll give it some thought,' Zac joked around the lump growing in his throat. This was his closest mate talking about marriage. It was great news.

'You do that.'

Spending time with Liam was always good as he missed him now they lived in different parts of the country. They'd always got on well and understood each other. They'd spent the morning on the boat talking about everything and anything—except Maisie—and didn't catch any fish no matter how hard they tried.

'Hey, you look lonely.' Maisie came up beside him.

'Hardly. Just miles away.' Looking at her took his breath away. She was dressed to the nines in a stunning short blue and white dress that clung to her hips and breasts in a very seductive manner. This got harder by the day. 'How was your morning in town?'

'We did a bit of shopping, had a long coffee break, then lunch. Sasha's lovely, and Liam's so happy it makes *me* happy.'

'I got the same message. Another one down, you think?'

Her smile jerked, returned into place. 'I reckon. Zac...' She hesitated.

Wary of what was to come, he stalled her. 'I ordered you a wine. Is that okay?'

'Perfect.' Placing her hand over his and raising the hairs on his arm, she said with no smile, 'About last night. I don't want it hanging between us like a bomb about to go off.' She held up her other hand. 'We're okay today, but it's there, if you know what I mean.'

'I do.' The urge to detonate the bomb was huge.

At last she took her hand away, only to smooth that amazing dress over her thighs, tightening him further. 'You do?'

'Absolutely.' Reaching for the glass of beer as the barman placed it on the counter, he took a mouthful.

'Right.' She sounded disappointed about something.

What had he missed? Was he supposed to have leapt in and said, 'No, I don't know why I drew away when your mouth was so damned close I ached to cover it with mine, to taste you, to feel you react to me.' Because those were the words hovering on his lips right now. Words that once out there would not be retracted. Nor would he want them to be.

'You're fading out on me.' Her fingers ran across the back of his hand like she was playing a piano.

Playing with fire, more like. Shaking his head, he turned his hand over and held hers. 'Not even close, Maisie.'

Her eyes widened as she stared at their joined hands, and the tip of her tongue dampened her lower lip. 'Tell me. You want to follow up on last night?'

He didn't move, soaked up the warmth for a moment. 'Yes. I do.'

Her gaze turned onto him, and she smiled, a smile that cut to his heart and ramped up hope.

'Evening, you two.' Pippa and Ross cut through the need filling him like a wet blanket.

Maisie slowly withdrew her hand, the heat in her eyes fading just a little.

As was the heat below his belt.

The parents were quickly followed by Liam and Sasha, and everyone was shown to their table looking out at Lake Wakatipu. When Maisie looked to sit between her father and Liam her mother nudged her along to the seat next to where Zac was waiting. It was as though Pippa wanted them to be together.

'What wine are you drinking?' Ross asked his daughter.

Zac gave him the brand.

Ross's eyebrow rose and he looked to Maisie, then back at him, before giving a brief nod. 'Good choice. I'll get a bottle for the table.'

Liam piped up. 'Zac, you spoiling my sister, by any chance?'

Maisie leapt in. 'He knows better than to go for the cheap option when I'm around.'

'Wise man.' Liam grinned.

'I heard you're basically one of the family,' Sasha said to him.

'Absolutely. They all know me too well to be able to get away with anything.'

'Can we have that in writing?' Liam asked.

'I don't think so.' Zac glanced to his side and saw Maisie blush as she turned to talk to her mother. He upped the stakes. 'Naturally I spoil Maisie. It's my way of getting her attention.'

Her hair flicked over her shoulder as her head shot up, that blush deepening. The yellow specks in her eyes were brighter than normal. 'Keep bringing that wine and I'll do anything you ask.' Her next smile rocked him. Again they were on the same page.

So she would've kissed him last night if he hadn't pulled away? Hopefully she'd be willing later tonight if they managed to be alone. He slapped his forehead lightly while wanting to bang his thighs with frustration. Stepping up to the mark, showing his love, shouldn't be full of all these questions. He'd decided to go for Maisie, show her his love, and that meant doing something about it, not worrying about every breath either of them took.

'Anyone looked at the menu yet?' Liam asked.

'We've barely sat down.' Zac reached for his menu, and pretended to peruse it, glad the conversation had moved away from them.

Maisie touched his hand before turning away to her mother. 'When are we going to Dunedin next? I want to get some new jeans.'

Zac stared at the back of her head and thought about how that silky hair would feel running through his fingers. Straight hair that fell to her shoulders, a blond contrast to the blue of her dress shining in the gleam from the overhead lights. His hands tightened as he held onto the yearning gripping him. Now was not the time or place. Reaching for his glass he looked around and found Liam watching him, a cheeky smile on his face. Raising his glass, Zac nodded. 'Set a date soon, will you?' The man needed reminding who'd been talking about marriage that morning.

His friend raised his beer in return. 'You'll be the second to know.'

Zac sighed. If only it was that simple. To be so certain of his future would let him sleep at night again.

'Glad we brought two cars,' Maisie said quietly to Zac when everyone was preparing to leave the restaurant. 'I don't want to be a spare wheel with Liam and Sasha. It's enough to be sharing the apartment.'

'There's still my spare room.' He'd get to spend time alone with her. Another reason apart from driving not to have had more than one beer all night.

Maisie raised her face to look straight at him. 'I know.' Her breasts rose on a sigh.

A knot tightened in his gut. Another near-kiss coming up? He sensed yes was the answer to that too. Near-kiss or go for broke and really kiss her. Deep and long. Learn more about *his* Maisie.

Liam's laughter broke through his daydream, reminding him that Maisie would probably go back to her bed tonight. He took her hand, then dropped it and took her elbow. 'Let's get out of here.'

Her smile was soft and full of warmth as she slid her hand back into his. 'Let's.'

He didn't break any speed limits but it seemed as though they got to the apartment quicker than usual. Inside he switched on only the kitchen light, leaving the lounge in a soft half-light. While he made coffee Maisie sat on a stool, watching him. Did she feel something for him? He'd never been so insecure, not even with his parents. She hadn't slapped him down for holding her face and nearly kissing her last night. 'Maisie.' He went around to her side of the counter. 'About last night...' He paused because she was regarding him with tenderness and something like hope in her face.

'What about it?' she asked when he didn't continue.

'I didn't finish what I started.'

'*We* didn't.'

Her hand caressed his chin. Then his cheek. Then her finger traced his mouth. 'I know I didn't show it, but I didn't like it when you left.'

His lungs squeezed, sending air gushing out. Reaching for her, his hands on her waist, he brought her close to him so he felt her breasts pushing against his chest, her hips touching his, her stomach touching him where he was pulsing. Lowering his head, he placed his mouth on those gorgeous lips and savoured her. Her lips were soft and full and were kissing him back. He wanted more. Needed to taste her, to lose himself in her kiss. His tongue pressed between her lips, touched her heat. His arms wound around her body to bring her into him.

This was his Maisie. The woman he dreamed about, longed to know completely. The woman he needed to share himself with. To love and be loved by.

Zac pulled his mouth away. Felt the loss immediately. He stared into the beautiful face so close to his. Maisie. If there'd been any doubt before there wasn't a drop now. He loved her. Totally. She was his life. And he had to protect her. From being hurt again if they got things wrong. But they wouldn't. He loved her.

'Zac? What's wrong?' The doubt and worry in her voice made him drop his arms fast before he could pull her back into his embrace and kiss her senseless.

Stepping back, he rubbed his hands down his face. Like he was trying to remove that kiss. But he wasn't; it was there to stay. 'Sorry, this is tricky.' It was all very well deciding to go forward with Maisie and put his love on the line, but when it came to it, he was afraid of losing her altogether.

'Thanks a lot.' Her lips were quivering. 'I think I'd better go if that's the best you can come up with.'

'Maisie, think about it. We're friends, always have been. I don't want to lose that. Do you?'

'Do we have to?'

'I don't know, and that's why I've stopped. I can't risk it.'

She stood up and took his hands in hers. 'I am going to kiss you. Zac.' She paused, her eyes intense, her mouth soft.

He didn't move for a long moment. His heart was pumping hard, his head light. Everything he wanted was right there, waiting for him. 'The hell with this.'

Reaching for her, he lowered his mouth to hers. 'Not before I kiss you first.'

She fell into him as her arms slipped behind his head. Soft, hard, gentle, strong. Her mouth opened under his lips.

The taste of her. Man alive. This was nectar. Maisie beyond his dreams.

The softness of her backside under his hands. Hot, firm, unbelievable.

More than his dreams had ever come up with. More than he could have believed.

'Maisie.' His Maisie.

'Shut up and keep kissing me.'

No problem. It was all he wanted to do right now.

Bang.

'What the...?' Zac jerked back.

'Maisie, you here? I forgot my key?'

Liam Bloody Rogers.

Zac held Maisie to him, not wanting to let her go for a second.

'In my bag by the door,' she called, her hand gripping his waist.

'You guys joining us for a nightcap? Or shall we come up?'

Zac sighed. 'No getting away from them this time.' For once he would've enjoyed telling his friend to go away. 'Come on up.'

Against him, Maisie sighed in frustration. 'Everything seems against us.'

CHAPTER SEVEN

MAISIE'S HEART TRIPPED. The screen on her phone showed Zac. He hadn't been over earlier to spend more time with Liam and Sasha before they left for the airport which had made her uncomfortable. Did he regret their kisses? She'd been steamed up and ready to go where she'd never been before with Zac when her brother interrupted them. Had Liam's arrival caused Zac to rethink what was happening between them?

Zac, who was calling her right now. Deep breath, fingers crossed that he might want to spend some time with her. 'Hello, where were you at breakfast time?'

'Sorry about that but I got called into work. Now I'm ringing around getting the S and R team ready. You available?'

'Of course.' Settle, heart. 'What've we got?'

'A thirty-year-old man has been missing on Ben Lomond since late yesterday afternoon. Gear up for wind and snow, and possibly an overnighter. I'll pick you up in fifteen.' Gone.

Fair enough. Zac would have others to phone and plans to make.

But her heart was sluggish as she gathered up her outdoor gear and stuffed a jersey and jacket in her backpack. This wasn't getting her anywhere. If Zac wasn't prepared to talk to her, then why had he kissed her in the first place? Like, seriously kissed her as though she meant everything to him. Or was he just a good kisser and she'd fallen further under his spell? No, Zac wouldn't treat her like that. He'd meant every last touch and taste when he kissed her. As she had, returning his kiss with everything she had, everything she felt for Zac, even the confusion about where they were headed.

Filling her water bottle, Maisie focused on the job in hand, because right now that was more important. Someone had been missing since yesterday close to town and the search crew hadn't been called in hours ago? What was wrong with people? This happened more often than she'd realised until she became an S and R member. Someone thought another person would've heard and didn't follow up to find out, and then suddenly urgency flared when it became clear their friend hadn't returned. Hard to imagine what they were feeling now they knew there might be a serious problem with their friend.

This would be her first hike up the mountains on a search. Quietly confident about her walking for many hours and her medical abilities, a vague unease sat in her mind. She was used to tragic scenarios in a hospital with all the backup she required, but out in the wilderness would be different. No fancy equipment, no doctors to make decisions.

Zac's smile when he pulled in with Jamie to pick her up had her toes curling. 'Morning, Mais.'

Happiness swamped her. All was good. She'd been overthinking things. 'Morning, Zac. And Jamie,' she added as an afterthought when he looked over the seat at her.

'The man's friends didn't think anything of it when he didn't turn up for a prearranged dinner last night. Figured he was too tired after his walk up the mountain. It was only this morning when a friend went to see why he hadn't been at breakfast that it was realised he'd never returned from his walk,' Zac told her and Jamie as he drove them to the collection point at the bottom of Ben Lomond. 'Apparently he often goes on walks alone. The problem being he's an Australian from Perth and not used to our mountainous terrain and he wouldn't have recognised that snow was on its way.'

'Didn't people warn him?' It never failed to amaze Maisie how some people went for a walk without first checking out weather conditions which around this area could change from calm to stormy in very little time.

'Seems not. He was heading up the track to the top which, since he's supposedly fit, should've taken four to five hours,' Zac said.

'Next you're going to say he didn't have any food with him,' Jamie said.

'You got it.'

'You've got to be kidding,' Maisie muttered.

'Welcome to Search and Rescue.' Zac tossed her a grin. 'He's not the first, and he won't be the last. How many sandwiches did you pack?'

'More than enough to share around.' She laughed to ease the tension in her shoulders, put there more by Zac's presence than the missing man's situation at this point. 'I presume there's a thermal blanket in the medical kit?' There was one in her day pack if needed, and an extra bottle of water.

'First thing to get packed every time. The dogs are coming too, though not Shade. Mallory had her at the vet yesterday.'

'She's got an infected foot where she tore a pad playing on the beach.' Mallory had phoned yesterday afternoon, needing a shoulder to cry on since Josue was at work. The baby had colic and wouldn't settle. Shade's problems weren't too bad but Mallory always worried about her pet. They'd talked for nearly an hour with baby Jess crying her lungs out for most of the time while Mallory paced the house.

'What's the plan of attack?' Jamie asked.

'The guy sent photos to a work mate from the top yesterday and mentioned it was getting very windy. We start at the bottom and work our way up, some on the track heading up fast to begin looking around up there while others branch out left and right. Though how anyone could lose their way when the track is very clear is beyond me. It's well marked all the way.'

'I hope he had extra warm clothing,' Maisie thought aloud. 'Otherwise he's going to be hypothermic. Probably will be anyway. That snowstorm might've been short but on the news they were saying it was brutal.' She shivered, thinking about being stranded in that.

Zac pulled in behind other four-wheel-drive vehicles. 'Let's get this happening.'

Maisie followed as he strode across to the group of searchers all dressed in heavy outdoor clothing and strong boots. His head was high and his shoulders back. Zac in action mode. He loved getting out amongst it and helping people, using his skills and knowledge for others. This was happy Zac. Then she shivered. As long as the outcome went well. Not that he'd blame himself if it didn't. They should've been called in hours ago.

'Here's what we know.' Zac rattled off the scant facts, and then put everyone in teams. 'Maisie, you stay with me in case your medical skills are required. We're going up the track to the top with Jamie and Terry and his dog. The guy's name is Martin Cross. Spread out, everyone, and keep in touch.'

Yes. She mentally fist-pumped. More time with Zac. Great. Maisie slipped her backpack on and then lifted the medical kit out of the vehicle. Guess her medical skills were the focus on who she went with and as they were heading straight up to where the chances of finding this man were more likely it made sense. Glad something did, she sighed.

'I'll take that.' Zac reached for the kit, his arm brushing hers.

'I can carry it,' she laughed. 'I'm not a toddler.'

'Maybe, but that's why I've got a large pack—it fits in neatly.' His hand touched hers as he took the strap, sending sparks up her arm. It was as though he couldn't help himself, needed to be making contact.

She got it. They were going to be walking up Ben

Lomond together and she was already in a lather about him. Hard not to be when her hands could still feel his muscular shoulders where she'd held tight last night. 'Fine.' She let go her grip on the kit. Arguing over who carried it was a waste of precious time. The most important thing to be doing was to get moving and find the Aussie alive.

Following Zac was hard work. His long legs ate up the ground at a steady pace that wasn't too difficult to keep up with. But just being right behind him and watching how his muscles worked under the fitted fabric of his trousers made her mouth water. It had to be the walking that had her heart beating harder than normal. Had to be. A groan filled with lust escaped her. Okay, maybe not.

Zac glanced over his shoulder. 'You okay?'

'Yes.' Sort of. This was going to be a long day. Unless they found the Aussie in the next half hour. What were the chances? Pretty slim, she reckoned. There were no footprints in what was left of the snow on the track. He had to be above them, or had gone off the track before the snow arrived so any signs of his movements would've been covered during the storm. After a night in the freezing temperatures he'd most likely be struggling to walk down. The best thing he could've done was to find shelter under a tree or bush and curl up to hold in what warmth he could, but people struggled with that concept. Their first reaction was to move, try and find their way out, not realising that made it harder for rescuers to track them down. To remain in one place, alone, hungry, thirsty, frightened, even injured had to be very hard to do, yet it gave people the best chance of survival.

The track widened so Maisie stepped up to walk beside Zac, to heck with not talking. No muscles in sight now which was a bonus for her heart rate. 'I'm picking this guy will be hypothermic.' Hadn't she already said that earlier? 'And possibly injured.'

'Nothing we can do until we find him,' Zac said.

'I get that, and I was just chatting.'

'Sure.' Of course he was experienced in these rescues and wouldn't want to discuss the obvious. He probably suspected she might want to talk about them, and was trying to avoid that.

Maisie slowed to let him go ahead again. Better to watch his legs than talk about the obvious and have him wishing she hadn't joined S and R. Concentrating on where she put her feet, Maisie focused on the climb and tried to ignore Zac. Which was a complete fail. How could she when he was only metres in front of her, striding out while constantly scanning their surroundings? Tall, strong, beautiful. The man of her dreams. He'd always been there, and now this was for real.

Someone to the side of them called out, 'Martin, can you hear me?'

Maisie held her breath, and felt the silence chill her.

After two hours they stopped for a break, sipped water while Zac called up the rest of the search teams one by one to see how they were doing. Everyone was making good progress, but bottom line, there'd been no sign of the missing man.

'Not even a footprint,' Zac muttered as they climbed higher and higher.

Maisie shivered, pulled her jacket sleeves further down around her wrists. 'He's not going to be in good shape.'

'So you keep saying.' Zac elbowed her arm lightly. 'Try a bit of positivity here, will you?' he added with a smile.

'You're right. He's probably got a fire going and is cooking a rabbit over it as we speak.'

Zac actually laughed, a full happy Zac laugh. 'Hope he leaves some for us.'

Maisie pulled a face. 'I don't think so.' She was besotted with him and still afraid of the consequences if they didn't get it right. Not as tough as she'd thought, huh? Focusing on the track she saved her breath for the walk. Better than saying something that'd change the mood between them again.

Despondency fell over the rescuers when they all congregated at the top.

'No signs of anyone up here on the main track since the snow began,' Jamie said after other searchers had reported negative results.

'Not even the dogs are picking up on a scent to follow,' a dog handler commented. 'Are we sure this guy didn't make it back to town and has left to go elsewhere with no one knowing?'

Zac was wandering along the ridge. 'He's not answering his phone. There could always be a reason for that, I suppose.' He pointed to the far side of the mountain they'd come up. 'Surely he wouldn't have gone down that way? That's the way to all sorts of difficulties for an inexperienced climber.'

'Why would he do that? There are signs showing the track goes back down the way he'd have come up. Nothing indicates a way down to town there,' Maisie said.

'It's possible if he's disorientated,' Jamie said.

'True.' Back to the hypothermia. Or, 'Could he have fallen? Hit his head? Broken a leg and tried to crawl back to the track and lost his way?'

'We won't know until we find him,' Zac said. 'We'll take a break and have some food and hot drinks.'

The day wore on, and no sign of the missing man. Everyone was getting tired and despair was rife.

'Where is he?' Zac growled. 'No one's seen him in town.' He held his phone up. 'His girlfriend's waiting at home for him and she's heard nothing.'

They'd been up and down the mountainside, scrambled over banks and slogged through the long grass out in the open. As the sun dropped behind the ranges everyone met up at a bush hut on the far side of Ben Lomond. 'Take a well-earned break,' Zac told them, while Maisie heated up water for tea and coffee.

Earlier a chopper pilot had flown in precooked food for everyone and it was quickly devoured.

Sitting down beside Zac, Maisie struggled to suppress a yawn. 'I'm going to feel every muscle tomorrow.'

Zac's gaze cruised her legs, up her body and stopped when her eyes locked with him. 'You're doing fine. We all feel it when we're out so long.'

The shiver that rocked her had nothing to do with

the chill in the air. The heat in Zac's gaze made her blood simmer while her skin tightened with longing. Not what she should be feeling while out trying to find a man who'd been lost now for more than twenty-four hours. 'I need to get fitter.' And more used to seeing that look in Zac's face.

'Nothing wrong with you.'

My fitness? Or me in general?

Glancing around, she was reminded they weren't alone. So no questions. 'How long will we stop this time?'

'About an hour. We all need to recharge our batteries. We may be fit and agile, but our bodies need nourishing and a rest. There could be many hours walking ahead.' Zac chattered easily now. 'The helicopter's returning around then to use the night vision gear to sweep the mountainside and cover areas none of us have been able to get to. Including the back of the mountain, just in case.'

'I guess there's no such thing as an impossible area when searching for someone like this. The man must be frightened, worried sick about whether he'll make it out.' She couldn't imagine being in that situation. Stuck, alone, lost, maybe in pain. This time her shiver was for the Aussie. 'We've got to find him—alive.'

'We will.'

'That's your go-to, isn't it?' Typical Zac. Positive until proven wrong. Could he apply that to them and their changing relationship? Or could he already have done so, and become worried it could all go wrong, hence his partial withdrawal today?

'What other choice is there?' His grin was a little crooked, his eyes a little darker. 'Probably why I take losing so hard.'

'You didn't lose your last case.' Reaching over she squeezed his hand before withdrawing, hopefully giving Zac something to think about. Something that'd warm him and straighten that grin.

One of the dogs stood up, nose in the air.

'What's up, Boss?' Terry asked.

Woof-woof. Sniff, sniff.

'He's scenting the breeze,' Terry noted.

Zac was instantly alert, hope filling his face.

Everyone was on their feet, looking around, peering through the near darkness.

'Hello. Anyone out there? Martin, is that you?'

Maisie was holding her breath, her lungs beginning to ache. Silence reigned other than the breeze stirring the grass and bushes.

'Terry, give Boss his head,' Zac advised. 'Let's see what he finds. Everyone else spread out behind him.'

Zac called out, 'Come on, everyone. Leave your gear here. If we don't find him soon we'll spend the night in the hut.' He pulled a map out of his pack. 'I'll take another look at the map and see if we're missing something. Though I've done countless searches up here and must know the place fairly well,' he added in an aside to her.

'Every person's reactions to being lost will be different though. What if he's hidden himself for shelter and can't get out again because of an injury? Not easy to find then.'

The quiet night was broken with the thumping of rotors as the helicopter suddenly rose up over the back of Ben Lomond. Everyone paused, watching the movements of the aircraft and where the pilot was concentrating his search. No one wanted to create difficulties by showing up on the second pilot's night goggles.

Zac bent down in a huddle to talk to the pilot on his radio. 'They're going to sweep the steep areas further down the back, leaving the higher inclines to us,' he informed everyone. 'Spread out.'

Torches began lighting up the area randomly, slicing the darkness with sharp beams. Forty minutes later… *Woof-woof.* Boss was sniffing the air, this time in the direction of an area where there was no track.

Maisie moved forward to peer around, picking out bushes, searching their shadows with her torch. Nothing. Boss paced ahead, nose sniffing, head up, and she followed behind Terry. 'Where, boy? Show me.'

They went downwards, across the open grass, towards the bush line, in the opposite direction of the chopper. Behind she heard others talking, saw their torchlight flitting everywhere. 'Hello? Martin, are you there?'

Woof-woof. The dog ran to a bush, stopped and wagged his tail.

Really? Could they have found their man?

A cough. From behind the bush.

'Martin? Is that you?' She ran around the gorse and stumbled to a halt. 'Oh, thank goodness.' A man sat with his jacket wrapped tight around his body, shaking and crying. 'We've found you at last.'

Terry brushed past her. 'Man, are we glad to see you.'

Then Zac was there. 'You're Martin Cross?'

The man nodded, and wiped his sleeve across his face. 'I so happy to see you guys. I thought I was done for.' His voice was hoarse, his body shaking.

Zac pulled out his radio and called the pilots. 'We've found our man. Will let you know what the situation is shortly.'

Maisie dropped to her knees beside him. 'Hi, I'm Maisie and I'm a nurse. Have you hurt yourself anywhere?'

'I think my arm's broken.' He'd tucked the right arm under his jersey.

She'd leave it as it was. Moving it would cause unnecessary pain. 'Did you fall?'

He nodded. 'I think so. Sort of remember sliding down the hill.' His memory wasn't great.

'Anything else hurting?' Maisie took his wrist to check his pulse.

'Just a h-headache, and sometimes I seemed to forget where I am. I can't believe you found me.' His speech was slurred and his eyes blinking.

'Have you been drinking water all the time you've been out here?'

'I lost my bottle when I fell. I tried m-melting snow in my m-mouth.'

'What about food?'

'A s-sandwich and a-apple y-yesterday when I r-reached the top.'

Maisie turned to Zac. 'Can we have—?' She smiled and took the thermal blanket he was holding out to her.

'Thanks.' *Great minds think alike.* 'Martin, we need to get you wrapped in this. It'll give you some warmth.'

'I've never struck temperatures like they were last night, and today hasn't been much better.' The man gave a weak smile.

Zac had a bottle of water at the ready. 'I'll help you with that blanket,' he said.

'Thanks, mate.'

'What do you think?' Zac asked as she helped wind the blanket tight around Martin's shoulders. 'Anything other than hypothermia and a fractured arm—if it is?'

'I'm treating it as broken for now. He might have a mild concussion.' She'd checked Martin over. 'He moves his legs freely enough, pulse and breathing are normal. I think we can get him to walk to the clearing to be airlifted out, but I'll be keeping an eye on him every step of the way.'

'I'll let them know.'

'Mostly, he needs to be warm and dry, and get some liquids and food on board.'

'Aka a chopper ride to hospital.' Zac smiled at her. 'The best outcome.'

Her stomach squeezed. 'Yes, definitely.' In lots of ways. They were comfortable together. Sexual tension had come into their relationship and it felt wonderful. As if she'd turned a corner with Zac. This feeling was underlining her feelings and waking her up to how hard it might be to remain uninvolved. She didn't want to walk away from that kiss and the emotions Zac had provoked. She wanted to follow up and have more encounters like that, encounters that led to deeper love and a future. But also, she could never lose him as a friend. Lovers could be friends, but could lovers go back to being just friends if this new relationship didn't pan out?

Confusion almost overwhelmed her. Throw in aching muscles from all the walking she'd done today. Add the relief over finding their man alive and well. Then more relief at how she and Zac had finally gone from cold to warm with each other again, and she was shattered. A hot chocolate and a plate of fries wasn't going to suddenly appear to fix this, but the canned soup and tea back in the hut might go some way to easing the stiffness in her body. A hug from Zac would definitely work to make her feel more comfortable.

'Guess we're up for a night in the hut,' Zac announced to the group after Martin had been airlifted off the mountain. They'd reached the hut where everyone had left their gear. 'Unless anyone wants to walk out now, but I wouldn't recommend it in these pitch-dark conditions.'

Maisie sat down beside Zac with a sigh and leaned against him. 'It's too good to get the weight off my feet to be wanting to walk further now.'

'I should've sent you back on the chopper. As a nurse,' he added when she raised her head to stare at him.

'I wouldn't have gone, so don't go all protective on me. Anyway, there wasn't any room with Lynn on board as well.' The woman had slipped and sprained her ankle as they'd made their way to the helicopter with Martin. Perfect timing, really.

Zac pulled her back beside him. 'Glad you're here?'

'You bet.' She winked. 'So, shall I start heating soup for everyone?'

'Got to get the fire going first,' Zac pointed out.

'On to it,' someone called out from inside the hut. 'We're going to be squashed in on the bunks tonight.'

Zac stood up and reached for both their packs. 'We're in the corner.'

Together? Better than being squeezed between two people she didn't know well. 'Sounds perfect.' Lying next to Zac, maybe cuddle up a bit once everyone was asleep, had to be the best end to a long day. The best they could manage in a hut full of people.

Everyone made short work of the soup and mugs of tea and were soon sprawled out in sleeping bags on the wooden bunks made for six people. 'What's wrong with ordinary bunks?' Maisie asked as she wriggled into her sleeping bag. Not that she was complaining since Zac had scored the two spots nearest the wall. On a regular bunk they wouldn't have been sharing a mattress.

'There's only space for three of those, whereas this way means up to a dozen can fit in,' Jamie answered. 'Crammed as it may be.'

'Lights out, guys,' Zac laughed as he lay down beside her.

The fire was still burning, giving off quite a glow, but hopefully it would die down fast as no one had restacked it once the soup and water had been heated.

Maisie was next to the wall. For once she was grateful for Zac taking over because it meant she didn't have a stranger on that side, and only Zac could touch her or bump into her through the night. How cosy, lying here with him, even though they were in sleeping bags and there were ten other people in the hut.

It got even cosier when the room got darker and Zac wrapped an arm around her waist, snuggled in behind her. His breath was light on her neck where her hair had fallen onto the bundle of clothes that was her pillow. Rolling carefully, she touched his face with her fingers. 'Hey,' she whispered.

'Hey, yourself,' he whispered back.

Along the bench someone was snoring, and someone else muttered, 'Shut up, Harry.'

Rolling onto her back, she laughed softly. 'This reminds me of going camping with my classmates at high school.'

'Who held you then?'

'No one.' She hadn't had a serious boyfriend back then. And Zac had turned her down.

'I probably scared him off,' Zac laughed not so quietly, raising a growl from the other end of the hut.

Maisie smiled to herself. The first time she got to sleep with Zac and they were in a hut with a crowd. 'We're not very good at this.' If he was going to back off again, then she was going to make it hard for him. Okay, rephrase that. Make it difficult. There had been longing in his face last night when he'd kissed her. He couldn't deny it. There was longing for Zac in her heart she wasn't going to deny either. They had to follow through and see where they got.

'Roll over,' he whispered. 'I'm going to hold you.'

'Yes, boss.' She wriggled and turned, trying not to tangle her legs in the sleeping bag.

'Better believe it.' A light kiss landed on the back of her neck.

Her heart slowed, soft with love. Yes, Zac was the man for her. They had a long way to go to be one hundred percent certain of what they were doing but she was ready to try. Then she tensed. She was still guessing at what Zac felt. Could've got it all wrong.

'Maisie?'

Twisting so she could speak quietly, she asked, 'Is this for real?'

The ensuing silence was finally interrupted by a loud snore.

Her heart thudded heavily. He wasn't answering. She was wrong. She'd have to forget pushing forward. Giving up that easily? No, she wouldn't. No.

'Yes, I think it is.' The words were soft and slow, and purred across her skin.

Relief sighed out of her lungs, and she snuggled closer to that divine body behind her. If only the sleeping bags weren't between them.

CHAPTER EIGHT

IT SEEMED TO take for ever to hike back down to the car park where their vehicles were. Maisie chuckled to herself. Zac thought she didn't realise he was keeping an eye out for her, making sure she was managing now that the search was over. She was feeling a bit flat. Her adrenaline had deserted her after they'd found the Australian, but lying with Zac had made her happy so all in all she felt pretty damned good.

Shoving her pack into the back of his four-wheel-drive, she dug her phone out of her jacket pocket and pressed the number for work. 'Hello, Jill. Sorry but I'm going to be late.' She went on to explain where she was.

'Not a problem. We're not busy yet. Take as long as you want when you get home. I'll call if you're needed later.'

'Thanks. You're a champ.'

'You owe me,' Jill laughed and hung up.

Placing her phone in the console, she clipped her seat belt in place and leaned back to close her eyes. 'I can smell bacon and eggs.' As if. But wouldn't they be great right about now.

'You cooking?' Zac asked.

'Not likely. There's not much left in my fridge after my visitors. I'll grab something at the canteen when I get to the hospital.'

'Unfortunately work doesn't stop because we've been out all night.' Zac turned onto the metal road, heading back to town. That hand that had been splayed across her stomach most of the night was now spread over his thigh. 'You're on day shift, then?'

'Yep. I'll hang around at the end to make up for my late arrival—unless it's so quiet I'm not needed. That doesn't happen often though.' None of them usually walked off on time, mainly because they didn't just finish a conversation with a child or their parents when the time hit three o'clock or whatever shift-finish they had. 'What about you?'

'Depends what's going down, but I usually make up any hours I've missed. I've got a court appearance in Dunedin tomorrow that I need to run through all the details for again, so it's probably going to be a long day for me.' He glanced across, then in the rearview mirror. 'Jamie? You on days or nights this week?'

'Nights, so I get to go home and unwind over bacon and eggs and anything else Kayla might spoil me with.' He laughed.

Maisie had almost forgotten he was with them. She turned to growl, 'You're so mean.'

'I know.' He was smiling.

Facing forward, she closed her eyes again, mainly to stop staring at Zac. She'd got it bad, if she had to do that. Not that it mattered she wasn't looking at him.

Her head was full of memories of being held against him, feeling his stomach against her lower back, his thighs against hers, his breath on her neck. And that hand spread wide over her front. Her mouth slipped on a smile. Oh, yes, she'd had a wonderful night and not done much at all. Life was getting better by the day. Make that, by the hour.

Zac pulled up outside the fire station where Jamie's vehicle was parked. 'See you later.'

'S and R training this week,' Jamie reminded them.

She couldn't complain about not having enough to keep her busy, and even better, Zac would be there too.

'I probably won't make it. I'm in Dunedin tomorrow and Wednesday.'

Okay, so Zac wouldn't be at training. She'd survive. This sense of being a part of his life was surreal when they'd always been there for each other but not as a couple.

You're not quite a couple yet.

True. Reality didn't dampen her mood. Happiness had a way of keeping the doomsayer in her head quiet.

As they drove away, Zac said, 'I can rustle up some breakfast while you're in the shower. It won't make you any later than grabbing a bite in the canteen, and will be tastier.'

She didn't need to rush now that Jill knew what was going on. 'Won't you be late?'

'Do I look worried? The later I start the later I'll leave tonight, that's all.'

She smiled. 'You're on.' Then she yawned. 'If I don't turn up within half an hour I've probably fallen asleep in the shower.' Now there was a thought. Wet skin, warm water, slick hands. *Shut up.* She blushed. This blushing was becoming a habit. Hadn't had a shower with Zac ever. The heat deepened. 'I'll set the alarm on my phone just in case.'

'Damn.'

'What?'

'Nothing.' He swung into their communal driveway. 'See you soon.'

Okay, obviously she was meant to get out fast and not ask what he meant. It was tempting to stir some trouble, but in real life she had a job to get to sooner than later. 'I'll be fast.' But not so fast that she didn't soak away the aches in her calf muscles and back. Or wash her hair to get rid of the knots accumulated from rubbing against her makeshift pillow during the night. She must look like something out of a horror movie this morning, especially once she removed her woollen hat.

'Take your time. I'll grab a shower too before I start cooking breakfast.'

Closing the door before she came out with something about showers and them getting closer, she went into her apartment and dropped the pack on the entrance floor. She'd deal to it when she got home from work.

The plate Zac handed her a while later was laden. 'Get that into you.'

'A full English breakfast. That looks delicious.' Hard to imagine she'd eat even half of it, but she was about to give it a try. 'I'll get the coffee.'

'Sit down. I've got it sorted.'

They ate in a comfortable silence, Maisie barely

aware of the time ticking by. She had been told when she started the job that hospital management understood she was a volunteer with S and R and would make certain she could work with both, but she didn't want to abuse their acceptance.

Zac suddenly broke the silence. 'About the award ceremony.'

'I got the feeling you only mentioned it because you knew Liam would say something.'

He swallowed his mouthful and put down his knife and fork, pushed the plate aside. Picking up his coffee, he took a gulp. 'I feel uncomfortable about being recognised for bravery.' She opened her mouth to say something but he shook his head. 'Listen. I know I took the bullet that was meant for the captain, but still, it was a shocking scene with all hell going down. Everyone reacted instinctively. I didn't deliberately think, "The boss's going to get killed so I'll step in front of him and take the knock." It just happened.'

'I guess so.'

'That's it? I'm not going to get a speech?' Relief filled his smile.

'We've been over this enough times for me to know how you feel. It's awesome your bravery is being recognised, and don't argue, you are brave. Others might've kept out of the way and saved their own bacon—instinctively or not.'

'Knew I shouldn't have relaxed so soon. You were always going to have a crack at me.' He was still smiling though. 'Right, further to that. So we'll be away for the night. I'll book rooms at the hotel the ceremony's being held.'

Shock made her eyes pop wide, and her mouth open. Forget how her heart was reacting. It was going nuts. She hadn't thought about where they'd stay. Zac had said rooms. What about one room to share? 'I can't wait.' Unexpected happiness surged through her. She'd be his partner for the night. *Woo-hoo*. 'Will it be a formal occasion?' A new dress was a must-have. She'd definitely need to go to Dunedin shopping with her mother now.

'Black tie event. I'll have to hire a suit.'

'Hire one? Go all out for once and buy one. Shoes, the black tie, a perfect shirt, the whole works.' Zac didn't go overboard with clothes, more an off the rack kind of guy.

'Now who's being bossy?' He was laughing, like suddenly he wanted to go to this ceremony. With her at his side!

Maisie watched him over the rim of her mug. Sitting beside him at the table, standing up to applaud as he walked up to get his award. How amazing was that? 'Another step in the right direction for us.'

'Are you okay with that?'

'More than okay, ecstatic,' she admitted. 'We are changing, being together in a different way. I'm still not sure where we're headed yet but I'm liking how we're doing.' *And* she knew where she wanted to go.

He suddenly looked floored, making her feel like a spoilsport.

Had she gone too far? Probably, but that was how she tried to deal with problems these days. 'Funny how we've known each other all our lives and yet now I feel I don't know you. Not entirely, or how I thought I did anyhow.'

'Do we ever know a person that well? I doubt it. There must be things a person keeps to themselves, even those they grow up with.'

Talk about the strangest conversation. Could be it was time no matter what went down. Except they both had to get to work. Draining her mug, Maisie smiled. 'As usual, our timing sucks.'

Standing up, he reached for her hand. 'You're right. We both need get out of here and on our way to our other lives.'

Slipping off her chair, Maisie cuddled into him, still holding his hand. 'Thanks for breakfast.'

Zac wound his arms around her, drew her close before lowering his mouth to hers. She pushed up into his kiss, devouring him with her lips, setting her blood humming, her heart banging. She wanted him. Even better, he wanted her. It was obvious in the solid shape pushing into her stomach. When his hands rubbed over her butt, she struggled to remain upright, the need pouring through, her buckling her knees. Who knew kisses could be like this? Not her, for sure.

Pulling back, Zac tucked a stray strand of hair behind Maisie's ear. 'You don't know what you're doing to me.'

Her fingers traced his jawline. 'Oh, I think do, because you're doing it back just as much.'

'How long have you felt this way about me?' he asked.

That was direct. 'For a while. You want a date for when I started noticing you as a man, not a friend?'

'This is an unusual situation to find ourselves in and I don't want either of us to end up regretting anything we might do.'

'I agree, but I want to find out if we're on the right track.'

'How about we date? Go out for dinner, to the pub, for walks, whatever takes our interest, and see how that goes?'

Yes. She mentally fist-pumped. 'Perfect.'

'Can we treat this relationship as though we're new to each other?'

'You're still saying we're not to rush things?' Like that'll be easy after she knew his kisses were dynamite.

'Something like that.' A wry look filled his face. 'Not saying it'll be a piece of cake to hold off from rushing you into bed, but I don't want to wake up there one morning to find we got it wrong. Know what I mean?'

'Wednesday night when you get back from Dunedin let's go to dinner at Scuzzi's. Might as well start out how I intend to go on.'

Zac stared at her, laughter filling his eyes and lifting his mouth. 'You have changed. Or I never really knew you. Bring it on.' He glanced at his watch. 'And now we'd better get a wiggle on or the bosses will be sending squad cars out to pick us up and deliver us to our respective jobs.'

She brushed a light kiss over his chin. 'See you tonight.'

I know I want you, Zac Lowe, more than I've ever wanted a man before.

Maisie hummed as she drove to the hospital. Not

even Paul had rattled her this much. He'd never made her feel as if her world was crumbling inwards into a pool of heat and love, into what her life was meant to be. Something about the serious way Zac'd said they'd start dating more told her he loved her, wanted the whole deal. As did she.

Going on dates would be exciting. It was very different to having a beer at the pub with others or picking up each other's dry cleaning in town. She hadn't dated in years, and could still remember the magic of meeting a man and getting to know him, deciding if there was more to find or it was time to leave. She couldn't see herself ever leaving Zac.

Zac dressed in new navy trousers and a crisp new light blue shirt, then slipped into his black leather jacket, and studied the image in the mirror. 'Not bad.' Hopefully Maisie would be impressed.

Tossing the car keys in the air he caught them and whistled his favourite tune. 'I'm going on a date with the woman of my dreams.'

Maisie took his breath away as she stepped down her stairway to meet him at the front door. Her hair shone under the light. The lime-green dress she wore accentuated every curve and swelling so his heart could barely beat it was so full of need and love. And they were supposed to play good? Not going to be easy, if even possible. But he would because this was the most important thing he'd ever done, making sure they both understood what they were getting into. Love, commitment and family, hopefully with her family's encouragement.

'You look fabulous.' He took her hand and led her outside to the car. 'You know it's a long time since I've been on a date like this.'

Where I'm not thinking just about having a good time and not getting involved.

'Long time since I dated, full stop.'

And she'd broken the drought with him. *Yes.* Opening the passenger door, he said, 'Your chariot awaits.'

She laughed. 'Don't go overboard or I might change my mind about who I'm dating.'

'Not in this lifetime.'

They kept up the banter on the short drive to the restaurant, and then throughout the meal. It was relaxing and fun, and something he hadn't known for a long time. But as they were sipping coffee after their dessert, Zac suddenly asked, 'What do you honestly think your family will think about us being together?'

'They'll be happy.' Hazel eyes were firmly locked on him. 'Why do you ask? No one was glowering at us at dinner.'

'Just wondering if they might be shocked since I've been a part of your family most of my life.' He was backing off, not explaining everything suddenly welling up inside him.

'I'm not buying that, Zac. I understand what you're saying in that we've always been close but that won't stop my family from accepting you as my partner.'

'My feelings for you have changed, become more intense.' So much for holding back. 'Along with that, I worry if we get it wrong, then I'll lose you as a friend, as well as Liam, Pippa and Ross. Just saying.'

Those beautiful eyes locked on him. 'Zac, I'm more than ready to go on this journey together. I'm presuming you want more than a hot fling?'

He reached for her hand, squeezed tight. 'Absolutely. I haven't lied about my feelings once.'

Maisie blinked, then straightened her back. 'You know what? We're adults and make our own choices in life. I don't have a problem with my family and nor should you. I've made stuff up before and still have good relationships with them. The same goes for you. I've been afraid to step across the line and admit how I feel about you, but not any more. I care for you, Zac. A lot.'

A smile began lifting the corners of his mouth and wiping away the frown that had settled on his brow. 'Want to go for a walk along the lake edge?'

'No, take me back to your apartment, Zac.'

His apartment. Zac's heart soared. At the top of the stairs he swung Maisie up in his arms and sought her mouth with his, tasted her, breathed that scent, absorbed her heat.

She was kissing him like she never wanted to stop, devouring him, her lips full and giving, her hands pummelling his shoulders.

Bringing him to a peak, tightening every muscle, heating his blood. 'Maisie,' he groaned between their mouths. He needed to be touching her, *all* of her, learning her body, her needs.

She tore her mouth away, stunned eyes meeting his. 'You're sure?'

Lowering his head, he kissed her like she was his other half. Which she was. Kissed her until he couldn't breathe. Until she melted into him, became a part of him. Then he kissed her some more.

His hand was being wrapped in Maisie's. When had she shifted to be standing in his embrace, her whole body length moulded to his?

She tugged him gently, stepping backwards across the room towards his couch.

'Bedroom,' he gasped.

'Too far.' Hot lips trailed over his chin, down his neck to the vee of his shirt and the skin on his chest. Her free hand cupped his butt, fingers kneading softly.

Keep this up and he wasn't going to last. Lifting Maisie into his arms he strode to the couch and lay her down on the cushions, holding both her hands with one of his to keep her from touching him while he began slowly kissing, tasting, her neck, then the hollow of her throat, following the path she'd been on with him moments ago.

Clothes got in the way. He had to remove some, discover more of that hot, supple body under his fingers.

Maisie tugged her hands free and solved the problem, unzipping her dress, pulling it over her head to toss.

His mouth was dry, his heart pounding as he saw Maisie for the first time. Tanned skin everywhere, full breasts, the dark curls inviting him lower. Lifting his head, he met her steady gaze and fell into her heat. 'Maisie.'

Hands were on his chest, fingers massaging his nipples, sending spears of heat up, down, throughout his body. Lips were caressing his stomach. He was hard, ready. When had he removed his shirt? His trousers were in a pool at his knees where he knelt beside the couch. He stood, stepped out of them and lowered himself beside Maisie. His hands sought her hips, lifted her over him.

Her body on top of him, he slid his hand between her legs, sought her heat, touched, caressed.

She cried out, a loud, long cry. 'Zac.' Then she was shifting, sitting over him, sliding down his length and taking him into her.

His love. Only love. Maisie.

CHAPTER NINE

'I'VE DIED AND gone to heaven.' Two weeks later, Maisie sighed into Zac's chest as they sat on her couch after making love.

'Hate to disappoint, but I'm just your down to earth kind of guy.' He hugged her tight, breathing in deeply.

'If this is down to earth, then I've been lost.'

'Me too.' Those strong arms tightened around her lethargic body, giving her a heartfelt warmth she hadn't known in a long time, if ever.

A deep yawn rolled up her throat and over her lips.

'What shifts are you doing this week?'

'Day shift for three days, followed by two nights.' Just thinking about running around after sick children made her tired. How did mothers do it when they were feeding babies every few hours and with a toddler requiring attention? Guess love got them through most of the exhaustion, and the sweet moments would be a bonus they'd never forget. Bring it on. She jerked.

'Maisie?'

'Nothing.' Bringing the idea of parenthood into the room now might put an end to the fun. Still too soon for her and Zac. Their lovemaking was beyond wonderful, and they were getting closer all the time, but she wasn't rushing things. She wanted to enjoy what they'd found and let the future unravel day by day.

'You sure?' Doubt lowered his tone.

'Absolutely. I might've nodded off for a couple of seconds.' Now she was fibbing, something she hadn't done since she was a kid trying to get his and Liam's attention. Only protecting herself, and Zac. After all, why spoil another great day?

'Okay, I'll leave you to go to bed.' His breath tickled her neck as his lips trailed light kisses from her ear to the corner of her mouth.

Bed without him? That had only happened when she was working nightshift since they'd first made love. 'I don't think so.' Deep warmth was stealing over her, softening the tightness, loosening her arms around Zac. She was in a good place, safe and happy, with the man she loved. 'Come here.'

'Oh, sweetheart,' Zac whispered.

Sweetheart? That's me? A smile tripped onto her mouth as she reached for him again. *I'm Zac's sweetheart.*

Words that stayed with her at work a few hours later as she nursed seven-year-old Courtney after an appendectomy.

The young girl had been brought into hospital about four that morning and been sedated until the local general surgeon arrived from Wanaka where he'd been for the weekend. Now she was starting to waken and needed to be watched in case she became distressed.

'You look shattered,' Jill commented from the next bed where a girl was lying with her broken leg held above her body. 'Have a fun weekend?'

'Absolutely.'

'I saw you at the pub with Zac Lowe last night.'

'Where's Mum?' Courtney was awake.

Thank goodness for little girls, Maisie thought as she turned back to her patient. 'Your mum's waiting in the next room, Courtney. I'm Maisie, and I'm looking after you for a while.'

'I want Mummy.'

'In a few minutes we'll shift you to a different room and then you can see her. Can you sip some water for me?' Maisie held the plastic cup and placed the end of a straw in Courtney's mouth. 'That's the girl.'

'Why am I here? I haven't got a tummy ache any more.'

'The doctors took your appendix out, and they gave you something to make the pain go away. I'm going to see how your pulse is now you're awake.'

'What's a pulse?'

'Feel here.' Placing Courtney's finger on her pulse, she asked, 'Can you feel that going bump, bump?'

The girl nodded. 'What is it?'

'That's your heart pushing the blood around your body to take food and water everywhere. Right, that's all good so we can go back to the ward now.'

Meg, Courtney's mother, stood up the moment the orderly pushed the bed out of recovery. 'Hello, darling.' Turning to Maisie, she asked, 'Is she all right? The surgeon said the op went well but I don't want her in pain.'

'She's receiving a light painkiller and antibiotics intravenously and everything's normal. It's just a matter of taking it quietly for the next couple of days and then she'll be running around as per usual.'

'And I'll be wishing for something to shut her up.' Meg smiled. 'She's usually such a busy soul, I struggle to keep up with her.'

'Better that way than moping on the couch all day,' Maisie said. Kids should be active and spend a lot of time outside in the fresh air.

Thinking about children again, Maisie.

Why not? If what she and Zac had going already, then it was a natural process. Love, lovemaking, babies. Holding their baby in her arms, against her breasts. Oh, yes. Her breasts ached at the thought. So much for taking things slowly. Here she was taking giant leaps, acknowledging he'd be a wonderful father, loving and caring. Her heart flipped. He was her man. She adored him. He made her feel good about herself again. Like she was floating on air all the time. Her confidence was back; she was in charge of her life and sharing it with the man of her dreams. Her trust issues were gone. Happiness was there when she woke in the mornings, stayed with her all day, went to bed with her every night.

So who would their baby be like? Tough and dark haired with big blue eyes like his or her father? Or dark blond and slight like her? Intense and out there like Dad? Or shy and non-confrontational like Mum? Boy or girl? Yearning filled her, swamped her heart. Her hopes were lifting all the time, her worries about losing a friend apparently gone. Her love for Zac was real and deep, and she felt safe giving him her heart. She didn't want safe any more. She wanted to leap from the clifftops, shouting her love to the world.

'I'm hungry.' Courtney broke into her thoughts and reminded her what she should be focused on.

'You can't have too much yet as your tummy's got to settle down. You chat with Mum while I go and see what I can find in the fridge.' There wouldn't have been anything from the kitchen delivered at breakfast time for this one as orders were put in the night before. Yogurts and fruit were kept in the staff fridge, along with cereal and sometimes bread in the cupboard for these circumstances. In the kitchen she put on the kettle for a coffee as her break was due, then retrieved a yogurt and banana for Courtney.

'Here you go, my girl.' Fingers crossed she ate these foods. Picky eaters weren't so easy to cater for around here.

'Yum.'

Phew. 'Right, while you eat that I'm going to have something to eat too. I'll see you shortly, okay?'

'She's coming right fast,' Meg said.

'They usually do, but be aware the after-effects of anaesthesia can make her drowsy on and off for the rest of the day. She might also feel nauseous, though the way that yogurt's disappearing I doubt there's anything out of order with her stomach.'

Meg chuckled. 'I hope you're right.'

'Want a coffee?' Maisie asked Jill as she went past the desk where she was working on the computer.

'Sure do. Be with you in a minute.'

Grabbing her phone from her locker, Maisie checked to see if she'd missed any messages. Heat warmed her cheeks. Zac had texted.

How's your morning going? We've got four burglaries to sort out. Could be busy tonight. Be in touch.

Okay, not quite what she'd expected. That was a normal Zac message, not one filled with xxx's. Guess he was focused on trying to track down the bad guys.

Chugging along. Missing you. Xx

Only being truthful, not over the top. Disappointment hovered in her mind. This was getting out of hand. She was overthinking things just because Zac's message hadn't been filled with love and kisses. Dropping the phone back in her bag, she shut her locker and went to make coffee. Jill always had plenty to talk about after a weekend and she could do with the distraction.

Jill poked her head around the door. 'We need to get ready for two five-year-olds. Knocked off their bikes by a van which didn't stop. Injuries include fractures and abrasions.'

Maisie's stomach tightened as she rushed after Jill. Not quite the distraction she'd hoped for.

It had been a hectic week with long hours culminating in the arrest of three men responsible for stealing to-order high-end televisions and music systems from across the South Island, and Zac was happy to be out on the water with Maisie. He idled the motor while she dropped the anchor off Glenorchy. 'Give it a few metres extra,' he called. Too short a rope made for uncomfortable swinging.

Maisie flipped him a finger. 'How many times have I done this?'

Often. 'Don't want to spoil our picnic bobbing around.' He grinned at her cute derriere sticking out from the front of the boat. He had been looking forward to this downtime with her for days.

A slight hand covered his and twisted so that the motor stopped. 'You going to stand there all day? I'm looking forward to fish for dinner.'

Now there was a challenge if ever he heard one. 'Wait and see.'

She delved into the chilly bin for two bottles of water and handed him one, then made herself comfortable on one of the seats. 'This should be fun. I prefer rainbow to brown trout, by the way. And I'm not helping when you land it. Yuk.'

He shook his head at her as he lifted his rod and checked the fly was secure. 'You want to catch your own?'

'No way. I'm quite comfortable doing nothing, thanks.'

She looked it too, and gorgeous in fitted black jeans and a thick merino jersey the colour of her eyes. His heart did a little skip. Everything was perfect. The sunny day and the calm lake, the easy camaraderie between them, knowing they were becoming closer as a couple—yes, perfect. As long as he caught a trout.

As Zac was about to admit defeat an hour later he felt a tug on his line and raised his rod sharply. 'Got you.'

'You've got one?' Maisie stood to peer over the edge of the boat. 'Want me to get the net ready for when you bring it to the surface?'

'Good idea.' He was winding, then pausing to give the fish its lead, winding again. Slowly, slowly did it. He'd lost enough to know the score. And today he really wanted to put dinner on Maisie's plate. It was a big trout.

'Not bad,' she told him. 'Allowable size anyway.'

He'd have swatted her backside for that if he didn't need two hands to bring in his catch. 'Get ready with that net.'

And don't take it from the mouth end, he nearly added, but she already knew how it worked. Knock the hook out of the mouth and there went dinner. The fish leapt out of the water, splashed down again.

'That's more than takeable.' He grinned, winding in the loose line.

'I know.' Maisie held the net just above the water, ready to scoop as soon as the trout reappeared. It was right there.

'Now.'

She already had it and was lifting it onto the boat. Then she high-fived him. 'Great going.' She got him a low-alcohol beer from the bin. 'Your reward.'

No, that'd be seeing her face fill with pleasure when she ate dinner tonight after he baked the trout. 'Might as well set up lunch now that I've done what I came to do.' He broke down the rod, dealt to the fish and cleaned up the deck.

Maisie opened the picnic hamper and unpacked the food. 'Oh, yum, my favourite pasta. And ciabatta. Marinated mussels.' She gaped at him. 'Spoiling me by any chance?'

'Why wouldn't I?'

She nodded. 'Can't think of any reason.'

They were on the same page—again. Happening a lot lately. He couldn't remember being so happy. Sitting down beside Maisie he took her hand in his. 'We're doing okay, aren't we?'

A frown formed on her brow. 'Stop looking for trouble, Zac. Everything's wonderful.'

She was right. His ingrained fear of hurting Maisie and losing everything was a pain in the butt. Once, when he was sixteen and still angry at his parents for not loving him how he expected, Ross had told him his anger was pointless, and he should put his energy into doing the things he could. Ross had been his mentor, and usually right, but he'd also made certain he and Liam kept an eye out for Maisie. Zac had never been able to let that go. He owed Ross and Pippa for their big hearts at a time they were suffering for Cassey. But he owed himself a life too, and they'd be the last to tell him otherwise.

Sipping his water, he looked at this woman turning his world upside down in ways he'd never imagined possible. He was lucky to have her, to know her and be able share parts of himself he didn't usually do.

A loud roaring sound began penetrating his consciousness, getting closer and louder all the time.

'Someone's in a hurry,' he noted as he saw a speed boat barrelling across the water half a kilometre away.

Maisie stood up and stared across the water. 'Hope he knows what he's doing,' she muttered. 'There are other boats anchored where he appears to be heading.'

Apprehension flickered in Zac's gut. The boat's speed was sending out big waves behind the craft that would rock the other boats hard. 'Look out,' he yelled, knowing he couldn't be heard. 'I think we need to—'

An almighty crash shook the air, and the sound of metal impacting on metal rang out across the water. 'I'll pull the anchor, you start the motor,' he told Maisie. 'Someone's got to be injured for certain.'

She didn't waste time talking, went straight to the control panel and, after checking the gears were in neutral, switched the key. Then she quickly packed up their meal and put the chilly bin up the front of the boat out of the way.

'Go,' Zac called as he stowed the anchor and hooked the lid in place.

The boat moved forward, and Maisie increased the speed a little. The sooner they got to the scene the better for anyone in the water, and at the speed she was doing, they weren't going to create waves and add to anyone's distress.

'You take it,' she said when he stood beside her. 'I'll keep an eye out for anyone in the water.'

Another boat had pulled anchor to make their way closer to the accident. The speedboat had come to an abrupt stop, its nose high out of the water with a gaping hole on the underside, and the engine half submerged at the back. The small launch it had run into was on its side and two heads were bobbing in the water, alongside the boat.

Zac slowed right down and scanned the water between them and the launch. 'I'm going to them first. See anyone with the speedboat?'

'Not yet. Hang on. There's someone floating face down. Left, Zac, left, that's it. You're on track, pull back on the throttle. Stop, we'll float the last bit.' Maisie was doing up the life jacket she'd just pulled on. 'I'm going in.'

'No, Mais. I'll go. You could get caught up in something from the boats.'

Too late. She was over the side and in the water, making for the incapacitated man.

'You're supposed to stay safe,' he growled. She'd have swiped at him if she'd heard.

Zac left the motor idling and went to stand on the flat space beyond the deck where it would be easiest to bring the man on board. Definitely a male by the width of the shoulders and the short hairstyle, though that might be being sexist.

Maisie reached the guy and immediately began turning him over. She struggled and Zac dived in, swam across the small gap to help. Between them they rolled him over, and began dog-paddling back to the boat, pulling him along between them.

'Hello? Can you hear me?' Maisie asked. She was looking at his head, then down his upper body. 'He's unconscious which suggests he breathed in water without knowing.'

Zac climbed onto the boat and grabbed hold of the guy while Maisie did the same. 'This isn't going to be easy.' There wasn't a lot of space between the large motor and the edge of the boat. 'I'll take his shoulders and try lifting while you see if you can pick up his legs when I get them a little way out of the water.'

Maisie held onto a welded pipe with one hand so she could lean out ready to grab the trousers when Zac pulled the man up and back into the boat. He began pulling, lifting, doing whatever it took. His lungs began burning with the effort, his legs shaking with strain, and still he hadn't got far. He took one step back, pulled.

'Got him,' Maisie yelled as she leaned further forward.

Don't fall in.

He fixed his gaze on the man coming further into the boat, inch by long inch, until suddenly he was tripping backwards as Maisie lifted the legs over the side into the boat. 'Done,' Zac grunted, drawing in a lungful of air.

Maisie was already kneeling on the deck beside the guy, tilting his head back, listening for breathing. Then she rolled him on his side and banged his back.

The man gasped and spewed water everywhere.

'Hello, can you hear me?' she asked.

Shocked eyes opened, stared at her.

'You've been in an accident and ended up in the water face down,' she explained. 'I'm going to keep you on your side in case there's any more water in your lungs. Understand?'

A short nod.

'How many were on your boat?' Zac asked. He

hadn't seen anyone else by the speedboat but with the speed the accident happened someone else could easily be in the water and some distance away.

'Just me,' the guy croaked.

'I'm going to take a look around and see if the others by the launch are all right,' Zac told Maisie. 'I'll go very slowly so as not to cause waves or rock the boat. Okay with you?'

'Yes. I'll check this man over.' She was fingering the skull wound. 'Can you feel pain anywhere else other than your head?' she asked her patient.

The man coughed and more water appeared from his mouth. 'I'm not sure. Everything feels odd.'

'Explain.' She sounded so calm.

'My sight's blurry. Sharp pain in my chest. Something's happening.'

Maisie reached for wrist. 'I'm checking your pulse.'

The man tried to sit up.

'Stay still.' Maisie's hand splayed across the man's ribs, keeping him down, while with her other one she found his pulse.

'Chest hurts,' he repeated.

Zac was keeping an eye on the water, flicking looks at Maisie and the man, and calling the emergency services. 'I've got the ambulance service on the line.'

'Tell them we need the rescue helicopter with a medic.' She didn't look away from the guy.

After passing on her request, Zac put the boat into neutral and picked up the handpiece for the marine radio. 'Queenstown marine, this is Zac Lowe. Come in.'

'Marine base, Zac. What's up?'

'There's been an accident offshore at Glenorchy and people and boats are in urgent need of help.'

'Help's already on its way.'

'Zac,' Maisie called. 'He's having a cardiac event.' She was tearing the shirt from the man's chest. 'He's arrested.'

'Cardiac arrest. Inform the rescue helicopter crew,' he yelled into the handpiece before dropping it and going to Maisie's aid. Kneeling down he took the man's head and tipped it back to open the airway.

Maisie was pressing hard into the exposed chest with her interlocked hands. 'When I say, give him two breaths of air, then sit back while I do compressions again.'

'Tell me if you want a break from the compressions,' he told her.

Sweat was beading on Maisie's forehead. Doing CPR was no picnic, but Maisie was handling it like a pro, which she was. The man didn't know how lucky he was to have a nurse on hand when his heart conked out.

'Two breaths.' She nodded.

One, two. Zac sat back on his haunches, holding the man's head again.

Push, push, push. Maisie had a steady rhythm going.

Gasp. Cough. Water spilled out of the man's mouth as Zac hurriedly turned his head sideways.

'Yahoo, well done.' He grinned with relief.

'We're not out of the woods yet,' Maisie warned, but she was smiling. Tugging a roll of paper towels that was tucked into the side panel of the boat, she wiped the man's mouth and then face. 'He's been sweating and

I didn't notice, just thought he was soaking wet from being in the water.'

'No one would've thought differently,' Zac said. The man's clothes were drenched, as was his hair and skin.

'What's the story about the helicopter?' Maisie asked, her finger on the man's pulse.

'I'll find out.' He scrambled to his feet.

As Zac made the call, he looked around and saw that other boats were with the launch the speedboat had hit. No one was panicking so hopefully that meant no other serious injuries and Maisie wasn't needed, because she had her hands full. She couldn't leave this guy to go help someone else.

'The helicopter's on its way, should be about ten minutes away,' he was informed. 'The pilot wants you to head to shore at Glenorchy where people are waiting to take the man off the boat to the helicopter when it lands.'

'Will do.' Zac filled Maisie in. 'That work for you?'

'Definitely.' She smiled at him. 'Well done, partner.'

Partner. His heart squeezed. Raising his thumb in acknowledgement, he said through a wide smile, 'We make a good team.' In so many ways. He was giving it everything, no more doubts or holding back or worrying about what could go wrong. Ready to take a chance on being together for ever. 'A great, loving team.' He turned the motor on.

'We sure are,' she agreed.

Zac couldn't believe how happy he was. The days were brighter, the nights warmer. Maisie was the only woman he'd truly loved, and now that he was putting it out there for her to see and be a part of, it felt wonderful. Something he'd longed for all his adult life was coming to fruition. Better still, she reciprocated by being loving and exciting. She had his back, even when he didn't need it, sensed his needs almost before he was aware of them. Stuck up for them as a couple whenever he voiced concerns over her family. She gave herself to him, trusting and open, not trying to prove to him she was as good as him as she'd done for years. He couldn't ask for anything more.

'There you are.' Maisie's soft voice caressed him as she approached him at his dining table from the top of his stairs.

Nice pants. Tight enough to accentuate those shapely legs and not look like she'd squeezed herself into something two sizes too small. Sexy came to mind, and tightened other parts of his body. 'Hello, gorgeous.'

She kissed him before pulling out a chair opposite. 'The rescue chopper brought in two teenagers from Coronet Peak this morning. They'd been racing down the slope and lost control. Severe injuries for both.'

'I heard the paramedics had been called out. What were they doing up there? There's not enough snow for snowboarding yet.' He should be used to people behaving idiotically by now, but he wasn't.

'A lot of people are asking the same thing, but then teenagers being what they are, there probably won't be any sensible answers.'

'I remember those days. Liam and I doing donuts

in the car on the back road and wondering why we got caught.'

'Because Dad was a local cop you got a bigger telling-off than most and made to do community service for a month.' Maisie was laughing. 'But you never did it again, did you?'

'Actually, we did, but we went somewhere no one would find us so it wasn't as much fun. Deflating, really, so your dad won that one.' And a few others he wasn't going to mention. 'At least I'm tolerant of teens these days. Hope I'll be the same with my own.' Most of the time.

'Why wouldn't you be? You'll want to make up for your parents by being the best dad out there.'

That stumped him. Her lovely eyes were underlining her statement, showing she meant every word. His heart was slamming. He was lost for words.

'Only saying it as I see it.' Her mouth curved into a gut-wrenching smile.

He needed space, time to absorb her belief in his ability to be a good parent. 'So what brings you here? I thought you were going to see Mallory after work.'

'I'm on the way, just wanted to drop in to see you first.' Now she eyed him up as though there were other things going on in her head.

Things he didn't want to hear about because he was already getting hot for her. He sighed his frustration.

'Problem?'

'All's good.'

I love you, Maisie. How do I tell you that? Are you ready to hear it? We're getting on so well, but—

The old 'but' scenario. And he'd thought he'd buried it. Most days were free of doubt. Damn, he needed to move on, grow a backbone, do something more than go round in circles.

She knew him better. 'I can see that.' Sarcasm wasn't usually her strong point, but being wound up about this made her sound like she was asking too much of him.

He didn't do sharing when it came to his emotions, especially love. 'Drop it, Maisie.'

A soft hand touched his arm. 'If that's what you want, but, Zac, we're becoming a couple, we share more than ever.' She paused, obviously waiting for him to agree.

He did, and then again there were things he couldn't share yet. Once said it would be out there, and if Maisie didn't love him as he did her, then this was over. He wasn't ready for that. Would never be ready.

Her hand disappeared. 'I see.' She stood up. 'I'm obviously wrong. I don't have a clue what's going on here, but I'll leave you to get on with whatever you've got planned and go visit Mallory.'

He'd gone and done the one thing he was desperate not to—hurt her. Leaping to his feet, he reached for her. 'I'm sorry. I've been getting wound up about things and took it out on you.' Leaning closer to brush a kiss on her mouth, he found himself kissing air as she stepped back.

'Not so fast. What's bugging you? Us? Our relationship? It can't be work because you usually talk to me about that.'

The problem was Maisie knew him too damned well. But she didn't know he loved her.

'I see.' She spun away and headed for the stairs.

No, you don't.

He went after her, his gut in knots. What if she walked away and that was it? 'Maisie, stop.'

She did, turning to eyeball him. 'I'm listening.'

'I get nervous about us and what's happening. It's such a huge change in our relationship I worry sometimes about what lies ahead.' He didn't tell her he loved her, he showed it. Didn't he? Possibly not, if she was unaware. 'You've been hurt before. I don't want that happening again.'

One shapely eyebrow rose slightly. 'You believe I don't have moments where I pause to take a breath? Don't wonder about this and where we're headed?'

Of course she would. It was in her make-up to wonder if she was doing the right thing for others, and herself. He'd slipped up there. 'I'm an idiot. It's just that you seem so relaxed about everything and I've been reluctant to burst the bubble by expressing my concerns.'

And my love.

'That's not how relationships should work. Not for me at least.' She bit her bottom lip. 'I don't want a repeat of my previous marriage. We have to talk about what bothers us.'

He took her hands in his. 'I'm not trying to hide anything, Maisie. It's all happened so fast that I have to keep pinching myself to see if it's true.'

Doubt crossed her face, disappeared again. 'You're worried I might get cold feet?'

'Not at all. When you give yourself, you give everything.' It dawned on him that's how she'd been with

Paul, which only made what the man did all the worse. And him suddenly more cautious. Was he seriously good enough for Maisie to love? He hadn't been for his parents. They hadn't been able to love him without hesitation. It was different with Maisie. The sane side of his mind knew that. But the doubts from his childhood knew when to creep in with their negativity. He'd hate for Maisie not to love him as much as he loved her.

'Not quite so much any more,' she admitted, squeezing his hands. 'I might've toughened up, but I'm wary of putting myself on the line now, even with you.'

'I get that. I have the same thoughts.' Watching her, he saw the moment she relaxed and let him off the hook—for now anyway. 'That's why we were supposedly going slowly.'

'We don't know the meaning of the word.' Her face softened and a small spark came into her gaze. 'I suppose knowing each other so well complicates falling in love in unexpected ways.'

Thump. Falling in love. Was she in love with him? His hands jerked, then relaxed in hers again. Of course he loved her and wanted the same in return, but what if she woke up one morning and found she wasn't ready? Or had made a mistake and this was a rebound moment?

Maisie pulled her hands free of his.

She was going to leave, go to Mallory's.

Then she slid her arms around his neck and reached up on her toes to place her mouth over his. 'Relax, Zac. It's early days. But forget slow. It ain't happening.'

His body agreed, every part of him roaring into life,

crying out for her, obliterating his concerns in an inferno of need.

He hugged her tight. 'This is why I care for you so much.'

CHAPTER TEN

'HANDSOME DOESN'T BEGIN to describe you,' Maisie said as she straightened Zac's bow tie. Her stomach was doing its washing machine number on her, and her fingers wouldn't stop shaking. This was Zac's big night and she would be there, right at his side, and the excitement levels kept growing as the time to head downstairs to the hotel's conference room and the awards dinner approached way too fast.

'Then what does?' Zac teased. 'And don't say I should wear an evening suit all the time.'

'I think you should.' The black suit and crisp white shirt turned handsome into mouthwatering, stunning and sexy as it was possible to get. 'I've never seen you look so suave. Every woman in the room will want you.' They'd have to fight her for him first.

'I'm not the only cop getting an award tonight.' His smile faded a little. 'Thank goodness.' He really didn't want to be the centre of attention.

She got that. 'You're the only one that matters to me.'

He glanced at his watch and breathed deep. 'Ready?'

So he was ignoring her compliment. 'As ready as I'll ever be.'

It had been an intense couple of hours as their flight from Queenstown had been delayed by weather for ninety minutes and then there'd been no taxis at the airport when they landed. Liam came to their rescue, picking them up and delivering them to the hotel with little time to get dressed. Maisie hugged him. 'Relax, gorgeous. Tonight's all about you.' His to enjoy and be celebrated for his bravery.

Her parents were also here. Liam had got them seats at their table because, as he'd said, they were as much Zac's parents as theirs. She knew he'd be ecstatic they'd come. Like they'd miss this occasion.

Zac took her hand and looked her up and down. 'You are so beautiful you make my heart sing.' He kissed her softly. 'Truly, you do.'

Her heart expanded with love. 'Don't make me cry or my mascara will run.'

And I'll be all choked up for hours.

'Let's do this.' As Zac's fingers slipped between hers, she sighed with happiness. Sometimes he worried her with his concerns about her getting hurt or her family not accepting their relationship but he was so wrong. Her life had become wonderful in such a short time it seemed unreal. It couldn't be any better, and she just wanted to take the lift to the rooftop and shout out across Christchurch, 'I'm in love with the most wonderful man on earth.'

Instead Zac pressed the button that'd take them down

to the first floor. 'Showtime.' He grinned. 'I'm glad you're with me. I did not want to do this on my own.'

'You were never going to do that. The family's here, and so are your old mates from when you worked here.'

'Not the same,' he said, a little frown appearing.

'What's worrying you?'

And don't say, 'Nothing.'

'Nothing.' He bent to kiss her cheek. 'Promise.'

She didn't believe him, but the lift bumped to a halt and the doors slid open to reveal a well-dressed crowd of men and women standing around talking and laughing with glasses of champagne or beer in their hands. It was not time to have an argument over something that could just as easily turn out to be unimportant.

'About time.' Liam stepped away from a circle of people and came towards them.

Zac's hand tightened around hers like a reflex motion, and then he began to withdraw his hold.

Maisie tightened her grip. They were a couple, and she wasn't going to hide it. If the family hadn't got the idea already, then it was time they opened their eyes. But she believed they all knew she and Zac were an item. 'Hi, Liam. Where's Sasha?'

'Talking to her sister. The cop that introduced us, remember?' He wrapped an arm around Maisie in a hug. 'Good to see you here with Zac,' he said quietly. It was approval.

Letting Zac's hand go, she hugged her brother tight. 'Thanks.' Stepping away she felt the full force of Zac's eyes on them and knew he was expecting some kind of reaction from Liam. 'Zac's gone the whole distance with his attire tonight.' Her stomach was still doing its thing whenever she looked at him, he looked so gorgeous.

'You've scrubbed up all right.' Liam gave Zac a man hug. 'You ready for this?' There was understanding in her brother's eyes. He knew the memories would hit Zac when the speeches were made, but he also got it that Zac was moving on and tonight would help.

Zac grimaced, then looked from Liam to her and back, and stood a little taller. 'Yes, I am.'

'Good. Let's have a drink. I was about to give up waiting for you two to turn up.' Liam signalled a waitress, obviously taking command so that Zac could relax. It was how these two operated, their way of supporting each other.

'Champagne for me,' Maisie laughed. 'I'm celebrating tonight.'

'Zac, there you are.' Her mother pushed through the crowd to wrap her arms around him. 'You didn't think we'd miss this, did you?'

Zac blinked, then brushed his eyes with the back of a hand. 'Pippa, Ross, thank you for coming. You've made my night.'

Maisie grinned. 'You thought you couldn't get any more tickets for our table but Liam had already beaten you to it.' Zac had mentioned inviting them, and her mum had said they were going away for the weekend, fully intending to surprise him.

'Should've known.' Zac grinned. 'Families, eh?'

'You bet.' Her father shook his hand. 'We're yours.'

Zac blinked, turned away.

'Hi, Maisie, great to see you.' Sasha appeared beside

her. 'What a stunning dress. That shade of blue suits you perfectly, and I'm a little jealous of how you can wear something so fitting and look perfect.'

Maisie blushed. 'Come on. You look wonderful too.'

Sasha laughed. 'Now we've got that out of the way, let's enjoy the night.' She was looking at Zac. 'Your man is looking exceptional tonight, isn't he?'

My man?

Yes, he was her man, and exceptional in more ways than one. 'I think so.'

A gong sounded. 'Would everyone go in and take their places at the tables now, thank you.'

'We *were* running close to the wire for getting here.' Zac took her elbow. What happened to holding her hand? Was he getting nervous? 'Ready for this?'

'Yes, I am.' She locked her eyes on him. 'So are you.'

His chest rose. 'You know what? I am. I can do anything with you by my side.'

I am not going to cry. I'm not. She wiped a tear away. *Okay, not much.*

'We're holding people up from getting to their tables.' They'd stopped in the middle of the main aisle running down the centre of the large room.

Zac grinned. 'Do I care?' Confident Zac to the fore. Completely to the fore. He talked and laughed with everyone around their table, accepted congratulations from strangers and friends alike, and all the time kept an eye out for her.

The evening flew by. The dinner courses came and went, her glass was constantly topped up by hovering waiters and the talk and laughter around their table was funny and enjoyable.

Then a man stepped onto the stage and tapped his glass. 'Can I have everyone's attention, please?'

'Here we go.' Liam tipped his head in Zac's direction.

'Ladies and gentlemen, let me introduce myself. I'm John Collins, Police District Commander.' Polite applause followed. Then, 'I'm not going to talk all night.'

A few good-natured comments came from around the room.

'But I am going to say that without all of you our district wouldn't be as safe for the public as it is. Not that it's perfect by a long way, but I know from personal experience that all of you do your utmost for our people.'

'Get on with it,' Zac muttered.

Maisie reached for his hand, and he squeezed tight.

'Tonight we are recognising some exceptional members of the force.' Collins continued for a couple of minutes, then paused. 'Right, that's enough from me, except to say thank you to all of you, and especially to those receiving awards tonight. I'm now handing over to department director, Jeremy Harlen.'

'He's in charge of the station I worked at here in Christchurch,' Zac told her.

Harlen talked about the men and women to be honoured, then began calling each individual to the stage to get their pin and certificate. Maisie watched and listened, her heart pounding as it got closer to Zac's turn. It seemed to take for ever, then suddenly the wait was over.

'Detective Zachary Lowe, please come forward.'

Maisie squeezed his hand. 'Go you.'

'Want to come with me?'

'No, this is your show.'

His smile was crooked, but he nodded. 'True.'

By the time he reached the stage everyone was clapping. Maisie was crying. Damn it, she'd sworn she wouldn't do this. Impossible not to when Zac looked strong and confident, and so damned wonderful striding across to shake the commander's hand. She scrunched up the paper serviette her dad passed across to dab at her eyes.

Jeremy Harlen shook Zac's hand. So did John Collins before taking over the microphone. 'Now I am going to say a bit more than I've done so far. Most of you know the story of how one night fourteen months ago my team was called out to an armed holdup that went horribly wrong. Every man on our team worked hard to get a good outcome but we were on the back foot from the beginning. The men were armed and dangerous, and were not interested in reasoning their way out of the situation. One of ours lost his life.' John paused, swallowed hard. 'This man, Zac Lowe, took a bullet for me. I owe him my life.'

Collins wrapped Zac in a man hug as the room erupted with shouts of 'Bravo!' and 'Zac! Zac! Zac!'

Maisie gripped her hands together on her lap and stared at Zac. He seemed to grow under the applause, like this was the last step in leaving the past behind.

The commander stepped forward and clasped Zac's hand, shook hard. 'We need men like you in our force.' He reached behind and picked up what looked like a medal and pinned it on Zac's jacket. 'For courage and bravery while serving our country.'

Again the room erupted with cheers and clapping. Zac raised a hand and gave a wave. 'Thank you, everyone. I appreciate this and the kind words, but I know others would've done the same if they'd been in the same position.' He shook hands with Collins and Harlen once more and walked off the stage.

'We won't see him for a while,' Liam laughed. 'Everyone will want a word with him.'

'Then let's get another round of drinks and have our own little party.' Sasha waved to a waitress. 'What do you think, Maisie?'

'Good idea.' Her glass was empty and she was in the mood to have some fun and let her hair down a little.

'Zac, got a minute?' Jeremy tilted his head towards a couple of empty chairs away from the tables.

Why did this feel like he was about to be put on the spot? Zac wondered as he said, 'Sure.' If he was being honest, he'd half expected Jeremy to want to have a chat. He was way overdue telling the chief his decision. He looked over to the table where Maisie sat with Liam and Sasha and his stomach knotted with love. He was doing the right thing, for them both. Maisie was the love of his life. Always had been, always would be.

'Want a beer?' Jeremy had the attention of a waiter.

'Make it a wine, thanks.' He wasn't driving anything more lethal than the lift up to his room tonight. And he was hyped. All the good-natured cheers and back-slapping had put him in high spirits. For the first time since the shooting he completely accepted what had happened and his role in it. He'd done his best and it had turned out to be good.

They parked their butts with their backs slightly to the room so that hopefully everyone got the idea and left them alone for a little while. Zac sipped his wine and waited for the inevitable.

'You're ready to come back,' Jeremy said. As an opener it was direct and blunt. Typical Jeremy.

He did miss the big cases, the long hours that became nights and days as the team dug deeper into murders and drug dealers and all the other big crimes that went down in a city and which Queenstown was lucky not to experience very often. When he'd gone home to recover and make the decision about whether he wanted to continue his career in the CIB, he'd found he mostly preferred the quieter lifestyle of his hometown where there were people he knew and time to do more than work. Though there were days when he longed for the detecting work he'd been good at. Sometimes he thought he should return to doing that. But Maisie made his decision straightforward.

'I don't see you rushing to pack your bags,' Jeremy commented after a long moment of silence.

'I have a life down south.' It was true. In the space of fourteen months he'd established himself in S and R, had gained a reputation as a fair but hard cop, felt more at home than he had anywhere else. And again, there was Maisie. Whichever way he turned, everything came back to Maisie. She'd returned home to get back on her feet amongst those she loved. Queenstown was in her blood. She adored the mountains and space. None of those in Christchurch, no close friends or parents. Even if he was busting to take up this offer, he couldn't ask her to move again. The job was tempting but not tempting enough to tip Maisie's life sideways again.

'You had one here.'

'All work and no play.' That's how he'd chosen to live back then. He'd never been concerned that he was alone because his career came first over everything. Strange how that all changed with one bullet. He'd gone back to his roots where people knew him as more than a detective. Back to where his career didn't run his life twenty-four-seven, and where he could be useful in other areas. He'd gone back to Queenstown because one day Maisie would come home. And she had.

'Bring her with you.' Jeremy inclined his head towards the table where Maisie sat.

So he'd noticed Maisie, and that they were together. Their changed relationship was no secret. Zac glanced over his shoulder to find her. She was watching him, a smile lightening her face. His gut squeezed. Bring Maisie to Christchurch when she'd only recently settled back in Queenstown where she always felt happiest? Where she could walk with her head high and not have to cope with the meanness of people who thought she was nearly as guilty as Paul. She'd have that here. More so as no one knew her. Which wasn't a reason to drag her away from having Mallory and Kayla nearby. They shared so much, had a lot of background that couldn't be beaten by new friends in a new city. 'That isn't an option. For either of us.'

Jeremy waved a carrot in front of him. 'You'll have your own team.' Two carrots. 'An increase in salary. Plus me to talk over any problems arising with staff or cases.'

He couldn't want for more. Best job, best conditions. Crunch time. Get it over and done with. 'Thanks, but no thanks. I am happy where I am. I won't be returning to Christchurch to work.' Definite decision. His chest felt light and free. When he'd left after the shooting, it had been with the knowledge there was a position back here when he was ready. At first he'd thought he'd only be away a few months but he'd barely thought about it since, that's how right it felt to be in Queenstown. Zac stood up and shook Jeremy's hand. 'I appreciate your offer, but it wouldn't work out for me.'

On the way back to his woman, he picked up two glasses of champagne off a waiter's tray. Handing her one, he tapped it with his. 'To us.'

'And to Zac for what tonight means,' said Liam. The family, his family, were all raising their glasses in his direction. Maisie was beaming. His heart stuttered when he met Ross's eye. It said, 'Be careful with Maisie.'

I'm doing my best.

Was it enough?

'So how's my hero?' Maisie snuggled into Zac as the lift shot them up to the eleventh floor. It had been quite the night and she was buzzing, more than ready for some hot activity with Zac.

'Wired.' He grinned and pulled her close, his mouth covering hers.

'Perfect.' She pressed closer, her breasts hard against his chest, her mouth opening under his. Felt his need pressing into her belly. Felt her own grow, spreading heat over her body. Her legs trembled; her skin tightened.

Zac lifted his head far enough to murmur, 'Maisie, Maisie,' then went back to kissing her senseless.

She was floating on air. This kiss beat the heck out of others they'd shared. She was with Zac, in a hotel, and about to make love. Love. As in hearts joined for ever. Not that Zac ever mentioned love, but he showed her in a million little ways—his smile, bringing a coffee over from his apartment when he got up to go to work if they hadn't spent the night together, his sensational, toe-curling kisses. So tonight she was celebrating *them*.

'Um…excuse us.'

Maisie jerked back, looked around. The lift was open, people were standing outside waiting to come in. Had they gone up to their level and returned without noticing? Or hadn't they left the conference room floor?

'Ah, sorry about that.' Zac reached for her, pressed her head against his chest. 'Do you want to share the lift?' His chest and stomach were making small convulsions like he was silently laughing.

She couldn't help it. She began laughing too. What the heck? Might as well make a complete idiot herself. Slipping her hand into Zac's, she leaned back against the wall and tapped her foot as the lift filled and began to move upwards, stopping at every damned floor on the way to theirs. She couldn't even blame anyone for the delay. She and Zac had lost all awareness of where they were, only wanting to be close together.

Being dragged back to reality made her smile. She'd make time to change out of her dress before they got too hot and busy. She'd gone shopping yesterday for some fancy lingerie that cost a bundle and was worth every cent. Even if she said so, she looked sexy in the red satin and lace shorts and top with thin straps that showed her cleavage to perfection.

She headed for her case before he had the door to their room closed. 'Give me five.'

'Five? I can't wait thirty seconds.' He reached for her.

'Tough.' Ducking out of the way, she snatched up the lingerie and stepped into the bathroom. 'You're going to have to.' Emotion clogged her throat as she tugged her dress over her head and tossed it aside. Reaching for the lingerie she rubbed the soft satin against her feverish skin. Cool and sensual. The strawberry shade highlighted her blond hair as she gave it a quick brush. Then she applied a new shade of lipstick to match and she was ready to go.

Pausing, she stared at herself in the mirror. This was it. A commitment to the man she truly loved. Zac was her man.

The thin heels of her shoes clicked on the tiles as she left the bathroom. Holding her head high, and her shoulders up, she crossed to the bedroom room and right up to him.

Zac's heart leapt in his chest. 'Maisie, sweetheart, you're so beautiful you take my breath away.' Literally. He was struggling to get any air into his lungs. Placing his hands on her hips, he held her back far enough to gaze down that red-covered length, over the curves of her breasts, the flat stomach and beyond.

She was stretching up into the points of those incredible shoes, her mouth seeking his. Her sweet mouth, now hot and fierce, as though she was claiming him. Which she was. He was hers for her to do with as she wanted. Starting with this kiss.

Soft. Gentle. Demanding. Sexy. Everything he'd ever hoped for—and more. Lots more. Holding her body up against his, his mouth covering, taking, hers, his hands spread across her back, he began walking slowly backwards to the massive bed where chocolates lay on the pillows and seductive lights highlighted the beauty he held. Absorbing her heat and softness, tasting her sweetness and fire, he put one foot back, then the other, taking her with him as he kissed her. A deep, hot, for ever kiss. A kiss to seal their relationship. 'Maisie, you are so beautiful.'

Her mouth spread into a wide smile under his lips. He thought she whispered 'Zac' into his mouth, or he could've been dreaming because everything was like a dream right now, only so much better, hotter, softer, more loving. Real.

Cooler air slid across his lower back. Maisie's hands were splayed across his heated skin, tightening his abs, centring his being, hardening his need. 'Slow down, woman.' He couldn't lose control. Maisie came first. He swung her up into his arms, and strode the last few metres to lay her on the bed, before shucking off his clothes as fast as possible.

She reached up, pulled him so he sprawled across her, feeling her breasts pressing against his chest, those slim legs under his thighs. And still she kissed him, teased him. 'Zac,' she whispered against his skin. 'I want you.' She was pushing up onto an elbow to lean over and lick his nipples, flaming the fire in his belly.

Reaching for her, he rolled over, tucked her under him and began to slowly return the compliment, licking, kissing, devouring her body. Stopping there to touch that pale soft skin, moving to kiss a trail down from her neck to her breasts and on down the cleft between them to her belly button. Kissing all the way as she arched up beneath him, pushing against him, crying out with longing filling her voice, touching his erection. Stirring him harder. Had him caressing those thighs that had often made him long to touch her. Smooth, hot.

'Please, Zac,' she begged. 'Take me, now. I can't wait.'

Nor could he. But he would. Finding her centre, touching her, feeling her moist heat, nearly undid him. And when she quivered against his hand he rose over her and slid inside his Maisie. Pulling back, he gasped for air, and drove into her again. And again until she cried out, and then he let go and joined her. He'd found what he'd been searching for. Maisie and love all in one.

CHAPTER ELEVEN

MAISIE AWOKE SLOWLY, stretching her legs to the end of the bed and her arms over her head. There were aches in places she didn't know existed. Good aches. Rolling her head, she blinked. 'Zac?' Where was he? The bathroom door was open.

'Hey.' A quiet word from by the window where he sat. The curtain was drawn back enough for him to look out.

Shuffling her backside up the bed, she leaned against the headboard. 'You been awake long?'

'About an hour.' His voice was flat. After last night and making love twice?

Something wasn't right. 'What's up?'

'It was a big night. I think it's all catching up with me.' He didn't give her a blinding smile to say it had been fantastic.

She wasn't about to let him spoil the day, or the night before. 'What time are we meeting the others for brunch?'

'In an hour. I was about to shake you awake.'

'Kissing me awake would work better.' She smiled.

'Then we might not make it to brunch.'

So they were still okay. He was just worn out. And she'd been thinking of herself, not him. Climbing out of bed, she crossed to wrap her arms around him from behind. 'You're amazing. I haven't had such a wonderful time in for ever.'

Turning, he looked up at her. 'Nor have I.'

Leaning down she kissed his cheek, then his mouth. 'I think we're past the dating phase, don't you?'

Zac stood up, pulled her in close. 'Well and truly.' He kissed her, long and deep.

All was good. 'I'd better grab a shower.'

He took her hand and headed for the bathroom. 'We're going to be late.'

A while later, as they were dressing, Maisie asked, 'What did Jeremy Harlen want last night? You two were in a huddle for quite a while.'

Zac winced. 'He offered me my old job back. I knew it was likely to happen, been expecting it for months.'

'Zac?' Alarm bells were ringing. He'd never mentioned this before, though when he first returned to Queenstown he had said something about how long he might stay in town. She'd forgotten all about that. 'You accepted it?'

He shook his head abruptly, concentrated too much on doing up his shirt buttons. 'No, I turned it down.'

'Why?'

Zac shrugged. 'I'm happy where I am.'

Deep breath. 'Are you sure?'

He came to her then and took her face in his hands, his eyes locking with hers. 'Yes, absolutely.'

So kiss me.

He didn't.

'That's good, but I know how much you loved that job.' The quaver in her voice was a dead giveaway. She was fearful for what lay ahead, that he might change his mind despite his insistence he wouldn't. He had loved working up here. An ache was starting up in her heart. She trusted Zac not to hurt her.

'I did, but it's over. I live and work in Queenstown now.' His hands fell away but he was still watching her.

Doubts slammed in left and right. Was she the woman he wanted? Had he had a sudden change of heart and she was no longer important enough to be with? Did he really want to leave her to come back here and was putting off telling her? Had Zac already reached the point where he didn't think she was enough for him?

Slow down. You're going off the deep end without reason.

Fear of being hurt again wasn't reason? Fear of having her trust thrown in her face didn't count? She drew a steadying breath, huffed it out. 'This isn't anything to do with us, is it?'

'Maisie, I don't want to leave you, not for anything. And I couldn't expect you to pack up and move again when you've only just returned home.'

'Is that why you turned the position down? Because of me?' And she'd thought they should talk about everything.

'*One* of the reasons. Not the main one.'

Forget the main one. 'You made a decision involving both of us without talking to me first? My opinion doesn't count?'

'You don't know anyone in Christchurch.' Desperation filled his eyes. 'I was thinking of you.'

'Over-protecting me again, that's what you're doing.' She glared at him. 'Will you never accept I'm all grown up and quite capable of making and living with my own choices?'

'I don't want you unhappy, Mais.'

'What do you think you're saving me from? A challenge? Fun and excitement at starting something new with you? This isn't how close, loving relationships work, Zac. We're meant to work together on everything—talk about the big issues, come to conclusions together.' Sinking onto the side of the bed, she stared at the floor. 'I didn't even know you might've wanted to come back here.'

She'd given one hundred percent of herself to Zac—like she had to Paul. Too much? Or had she made another monumental mistake? Trusted Zac to believe in her too easily?

'I tossed the idea around a bit at first, but wasn't rushing to grab the opportunity. Then when you came home, I more or less forgot about it. You're what's important to me, Maisie. You and me as a couple.'

'We're not a couple when you don't discuss important issues with me, and a job offer is right up there.' She couldn't believe he'd hurt her. She'd trusted him not to. 'I have to know what's going on or I feel like I'm not in a partnership.' Which was just how Paul had treated her—someone supposed to follow, not stand beside him. She could not go with that again. Not even with Zac, whom she trusted.

Silence fell between them.

Except for the crashing under her ribs.

Say something, Zac.

Nothing.

She stood up. 'We'd better get a move on. The others will be wondering what's happened to us.'

'Maisie,' Zac whispered. 'I'm sorry.'

'It would be better if you just talked to me.'

He took her face in his gentle hands and leaned in to kiss her. Slowly, tentatively, as if he hadn't done this before.

She stepped back. If he wasn't going let her into his life fully, then they didn't really have a relationship—not one she could live with.

Zac's head was thumping. He'd made the biggest mistake of his life and didn't know how to rectify it. Maisie was hurt. He'd broken her trust in him by making decisions involving her without her input. He wasn't good at loving her.

Head high, she strode into the café ahead of him, having remained silent on the short walk from the hotel. He'd never known her to cut him off like this before. The disappointment directed at him when she learned why he'd turned down the job would stay with him for a long time.

Hard to believe they'd made love twice during the night. He hadn't been able resist her the first time when she came out of the bathroom in that sexy-as-could-be red lingerie and they'd fallen together, everything coming together so fast. Then when she was curled into his body and holding him like he was the most important person in her life, he'd had to have her again, and he'd made love extra gently and drawn out her orgasm until she was begging him for release.

He'd been so relaxed and happy. But as the hours crept by with Maisie tucked in against him, he'd thought about the conversation he'd had with Jeremy. How he'd be able to run his own department, something he'd been aiming for before the shooting. Then he'd thought about his job in Queenstown and how much he enjoyed being back home. Especially now that he and Maisie were getting along like a house on fire. *Had been* getting along. Because right now there was nothing but ice in her eyes, in her tense shoulders and white-knuckled fingers gripping her bag.

'Morning-after blues got you?' Liam asked quietly.

'Something like that,' he admitted. 'It was quite a night.' In more ways than one.

'Maisie's very quiet too.' Brother to the fore.

As if Zac needed reminding that Liam would cut him out if he hurt his sister. Something else to worry about. 'She didn't sleep very well.' They'd been busy.

'Look after her, Zac.' The warning was there, loaded and ready to explode into him.

'Of course.' He had been when he told Jeremy no thanks. *'Stop protecting me.'* Maisie had a point. He had tried to back off on that lately but it was hard to give up what he'd been doing since he was seventeen. He was between a rock and a hard place. He hadn't used her as the only reason not to return here. He genuinely liked his job in Queenstown, the different pace suited him now. And yes, there were things he'd regret about not taking up the position he'd been offered last night, but they weren't the most important facts. That was living where Maisie was, and say what she liked, leaving home when she'd just arrived back wouldn't be easy for her. Queenstown was home to both of them, and he wanted their family nearby if they set up house together and got married. Also if they had kids. Except right now that was looking impossible.

The eggs were glue in his mouth. Coffee didn't wash them down. His stomach was rotating, his head thumping.

Maisie was pushing a hash brown around her plate, looking at it as though it might bite.

'Not hungry?' Ross asked from across the table.

'Not really,' he admitted.

Maisie didn't answer.

He stood abruptly. 'I'll go and check us out of the hotel.' There hadn't been time to do it when they left and he couldn't sit still another moment.

'I'll come with you.' Maisie put down her knife and fork, drained her coffee and got up to hug her brother. 'See you for Mum and Dad's anniversary.'

'I can drop you at the airport,' Liam replied, one eye on his sister and one on him.

Maisie shook her head. 'Thanks, but we've got plenty of time and you need to go with Sasha to see her family.'

Liam nodded. 'True,' He looked in two minds about leaving his sister with Zac.

Zac stepped up. 'Maisie and I'll be fine. Plenty of taxis on the rank last time I looked.'

Sasha was hugging Maisie and they were talking quietly.

'Zac? What's going on? You two had a lover's tiff?'

'Nothing like that, mate.'

'Whatever's putting that look on your faces, fix it. It doesn't suit either of you.' Liam turned away to take Sasha's hand, looked back at him. 'See you both when we come down for the anniversary shindig.'

'Will do.' If he was still welcome when the family learned why he and Maisie weren't talking at the moment. In three weeks Liam and Maisie's parents would be celebrating forty years married. Forty years of happiness and love, with life's problems thrown in which they'd managed to work their way through and remain loyal and in love.

Maisie hugged her mum and dad. 'See you when you get back on Friday.' They were taking a short road trip on the way south.

Ross looked over to him, said, 'It was a good night.' Then he looked at his daughter and back to him. 'Keep it that way.'

That sharp tone took him back to his teenage years and Ross warning him to stay clear of Maisie. But no one appeared to mind them being together now—unless he screwed up big time. Then who knew? 'Of course.' He'd do his best anyhow. Problem being Maisie had a mind of her own and he'd hurt her by not involving her in his decision. It wasn't going to be easy to get past this blunder, given her past with Paul.

She walked beside him out of the café, head high again, shoulders tight, and gripping her handbag as though someone was about to steal it.

He strode along, slowed when he realised he was walking too fast and making her have to take longer steps than were comfortable. 'Sorry,' he muttered.

'Where did I go wrong?'

Gulp. 'You didn't. Haven't.'

'You've made a choice and it isn't what I thought we were doing together.'

'I did.'

'Should be an exciting flight home.'

An hour later they sat awkwardly on hard plastic row chairs in a corner of the departure lounge at Christchurch Airport, cardboard mugs of unwanted coffee on the seats either side of them. Zac's legs stretched ahead of him as he stared at his shoes, wondering how he'd got into this position. He loved Maisie. Everything had been going well between them. It should be simple to tell her he loved her and drop everything else. If only he knew how to say 'I love you' without worrying that he wasn't loveable. He'd been eight when he'd told his mother he loved her and she'd walked away without a smile, nor had she said a word. The pain had been deep and lasting. 'I want so much for this to work out between us.'

The colour left her cheeks. 'What are you saying?'

He tried, and failed, to ignore the sorrow in her eyes. 'This has shown me I'm not the man you deserve,' he growled through the tears stuck in the back of his throat.

She didn't even blink.

He didn't know what he'd expected, but nothing wasn't it. 'You're not surprised, judging by your reaction.'

'Surprised?' Now she blinked. 'Surprised?' she almost shouted. 'Try disappointed. Hurt. I trusted you, Zac.'

Slam. His heart stalled. Trusted. In the past.

'Where does this leave us? Our friendship? The family?' Her questions were so quiet he had to lean in to hear her, and was rewarded with the familiar scent he'd come to adore. It teased him, reminding him of what was at stake. 'Don't say we can have a conversation and get on with where we left off. It's not that easy. I've been there before, had the conversations with Paul, heard how he hadn't done anything wrong and that I had to believe in him, and look where that left me. I said I'd never go there again, Zac, and this mightn't seem like a big deal to you, but it reeks of being let down badly to me.'

'Maisie, you came home to get your mojo back.' *Try harder, man.* 'You're happy in Queenstown with Mallory and Kayla settled there, your parents only a few minutes away. Then we get together.' He still hadn't told her his true feelings, but if he did now she'd probably see it as an attempt to win her back. Which it would be. He opened his mouth, saw Liam and Ross in his mind and closed it again. Don't hurt her any more.

'They are my closest friends, not my reason for getting up in the morning.' Her hands were making folds in the hem of her shirt. Her face was white, and her eyes dull with sadness when her gaze locked on him. 'You're not being entirely honest with me, Zac, and that's the cruellest part. It's the first time that I know of when you haven't told me what you're really feeling. That is hard to take or understand.' Her breasts rose as she drew a breath. 'Are you being honest with yourself?'

He winced.

'Your silence speaks volumes. It says you don't really love me enough to continue our relationship. I thought you'd have the guts to tell me, but I wonder if I've ever really known you as well as I believed. Which is awful because I relied on my impression of you as honest and reliable, and caring and loving. I believed you were the man I loved and wanted to spend the rest of my life with.' She stood up and reached for her carry-on bag. 'I thought I could trust you. I guess I was wrong.'

'I don't bloody believe it,' Maisie cried into her sodden pillow three nights later. 'When I fall for Zac, the most trustful man I know, he goes and leaves me hanging.' She couldn't accept that he mightn't talk about the important things they'd face if they shared a life together. He often held worries close to his chest, but they didn't involve her. Or so she'd thought.

She loved him. That hadn't changed. It wouldn't go away overnight. It wouldn't go away at all. She'd never told him in those exact words, but surely he'd seen how much she did love him. He'd never mentioned the L word either, yet most of the time she'd believed he did love her.

It just went to show she couldn't trust a man with her heart again. If Zac could do this, then what chance was there of her ever getting it right? None. Nada. Zero.

Her heart hadn't stopped aching since Sunday morning. It ached when she was nursing her little patients, when she shopped for groceries she then didn't eat, and all night long it kept her awake. She'd lost the man she'd come to love as much as life because it turned out Zac was afraid to take a chance on her loving him enough so he could be open about what he wanted to do with his career and, therefore, their future. He'd also obviously forgotten she needed to be in the picture all the time if they were going to have a stable relationship. But in the end, she loved Zac and someone had to make a move to sort this out. She could be the one to do that by knocking on Zac's door and suggesting they keep trying to make it work out. Yet she was reluctant. If he didn't trust her, she could be losing a future that would mean Zac and children. A family of her own to cherish all her life. She doubted she'd have that with anyone now because she'd always be waiting for the axe to fall.

Her phone beeped as a text came in.

She ignored it.

As she had Mallory and Kayla for days now. Fobbing them off with fibs about work and double shifts, because she felt such an idiot for even believing she could trust Zac. She wasn't going to get away with it for much longer though. They also knew her too well.

Next she'd have to face her parents and pretend to be happy and all was good in her world. Might have to visit a make-up artist first and get painted up so the worry wasn't showing so much.

Why don't you like talking to me about us, Zac? You talked about the shooting and your fear and shock. Surely that was far more difficult than asking me if I'd

move to Christchurch with you? That hurts as much as
anything. Aren't I good enough for you?

She stared at the ceiling. No answers up there.

Tossing the covers aside, she crawled out of bed and
groaned. She was so damned tired every muscle ached,
her head throbbed and her heart was heavy. Might be
time to join a gym or take up running to expend some
energy and make sleeping a natural part of her routine
again. Except she didn't have any energy, which had
to be the reason sleep had evaded her since Zac did his
number on her.

Pulling a jersey over her PJ top and picking up her
phone, she trudged into the kitchen to make coffee. Her
phone began blinking. More texts.

Grr... Leave me alone.

Another one from Kayla. She'd better deal with her
friends. *Tap, tap.*

Need a catch-up. Things to talk about.

Time to tell them she and Zac were over. She'd held
out on the misguided belief that Zac would come knocking on her door to promise he'd never make that mistake
again, but he was probably waiting for her to go over
and forgive him. She could do that, but she'd always be
afraid of him doing it again. Her heart was broken and
she needed to talk to someone.

The doorbell buzzed. Wouldn't be Zac. He'd just
come straight on up. Might not with the way things
were though.

The ringing didn't stop, was a continuous high-pitched noise slicing into her head. 'Coming.'

The ringing still didn't stop.

Unlocking the door, she pulled it open to find the young girl from next door staring up at her, tears running down her face.

Bending down, she said, 'Matilda? What's the matter?'

'Mummy's hurt. She's not talking.'

Slamming the door shut behind her, she took Matilda's hand. 'Come on, we'll go and see what's the matter.' Anna was hurt, not talking. It didn't sound good, if Matilda had got it right. The girl looked terrified. Reaching down she lifted her into her arms as she strode to her neighbour's front door. 'Is Daddy at home?'

'No. He went to work.'

She charged up the stairs. 'Anna? Can you hear me?'

'She won't talk to me,' Matilda said.

'Where is she?'

'In the kitchen.'

Anna lay sprawled across the floor, eyes closed, blood gushing from a head wound, and her right arm tucked under her back.

Maisie put Matilda down on a chair at the table. 'Stay there, sweetheart, while I ring for help and look after Mummy, okay?'

Matilda nodded slowly.

Kneeling down beside Anna, Maisie noted a yellowish puddle on the floor. Cooking oil, by the look of it. Anna must've skidded in it. 'Anna? It's Maisie.'

No movement, no recognition of her voice.

Maisie still had her phone in her hand. Quickly she

punched a number. 'Zac, I'm at Anna and Mathew's. Get over here fast.' Click. She pressed one-one-one and holding the phone to her ear began feeling for Anna's pulse. Multi-tasking came easily to her.

'Emergency services. Which service do you require?'

'Ambulance.' Pulse steady.

'What's up?' Zac blasted into the room. 'Oh, crikey. Hey, Matilda, come here, little one.' He scooped her up into his arms and held her so she couldn't see her mother, all the while looking at Anna. 'Want me to take the phone? I'm presuming you're on to the ambulance?'

'Yes.' Giving him the phone, she added, 'Tell them Anna's unconscious, has a head wound. Looks like she slipped and hit the edge of the bench.' There was a red smear on the rim of the bench.

Lifting Anna's eyelids, she saw her eyes were dilated. Breathing slow but not dangerous. Heart rate rapid. One wound on the skull. Left arm uninjured. Right arm twisted badly at the shoulder. She'd leave that until the paramedics arrived. No abdominal swelling. Legs were straight. 'Head and shoulder, arm injury,' she told Zac.

He was giving the service Anna's address. 'There's a nurse with her.' He mentioned the injuries. 'You want me to stay on the line? Fine.'

Maisie got up to get the roll of paper towels from the bench. 'These will have to do for a wad until the ambulance gets here. I hope Kayla's on.' She was a first-rate advanced paramedic who never got fazed in urgent situations.

'You know where Mathew is?'

'Matilda said he went to work.'

'I don't have his number.'

'It's on the fridge door,' Matilda piped up. 'And Mummy's. There, under the princess.'

Maisie smiled as she reached for the notepaper with two phone numbers written clearly on it. Handing it to Zac, she rubbed her hand over Matilda's arm. 'You're a very brave girl. You did the right thing coming to get me.'

On the floor Anna began gasping and shaking.

Convulsions. Just what she didn't need, but not uncommon after head injury. Maisie held her head to the side and, using her finger, scooped Anna's tongue straight so she didn't choke. Even then she didn't relax, kept watching until Anna stopped convulsing.

'Hello, this is Zac Lowe, from the police station. I need to speak to Mathew, please.' He had his phone against his ear now.

Maisie held Anna's head until she settled completely.

'Get him out of the meeting. This is an emergency.' Then, 'Thank you.' He did an elaborate eye roll. 'Honestly.'

Picking up the roll of towels, Maisie tore off the first two and put them aside, then made a wad from the uncontaminated ones. 'Careful of little ears when talking to Dad.' Telling a policeman what to say? *Good one, Maisie.* She glanced at him.

He was smiling at her ever so cautiously.

There was a turn around. Any smile at all had to be better than none. She got on with stemming the blood flow from Anna's head.

'Mathew, Zac. Anna's had a fall. You need to come

home.' Pause. 'Good man. See you shortly.' Another pause. 'Yes, she's fine. She's the hero in this. Tell you when you get here.' He hung up and slipped his phone in his pocket. 'On his way.'

A siren was coming closer by the second. 'Thank goodness,' Maisie muttered. 'We need them now.'

He shut off Maisie's phone. 'I'll go down to show them the way.' He still held Matilda close.

Hopefully the trauma of seeing an ambulance would be far less than watching her mother lying on the floor, though from the moment Zac had picked her up, Matilda hadn't been able to see Anna.

Heavy footsteps told her she had company. 'Thank goodness it's you,' she told Kayla as her friend stepped into the kitchen. 'Watch out. There's oil on the floor I haven't had time to clean up.'

'Will do.' Kayla was already sussing out their patient. 'Fill me in.'

It didn't take long, the details being scant. 'Not sure about that shoulder. Could be the upper arm that's damaged. Thought it best to wait until we roll her onto the stretcher. Especially with that head wound.' She wasn't sure how severe it was and didn't want to make matters worse.

'I agree.' Kayla was making her own observations while the other ambulance officer was attaching monitor pads to Anna's chest to take readings of heart rate, pulse and temperature.

Fast and efficient, they soon had Anna ready to roll onto her side so Maisie and Kayla could carefully move her arm to the side.

'Fractured wrist. Possible fracture to the humerus, definitely severe bruising to the upper arm muscles,' Kayla noted. 'Head wound's the major concern. Right, let's get her on the stretcher and we'll be on our way.'

When they were ready to go downstairs, Zac handed Matilda to Maisie. 'Here you go, my girl. Maisie will look after you while I help Mummy.' Two female ambulance crew and he wasn't standing back while they did the heavy lifting.

Kneeling down to tackle the oil spillage, Maisie's heart turned over. Typical. He was a man's man, stepping up to help, and all the better for it. Damn, but she'd missed him these few days. It had been especially hard when she only had to look out the window to see him in his kitchen or on his deck whenever he was at home. She was being stubborn by staying away. All because she had trust issues that had nothing to do with Zac. He'd never deliberately hurt her, and if he did get it wrong like last week, then she needed to let go the past and talk to him openly and honestly.

The sound of brakes skidding on the drive cut through everything. Mathew called out, 'What's happened? Anna? Oh, hell, what's wrong with her?'

'Daddy?'

Maisie raced downstairs, Matilda bouncing on her hip. 'Mathew, over here.'

He rushed to grab his daughter out of her arms and hug Matilda tight. His face was white as he stared over Matilda's head to the back of the ambulance. 'Maisie? Tell me what happened.'

'I think Anna slipped on some cooking oil. There

was a puddle on the kitchen floor. She's hit her head as she fell.'

'Is she all right?'

Deep breath. 'Mathew, she's unconscious. I can't say more than that.' Life could change in a second. A person could lose everything without any warning. Where was Zac?

'What aren't you telling me?'

Zac came up just then. 'What Maisie's saying is she's not a doctor. She's done everything possible for Anna while waiting for the ambulance, and the paramedics have been brilliant too. Now it's important to get her to hospital so the doctors can take over.' As he spoke the ambulance began backing down the drive.

Again Maisie's heart softened. Zac was her man. He just didn't get it—yet. No, he did. It was her who had to let go the past completely and show him how much she loved him. Starting now. Would he let her in again? Or say she'd made his mistake into something too big to be able to forget in a hurry?

'And, Mathew,' Zac continued. 'Your daughter saved Anna. She ran to Maisie for help.'

Tears appeared in the corners of Mathew's eyes as he hugged his girl tighter.

Maisie gave him a moment, then said, 'Do you want a lift to the hospital?'

It took him a moment to gather himself. 'Thanks, but I'll drive us there. I'll just take a few minutes to calm down.'

'You're sure? I'd hate you to have an accident.'

'I'll take you.' Zac was on the same page.

'All right. Thanks. I'll get Matilda's car seat.' Mathew's voice was quavering, and his hands shaking.

'Wise move. I'll lock up after you've gone,' Maisie told him. Then she could go and get out of her PJ's and into a hot shower. This hadn't been the ideal start to her day.

Life could be damned short, Zac growled. No one knew when they got up in the morning what was going to happen during the day. According to Kayla when the paramedics took her into the emergency department, Anna was seriously ill. She might've slipped or she might've had a stroke. It would be a while before they knew, and Mathew was going to have to sit it out, poor man. Thankfully, he had family in town who were on their way to be with him. But what a shock to have to face.

Zac pulled into his drive. So why was he stuffing around waiting for Maisie to forgive him and not beating down her door to tell her he loved her more than anyone or anything? Why was he messing with something so beautiful? The love he'd longed for all his life had been in the palm of his hand and then he'd gone and blown it. She'd walked away because he'd acted like her ex.

He could blame his parents for not having love in his life when he was younger, but the fact remained he had been loved by others all his adult life and he'd been a coward to run from Maisie's hurt. He'd had support from a different quarter all his life, and it had seen him through everything. He loved Maisie. He loved her family, but they came second to what he felt for her. He should've known that from the start and acted accordingly. They wouldn't turn him away for loving their daughter and sister. They'd embrace him. And if he made mistakes—who didn't?—they'd be there to guide him as they had done with every damned thing throughout his life since the day he met them.

He had to persuade Maisie to give him another chance.

He'd hurt her big time. Yet she hadn't turned her back on him, not completely. He was the person she phoned first this morning to help with Anna. Admittedly, he lived next door, but a nurse lived over the road too. He was her go-to man, and he was going to remain as such for the rest of their lives.

Shoving the car door wide, he got out and straightened his shoulders. Here goes. He'd be honest and upfront. Maisie would understand that better than any other approach. He desperately needed her to understand and forgive him.

Her front door was locked. He pressed the bell continuously. Nothing. Probably in the shower washing the sleep out of her face and eyes. Dealing with Anna, still in her pyjamas with her hair coming out of the band she must've put it in before going to bed, she'd looked exhausted. His heart had cracked a little when he saw her talking on the phone to the emergency line. Hard to believe he'd managed to stay away for three whole days and nights.

And now she wasn't answering her doorbell. He couldn't blame her for avoiding him if that's what she was doing.

He crossed to his apartment and let himself in. Not locked, because he'd forgotten all about that when he drove Mathew and his daughter to the hospital. Tossing the car keys on the sideboard, he took the stairs two at a time, and tripped to a stop on the top one. Maisie sat slumped on a stool, a steaming mug in her hands. His black bathrobe was far too large on her slim frame. Her wet hair hung in a long twist down her back. Most of all, she looked shattered.

'Maisie, are you all right?'

'I locked myself out,' she muttered. 'Helped myself to your shower.'

Thank goodness for that. He strode across and took the mug out of her hands before wrapping her in his arms. 'Darling, I'm so damned sorry for being an idiot.'

Her head was moving from side to side. 'You've been saying that since you were a teen. But it's me who's the idiot this time.'

'No, you were looking out for yourself.' He drew a rough breath. 'I don't usually call you darling.'

Careful, you're not out of the mess by a long shot.

Using one hand, he pulled up another stool and sat down, still holding her.

'Don't try to charm me over, Zac. It isn't going to work.' Her eyes were dark but there was a glimmer of a spark in them.

'I was speaking from my heart.' It was true. He wasn't going to hold anything back any more. 'I made a hideous mistake and I want to rectify it. If I can.'

'Zac, I was wrong to get so steamed up and walk

away from you. It felt so like what's happened in the past I didn't stop to think about the fact that this is you, and you don't deliberately try to hurt people, especially me. It's my turn to say sorry.'

'I love you.' The words flew out, as they should, full of love, of emotion, of everything he had to give. Far easier to say than he'd ever have believed. 'Maisie.' He gripped her shaking hands. 'I do. I love you and have right from when we first met.'

Her head bobbed down once, then she locked a fierce look on him. 'I love you too, Zac. I think I probably always have too. That day at school when you walked away from me I wanted you to stay, not as a kind of brother, but as my boyfriend.'

The tension left him. 'I had to go or risk getting kicked out of your family, which frightened the hell out of me. I'd finally found the kind of love I'd been looking for since I was born. Your parents gave me that without question. I wasn't losing it, even for you then. We were young and there was no future for us back then. We had some growing up to do. But now's different. I'm ready for everything.'

'I panicked on Sunday. I'd had moments worrying about would happen if our relationship failed. Then you told me about why you'd turned down the job and everything came crashing in on top of me. I didn't mean to hurt you.'

'I did say I wanted to remain in Queenstown, that asking you to move away from here wasn't the only reason I said no to the position.'

'I ignored that.'

'You did, but that's okay. I've forgotten already.'

Maisie started to say something.

He cut her off. 'We are so close, so into each other, each other's other half, really. I only ever wanted you, and yet I wasn't one hundred percent ready to let go my fears about screwing up with you and therefore losing everyone. But after seeing Anna lying on the floor, I realise life's too short to waste on arguments and worrying about what might or might not happen. I want us to be together, facing life side by side, Maisie.'

'You need to learn to trust me, us.'

'I do now. Though I might need a nudge occasionally.'

She pulled her hands free and picked up her mug to take a sip. 'Paul broke my trust. I never believed you'd do that.'

'Yet I did.' His heart died a little bit. She wasn't going to forgive him.

'Yes, you did. You made me believe I'll never be able to trust my heart to any man again.'

He was in deep trouble. 'Maisie, I am so sorry. I do love you, and I won't ever let you down like that again.'

The mug turned back and forth in her hands. 'The thing is, at first I wondered if I was falling for you because I could trust you not to hurt me.' She looked away for a moment and when her gaze returned her eyes were sad and sorry.

He sucked in a sharp breath.

'But it didn't take long for me to know I love you for the man you are, all of you, all your quirky personality streaks and the honest ones, serious and not so smart ones.'

His lungs squeezed the air back out.

Her eyes softened, as did her face, and those gorgeous lips, her whole stance following. 'Zac, I have been dying to say this for weeks. I love you with all my heart. I've come home to you, with you, for you.'

Relief soared through him, set his heart beating wildly. Maisie loved him.

She hadn't finished, but that was his Maisie. 'We've both made mistakes. Let's not do that again. As friends we've always been able to talk. Let's keep doing that as lovers.'

He scooped her up in his arms and lowered his mouth to hers. 'Sweetheart, thank you. I love you so much it hurts.' His world was falling into place at last.

Except for one more thing. He pulled out of her arms, and dropped to his knee. 'Maisie Rogers, please marry me and have a family with me.'

She laughed. And cried. And ran her hands down both sides of his face. 'Get up. We're equals, remember.'

'You're killing me,' he said, scrambling onto his feet.

She stood up, breasts to his chest, and smiled through her tears. 'Of course I'll marry you and have some babies with you. Bring it all on.'

Then they were kissing like there was no tomorrow; only there would be. Plenty if Zac got his way.

* * *

An hour later Maisie picked up her phone from where she'd left it when Zac turned up.

Two identical texts from Mallory and Kayla:

What are we going to talk about?

Maisie laughed.

Wedding plans.

* * * * *

COMING SOON!

We really hope you enjoyed reading this book.
If you're looking for more romance, be sure to
head to the shops when new books are
available on

Thursday 25th
November

To see which titles are coming soon, please visit
millsandboon.co.uk/nextmonth

MILLS & BOON

THE HEART OF ROMANCE

A ROMANCE FOR EVERY READER

MODERN

Prepare to be swept off your feet by sophisticated, sexy and seductive heroes, in some of the world's most glamourous and roma locations, where power and passion collide.

HISTORICAL

Escape with historical heroes from time gone by. Whether your passi for wicked Regency Rakes, muscled Vikings or rugged Highlanders, the romance of the past.

MEDICAL

Set your pulse racing with dedicated, delectable doctors in the high-j sure world of medicine, where emotions run high and passion, comf love are the best medicine.

True Love

Celebrate true love with tender stories of heartfelt romance, from th rush of falling in love to the joy a new baby can bring, and a focus c emotional heart of a relationship.

Desire

Indulge in secrets and scandal, intense drama and plenty of sizzling action with powerful and passionate heroes who have it all: wealth, s good looks...everything but the right woman.

HEROES

Experience all the excitement of a gripping thriller, with an intense mance at its heart. Resourceful, true-to-life women and strong, fear face danger and desire - a killer combination!

To see which titles are coming soon, please visit

millsandboon.co.uk/nextmonth

MILLS & BOON

Coming next month

CHRISTMAS MIRACLE AT THE CASTLE
Alison Roberts

'Here… catch, Abby.'

But the mistletoe didn't quite make it into her waiting hands because it snagged on some lower, outer branches. They were just a few inches too high for Abby to reach, even standing on tiptoes.

'I'll find a stick.'

'I can reach it. I'll just get this smaller one before I come down. Maggie's bound to have plans that need more than one weird bird's nest.'

Abby hadn't moved by the time Euan shimmied down from the tree only a minute later, with a smaller ball of mistletoe in his hands. His nose and cheeks were reddened by both the physical effort and the cold and he was breathing hard.

'You look like a dragon,' Abby told him. 'Puffing steam.'

'Hmph.'

She was getting used to that grunt that was clearly an important part of Euan's vocabulary. He reached over her head to unsnag the first mistletoe he'd harvested and, as it began to fall, Abby also reached up, to catch it. So she was looking up, with her arms above her head, as Euan looked down to see where the ball had gone. He was much closer than Abby had realised. So close that…

… that the moment suddenly froze.

She couldn't move. Euan seemed to be as still as she was. It was a blink of time but more than long enough for something to click into place.

It wasn't conscious. It had to be the result of a lot of things. Things like how excited Abby was to be here, in this spectacular place. The way Euan's story had captured her heart so firmly and her determination to try and do something to help him. The fact that, despite his outward grumpiness and the impression he wasn't that happy to have her here, there was a level of attraction that was the final catalyst for what Abby realised might be the perfect way to make this Christmas more enjoyable for this man.

She hadn't lowered the mistletoe and that was the perfect excuse for what she did next.

Abby stood on her tiptoes and kissed him.

She'd only intended it to be a friendly sort of kiss. A brief, under-the- mistletoe, Christmassy sort of kiss. One that wasn't going to be significant in any way.

But the instant her lips touched his, everything changed…

Continue reading
CHRISTMAS MIRACLE AT THE CASTLE
Alison Roberts

Available next month
www.millsandboon.co.uk